Executive | Privilege

Executive | Privilege

PHILLIP MARGOLIN

HARPER

NEW YORK • LONDON • TORONTO • SYDNEY

EXECUTIVE PRIVILEGE. Copyright © 2008 by Phillip Margolin. All rights reserved. Printed in the United States of America. No part of this book may be used or reproduced in any manner whatsoever without written permission except in the case of brief quotations embodied in critical articles and reviews. For information, address HarperCollins Publishers, 10 East 53rd Street, New York, NY 10022.

HarperCollins books may be purchased for educational, business, or sales promotional use. For information, please write: Special Markets Department, HarperCollins Publishers, 10 East 53rd Street, New York, NY 10022.

FIRST INTERNATIONAL EDITION

Designed by Renato Stanisic

Library of Congress Cataloging-in-Publication Data is available upon request.

ISBN: 978-0-06-165337-7

08   09   10   11   12   WBC/RRD   10   9   8   7   6   5   4   3   2   1

On January 8, 2007, at 1:40 in the afternoon, Doreen,
my wife for thirty-eight years, passed away.
She was my hero, the personification of class,
and as close to perfect as a human being can be.
Everyone loved her. She lives on in my heart.

Executive | Privilege

Prologue

Brad Miller woke up at 6 A.M. even though his meeting with Roy Kineer, the retired Chief Justice of the United States Supreme Court, was scheduled for nine. He was too nervous to get back to sleep, so he went into the bathroom to get ready for the most important meeting of his life. Under normal circumstances Brad would have been anxious about being in the presence of an intellectual giant. Not so long ago, he had been reading Kineer's landmark opinions in law school. But it wasn't Kineer's stature that made Brad's hand shake as he shaved. What frightened him was the possibility that he was wrong, that he'd misinterpreted the evidence. And what if he was right?

Brad stared in the mirror at his half-shaved face. Nothing about his average looks or personal history was outstanding. He was twenty-six, with curly black hair, a straight nose, and clear blue eyes—not ugly but certainly not male model material. He was a fair athlete who was good enough to be the second best player on his college tennis team, but his athletic skills had never been championship caliber. Brad had done well enough in law school to make the *Law Review*, but he hadn't won any other academic prizes, and he was employed as a junior associate in Oregon's largest law firm, which meant that he occupied the lowest rung on a very high ladder. Until today, he had been a fairly insignificant member of the human race. If he was right, he was about to become a key figure in the biggest political scandal in American history.

The sound of running water woke Dana Cutler, who never slept easily. It took her a moment to remember that she was in the FBI safe house and another moment to decide that there was no threat. Brad Miller was in the room next to hers, and he was probably taking a shower. While her breathing eased, Dana lost herself in the shadows that were shifting across the pale white ceiling. When she was calm she got out of bed.

Dana had been sleeping in a T-shirt and panties and she looked sexy until she took off the T-shirt, revealing the scars on her breasts and stomach. Plastic surgery and time had turned most of them into pale, oddly shaped souvenirs of something really bad. While she washed and dressed, Dana turned her thoughts to the meeting she would attend later this morning. She prayed that it would usher in a return to normalcy. She was tired of the violence, tired of being hunted; she longed for calm and quiet days.

Brad finished in the bathroom and dressed in his best suit. Before going downstairs, he pulled the shade aside and looked out the window of the safe house, which was separated from the woods by a wide field. The leaves were changing from green to vivid reds and yellows. The sky was clear, and the colors looked even more intense in the strong sunlight. Below his window, an agent was patrolling the grounds. The guard exhaled and his breath turned white in the chill fall air.

Brad turned away from the window and headed down to the kitchen. He had no appetite, but he knew he had to eat. He would need all of his energy when he met with Justice Kineer, who had come out of retirement to head up the investigation that was occupying the front page of every newspaper in the country. United States presidents had been suspected of sexual infidelities, financial schemes, and criminal activity, but no president had ever been the subject of a murder investigation while serving in office.

Brad didn't recognize the agent who was making coffee on the kitchen counter. He must have come on duty after Brad went to sleep.

"Want some?" the agent asked, pointing at the pot.

"Yeah, thanks. What is there to eat?"

"There's a full larder. Take your pick—eggs, bacon, cold cereal."

Normally Brad was a pancake and omelet man, but he didn't have much of an appetite this morning so he settled for a bowl of cold cereal and then carried a mug of coffee into the living room. He would have liked to get a breath of fresh air, but Keith Evans, the agent-in-charge, had instructed him and Dana Cutler to stay inside and away from the windows. Brad suddenly felt sick when it dawned on him that he'd made himself a perfect target for a sniper when he'd pulled aside the shade to look outside earlier.

"How's the coffee?"

Brad turned and saw Dana descending the stairs. She was wearing a business suit, and it threw him. He had never seen her dressed up before.

"It's good, strong," he said. "I didn't sleep so well last night and it's just what I need."

"I didn't get much sleep either."

"You should have something to eat before we go."

Dana nodded and walked into the kitchen. Brad watched her. Even though they were on the same side, Dana made him nervous. He had grown up in a nice, middle-class family. Until the Clarence Little case entered his life, he had followed one of the approved middle-class routes through life—college, law school, employment in a good firm with plans for a family of his own and a house in the suburbs. There was no place in this design for acts of extreme violence, the exhumation of corpses, hanging out with serial killers, or trying to bring down the chief executive of the United States of America, things he'd been doing way too much of lately.

Brad heard the guard in the kitchen say good morning to Dana before walking toward the back of the house. Plates rattled on the kitchen table, Dana making something for breakfast. Brad knew for a fact that he wouldn't be sitting in this house surrounded by armed guards if it weren't for her. He would probably be in his broom closet–size office working on a memo for one of the partners concerning some minuscule aspect of a multimillion-dollar real estate closing. Of course, some would say that being bored to death was better than being dead for real.

Part One

A Simple Assignment

Washington, D.C.
Two and a Half Months Earlier

Chapter One

Dana Cutler's cell phone rang moments after Jake Teeny's pickup disappeared around the corner and seconds after she closed the door of Jake's house, where she was house-sitting while he was away on an assignment.

"Cutler?" a raspy voice asked as soon as Dana flipped open the phone.

"What's up, Andy?" she asked.

Andy Zipay was an ex-cop who'd left the D.C. police force under a cloud a year before Dana had resigned for far different reasons. Dana had been one of the few cops who hadn't shunned Zipay, and she'd sent business his way when he'd set up shop as a private investigator. Six months after her release from the hospital, Dana had told him that she wouldn't mind working private if he had some overflow and the jobs were quiet. Zipay gave her assignments when he could, and she appreciated the fact that he had never asked her what had happened at the farm.

"You up for another job for Dale Perry?"

"Perry's a pig."

"True, but he liked the last job you did for him and he pays well."

"What's the deal?"

"A tail. It sounds like easy money. He needs someone right away and I have a full plate. You in or out?"

Dana's bank account needed an infusion of cash. She sighed.

"Does he want me to come to his office?"

"No." Zipay told her where to go.

"You're kidding?"

It was two in the morning when Dana eased Jake Teeny's Harley into a parking space in front of a twenty-four-hour pancake joint in suburban Maryland. She was wearing a black leather jacket, a black T-shirt, and tight jeans, an outfit that made her look tough. Even without the Harley and the outfit as props, people would back off instinctively in Dana's presence. She was a hard twenty-nine, five ten, lean and muscular, and she always seemed on edge. The intensity in her emerald green eyes was intimidating.

Before entering the Pancake House, Dana removed her helmet and shook out her shoulder-length auburn hair. As soon as she stepped through the door, she spotted Dale Perry in the rear of the restaurant. She ignored the hostess and headed to his booth. The lawyer was in his late forties, short, overweight, balding, and working on his third divorce. His fat face reminded Dana of a bulldog, but she was certain that Perry didn't see what others saw when he looked in the mirror, because he came on to every halfway attractive woman he met. Perry had made a pass at her the last time she'd done a job for him. She'd deflected it deftly and had even dropped hints that she was a lesbian to dissuade him, but that only seemed to create a challenge for the lascivious lawyer.

Dana rarely smiled, but her lips momentarily curled upward in amusement when she considered the spot that Dale Perry had selected for their meeting and the way he was dressed. Perry, a senior partner in a big D.C. firm, was a close friend of the president and very influential behind the scenes in national politics. He was the type who dressed in three-thousand-dollar power suits and conducted business in the bar at the Hay-Adams hotel, where Washington's power brokers decided the fate of the world while sipping twenty-five-year-old, single malt scotch. Tonight, the lawyer was cradling a chipped mug filled with bad Pancake House coffee and wearing jeans, a Washington Redskins jacket, dark glasses, and a Washington Nationals baseball cap with the brim pulled low.

"*Qué pasa?*" Dana asked as she slipped into the booth across from Perry and deposited her motorcycle helmet on the cracked vinyl.

"It's about time," Perry growled. Dana didn't react. She was used to Perry pulling rank. He was a macho pig who loved dumping on underlings. Dana didn't consider herself an underling, but there was no profit in letting Perry know how she felt. She never let her ego get in the way of making a buck.

"So, Mr. Perry, what's the problem?" Dana asked as she took off her jacket.

A waitress appeared and Dana ordered coffee. When the waitress was out of earshot, the lawyer resumed their conversation. Even though there were no other customers in their vicinity, he lowered his voice and leaned forward.

"Remember that job you did for me last year?"

"Tailing the guy who worked for the senator?"

Perry nodded.

"How'd that work out?" Dana asked.

Perry smiled. "Very nicely. I played him the tape. He threatened to sue, have me arrested, blah, blah, blah. But, in the end, he caved."

"Glad to hear it worked out."

"You do good work."

Now it was Dana's turn to nod. She did do excellent work. Private investigation suited her. She could stay in the shadows a good part of the time when she was working at jobs that Perry's firm would never assign to their in-house investigators, and the pay for assignments that weren't completely kosher was higher than most hourly wages. They were also tax free because she was always paid off the books and in cash.

The waitress returned with Dana's coffee. When she left, Perry dug into a manila envelope that was lying on the seat next to him. He pushed a color photograph of a young woman across the table.

"Her name is Charlotte Walsh. She's nineteen, a student at American University. I'll give you her address and some other information before you leave."

Dana studied the photograph. The girl was pretty. No, more than pretty. She had a sweet, fresh-faced look, like the good girl in movies about teens in high school, blue eyes, soft blond hair. Dana bet she'd been a cheerleader.

"My client wants her followed everywhere she goes." Perry handed Dana a cell phone. "The client also wants a running account of everything Walsh does." Perry slid a piece of notepaper with a phone number across the table. "Leave voice mail messages anytime she makes a move with details about what she's doing. Pictures, too. You'll give me everything you've got. Don't keep any copies."

Dana frowned. "This kid's just a student?"

"Sophomore studying poli-sci."

Dana's brow furrowed. "Who's the client, her parents, worried about their little girl?"

"You don't need to know that. Just do your job."

"Sure, Mr. Perry."

The lawyer took a thick envelope stuffed with bills off the seat and handed it to Dana.

"Will that do?"

Dana lowered the envelope beneath the tabletop and counted the cash. When she was done, she nodded. Perry handed her the manila envelope from which he'd taken Walsh's photograph.

"There's more information about the subject in here. Get rid of everything after you've read it."

"Do you want any reports?" she asked.

"No, just the photographs. I don't want anything on paper. Keep me out of it unless there's a problem."

"Sure thing." Dana stood up, leaving three-quarters of the coffee in her mug. She put on her jacket, stuffed the money in a pocket, and zipped the pocket shut. Perry didn't say good-bye.

Dana reviewed the meeting on the ride back to Jake Teeny's house. The job seemed easy enough, but she knew there was more to this assignment than figuring out how a cute coed spent her days. The money Perry had given her was more than a simple tail merited, and there was no way Perry would want to meet at two in the morning in a bad pancake restaurant in the suburbs if this was an ordinary assignment. If she needed more proof that something was up, Perry hadn't hit on her. Still, the money was good, and tailing a college kid should be easy. Dana forgot about the job, goosed the Harley, and gave herself over to the ride.

Chapter Two

Charlotte Walsh looked up from the economic report she had been pretending to read and glanced around the campaign headquarters of the Senator Gaylord for President Committee. It was five-thirty and most of the volunteers and employees were either at dinner or headed home, leaving only a skeleton staff. When she was certain that no one was near the office of Reggie Styles, Senator Maureen Gaylord's campaign coordinator, Walsh took a deep breath and crossed the room. Styles was out of the office at a meeting and the desks near his office were deserted for the moment, but that could change in a heartbeat. The suite was usually filled with noisy volunteers.

The only reason Walsh had the economic report was because it was a thick stack of loose pages. She carried the report into Styles's office. If she was caught, she would say she was leaving it for him. She felt light-headed and a little nauseated. She also felt guilty. She had never meant to be a spy when she volunteered for President Farrington's reelection campaign, but Chuck Hawkins, the president's top aide, had asked her to infiltrate Gaylord's headquarters as a personal favor to the president. There had been a promise of a job at the White House as a reward. And then there had been the private meeting with President Farrington in Chicago.

Walsh swallowed hard as she remembered that midnight meeting in the president's hotel suite. Then she forced herself to concentrate. She had seen Styles put the spreadsheets for the secret slush fund into the lower right drawer of his desk. Walsh looked over her shoulder. When she was certain no one was looking, she used the key she'd copied and took the five sheets out of the desk. When she'd slipped them randomly between the pages of the economic report she hurried to the copying machine and started feeding the sheaf of papers into it. When the copy was finished she would take it with her after returning the originals of the purloined material to Styles's desk.

"Working late?"

Charlotte jumped. She'd been so focused she had not heard Tim Moultrie slip up behind her. Moultrie was a junior at Georgetown who was an avid supporter of Senator Gaylord. He also had the hots for Charlotte and had hit on her as soon as she started working as a volunteer. Moultrie wasn't bad-looking, and he was awfully smart, but he was just a college boy, and boys her age didn't interest Charlotte anymore.

"Hi, Tim," she answered, unable to keep a tremor out of her voice.

"I didn't mean to startle you," he said, laughing. "I guess I just have that effect on women."

Charlotte managed a weak smile. Out of the corner of her eye she saw the pages collating in the plastic tray attached to the copier.

"What are you up to?" Tim asked.

"Just copying a report on the Asian trade deficit. Senator Gaylord wants to hammer Farrington on his trade policy."

"That should be easy. Farrington's trade policies have been a disaster. If he gets elected we'll be a Chinese territory before his term is through."

"I agree completely," Charlotte said, egging Tim on in the hopes that he'd be so busy expounding his theories that he wouldn't pay any attention to the papers she was copying.

The ploy worked, and the last page shot out of the machine halfway through Tim's tirade against the evils of the subsidy Japan was giving to one of its industries.

"I'm glad you're around to explain this economic stuff to me," said Charlotte, who'd aced her course in international economic theory.

"Not a problem," Tim answered as Charlotte stacked the original and the copy in two neat piles.

"Say, it's almost dinnertime. Want to grab a bite?" he asked.

Charlotte glanced at the wall clock. It was only a little after six and she had a few hours to kill before her meeting.

"Gee, I'd love to. Where do you want to go?"

Tim named a Thai restaurant a few blocks from campaign head-quarters.

"Thai sounds great. Give me a few minutes to straighten my desk and do a few odds and ends. Can I meet you in the lobby?"

"Sure thing." Tim beamed.

Charlotte stalled for time in the copy room by leafing through one of the paper piles. As soon as Tim was out of sight, she extracted the five stolen pages from the stack of originals and returned to Reggie Styles's office. She had just finished putting them back in the lower drawer when Tim walked up.

"What are you doing?" he asked, sounding suspicious this time.

"God, Tim! You've got to stop sneaking up on me. You'll give me a heart attack. Instead of having dinner with you, I'll be in the hospital."

Tim's face cleared and he smiled. "Wouldn't want that to happen," he said.

Charlotte placed the economic report in a stack of papers in Styles's in-box and carried the copy with the list of slush fund con-tributors to her desk.

"I'll see you in a minute," she said as she slipped the documents into her backpack and began straightening papers in a way that made her look as if she were actually doing something.

"See you in the lobby."

The door closed behind Tim. Charlotte sagged with relief. She'd done it. Of course, she'd have to fake enjoying dinner with Tim. She couldn't think of a way to get out of it without raising his suspicions, but that was a small sacrifice. Her adventure in political espionage had made her ravenously hungry anyway, and she was sure Tim would insist on paying for the meal. A narrow escape and a free meal; not a bad evening so far, she reckoned, and it would only get better in a few hours.

Chapter Three

Early in his presidency, Christopher Farrington had felt like a fraud, and he'd wondered how many other presidents had felt this way. Farrington was certain that every person who went into politics harbored a secret dream of one day being the president of the United States, but once the chosen few achieved their dream, he wondered if holding the office felt as surreal to them as his ascension to the presidency felt to him.

In his case the dreamlike quality of his presidency had been heightened by the fact that there had been no election, only an early morning visit from a Secret Service agent telling him that President Nolan had suffered a fatal heart attack and he was now the commander in chief. One minute he was serving in the relative anonymity of the vice presidency and the next minute he was the Leader of the Free World.

No one watching Christopher Farrington walk down the hall to his son's room would have guessed that he harbored doubts about his ability to lead the nation. Farrington looked presidential. He was tall and broad shouldered, his full head of glossy black hair had enough gray to give a simultaneous impression of vigor and maturity, and his welcoming smile told you that he might have risen to the heights, but he was still a guy with whom you could share a cup of coffee at your kitchen table. Tonight, as he stood in the doorway watching his wife tuck in the covers around Patrick, their six-year-old son, he also looked like any proud parent. His chest swelled with pride when Claire leaned over and kissed Patrick's forehead.

President Farrington's son would have none of the childhood memories the president had. Chris had grown up poor in rural Oregon with only a dim recollection of the father who'd deserted him, his mother, and his brothers and sisters. Most evenings, his mother had been too tired from working two jobs to tuck in Chris or his siblings. On the occasions when she'd bothered, her breath had been a mixture of mint and cheap liquor.

Sports had saved Farrington's life. He was six five and had a good enough jump shot to corral a scholarship at Oregon State, where he'd guided OSU to two appearances in the NCAA tournament. He was no slouch in the classroom either and his grades and financial need had earned him a full ride to law school in Oregon. There was a good chance that he could have gotten into one of the nation's elite law schools, but political office had been Christopher Farrington's goal since being elected class president in high school. A degree from Harvard or Yale didn't appeal to him as much as the possibility of making influential contacts during his three years in law school, and at this he succeeded. Powerful backers and his notoriety as a sports hero helped him win a spot in the state senate on his first try. He'd risen to the position of majority leader when he decided to take on an incumbent governor, who was brought low by a financial scandal uncovered by an intrepid reporter two months before the election. Farrington's closest friend and top aide, Charles Hawkins, had learned about the governor's peccadilloes before advising his boss to make the run and had fed the information about them to the reporter when the time was right.

Claire lowered the shade in Patrick's room, and the spotlighted Washington Monument disappeared from view. She turned toward the doorway and smiled.

"How long have you been standing there?" she asked when they were in the hall.

"A few seconds," Farrington answered as he closed the door quietly behind them.

The hall outside the family bedrooms reminded the Farringtons of a floor in a colonial inn. A plush blue carpet went well with the old-fashioned, off-white wallpaper that President Nolan's wife had selected. A few oil paintings from the 1800s depicting rural America in all its glory were interspersed with portraits of some of the lesser-known presidents. Freestanding lamps and a few small chandeliers lit their way. The Farringtons didn't care much about interior decorating so there had been no change in the décor since Christopher had ascended to the presidency.

The president was dressed in a dark blue, pinstripe business suit. The first lady was dressed in a powder blue pants suit and a cream-colored silk blouse. As they strolled down the hall Farrington wrapped his arm around Claire's shoulder. It was easy to do, since Claire was only a few inches shorter than her husband.

The first lady was a powerfully built woman who had gone to Oregon State on a volleyball scholarship and ended up as a third team all-American in her senior year. Her shoulder-length brown hair was curly, her nose was a little too large, and her blue eyes were a tad small for her face. She had a high forehead and flat cheekbones. Though not plain, she was certainly not girlishly pretty, but she was charismatic, and her size and intellect dominated any gathering. She had been the captain of her high school and college volleyball teams, captain of her high school basketball team, valedictorian of her high school, and an honors student in college and medical school.

Chris and Claire had married while Claire was in medical school in Portland and Christopher was on the verge of his first run for office. Claire had cut back on her practice when Patrick was born and had given it up when the family moved to Washington, D.C., after Christopher was elected vice president.

"You could have come in and kissed Patrick good night," Claire said.

"You two seemed so at peace that I didn't want to spoil the moment."

The president kissed his wife on the forehead. "Have I ever told you what a great mother you are?"

"From time to time," Claire responded with a sly smile, "and you're going to get many more chances."

Farrington looked confused, and Claire laughed. "I'm pregnant."

Farrington stopped short. He looked stunned.

"You're serious?"

Claire stopped smiling. "You're not sorry, are you?"

"No, no, it's just . . . I thought you were on the pill."

"I decided to stop taking it two months ago." She put her hands on Chris's shoulders and looked him in the eye. "Are you mad?"

A mix of emotions swept across the president's face but the words he spoke were the right ones.

"We always wanted more kids. I just thought another pregnancy would be tough with everything you have to do as first lady."

"Don't worry about me. Being pregnant didn't slow me down during the gubernatorial campaign."

"True. It was actually a plus, if I recall."

"And it will be a plus this time. The women will applaud your family values and the men will be in awe of your virility."

Farrington laughed. Then he hugged Claire.

"You're a treasure." He stepped back until they were at arm's length. "Are you going to be okay tonight?"

"I'll be fine. My speech is short and it will be nice going out in public before I start looking like a whale."

"You don't feel sick?"

"I've had a little morning sickness, but I'm okay now. Chuck called ahead to the hotel and booked a suite in case I need to rest."

"I love you," Farrington said, hugging her again. "You know I wouldn't have dumped this on you at the last minute if this meeting wasn't important, but Gaylord's pulling out all the stops. Chuck says she's raising a lot of money."

Farrington sounded worried. Claire laid her palm against his cheek. It was warm, and the touch calmed him.

"Maureen is going to shit bullets when we announce I'm pregnant. Let's see her claim the family values high ground now."

"I'm going to send Chuck with you."

"Won't he be needed at the meeting?"

"I want him by your side, Claire. I want to know you're protected."

Claire kissed her husband's cheek. "Don't worry about me, and definitely don't worry about Maureen Gaylord."

Chapter Four

Dana Cutler was bored out of her skull. After three days of following Charlotte Walsh to class, the supermarket, restaurants, and her apartment, she was ready to shoot herself. This girl's life was so dull that Dana couldn't imagine why anyone was interested in it. She would have quit if the job didn't pay so well.

A little after 6 P.M., Dana had left a phone message for her mystery client at the number Dale Perry had given her, explaining that Walsh had walked out of Senator Gaylord's campaign headquarters in the company of a white male, approximately six feet tall with wavy blond hair and a neatly trimmed mustache. The subject and her escort had proceeded to the House of Thai where they were currently sharing what appeared to be pad thai, spring rolls, and some type of curry. Cutler was able to give this detailed report because she was seated in her car in a disabled parking spot viewing the couple through the lens of the Leica M8 digital camera that belonged to Jake Teeny. The disabled parking permit on her dashboard was courtesy of an acquaintance at the Department of Motor Vehicles who sold fake driver's licenses, disabled permits, and other DMV goodies to supplement her income. If anyone ever asked, Dana would claim she was recovering from hip-replacement surgery and she had a letter from a quack who was on her acquaintance's payroll to back her up.

Dana had taken a chance and peed in another restaurant two

doors down from the Thai place as soon as Walsh and her buddy ordered. Now, an hour later, she was free of the call of nature, but her
stomach was rumbling. Dana grabbed a doughnut from the box on
her passenger seat and was taking a bite when Walsh stood up. She
stopped in midbite. Walsh had grabbed her backpack and headed for
the door. Dana dropped the camera next to the box of doughnuts
and started the engine of her inconspicuous, brown Toyota. The car
looked like a piece of crap but Dana had installed an engine that
would have made a NASCAR driver envious. Her father had owned a
garage and raced cars when he was younger. Dana loved speed and
learned how a car worked almost as soon as she learned her ABC's.
Her dad had died of a stroke before she'd finished working on the
engine and she'd always been sad that she hadn't been able to take
him for a spin in her jalopy.

Thinking about her dad brought back memories of her childhood.
She was certain that her memories were far different from those of
Charlotte Walsh. Dana's mother had walked out on the family in
Dana's sophomore year in high school. They talked occasionally, but
Dana had never forgiven her for deserting the family. Walsh probably
had great Thanksgivings and Christmases with loving parents and
bright, overachieving siblings.

Dana's folks hadn't been poor, but there was never any money for
frills. Dana had to work during high school if she wanted spending
money. Long nights as a waitress had paid her tuition to a community college, and Dana had been an underachiever until she joined
the police force. Being a cop was something she was good at, but her
days on the force were behind her now and she'd never get them
back.

Walsh headed back toward Gaylord campaign headquarters on K
Street. A lot of the people who worked on K Street were lawyers, lob-
byists, and employees of think tanks, and many of them had returned
to the suburbs for dinner. The cafés where Washington's elite met for
power lunches were closed and a lot of the windows in the high-rise

office buildings were dark. Few pedestrians walked the streets, and the street vendors who hawked flowers and knockoffs of Rolex watches and Prada purses had closed up shop. Dana guessed that her quarry was going to the garage where she'd parked a few hours ago. Sure enough, Walsh disappeared into the garage and drove out a few minutes later.

There weren't many cars on the road so Dana hung back, speeding up anytime she felt in danger of losing sight of Walsh's taillights. She hoped Walsh was going home to bed so she could get some sleep, too. The Toyota hit a pothole and the camera bounced on the passenger seat. When she thought about the camera, she automatically thought about Jake Teeny. He was a photojournalist Dana had met when he'd been assigned to take the photos for an article on policewomen. When she left the force, he'd helped her through her hardest days.

It wasn't unusual for Jake to be away for weeks at a time in some exotic locale or war zone. When he was in D.C. and they both felt like it, Dana stayed at Jake's house, which was roomier than the small apartment she called home. They'd been friends and off-and-on lovers for years, but neither of them wanted anything permanent and the relationship was convenient for both of them. Jake was the only person to whom she'd opened up about what had happened at the farm, though she hadn't come close to telling him the whole story. She couldn't risk losing him, something that could very well happen if he learned everything she'd done.

When Walsh turned onto the E Street expressway Dana knew that her quarry wasn't headed back to her apartment. Her dream of an early night disappeared and she turned on the radio. A newscast was just ending with a story about the latest victim of the D.C. Ripper, a serial killer who'd been murdering women in the D.C. area. The announcer was explaining that the police appeared to be stymied when Dana turned the dial to DC101. After she left the hospital, Dana found that she had trouble listening to stories about violence to women. When she'd been a cop, she'd dealt with victims' tales of rape, wife beating, and the like with a professional detachment she could no longer summon up.

"Highway to Hell" by AC/DC started playing just as the city gave way to a tree-lined roadway when she merged onto 66-west. Walsh took the exit for the Dulles Toll Road and drove along VA-267, exiting fifteen miles later onto Sully Road. After they passed a few illuminated construction sites and half-built subdivisions the Dulles Towne Center suddenly appeared in the distance. Dana groaned when she realized that the mall was Walsh's destination.

It was late, so most of the sprawling lot was free of cars. Dana expected Walsh to park near the well-lit mall entrance where the vehicles of those still shopping congregated, but she surprised Dana by driving past JCPenney and Old Navy to a remote section of the lot where the glow from the Sears and Nordstrom signs did not reach. Dana drove away from Walsh, turned off her lights, and circled back to a spot many rows away that gave her an unobstructed view of the driver's side of the student's car.

As soon as she parked, Dana checked her watch. It was seven-forty-five, so it had taken almost forty-five minutes to drive to the mall from K Street. She took a few shots of the car before phoning her client to report where they were and where Walsh had parked in the lot. Then she took a drink of coffee from her thermos to help her stay awake and grabbed the doughnut she'd started outside the Thai restaurant. She finished the doughnut and perked up when she noticed that Walsh was still sitting in her car. This was the first interesting thing that had happened during her surveillance. If Walsh wasn't at the mall to shop she was probably waiting for someone. If she was meeting this someone in a dark and remote part of the mall parking lot instead of the interior of the mall she didn't want anyone to see the meeting. Maybe there was a reason to watch the coed after all.

Dana focused Teeny's camera on Walsh's car and was about to take a few more shots when movement in her peripheral vision caused her to look right. A dark blue Ford drove into Walsh's row and parked a space away from her. Teeny's camera lens had a 3.4 f-stop so Dana could see the license plate. From farther away, she wouldn't have been able to read the license, but she could take a picture of it and blow up the picture on her laptop. Dana jotted down the Ford's license plate number. A moment later, Walsh got out of her car, looked around nervously, and got into the Ford's backseat. The Ford drove off with Dana in pursuit, far enough back so, hopefully, her lights wouldn't give her away.

In almost no time, Dana found herself heading into Virginia on a two-lane highway. It became harder to stay close enough to see the Ford, but luckily there were a few other cars on the road to screen her. Trees soon began to outnumber man-made structures. She made a note of the route on a pad she'd placed on the passenger seat then fiddled with the dial until she found an oldies station playing a Springsteen classic.

Dana cruised along about a mile farther when the Ford's brake lights went on. She slowed to a crawl. The Ford turned onto a narrow country road, crossed a railroad track, and drove by the darkened storefronts that lined the main street of a sleepy village. Dana jotted down the name of the town. A few miles past the city limits the Ford took a right onto a dirt road that was barely wide enough for two cars. Dana noted the distance she'd traveled from the village to the turnoff before cutting her lights and following the other car's taillights.

After a quarter mile, the Ford's headlights illuminated a white slat fence and a quarter mile after that the car stopped at a gate. Dana was surprised to see an armed guard. While the guard was concentrating on the occupants of the Ford, she put the Toyota in reverse and backed into a side road. If she had to run she didn't want to waste time turning around. Dana stuffed the cell phone in her jacket pocket and grabbed a heavy flashlight and the camera. She crouched down, crossed the road, hopped the fence, and ducked into the woods, pushing through the foliage with the flashlight beam held low so it wouldn't attract attention. After a short hike, she found herself on top of a small hill looking down on a white clapboard house that was about a football field away. The Ford was parked next to the front door but no one was in it. Dana had been surprised that there was an armed guard at the gate and more surprised to find other guards patrolling the grounds.

It was chilly, and Dana turned up her collar before settling in with her back against a tree. The ground was rocky and she had to shift around before she was comfortable. Nothing happened for several minutes. Dana drew up her knees, balanced the camera lens on them, and passed the time studying the house. The building looked like something from colonial times that had been updated with additions that were almost indistinguishable from the original. The bottom floor was illuminated, but that was all she could tell because the thick curtains on the front windows shielded the interior from view while letting only a little light escape.

To kill more time, Dana phoned in a whispered report to the client then snapped a few shots of the house, the guards, and the license plate of a dark blue Lincoln sedan that was parked at the side of the house. She jotted down the number of the plate on the sheet where she'd written the number of the car that had taken Walsh to the house. Dana was about to take another shot when a light went on in an upstairs room. She framed the window in her lens. A man stood in it briefly with his back to her, but he moved away before she could snap a shot. Dana peered into the room, but all she could make out from her angle were two shifting shadows on the wall. The shadows separated then came together until there was one flat black mass flowing across it. Moments later, the shadows dropped below the level of the sill and the room went dark.

Dana leaned back against the tree. She wished she'd had the foresight to bring the thermos along. She also hoped that Walsh wasn't going to spend the night because camping out wasn't her thing. She was getting bored so she watched the guards patrol the grounds and tried to figure out their routine. One of the armed men was a redhead with a crew cut. When he reached the point in his patrol that brought him closest to Dana she checked out his arsenal. He appeared to have a Sig Sauer 9-mm handgun in his holster and he was carrying a Heckler and Koch MP5 semiautomatic machine gun. She was trying to get a better look at the guns through the telephoto lens when the lights in the upstairs room came on again. A shadow appeared on the wall seconds before Charlotte Walsh walked in front of the window. Dana couldn't hear what she was saying but she was waving her arms rapidly and she looked like she was yelling.

Dana checked her watch. It was nine-thirty. It had taken her a little over an hour to drive from the mall to the farmhouse and Walsh had been upstairs for about a half hour. She finished her calculations just as the front door opened and Walsh stormed out. Dana snapped a few pictures. Walsh turned back to the house and talked to a man who was standing in the doorway. She was bent forward slightly and her fists were clenched. Her anger traveled up the hill on the crisp, night air but Dana was too far away to make out what she was saying.

Dana shifted the lens to the man in the doorway. She could see his shirtsleeve and part of a pants leg but she couldn't see his face. One of the guards got into the driver's side of the car she had followed from the mall and Walsh threw herself into the backseat. As the car drove off, Dana used the cell phone to report that Walsh was probably heading back to the mall. While she talked, she kept an eye on the front door in hopes that the man Walsh had been with would put in an appearance. Just as she was finishing her report the man stepped out of the house. Dana dropped the phone and aimed her camera. The man turned his face in her direction. He was too far away for Dana to make out his features clearly, but something about him was familiar. She snapped off a quick shot and was going to take another when a branch snapped.

Dana froze for a second before rolling behind the tree against which she'd been leaning. The crackling of more leaves told her that someone was headed her way fast. She guessed it was a guard who was patrolling the woods and felt like a fool for assuming that the only guards were stationed around the house.

Dana peeked around the tree and spotted a man carrying an MP5 moving toward her. She cursed under her breath and stuffed the cell phone in her pocket as she ran through her choices. She was armed but she wasn't going to shoot the guard. Under the circumstances, it would be felony assault or cold-blooded murder. She couldn't run without being seen and he was so close he'd hit her for sure even if he was a lousy shot. When she realized that her choices boiled down to surrender or resistance she flashed back to the basement.

Dana felt light-headed and began to shake. Her flashbacks weren't memories. They were more like a dream in which what you dreamt seemed real. Dana could smell the dank odor of mold on the basement walls and the foul water that pooled against them. Worse still, she could smell the sweat coming off the men who had held her captive.

Whenever the flashbacks occurred, Dana forced herself to take deep breaths. She did that now because she could not afford to be paralyzed by fear. The deep breathing distracted her long enough for the guard to disappear from view. Dana panicked as she scanned the forest. The man reappeared, closer now and definitely stalking her position. When he moved behind another tree, she inched away. The guard dashed toward the spot where she'd been sitting moments before and stopped, shocked that she was gone.

Dana ran, zigzagging through the underbrush to give the guard as difficult a target as possible. The guard raced toward the sounds Dana made in retreat. She knew he'd catch her soon or get close enough to take a shot, so she slid behind a tree, hoping that the guard's heavy breathing would mask the fact that she wasn't making any more noise. When the guard ran past her tree Dana smashed the flashlight across the back of his skull. He dropped to his knees and the gun discharged, spraying tree trunks and bushes. She wrenched it away and hurled it into the woods. The guard struggled to his knees, and she hit him again. He collapsed just as snapping branches, crackling leaves, and muted gasps from the base of the hill told Dana that the other guards had heard the shots and were speeding toward her.

Dana broke out of the trees and vaulted the fence. She'd guessed where her car was and she was only off by a few yards. She wrenched open the driver's door, threw the camera and flashlight onto the passenger seat, and started the engine. As she peeled out of the side road she looked in the rearview mirror and saw the redheaded guard vault the fence. Dana floored the accelerator, and the souped-up engine did what it was built to do. She swerved back and forth, sending up clouds of dust in the hope that they would make it more difficult for the guard to get off a good shot, but he held his fire. When she looked in her rearview mirror again he was writing something in a notebook. If it was her license plate number she was screwed. She was miles from home. If an APB was broadcast there was a good chance she'd be stopped while driving or find the police waiting for her at her apartment.

Dana tapped into her GPS and took side streets until she reached a large housing development. When she was certain that no one was following her, she parked on a side street. She'd had some time to think and she made a decision. Dana dialed the mystery client and heard the familiar generic voice tell her to leave a message.

"This is me again," she said after the beep. "I was just chased through the woods by a man with a gun. I had to slug him to get away. Being chased by armed men was not in the job description I was given. This definitely isn't what I signed on for, so this is my last report.

"The subject looked pretty upset when she left. I'm guessing she's headed back to her car in the mall and she'll probably go home after that, so I don't expect there'll be much more to report today anyway. I'll get the photos I took to your lawyer and he can give them to you.

"I don't know what's going on here, but I have no idea who you are so I can't give you up. The attorney-client privilege should protect you, too, so you don't have to worry about anyone discovering your identity. Your lawyer should be able to find someone else to carry on the surveillance."

Dana couldn't think of anything more to say so she ended the call. Then she sat in the car and tried to figure out a plan that wouldn't involve her going to jail for assault and trespass, but she was too wound up to think straight. Dana closed her eyes and saw an image of the man Charlotte Walsh had met. Why did she feel she'd seen him before? He had to be someone important or he wouldn't have had all those guards. Who was he? Was he someone famous? Had she seen him on TV?

Dana got an idea. She put away the cell phone Dale Perry had given her, turned on her own, and made a call to Andy Zipay.

"Zip, it's Dana. Do you know someone who can run some license plates for me?"

"Is this for the Perry thing?"

"Yeah."

"There's a cop who'll do it for me, but I don't like to use him too much."

"It's important."

"Give me the numbers," Zipay said.

Dana told him the license number of the Ford that had taken Walsh to the house, the number of the Lincoln sedan that was parked at the house, and she threw in Walsh's license plate for good measure. Maybe Walsh's car was registered in her parents' name and she'd get a clue to why Walsh was so important. She knew she was done with the case but she was still curious to know what was going on.

"How soon do you need this?" Zipay asked.

"As soon as possible."

"I'll get right on it."

Dana ended the call and thought about what she'd do next. It had been dark when she escaped and she'd stirred up all that dust. Maybe the redheaded guard hadn't gotten her license plate number or maybe he'd written it down incorrectly. She'd find out soon enough, but she didn't want to find out tonight. The natural choice for a place to sleep was Jake's, since she was house-sitting anyway. Dana started the car and headed there, glad to be rid of Dale Perry's assignment.

Chapter Five

The light from dozens of crystal chandeliers illuminated the tuxedo-and-evening-gown-clad elite who filled the grand ballroom of the Theodore Roosevelt Hotel in downtown Washington. Every inch of the huge ballroom was covered with circular tables draped with white tablecloths and decorated with elegant floral arrangements. For $1,000 a seat or $10,000 to sponsor a table, the contributors to Christopher Farrington's campaign had been served a dinner of chicken or salmon, mashed potatoes, and asparagus. No one came to these fund-raisers for the food. Many of the attendees paid hard cash for rubber chicken because they expected the party to remember them fondly in the future. And if Farrington didn't prevail, more than one of those in attendance had hedged his bet by contributing to Maureen Gaylord's campaign chest, too.

Some of those in the crowd were ardent supporters of Christopher Farrington and were actually there to hear the president. They had been disappointed when it was announced that affairs of state had kept him from attending, but the mood changed quickly when the first lady began to speak. Claire Farrington had been funny and forceful, and the highlight of her speech had been her discussion of the president's education policy, which she'd led into by voicing her concerns about America's schools as a mother *and* a mother-to-be. Thunderous applause had greeted the announcement of her pregnancy and an equally raucous round of handclapping signaled the crowd's approval when her speech ended.

"You knocked their socks off," Charles Hawkins told Claire as he escorted her off the dais. Hawkins was six two, lean, and hard muscled and he wore his salt-and-pepper hair in a buzz cut. He'd been an army Ranger before a knee injury suffered on a combat mission forced him to retire from the service. Except for a barely noticeable limp he still looked like he was on patrol in enemy territory. His hard eyes were always scanning the terrain for threats to the first family, and he was ready to strike at anyone who threatened Claire Farrington or her husband.

"You really think I did okay?" Claire asked.

"You had them eating out of your hand, and breaking the news that you're going to be a mother again was a stroke of genius. That's going to be the lead story in every newspaper in the country tomorrow."

"I certainly hope so," Claire said as her six-person Secret Service detail surrounded her and guided her through a corridor behind the kitchen. "Poor Maureen, she's giving a major speech outlining her foreign policy at Georgetown, tonight. I bet it'll be buried somewhere on page six."

At the end of the back hall was the elevator that would take her to an elegantly appointed meeting room on the second floor of the hotel where she was scheduled to have her picture taken with a small group of major contributors. They had almost arrived at the elevator bank when Claire grimaced and her hand went to her stomach.

"Is anything wrong?" Hawkins asked, alarmed.

"I'd forgotten that morning sickness doesn't just happen in the morning. Let's make this quick, Chuck."

"I'll call off the photo op if you give me the word. Everyone will understand."

"How many photos will I have to sit for?"

"I think there are twenty-five, but they're all more interested in access to Chris than another photo for the mantel. We'll promise them a private photo shoot at the White House."

Claire put her hand on Hawkins's forearm. "No, I'll be okay. If it gets really bad I'll tell you. I've got the suite so I can lie down if I get exhausted."

"You're certain you want to do this?"

"I'm fine," she assured Hawkins. "Just move the line along and tell the photographer not to dawdle."

"Ray," she said, turning to Ray Cinnegar, the head of the Secret Service detail. "Can you take me to a restroom? I need a few minutes."

"Sure thing. Maxine," he called to the woman who was point leader for the detail and had checked out the route earlier. "Mrs. F. needs to make a restroom stop."

"There's one coming up at the next turn. I'll scope it out."

"Go."

By the time Claire made the turn, Maxine was inside the restroom. Cinnegar kept the first lady outside until Maxine assured him that the restroom was secure. Claire sighed with relief.

When they arrived at the Theodore Roosevelt Meeting Room Hawkins ushered the first lady inside. The spacious room was furnished with original pieces that President Roosevelt had brought with him to the White House from Sagamore Hill, his family home. A line of men and women stood between the wall and a red velvet rope supported by brass stanchions. The line ended near the hotel's most famous antique, a grandfather's clock that had stood in a sitting room in the White House and graced the cover of the hotel's brochure. The photographer was waiting in front of the clock, which rang nine times moments after the first lady entered.

Most of the men and women on the line were powerful attorneys, wealthy financiers, corporate executives and their spouses, but many of them looked like anxious children waiting to climb on Santa's knee. Claire was amused. She'd experienced this phenomenon many times during her White House years—rich and powerful men and women reduced to gawking tourists at a celebrity sighting.

Several other people were milling around the room sipping champagne or eating the hors d'oeuvres that had been set out for the upscale crowd. One of the men had just stuffed a piece of caviar-smeared toast into his mouth. When he saw the first lady he wiped his hands on a napkin and swallowed quickly before walking over to her.

"Dale!" she said when she saw the lawyer.

"Just thought I'd give you a heads up," Perry said. "The fifth guy in line is Herman Kava, an industrialist from Ohio and a client. Treat him nice."

"Treat him nice" was code for a big contribution alert. Claire smiled.

"Thank you, Dale."

"Glad to be of service. Hey, Chuck."

Hawkins nodded before leading the first lady to her position in front of the clock.

Roughly forty minutes later, Claire thanked the last person in the line. As soon as an aide led the contributor out of the room she sagged with relief.

"How are you feeling?" Hawkins asked.

"Exhausted. Let me sit down."

"Are you okay?" Dale Perry asked when Claire collapsed onto a chair.

"Oh, Dale, I thought you'd left."

"I did, but I wanted to tell you the good news. Kava will be writing a check and he says Chris will be very pleased."

"Good," she answered as she rested her head on the back of the chair and closed her eyes.

Hawkins was about to say something when his cell phone rang. He looked conflicted, but Perry waved him away.

"Take the call. I'll look after Claire."

Hawkins pressed the phone to his ear then he cursed. "There's no reception in here. I have to go outside."

"Its okay, Chuck," Claire assured him. "Dale will get me upstairs."

Hawkins hurried out and Claire struggled to her feet.

"What's upstairs?" asked Ray Cinnegar.

"I had Chuck book a suite for me in case I got sick or exhausted." Cinnegar scowled. "This is the first I've heard about a suite."

"I'm sorry. I did it at the last moment and I forgot to tell you."

"You're supposed to clear this type of thing with us so we can check it out in advance."

"I know, Ray. I'm sorry."

"I don't think I can let you go up. We don't know who's in the adjoining suite, we haven't checked the room for explosives . . ."

"Chuck also booked the adjoining suite and no one expected me to stay at the hotel. Check out the suite but do it quickly. I'm really not feeling well."

"You're certain you don't want to go back to the White House?" Cinnegar asked.

"I'm positive. I need to rest now."

"Where is it?" Cinnegar asked. She told Cinnegar and he gave instructions to one of his men.

"Let me help you," Dale Perry said as he offered her his arm. Claire headed for the door and the Secret Service detail closed around her. Cinnegar asked Claire if she was able to climb one flight of stairs. When she said she could, they walked up to the next floor. As soon as Cinnegar checked the hall the agent led them past the door to the suite across from the stairwell and around the corner to the suite the hotel had reserved for the first lady. Cinnegar had obtained a master key for the hotel the day before the fund-raiser and he opened the door. Two agents went into Claire's suite to check it. Two more agents were about to check the adjoining suite when the door opened and Chuck Hawkins stepped out.

"Where's the first lady?" Hawkins asked.

"Around the corner."

Hawkins walked around the corner and found Claire and Dale Perry waiting for the agents to finish examining the suite.

"Claire, I have to go. Is that okay?"

"Go. I'll be fine."

"You're certain?"

"Go," Claire said just as the agents gave the okay for her to go inside.

Hawkins disappeared moments before the team that had swept the adjoining suite gave their okay.

The front door to Claire's suite opened on a sitting room outfitted with a couch, an armoire that held a television, several armchairs, and a writing desk. Claire ignored this room and walked into the bedroom, which contained a king-size bed. She took off her shoes and jacket and sat down heavily on the bed.

"Dale, can you clear everyone out and make sure all of the lights are out. I want to crash. Tell Ray I'll let him know when I'm ready to go back to the White House."

"You got it. And congratulations on the baby."

Claire smiled. "Thanks, Dale. Now get everyone out so I can sleep."

"Sure thing," Dale said before walking into the sitting room where Cinnegar and a female agent were waiting.

"Mrs. F wants everyone out so she can nap," Claire heard Dale say as she stripped off her clothes. The front door closed a moment after she turned off the lights in the bedroom and closed the shades.

Chapter Six

As soon as Charlotte Walsh was in the backseat of the Ford she pressed against the door, wrapped her arms around her body, and started to cry. Her chest felt tight but she was hollow inside. He had never loved her. He'd just used her to spy for him then he'd used her like a whore. How could she have ever believed anything he'd said? In her dreams, he'd left his wife for her, but they were only pipe dreams, a ridiculous fantasy. She was ridiculous. She could see that now.

"Are you okay?" the driver asked.

She hadn't realized she was crying loud enough for him to hear.

"I'm all right," she managed to choke out as she ran a forearm across her eyes.

"Do you need some water? I've got a bottle up here."

"No, that's okay."

Charlotte took a few deep breaths and tried to calm down. She'd never seen it coming. She'd been so proud of herself for getting the records of Gaylord's secret slush fund that she'd preened like a peacock when the president praised her. She'd suspected nothing when they'd made love; although, in retrospect, calling what they'd done lovemaking was a joke.

Charlotte had been stunned when Farrington told her that this was the last time they could be together because his wife was pregnant.

He'd assured her that he loved her but asked her to understand that he couldn't leave Claire, now that she was carrying his child. What rot! She felt like a fool. No, she was a fool, a child. How could she have possibly believed that someone that powerful would throw everything away for a schoolgirl? She was an idiot, a self-deluded idiot.

Charlotte thought back to Chicago. Chuck Hawkins had told her that the president had been impressed with her when they'd met in the D.C. campaign headquarters and he wanted her to fly to Chicago to talk about a special project. Only a fool would have bought that line—the president had spoken to her for less than a minute—but she'd believed what she wanted to believe.

Hawkins had explained the necessity of sneaking her in the employees' entrance to the hotel. He'd said that her cover would be blown if anyone from Gaylord's camp saw her. What a chump she'd been to believe his story. It was clear now that Hawkins had been acting as Farrington's pimp, but she was so excited by the prospect of her important, secret mission that she wasn't thinking straight.

The president had met with her alone in his suite. He'd asked her to tell him all about herself and he'd listened intently to her every word while refilling her glass with the liquor she didn't want to drink but was embarrassed to reject. The heady thrill of being the confidante to a president as handsome as Christopher Farrington, her secret mission, and the alcohol had made it easy for him to seduce her. Hell, she wanted to be seduced. The seduction had been no challenge at all.

Charlotte took some deep breaths and they helped. So did the anger she was starting to feel. The Monica Lewinsky scandal flashed in her brain. It had almost destroyed Clinton. And there'd been Watergate before Lewinsky, a president covering up a burglary. What would happen to Mr. Family Values if the press learned that he'd slept with a teenage campaign volunteer to get her to steal secret documents from his opponent's campaign headquarters?

There were no tears now, just a white-hot rage that sharpened Charlotte's mind. She could ruin Farrington if she wanted to, but would it be worth it? Lewinsky had become a pariah, a laughing-stock, and the subject of cheap jokes on late-night television. Did she want everyone in the world to know about her pathetic sex life? And there was the possibility of criminal charges. She had stolen campaign documents. That must be a crime. Once she went to the press the president would do everything in his power to discredit and destroy her.

The thought of going to prison and the notoriety she would receive sobered Walsh. Her life would be ruined if she told what she knew. Charlotte closed her eyes and leaned back in her seat. She was wrung out emotionally, and she almost fell asleep, but the car braked for a stoplight and she opened her eyes. They were in the village they'd driven through a little while before turning onto the road to the farm.

Charlotte looked out the window at the darkened storefronts. The town looked so peaceful at night. She sighed. She was angry but maybe she shouldn't be. She'd had an adventure. Someday she would tell someone close about the brief period when she'd been the mistress of the president of the United States. She smiled. It was her dirty little secret, and right now she bet Farrington was wondering if she would keep it. Her smile widened as she realized that Christopher Farrington had a hell of a lot more to worry about than she did.

She stopped smiling. What had she said when she was yelling at him? Had she made any threats? She was certain she had. Suddenly, she was fearful, then she shook her head. Clearly she was too emotional to think straight. She had to relax so she could decide what she should do. Probably nothing, she concluded bitterly. Farrington had used her but it would cost her too much to fight back. She tried to think of what had happened to her as being no worse than being dumped by any other guy. Sure it hurt for a while, but she'd get over it.

"We're back," the driver announced. Charlotte had been so pre-occupied that she hadn't realized that they had returned to the mall.

The driver turned in his seat and studied Walsh. He looked forty. His face was lean but there was gray in his hair and lines on his face. He seemed concerned.

"You sure you're okay?" he asked.

"Yeah, I'll be fine," she said, and she felt that she might be after a little while. It was never fun to be discarded, and she'd been so excited about being the confidante of a president, but she should have known that it wouldn't last.

Charlotte got out and shut the back door. The driver waited until Charlotte was in her car before driving off.

Charlotte sat in the car and tried to pull herself together. It was late and she was exhausted. She would think more clearly in the morning, but she was certain she'd come to the same conclusion. She should put this behind her and get on with her life. The sex had been okay and she'd had her fifteen minutes of fame, although no one would ever know about it. She sighed and put the key in the ignition. Nothing happened. She tried again but the engine wouldn't start.

Oh, great, she thought. Then she laughed. What else could go wrong?

She was bending toward her purse to get her cell phone when the driver's door was ripped open.

Chapter Seven

When he arrived at the farm, Charles Hawkins was escorted to the library. Two walls were filled with books that actually appeared to have been read. A stone fireplace dominated another wall. Someone had built a fire. A picture window that looked out on a wide back lawn took up the fourth wall. An unusual aspect of the room was the bulletproof glass in the picture window.

"What took you so long?" Farrington asked as soon as Hawkins walked into the library. He was holding a glass half filled with scotch and Hawkins suspected it wasn't his first.

"I don't have wings, Chris," Hawkins answered calmly. He was used to Farrington's moods.

"I'm sorry," Farrington said. "I'm upset."

Hawkins dropped onto a sofa and studied his friend carefully. Farrington looked exhausted, his jacket was off, his tie was askew, and his hair was mussed, as if the president had been running his fingers through it a lot.

"Tell me why I'm here," Hawkins said.

"It's that girl, Walsh. You know we talked about the records for Maureen's slush fund?"

"She was going to get them for us."

"Yeah, well she called. She said she could get the records tonight. I told her to come here."

"Where did she call?"

"The White House."

"How did she get through to you?"

"I gave her my cell."

"Jesus, Chris. That line's not secure."

"Don't worry. She didn't use her real name."

"I thought we'd agreed I was going to handle this."

Farrington looked down at the floor.

"You screwed her, didn't you?" Hawkins said.

"I couldn't help myself."

"You didn't screw her in Chicago, too, did you?"

Farrington didn't answer.

"Goddamn it, Chris, you swore to me that you didn't touch her. You were only supposed to convince her to be our eyes and ears in Maureen's campaign headquarters."

"I know, I know."

"You promised me you wouldn't pull this shit anymore."

"I broke it off," Farrington answered. Hawkins noticed that the president still couldn't look him in the eye.

"So you let her steal for you, you screwed her, then you said, 'By the way, we're through.'"

"I was going to tell her that we had to stop seeing each other when she got here but she's so beautiful."

Hawkins sighed. Getting mad at Farrington was useless; he'd always been ruled by his penis, and short of castration Hawkins knew that there was no way to change him.

"Claire is pregnant, Chris," Hawkins said patiently. "She announced this little fact at the fund-raiser, tonight. It's going to be a major story in every newspaper and on every television news show in the country. Do you know what will happen if the voters find out that you're cheating on your pregnant wife?"

"I'm sorry. I know it was stupid."

Hawkins counted to ten. "How did Walsh take it?" he asked.

"Not well. She threatened to go public."

"Fuck."

"I don't know if she'll go through with the threat."

"Yeah, well you'd better hope she doesn't or you'll be back in Portland chasing ambulances. Where is she now?"

"I don't know, but she left her car at the Dulles Towne Center mall. And there's something else."

"You didn't hit her?" Hawkins asked, alarmed by the possibility that Farrington had been violent.

"No, it's nothing like that." The president paused. "There was someone in the woods."

"What do you mean?"

"Someone was taking pictures."

"Jesus Christ! Do you realize how bad this is? Pictures of you and Walsh would sell for thousands to a tabloid or they can be used for blackmail."

Farrington's head snapped up. He was angry. "I'm not stupid, Chuck. I know exactly how ugly this can get. That's why I need you to fix it."

"How do you know someone was taking pictures?"

"One of the Secret Service agents spotted her."

"It was a woman?"

"We think so."

"Why just 'think'?"

"One of the guards spotted someone on the hill taking pictures. She ran, so he never got real close, and it was dark. Then she hit him on the head and stunned him. But he thought the photographer was a woman.

"The other guards heard a commotion and ran up to check on what was happening. One of them chased the intruder. When he got to the road a car was driving away. He thinks he got the license number but it was dark and the car kicked up a lot of dust. The plate we ran belongs to a Dana Cutler. She's an ex-D.C. cop who works as a private detective, which would fit with her doing surveillance and taking pictures."

"That's a lot of ifs."

"It's what we have. Can't you do something?"

"About what?"

"Both problems, Charlotte and the P.I."

Hawkins knew exactly what Farrington wanted him to do. He stood up.

"It's late. If we're lucky neither woman will do anything until the morning. That gives me a few hours."

"Thank you, Chuck. I don't know what I'd do without you."

Hawkins didn't answer. He was too angry. Instead he shook his head in disgust and walked out of the room. As soon as he was certain he wouldn't be overheard, Hawkins took out his cell phone and made a call.

Christopher Farrington had been anxious when his misadventure began, but he felt confident that Chuck would fix everything. He always did. And while he may have had twinges of fear and moments of doubt, the president never felt guilty about the way he'd used Charlotte Walsh; guilt was an emotion alien to him.

Farrington returned to the White House a little before 2 A.M. He took a quick shower and tiptoed into bed, feeling much better now that he was clean, as if the hot water had washed away his sins along with the grime. Everything would turn out well, he told himself. Farrington was smiling when he slipped beneath the fresh sheets.

"How did your meeting go?" Claire asked in a voice heavy with sleep.

Farrington rolled toward her and rested a hand on her backside. He really did love her. The other women served to alleviate a physical need, but Claire was his strength, his helpmate. He'd be lost without her.

"I didn't wake you, did I? I tried to be quiet."

Claire kissed him. "Don't worry. I wanted to be awake when you got back but I must have drifted off."

"Did your speech go okay?"

"Didn't Chuck tell you?"

"I'm sorry, but I was so wrapped up in what we were doing I forgot to ask."

Claire touched his cheek. "You have nothing to apologize for. I know the pressure you're under. But just so you know, I knocked 'em dead. They didn't even miss you."

Farrington smiled. "I'm glad you're not running against me. I wouldn't get a single vote."

"You'd get mine," Claire whispered, and the president felt familiar fingers snake through the fly of his pajamas and caress him.

He laughed. "I thought pregnancy lowered a woman's sex drive."

"Then you don't remember the last time I was pregnant. Now do something about my itch or I'll go on TV and tell Barbara Walters you're impotent."

"What a bitch," he whispered as he moved back far enough so he could pull down his pajama bottoms.

Chapter Eight

Jake Teeny had an exciting job that took him to the most exotic and dangerous places in the world, but he lived in a boring ranch house in the Maryland suburbs, preferring—he'd told Dana—a mundane, risk-free existence when he wasn't braving the dangers of a war zone or enduring the extreme heat of Africa or bitter Arctic nights. Weekends when he was home, Jake puttered in his garden, watched the NBA and NFL, and lived the life suburban.

Dana parked down the street from Jake's place as a precaution in case there was an APB out for her car. She was exhausted but she had work to do so she went into the kitchen and made a cup of instant coffee. She was carrying her mug downstairs to Jake's office when her cell phone rang. Dana placed the mug on a step and answered it.

"What's going on, Dana?" Andy Zipay asked. He sounded nervous.

"What do you mean?"

"My guy ran those plates. One of them belongs to Charlotte Walsh and another is registered to Monarch Electronics, an outfit in Landover, Maryland, but the third car is registered to the Secret Service. And that electronics firm is the type of place the Service would use as a cover for the cars they don't use on protection details."

Dana felt a chill. "Which license is for the Secret Service car?"

Zipay read back the license number of the dark blue Lincoln sedan that had been parked at the farmhouse. Now Dana knew why the man Charlotte Walsh had harangued looked familiar.

"Thanks, Zip," she said automatically as her brain raced along to the only conclusion logic was suggesting.

"Are you going to tell me why you're interested in the Secret Service?"

"You don't want to know, okay?"

"Whatever you say, but this better not come back on me."

"It won't."

Dana ended the call and made her way down the rest of the stairs as quickly as possible. She flipped on the light in Jake's office and booted up his computer. While she waited, she glanced at the walls of the cramped room. They were covered by photos that had won awards or were Jake's favorites. The photos were so striking they drew her eye even though she'd seen them several times: a naked child drinking water from a puddle on a war-torn street in Somalia, a terrified bride and groom moments after a suicide bomber struck at their wedding in Fallujah, a blind climber on the summit of Everest.

The computer beeped, signaling that it was ready to go to work. Dana swiveled back to the keyboard and typed in some commands. After downloading the images from her camera she burned a DVD for Perry to give to his client then she went through the pictures. She took a sip from her mug as she reviewed the shots from the Thai restaurant. The close-ups were good, and she only had to zoom in on a few to get better details. The shots at the mall were also good even though it had been dark and she had a clear picture of the license plate of the car that had taken Walsh to the farmhouse.

Her first shots at the farmhouse were okay, but the pictures she'd taken through the second-floor window hadn't come out as well. Dana moved through the pictures quickly until she came to the photos she'd taken when Walsh stormed out of the farmhouse. When she got to the shot she'd taken just before she ran she leaned forward and squinted at the monitor. The mystery man was looking at the departing Ford, and his face was framed in the shot, but he was too far away to see clearly without enhancement. Dana zoomed in. The man's features sharpened. She enlarged the shot some more and sat back in her chair, her heart beating rapidly. Dana had no doubt about the identity of the man Walsh had met at the farmhouse. President Farrington's face was in the newspaper every day and on television every night. What had Perry gotten her into?

Dana tried to take a sip of her coffee but her hand shook and a wave of hot liquid slopped over onto her wrist and scalded her.

"Shit!"

She wiped her hand on her shirt and shook it to cool it off. She'd have a lot more to worry about than a burn if the people watching Farrington had her license number.

Dana stood up and started to pace. Could she get Perry to intercede for her? He was connected. Hell, he was a personal friend of the Farringtons. Then it occurred to her that Perry couldn't intercede on her behalf. If he did, he'd have to tell the president that he'd hired someone to spy on him. Perry would deny any connection to her and the surveillance and there was no way she could prove he was lying. Perry had met her where no one knew them. The waitress was the only witness, and she'd never be able to ID Dale. He'd been wearing shades and that baseball cap. And there was no paper trail. He'd paid her in cash. She was screwed.

Another idea occurred to her as soon as she calmed down enough to think. Maybe she could work this fiasco to her advantage. If Christopher Farrington was having an affair with Charlotte Walsh the photographs she'd taken were worth a lot of money. Farrington was always spouting off about family values. Proof he was having sex with a teenager would send the media into a feeding frenzy. A tabloid like *Exposed* would give her a fortune for the shots. And there were the right-wing television stations. She bet they'd come across.

Of course, the money wouldn't do her any good if she was in prison for attacking the guard or dead. Maybe she could use the pictures as a bargaining chip to stay out of jail or to get Farrington to leave her alone. Maybe she could get some money for them from Farrington *and* use the pictures as an insurance policy. Dana decided that she should put a copy of the photos in a safe place, maybe give them to a lawyer or lock them up in a safety-deposit box. But did she need a bargaining chip? She would if the Secret Service knew who she was, but she still wasn't certain that they had her license number. There was only one way to find out. She'd have to go to her apartment and see if it was under surveillance. She couldn't drive her car because it would be recognized. Jake's Harley was available, but she didn't want to get him in trouble. In the end, Dana decided to take the motorcycle.

Dana put a DVD with the photos and a cover letter in an envelope with Jake's name on it and left it on his desk. Jake would know how to exploit the pictures if something happened to her. She addressed another envelope with a second copy of the DVD to a lawyer who'd given her legal advice when she was deciding whether to quit the force. She dropped the envelope for the lawyer in a mailbox on her way to her apartment, which was on the third floor of a three-story brick apartment house on Wisconsin Avenue, a short haul from the National Cathedral. The bottom floor was occupied by a Greek restaurant and the entrance was between the restaurant and a dry cleaner. Dana cruised by her building slowly, taking in both sides of the street. At this hour, there wasn't much traffic and it should have been easy to spot a stakeout. As far as Dana could tell, the cars on both sides of her block were unoccupied and she didn't see any suspicious-looking vans.

Dana waited on a side street for fifteen minutes before circling the block and cruising back on the opposite side of the street. Nothing she saw raised her antennae. If someone was watching her apartment they weren't doing it from the street, but the surveillance could be from any of the apartments across the street. She tried to spot some suspicious activity in one of them but she couldn't see into the darkened interiors.

After making sure that the back wasn't being watched, Dana parked the Harley in the rear of her building and entered it through a metal door that opened into the basement. Maybe she was going to be okay. Maybe she'd been lucky and it had been too dark to make out her license plate.

Dana took the stairs and paused on the landing that ran in front of her door. The cheap linoleum floor was dimly lit by a few low-watt bulbs spaced along the water-stained ceiling. The linoleum would squeak when she walked along it, so she moved as quietly as she could. The hall doors were made of thin wood and provided little privacy. If she was in the hall, Dana could hear televisions playing and domestic quarrels. She pressed her ear to the door to her apartment for a minute and used her key when she didn't hear any sounds coming from inside.

Dana flipped on the light and stared down the narrow hallway that led from the front door to the bedroom at the back of the apartment. The kitchen was through the first doorway on the left and the entrance to a small living room was next to the kitchen door. Dana closed and locked the front door and listened for sounds in the apartment. When she heard nothing she breathed a sigh of relief and stepped into the kitchen.

The blow to her solar plexus took her breath away, and Dana sat down hard. A large hand grabbed her by the throat and hoisted her to her feet while she tried to suck in air.

"Where are the camera and the pictures, bitch?" asked a large man in a black T-shirt. He pushed his face into hers. He had a broken nose and dull, blue eyes. His breath was stale, and she could see the dark bristles on his cheeks.

Dana wanted to answer but she couldn't catch her breath. The man threw her to the floor and kicked her in the side. Her motorcycle jacket absorbed some of the blow but not enough to prevent pain from shooting through her ribs.

"We're not fucking around. Give us the camera and all of the pictures, now, or I'll rape you before I kick you to death."

Dana's mind played tricks on her and she thought her attacker sounded like one of the men who had chained her to the wall in the basement. She scuttled backward down the hall like a crab until she was pressed against the front door. Then she curled into a fetal ball. Her attacker looked over his shoulder at a second man, who was dressed in a light gray jacket, jeans, and running shoes. His blond hair almost touched his shoulders and his beard was neatly trimmed.

"I think she's holding out because she wants us to fuck her," said the man who'd hit her. "What do you think?"

"I didn't hear the young lady tell us where the pictures are, did you?"

"No, siree. I do believe she wants it." Her attacker grabbed his crotch and pulled up. "Mmm, mmm, she's gonna taste sweet."

Dana was terrified but she was also armed. Ever since her ordeal she had carried an assortment of weapons, and the one that was easiest to reach in a fetal position was the gun that was secured to her ankle.

Her attacker watched wide-eyed as Dana fired. The bullet bored through his thigh, and he screamed and crumpled to the floor. The explosion and scream in the confined space paralyzed the second man. By the time he was able to move, Dana was on her feet, her gun pointed at his heart. She looked homicidal.

"Take it easy," the second man begged, his voice unsteady and his hands, which he'd raised in supplication, shaking badly.

A red tide washed through Dana's brain and insane voices urged her to kill. Only the lessons learned in months of therapy stopped her from shooting the man, or doing something much worse.

"Easy?" she screamed. "It didn't sound like you were going to take it easy."

Dana's hand was trembling and the intruder's eyes were glued on her twitching trigger finger. He held his hands out toward her.

"You don't want to shoot me by mistake. Calm down."

"Tell me to calm down one more time and I'll gut shoot you."

The man turned pale. "Look, we weren't really going to rape you," he said, his voice shaking as badly as Dana's. "We're federal agents. We were trying to frighten you."

The man who'd hit her had grabbed his thigh with both hands and was rolling back and forth on the floor, moaning in pain. Dana kicked him in the face.

"Shut the fuck up," she yelled so she could be heard above his cries of pain. Blood spurted from his nose and he collapsed on his back.

The second man used Dana's momentary inattention to go for a weapon, but her gun was back on target before he was halfway. He hesitated before raising his hands again.

"Don't shoot. We're really Feds. Let me get my ID from my pocket."

"I don't give a fuck who you are. But you're sure not dressed like J. Edgar Hoover. You're dressed like a burglar-rapist and I'd be acting in self-defense if I shot your balls off."

"Be smart. Kill us and you'll have every law enforcement agency in the country hunting you down."

"They're doing that already."

Dana cocked the gun.

"Please, don't. I'm married. I have kids."

"You think I care?"

Dana heard sirens. Someone had heard the gunshots and the screams and called the cops. She made a decision.

"Do you have handcuffs?"

"Yeah."

"Take them out slowly then get down on the floor and cuff yourself to this asshole."

The second man was only too happy to comply. As soon as the two agents were hooked up Dana backed out of the apartment and sprinted down the stairs. She'd been tempted to kill her attackers but she didn't need any more ghosts in her nightmares.

As soon as she straddled the Harley Dana sped off, making random left and right turns until she was miles away from her place. She tried to remember how much money she had in her wallet. She'd used an ATM recently and she thought she had $150. If she used an ATM again the cops would know it but she had no choice. She needed as much cash as she could get her hands on. She would not be able to use her credit cards from now on.

Dana found a bank on the outskirts of Chevy Chase and got the maximum amount of cash from the ATM. Then she sped off with no plan. She was living the ultimate nightmare. The president of the United States was out to get her and he had the resources of the FBI, CIA, NSA, and every other letter in the alphabet at his disposal. Dana had $372.40, a .38 Special with four bullets, and a borrowed Harley with three-quarters of a tank of gas.

Part Two

A Hopeless Appeal

Oregon

Chapter Nine

Shortly after moving to Portland to take a job with Reed, Briggs, Stephens, Stottlemeyer and Compton—Oregon's largest law firm—Brad Miller rented a riverside apartment with a view of Mount Hood. When he opened his bedroom shades on this balmy morning in late June he beheld the sun rising behind the majestic, snowcapped mountain and a crew of eight women stroking with vigor along the far shore of the Willamette River. It was a scene that should have brought a smile to Brad's face but this morning he had a good reason for feeling sad and empty.

Brad had experienced good days and bad days since moving across the country for his job. The longer he was away from New York and the everyday sights that reminded him of Bridget Malloy, the more frequent were his good days, but today was the seven-month anniversary of the day Bridget had broken off their engagement, and there was no view, no matter how magnificent, that could prevent him from being depressed.

Brad showered away some of his gloom, dressed for work, and walked to his office, stopping on the way for breakfast at a favorite spot on Third Avenue. He usually grabbed a quick bite at home, but there was a lull in work at the office and he was in no rush this morning. He read the newspaper while he finished his eggs. The Yankees' extra-innings victory over Boston helped take his mind off Bridget. Brad may have left the East behind, but he was a Yankee fan for life.

When he'd finished his breakfast, Brad walked several blocks to a thirty-story, glass-and-steel office building in the heart of downtown Portland. Reed, Briggs's main entrance was on the thirtieth floor. The first person clients saw when they entered the spacious waiting area was a gorgeous receptionist who sat behind a magnificent polished wood dais that displayed the firm name in shiny metal letters. Behind the receptionist were several glass-walled conference rooms with magnificent views of three snowcapped mountains and the river. While they waited, the clients sat on soft leather sofas and thumbed through copies of *U.S. News & World Report* or *The Wall Street Journal*. It was on this floor that the partners made big deals for important people in huge offices furnished by interior decorators.

Brad did not take the elevator to the thirtieth floor. Junior associates entered Reed, Briggs's hallowed halls on twenty-seven and walked down a dull, windowless corridor to a plain door, where they tapped in an entry code on a keypad affixed to the wall. Inside, the support staff sat in cubicles that filled the center of the floor, surrounded by the unimpressive offices occupied by the firm's newest members.

Brad filled a mug with coffee in the lunchroom and carried it to his tiny office. A narrow window above his credenza looked down on the roof of a hotel parking lot. The rest of the office was filled to capacity by a desk, two client chairs, a gunmetal gray filing cabinet, and a bookcase stuffed with a set of the Oregon Revised Statutes and the tax code. Brad's only decorations were framed copies of his college and law school diplomas.

Brad's desk was usually stacked high with assignments from the partners, but when he'd left his office the night before he'd had fewer files than usual to work on. This was because the partner he'd been assisting had just settled the lawsuit that had taken up a good part of

Brad's time since he'd joined the firm. When Brad walked into the office he stopped short and groaned. Three new files covered his blotter. A quick look at the memo on top of the center file let him know that he was in for a late night.

Brad took a sip of coffee while his computer booted up. After checking his e-mail, he started going through a forty-page contract between a subcontractor and a construction company that was building condominiums on the coast near Lincoln City. He was on page seven when his intercom buzzed and the receptionist told him that Susan Tuchman wanted to see him. Brad sighed, placed a yellow Post-It on the paragraph he was reading, and headed for the stairs that would take him up to the thirtieth floor.

The associates had nicknamed Tuchman the "Dragon Lady" and the aerie where the Gods of Reed, Briggs ruled, "Heaven." Brad could have ascended there on the elevator but walking up stairs was one of the few types of exercise he was getting since he started working fourteen-hour days. Some of the other associates jogged or exercised in a gym before work, but Brad was not a morning person. He did play an occasional game of tennis at the Pettygrove Athletic Club, where all the partners and associates had memberships, and he did get in a run or two on the weekend, but he'd noticed that the numbers on his bathroom scale had been inching up and he was finding it harder and harder to run down cross-court forehands. By the time he opened the door to the thirtieth floor he had made a vow to watch his diet and get in at least four hours of exercise each week.

Susan Tuchman's corner office was an homage to minimalism. Two large windows met at one corner giving her a wraparound view of Portland. A black leather sofa stood against a third wall under an all-white painting. The senior partner's desk was a large sheet of glass supported by aluminum tubes and the only items on it were an in-box and out-box made of polished metal and a thick file. The only cluttered space was a wall decorated with awards Tuchman had won from the Inns of Court, the American Bar Association, and other legal groups, and photographs of Tuchman with celebrities from the worlds of politics, business, and entertainment.

Tuchman was five four and rail thin. Her blond hair was free of gray thanks to chemistry, and a Beverly Hills surgeon of national repute could claim credit for her skin being as tight as plastic wrap. The senior partner was wearing a black Armani pants suit with a white silk blouse and a necklace of black pearls. She was forty-nine but she'd been a partner for ten years as a result of a series of victories for a pharmaceutical client and a tobacco company. Tuchman's first husband had been an associate at another firm but she had divorced him rather than set up a situation where an opponent from her husband's firm could move to have her taken off a case on the grounds of a conflict of interest. A second, tempestuous marriage to a federal judge had lasted only as long as it took Tuchman to process the difference in the income contributions to their joint bank account.

"Sit," Tuchman ordered, indicating a client chair made of the same black leather as the couch and supported by aluminum tubing similar to the tubing that held up Tuchman's desk. Brad lowered himself onto the chair cautiously, expecting it to tip over backward at any second.

"I've had some good feedback about you from George Ogilvey," Tuchman said, mentioning the partner who had just settled the lawsuit on which Brad had been working. "He tells me you're an ace at research."

Brad shrugged, not from modesty but out of fear that any support he gave for George Ogilvey's opinion would encourage Tuchman to add to his workload.

Tuchman smiled. "I've been trying to pick an associate for an interesting project, and based on George's glowing recommendation, I've concluded that you're the man for the job."

With all the work Brad had already he didn't need any more projects, interesting or otherwise, but he knew it would be wise to keep that opinion to himself.

"You know that Reed, Briggs prides itself on being more than a money factory. We believe that our attorneys should give back to the community, so we take on pro bono projects. The projects are exciting and give our new associates a chance to work one-on-one with clients and get courtroom experience."

Brad knew all about these pro bono projects. They were good PR for the firm but they were also time-consuming and brought in no money, so the partners foisted them off on the newest associates.

Tuchman pushed the file that occupied the center of her desk toward Brad.

"You're not from Oregon, right?"

"New York. I'd never been on the West Coast before I interviewed for this job."

Tuchman nodded. "Does the name Clarence Little mean anything to you?"

"I don't think so."

Tuchman smiled. "Snap quiz, name the president of the United States."

Brad returned the smile. "Christopher Farrington."

"Well done. And you know he was the governor of Oregon before he was selected as President Nolan's VP?"

"Uh, yeah. I guess I knew that."

President Nolan had died of a heart attack halfway through his second year in office and Farrington had suddenly found himself president of the United States. Brad turned toward the photographs showing Tuchman schmoozing with important people and suddenly noticed how many contained a smiling Christopher Farrington.

Tuchman noticed where Brad was looking. "The president is a close personal friend. I was his finance chairman during his run for governor."

"What does President Farrington have to do with my assignment?"

"Mr. Little has filed a writ of habeas corpus, which is now in the Ninth Circuit Court of Appeals. He is a convicted serial killer and he's challenging a death sentence he received in Oregon. The murder took place while President Farrington was governor and the victim was the daughter of the governor's personal secretary. The case created quite a stir here because of the tie-in to the governor but it may not have gotten much space in the New York papers."

"I think I heard about it," Brad said so Tuchman wouldn't think that he was a typical New Yorker, who thought you fell off the edge of the Earth as soon as you left the five boroughs, but the case didn't really ring any bells.

"The firm has taken on the representation of Mr. Little in federal court. I think you'll find the assignment very challenging. Look through the file and get back to me if you have any questions."

"I'll get right on it," Brad said as he stood.

"I'll have the banker's boxes with the rest of the file delivered to your office."

Oh, no, Brad thought. Banker's boxes were big, and Tuchman had just said that there was more than one. He remembered all the new work he'd just found piled up on his desk.

"Remember, Brad, this is literally a matter of life and death, and," she added in a confidential tone, "it might get you up to the United States Supreme Court. Wouldn't that be something?"

"I'll work very hard on Mr. Little's case, don't worry," Brad said with great enthusiasm, which disappeared as soon as he was out the door of the senior partner's office.

"This is just what I need," Brad muttered as he descended the stairs. Not only was he loaded with work for other partners but he knew absolutely nothing about criminal law and cared less. He'd taken the required course in criminal law his first year in law school and a refresher course when he was studying for the bar, but he remembered almost nothing he'd learned. Then there was the added pressure of knowing that a person might die if he messed up. Of course, that person was a convicted serial killer, someone he had no interest in saving from the gallows. If the guy really did it, society would be better off if Little was executed.

"Why me, God?" Brad muttered as he shoved open the twenty-seventh floor door. When he received no answer, he concluded that either the Deity wasn't interested in his problems or the Gods on the thirtieth floor were more powerful than whoever he'd previously considered to be the Big Boss.

Brad spent the rest of the morning and afternoon working on the contract for the Lincoln City condominiums. It was five-forty-five when he finally e-mailed a memo outlining the problems that the construction company faced to the partner who'd given him the assignment. He was exhausted and he toyed with the idea of going home, but he had too much work and the assignments were going to keep coming.

Brad sighed and ordered a pizza. While he waited for the delivery, he went to the men's room, where he recycled the coffee he'd been guzzling and splashed water on his face. Then he grabbed a Coke for the caffeine from the lunchroom refrigerator and got to work on the banker's boxes that held the files for *Little v. Oregon*. One box contained the fifteen-volume transcript of the trial and the nine-volume transcript of Little's sentencing hearing. Another had files with the pleadings, legal motions, and memos. A third contained correspondence, the police reports, and miscellany like the autopsy report and the photographs of the autopsy and the crime scene.

Two hours later, Brad was still at his desk, casting anxious glances at a manila envelope that lay a few inches from him in the center of his blotter. The only dead body he had ever seen was at his great-grandmother's funeral, and he didn't have a clear memory of that because he'd been five when she died. He did know that his great-grandmother had died peacefully in her sleep. She hadn't been tortured and chopped up like Laurie Erickson, the teenage girl whose autopsy and crime scene photographs were in the envelope.

Brad knew Laurie Erickson had been hacked to pieces and tortured because he'd just finished reading the report of Laurie's autopsy. It was very unnerving and read a little like a graphic review of a slasher movie, which was one type of film Brad avoided like the plague. According to the medical examiner, the cause of Erickson's death was no mystery. She had almost been decapitated when Clarence Little had hacked away at every inch of her neck with a machete or similar object, tearing the skin to ribbons; there was a subdural hemorrhage over the brainstem for which the examiner could find no source, and not satisfied with simply killing the unfortunate young girl, Little had sliced off several body parts after Erickson was dead.

The temptation to view photographs of the ghastly crime drew Brad to the envelope in the same way a freeway accident drew the eye of every driver who passed by. What argued against opening the envelope were the autopsy's gory details and the fact that he'd recently ingested three slices of pepperoni pizza. In the end Brad's morbid curiosity won out. He pulled the envelope to him, opened the flap, and slid the top photo out while averting his eyes so he didn't have a clear view. Then he turned his head toward the photograph slowly so he wouldn't have to take it in all at once. The picture showed a young woman with skin the color of wax who was stretched out naked on a stainless steel table with her arms at her side. It took Brad a moment to register the hideous nature of the wounds the poor girl had suffered. When he did he grew light-headed, his stomach rolled, and he wished he'd followed his instincts and left the autopsy photos in the envelope.

"What have we here?" Ginny Striker asked from the doorway. Brad jumped in his seat and dropped the envelope. A torrent of truly horrid pictures spilled onto his blotter.

"Eeek," Ginny shrieked in mock terror. "Is that a plaintiff in one of our toxic spill cases?"

Brad's hand flew to his chest. "Geez, Ginny, you almost gave me a heart attack."

"And a great worker's comp case. Why are you looking at these disgusting photographs?"

"Susan Tuchman saddled me with a habeas corpus appeal," Brad said. Then he waved a hand at the files that covered his desk. "As if I don't have enough to do."

"An associate's work is never done. He must toil from sun to sun."

Brad indicated the open pizza box. "Want a slice? These photos made me lose my appetite."

Ginny grabbed a piece of cold pizza and a napkin and sat down on one of Brad's client chairs. She was a few years older than Brad, a tall, slender blonde from the Midwest with large, blue eyes. Ginny was aggressive, funny, and smart and had started at Reed, Briggs a month before Brad arrived in Portland. During his first week on the job, she'd showed him the ropes. Brad thought she was cute but rumors of a boyfriend in medical school back east and his own tragic history with Bridget Malloy had kept their relationship platonic.

"I didn't know you were so squeamish," Ginny said.

"I've just never seen anything like this before. Have you?"

"Oh, sure. I was a nurse before I went to law school. I've seen more than my share of gaping wounds and internal organs."

Brad blanched and Ginny laughed. Then she took a bite of pizza while Brad gathered up the gory photographs and stuffed them back in the envelope.

"What's your case about?"

Ginny's mouth was half full of pizza and it took Brad a moment to figure out what she'd just said.

"Clarence Little, my newest client, is a serial killer whose current address is death row at the Oregon State Pen. He's there for murdering several women, including an eighteen-year-old girl named Laurie Erickson. I've been told that the Erickson case was very high profile out here when it happened because the victim was babysitting for the governor when she disappeared."

"I heard about that! Wasn't she snatched from the governor's mansion?"

"That's what they think."

"They did a whole hour on one of the prime-time news shows about it. It was a few years ago, right?"

"Yeah, a year before Nolan picked Farrington as his running mate."

"This is so cool, and why are you complaining? A murder case is way more interesting than the usual shit we have to work on."

"I might find it as fascinating as you do if I had nothing else to keep me busy, but I'm swamped, and I'm also not that motivated to save the life of some degenerate who gets his kicks torturing innocent girls."

"Point taken. So, you're certain he did it?"

"I haven't read the transcript—it's twenty-four volumes—but I read the statement of facts in the brief that was filed in the Oregon supreme court after he got the death sentence. The state didn't have an open-and-shut case, but it was pretty strong."

"What happened?" Ginny asked as she grabbed a second slice of pizza.

"Laurie Erickson was the daughter of Marsha Erickson, who was Farrington's personal secretary when he was governor. I think she worked at his law firm before he was elected. Anyway, Laurie was a senior in high school and she babysat for Patrick, the Farringtons' kid, on occasion. The Farringtons were going to this fund-raiser at the Salem Public Library. The library isn't that far from the governor's mansion.

"Patrick was two at the time and he had a bad cold. He was asleep when Laurie started to watch him. You know the first lady is a doctor?"

Ginny nodded.

"Well, Dr. Farrington had gotten some prescription medicine that Laurie was supposed to give the kid if he was coughing when he woke up. The governor and his aide, Charles Hawkins, went down to the limo while his wife was in Patrick's room telling Laurie what to do with the medicine. Dr. Farrington testified that she told Laurie good night a little after seven P.M.

"This was in December, so it was already dark when the limo left for the library. The security detail at the mansion didn't see anyone lurking around the grounds, but the mansion is an historic building that's surrounded by woods. It was built by a timber baron in the 1800s on several acres and refurbished after a fund-raising campaign in the late 1990s. There are a lot of ways someone can sneak onto the grounds. There's a guard at the front gate, another guard who patrols the grounds, and some security cameras, but the system isn't state-of-the-art."

"So the guards didn't see anyone come to the mansion after the governor left?"

"Actually, someone did. Charles Hawkins, the governor's aide, returned around seven-thirty to pick up a sheet with statistics for the governor's speech that he had forgotten to bring with him. Hawkins parked in the rear of the mansion and entered through a back door that's used by the staff. He had to pass by Patrick's room on the way to his office. Mrs. Farrington asked him to check on Patrick. Hawkins testified that Laurie told him that Patrick was still asleep. After that he got the paper and drove back to the library in time to give it to the governor."

"Did anyone see Laurie alive after Hawkins left?"

"No, he was the last person to see her, other than the killer, of course. When the Farringtons returned that night Patrick was still asleep but Laurie was nowhere to be found. The grounds and the woods were searched, but the police couldn't find a trace of her. A few days later, hikers found her mutilated body in a state park, miles from the mansion."

"What do the police think happened?"

"There's an entrance to the basement in the rear of the mansion. It was open when the police searched the place, and traces of Erickson's blood were found on a laundry chute that emptied into the basement. According to the medical examiner, Erickson was small and thin enough to fit down it. The cops think Little came through the woods and entered the house through the basement, knocked out Erickson, threw her body down the chute, and took her out the basement door."

"That seems like a lot of work."

"The guy's crazy. He probably thought it was a good plan."

"How would he know she was babysitting? He'd also have to know about the laundry chute and that it was big enough to accommodate someone Erickson's size. How did he know the layout of the mansion?"

"I don't know," Brad answered, annoyed that Ginny was playing detective.

"Why did the police arrest Little for Erickson's murder if no one saw him go into the mansion or leave with Erickson?"

"The big thing was the pinkie. He'd kidnap the girls, kill them, then cut off their pinkies after they were dead. The police think he kept them as souvenirs but they never found them. Erickson was missing her pinkie, and she'd been cut up the way Little had mutilated the other victims."

"The case still sounds weak to me."

"You're right. I think Little would have had a good chance to beat it if it was his only charge, but Little was arrested for killing thirteen girls, and the state had a very strong case in several of the other murders. They didn't prosecute Little for Erickson's murder until he'd been convicted of two other killings. Then the prosecutor introduced evidence from those cases at Little's trial for Erickson's death. The MOs were so similar that they pointed to one person committing all of the crimes."

"What's going on with his other cases?"

"The Oregon supreme court affirmed so—barring a miracle in federal court—he's going to be executed."

Ginny looked confused. "If he's going to be executed twice why is he appealing this case?"

Brad shrugged. "Beats me."

"Is there a chance he's innocent?"

"Who else could have done it?"

"Hawkins was the last person to see her alive," Ginny said in between bites. "One of the guards could have crept up the stairs when the others weren't looking. And if Little snuck into the mansion, so could someone else."

"Some other serial killer who just happens to have an MO identical to Clarence Little's?"

"Good point."

"Anyway, none of that matters. I can't reargue the facts in a habeas corpus case. I can only raise constitutional issues that were argued by Little in the habeas corpus hearing."

"Why does Little think he should get a new trial?"

"He claims that he had an alibi for the night Erickson was murdered and his trial lawyer didn't pursue it."

"So he's going with incompetence of counsel?"

"Yeah, but he doesn't have any case. The trial attorney testified at the hearing. He said that Little did claim that he had an alibi but wouldn't tell him what it was. He says he kept pressing Little for more information but Little was always so vague that he couldn't use an alibi defense."

"What did Little say?"

"Not much. I read his testimony. He just asserted that he had given the lawyer enough information but he wouldn't tell the judge where he was supposed to have been, and he fenced with the prosecutor. He comes across as real evasive in the transcript. The judge accused him of playing games with the court. He ruled that Little's attorney was competent and that was that."

"Are there any other issues?"

"Not that I can see."

"So, what are you going to do?"

Brad shrugged. "I guess I'll skim the transcript and read all this stuff just to be sure. The guy is on death row. I've got to leave no stone unturned, right? But I think I'm just spinning my wheels. I'll do some research. I owe the client that. If I don't find anything I'll meet with Tuchman and tell her we should advise the client to drop the appeal."

Ginny wiped her hands and mouth on a napkin. "I have a brilliant suggestion."

"About the case?"

"No, about life. It's almost nine and you look like shit. I think the Dragon Lady can wait a day to hear your views on Mr. Little's case, but I don't think you can last much longer without a beer. So, I want you to pack up your case file and escort me over to the bar at the Shanghai Clipper."

Brad looked at his watch. He'd lost track of time and his enthusiasm for work.

"That is a brilliant suggestion. You must have been top of your class."

"I did ace drinking law." Ginny stood up. "I'll get my coat and meet you by the elevator."

The Shanghai Clipper, an Asian fusion restaurant with a modern decor, was on the second floor of an office tower a few blocks from the Reed, Briggs offices. Large windows looked down on a section of the Park Blocks, a row of parks that started at Portland State University and stretched from north to south through the city with only a few interruptions. Brad and Ginny found a table in a dark corner of the bar next to a window and ordered beers and a few appetizers.

"Alone at last," Ginny said.

"It is good to get out of the office."

"You've got to watch yourself, pardner. A little overtime is okay, but you don't want to court a nervous breakdown."

"Is this advice of the 'do as I say, not as I do' variety? You worked as late as I did."

"Touché."

"Besides, it doesn't much matter whether I'm at home or the office."

"Whoa, you're not feeling sorry for yourself, are you?"

"Actually, I am. Today is the anniversary of a really rotten event."

The waiter appeared and placed between the lawyers two cold bottles of Widmer Hefeweizen, a selection of sushi, and a plate of fried won tons with a dipping sauce. When he left, Ginny cocked her head to one side and studied Brad for a moment. Then she closed her eyes, tipped her head back, and placed her fingertips on her forehead.

"I am seeing an image of a woman," she said in a fake Hungarian accent.

Brad sighed. "It's that obvious, huh?"

"When a guy is morose it's usually a safe bet that a woman is the cause."

"You got me."

"Want to talk about it? I'm a good listener."

"Yeah, sure, why not bore you with my tale of woe. Once upon a time I was madly in love with Bridget Malloy. She was—is still I guess—the girl of my dreams. She's smart and beautiful and she accepted my marriage proposal the third time I made it."

"Uh-oh."

"Yeah, I know, I should have taken no for an answer the first time, or at least the second time, but I can't think straight where Bridget is concerned."

"This story has to have an unhappy ending."

"It does. We were going to be married after I graduated from law school. The hotel was rented, the save-the-dates sent off, the wedding planner hired. Then Bridget asked me to meet her for drinks in the restaurant where I'd proposed for the second time."

Ginny put her hand in front of her eyes. "I can't look."

Brad laughed bitterly. "You've obviously figured out the punch line to this sorry joke. Bridget told me that she couldn't go through with the wedding. I think she said something about me being a great guy who was sure to find someone more worthy and something else about not being ready to settle down, but I can't really be certain. After Bridget dropped her bombshell the rest of the evening is a blur."

"I'm guessing you didn't handle this well."

"Nope. At least not right away. I spent the next two days drunk or in bed. I was in really bad shape. But then the clouds cleared, the sun came out, and I had an epiphany. Bridget said she was too young to settle down and I decided she was right and that maybe I was too young, too.

"Before Bridget backed out of the marriage, we'd planned to live in my apartment in the city. I was on my third callback to four Manhattan law firms and I was going to take the best job offer and work my way up to partner while Bridget completed her masters of fine arts and pursued her dream of being a writer. We'd have a child or two and move to the suburbs where we'd both grown up. There was a large home in a wealthy area of the North Shore and a country club membership somewhere in the plan. Then middle age and retirement after the kids were finished with grad school. It was all very tidy and awfully similar to the lives our parents had lived.

"After I sobered up I looked back over my life. I'd gone to high school in Westbury, Long Island, and college at Hofstra, also on Long Island and not too far from home. Except for a trip to Europe with my folks and a trip to the Continent on my own after college, I'd spent most of my life on the East Coast of the United States. Now that I wasn't on the marriage-career track anymore I asked myself why I should stay in Manhattan when there was a whole world out there. So, I went online and scoped out firms in Colorado, California, Oregon, and Washington state. When Reed, Briggs asked me to interview, I flew west and returned with a job offer. And here I am."

"But you're not completely over Bridget yet?"

"I am a good part of the time. Most of what I see in Portland doesn't remind me of her. That helps. But every once in a while I'll hear her favorite song on the radio or an old movie we watched together shows up on TV and it all comes back."

"And there's this anniversary."

"Yup."

"Is that why you buried yourself under Clarence Little's files?"

"Reading about the case helped me forget."

"Until I pulled the scab off your wound. I'm sorry."

"Don't be. It helped to talk about it. Getting it off my chest is better than holding everything in."

"Glad I could help, then."

"What about you, any tragic love affairs in your past?"

Ginny took a swig of her beer before answering. "I'm not sure."

"And that means . . ."

"I do have a boyfriend. He's in med school in Philadelphia."

"That's pretty far away."

"Yes it is. We're taking a break from each other to see if absence makes the heart grow fonder."

"At your suggestion or his?"

"My, aren't you getting personal."

"I spilled my guts. You can spill yours."

"It's sort of mutual. I mean, he proposed it, but I didn't fight very hard."

"How long have you been going out?"

"Freshman year of college."

"That's a long time."

"Yeah, but people change. Besides, that's seven years of togetherness.

Seven years is when the seven-year itch kicks in for married folk. There must be a reason for that, don't you think?"

"So you're in Portland to see if you miss him?"

She picked up her beer bottle and nodded.

"And . . . ?"

Ginny shrugged. "I'm not certain. We talk on the phone a lot, and that's nice. But I think he's seeing someone."

"Oh?"

She shrugged. "Matt's a lousy liar. What bothers me is that I don't care. I think I'm relieved, actually. Maybe he was right and we need to move on." She sighed. "Time will tell. Tune in next week."

Brad smiled. "We're two pathetic losers, huh?"

"Speak for yourself, Bud. I see myself as someone on the verge of a new adventure in living." She looked at her watch. "I also see that it's way past my bedtime."

Brad started to reach for the bill but Ginny beat him to it. "You bought the greasy pizza. This is my treat. You can get it next time."

"Deal," Brad said, knowing that Ginny was too strong-minded to back down and happy that she was thinking that there'd be a next time.

Chapter Ten

The trip down I-5 from Portland to the state penitentiary in Salem, Oregon's capital, took an hour. During the ride, Brad Miller's thoughts seesawed between his upcoming visit with Clarence Little and the meeting he'd had two days before with the Dragon Lady. As soon as he'd completed his research, Brad had told Susan Tuchman that he didn't think there was any issue in Clarence Little's case that he could argue with a straight face to an appellate court. He'd assumed that Tuchman would tell him to file a motion to dismiss the appeal after writing a letter to Little explaining that he had no case. Neither of these actions would require Brad to come within fifty miles of his homicidal client. Instead, Tuchman had ordered him to drive to the penitentiary and explain his conclusion to the death row inmate in person. Brad had tried to convince his boss that he should be billing hours for the firm rather than spending nonbillable hours locked behind high concrete walls with someone whose idea of a good time was chopping off the pinkies of the women he'd murdered. Tuchman had smiled—sadistically Brad had thought—while explaining how client contact would aid his growth as a lawyer.

Brad's knowledge of prison came mostly from movies in which brutal inmates either raped one another in the shower or took innocent civilians hostage during riots. The only criminal Brad could remember meeting was a tough kid in his high school gym class who—rumor had it—had gone to jail for stealing a car a year or so after graduation. The thought of being locked in with psychotic killers, deranged rapists, and violent drug dealers did not appeal to him in the least, and the idea of sitting across from a mass murderer made him very uneasy. The corrections officer who'd set up Brad's visit with Clarence Little assured Brad that there would be bulletproof glass and concrete separating them, but Brad had seen *The Silence of the Lambs* and didn't have complete confidence in the ability of law enforcement agencies to keep really wily serial killers behind bars.

The night before he drove to the penitentiary, Brad had a vivid dream about Laurie Erickson's autopsy. In parts of his nightmare Laurie was on the slab, but in other lurid dream sequences there was a man who vaguely resembled Brad lying beneath the coroner's blood-stained scalpel. Brad had startled out of sleep several times during the night, and each time he burst into consciousness his heart was racing and his sheets were damp with sweat. When he finally gave up on sleep at 5:45 A.M. he was exhausted and worried. By the time he parked in the visitors' lot at the penitentiary he was a wreck.

Brad made certain that his car was locked before walking down the tree-lined lane from the lot to the front door of the prison. The sun was warm, and there was a light breeze. On either side of the lane were pleasant white houses that were once residences and now served as offices for the staff. It would have been an idyllic setting if the prison's intimidating egg yolk yellow walls, topped with razor wire and guarded by gun towers, weren't looming over the charming houses with their neatly trimmed lawns.

Brad walked up a short flight of steps to a door that opened into a waiting room tiled in green and lined with cheap couches covered in rust-colored upholstery that had been made in the prison. Two guards stood behind a circular counter in the center of the room. After Brad explained the purpose of his visit and showed his bar card and driver's license he was told to have a seat.

Two heavyset older women occupied one of the couches. One was

African-American and the other was white. They seemed to know each other. Brad guessed that their sons were in prison and they'd struck up a friendship during prior visits. A woman in her early twenties sat on another couch fussing with a boy who looked to be four or five. The woman was attractive but wore too much makeup. The boy was whining and straining against the hand that held him firmly. His mother looked harried and on the verge of using violence to make the boy do what she wanted.

Brad found an unoccupied couch as far from the mother and her child as possible and studied his notes for the meeting. The kid was screaming now and it was hard to concentrate so he was relieved when one of the guards walked over to a metal detector and called out his name and several others. The older women had headed for the metal detector as soon as the guard left his post behind the counter. The mother picked up her son and carried him to the end of the line the older women had formed. Brad joined them. When it was his turn the guard told him to take off his shoes and belt and empty his pockets before walking through the machine. When Brad had his belt and shoes back on, the guard led the visitors down a ramp. At the end of the ramp was a set of sliding steel bars. Their escort signaled another guard who sat in a control room. Moments later the gate rolled aside with a metallic groan and they entered a holding area. As soon as the first gate closed a second gate opened and the group followed the guard down a short hall where they waited while he unlocked the thick metal door to the visiting area.

A corrections officer sat on a raised platform at one end of a large open room crowded with more prison-made couches and flimsy wooden coffee tables. Vending machines dispensing soft drinks, coffee, and candy stood along one wall. A gray-haired man shuffled over to the coffee machine. It was easy to tell he was a prisoner because the inmates wore blue work shirts and jeans.

Brad waited until the women had talked to the guard before telling him that he had an appointment to meet with Clarence Little.

Brad expected the guard to be impressed or horrified when he heard the name of Brad's client, but he just looked bored when he called death row to request Little's transport.

"You're across the hall," he said when he hung up. "It'll take about fifteen minutes to get him down here. Do you want to wait here or in the noncontact room?"

Brad glanced briefly at the occupants of the visiting room, which he had expected to be filled with tattooed Hells Angels and wild-eyed psychos with shaved heads, but none of the prisoners looked threatening. Several men sat on the floor playing with young children. Others leaned across coffee tables holding whispered conversations with wives and girlfriends. Still, it made Brad nervous to be in close proximity to someone who'd done something bad enough to get him sent to prison.

"I'll wait in the noncontact room," he told the guard.

Across the hall from the general visiting room was another visiting area. Windows made of bulletproof glass were set in two of the walls. Behind some of these windows sat prisoners deemed too dangerous to be allowed in the open visiting area. Their visitors sat on folding chairs, and the conversations were carried on over phone receivers. At the end were two rooms barely big enough to accommodate a bridge chair. The guard opened the door to one of them and ushered Brad inside. The chair faced a glass window set in concrete blocks painted institutional brown. A slot for passing papers had been built into the bottom of the window and a metal ledge just wide enough to accommodate a legal pad jutted out from the wall underneath the window. A phone receiver like those Brad had seen the other visitors using was attached to the wall.

The guard left and Brad stared anxiously through the glass at a door that allowed entry into an identical room on the other side. There were no photographs of his client in his file and Brad's imagination had created a murderer who was an amalgamation of Hannibal Lecter, Jason, and Freddy Krueger. The man who was led into the room by two corrections officers was five eleven, slender, and looked like an accountant. His brown hair was combed carefully so that the part was clearly displayed. His skin was smooth, his nose small and undistinguished. Gray-blue eyes examined Brad through plain, wire-rimmed glasses while the guards unlocked his ankle chains and handcuffs. One of the guards was carrying a folder. The edges were frayed and it was covered with writing. The guard handed the file to Little.

Neither Brad nor his client spoke while the guards were present. As soon as they closed the door behind them Little pulled his folding chair close to the phone and sat down. He placed the file on the ledge in front of him and picked up the receiver. Brad's stomach tightened.

"Mr. Little, my name is Brad Miller," he said, hoping that his client wouldn't notice the slight tremor in his voice. "I'm an associate at Reed, Briggs, Stephens, Stottlemeyer and Compton in Portland. The firm was asked to handle your habeas corpus suit in the United States Court of Appeals for the Ninth Circuit."

Little smiled. "Your firm has an excellent reputation for doing quality work, Mr. Miller. I'm flattered that the court appointed Reed, Briggs to represent me. And I appreciate the fact that you've taken time from your busy day to visit me."

Brad was relieved that Little was so gracious.

"You're our client," he said magnanimously, "and you couldn't really come to our office, could you?" Brad asked with a smile, hoping that a little humor would lighten the depressing surroundings.

Little grinned. "I guess not."

Brad began to relax. Maybe this wouldn't be so bad after all. Then he remembered that he hadn't given the bad news to the mass murderer sitting on the other side of the glass.

"I came to Salem to discuss some problems I'm having with your case," Brad started diplomatically.

"What problems?"

"Well, the writ of habeas corpus that you filed alleged incompetence of counsel."

Little nodded in agreement.

"And the judge who conducted the hearing disagreed with you about the quality of your representation at trial."

"He was wrong."

"Uh, yes, I know that's your position, but we have a problem. The United States Supreme Court wrote an opinion in a case called *Strickland versus Washington*. In that case they said that—and I'll quote this"—Brad said, pulling a copy of the opinion out of his file— "'a court deciding an actual ineffectiveness claim must judge the reasonableness of counsel's challenged conduct on the facts of the particular case, viewed as of the time of counsel's conduct. A convicted defendant making a claim of ineffective assistance must identify the acts or omissions of counsel that are alleged not to have been the result of reasonable professional judgment. The court must then determine whether, in the light of all the circumstances, the identified acts or omissions were outside the range of professionally competent assistance . . .'"

"I've read *Strickland*," Little said.

"Good. Then you understand that you can't just accuse your lawyer of screwing up. You have to tell the court very specifically what he did that constituted ineffective assistance."

"I did. I told my lawyer that I had an alibi for the time that I was accused of kidnapping and murdering Laurie Erickson and he didn't investigate my claim."

"Okay, that's the problem. There's no question that your lawyer had an absolute duty to make a reasonable investigation of facts in your case that could establish an alibi—and he testified that you said you had an alibi—but he said that you didn't give him any facts he could investigate. I've read the transcript of your habeas corpus hearing. The judge asked you where you were and you avoided answering the question. So, I guess the bottom line is that I don't see any way we can win your case on appeal because the Ninth Circuit is just going to say that you didn't make an adequate record to show your lawyer did anything wrong."

"I still want to appeal."

"Maybe I didn't make myself clear, Mr. Little. I read the transcript of your case. Then I did a lot of research on this issue. After that I conferred with other attorneys in the firm. No one thinks you can win. It would be a waste of time to pursue your appeal."

Little wasn't smiling now. "How long have you been out of law school, Mr. Miller?"

"Uh, not that long."

"And how many criminal cases have you handled?"

"Well, actually, this is my first."

Little nodded. "I thought so. Tell me, are you still new enough to your chosen profession to believe in the pursuit of Justice?"

"Sure, of course."

"And I take it that you wouldn't approve of an innocent man being framed for something he didn't do?"

"Of course not."

"And you wouldn't want an innocent man to be executed for a crime he didn't commit."

"No one would want that."

"The person who murdered Laurie Erickson might."

Brad frowned. "Are you saying you didn't kill Miss Erickson?"

Little kept his eyes locked on Brad's and nodded slowly.

"So you really have an alibi for the time she disappeared?" Brad said even though he didn't believe a word of his client's assertion.

"Yes, I do."

"Why the big secret? If you had evidence that would have led to your acquittal why didn't you tell your lawyer at trial or explain it to the judge at the hearing?"

"That's a little tricky."

"Look, I don't want to sound judgmental but you seem to be evading my questions about your alibi in the same way you avoided answering the judge's questions at your hearing. If you're not honest with me I can't help you."

"Here's my problem, Mr. Miller. There was a witness who could clear me completely, but my involvement with her would implicate me in another crime."

"Mr. Little, what do you have to lose? You're on death row not only for the murder of Laurie Erickson. You were sentenced to death for two other murders. The Supreme Court affirmed those convictions a week after your habeas corpus hearing. Even if I win this case, you'll still be executed."

"But not for something I didn't do. It's a matter of honor, Mr. Miller."

"Okay, I can see where you wouldn't want to let someone get away with framing you. What I don't understand is why you didn't tell your lawyer your alibi if you feel so strongly about this. Anything you told him would have been confidential, even if you confessed to another crime."

"I assume that would hold for you, too?"

"Yes. I'm your attorney, so everything you tell me is confidential. If you tell me about a crime you've committed I'm forbidden by law to reveal that confidence to anyone. And I'm sure your trial attorney told you the same thing. So, why didn't you tell him the name of the witness?"

"Because he's an idiot. The court stuck me with a complete incompetent. I had no faith that he would follow up properly if I confided in him. And my other cases were on appeal, so I didn't want to incriminate myself in another crime until I knew what was going to happen in those cases."

Little hesitated. Brad could see he was going through some kind of internal struggle.

"There's another thing," Little said. "In order to prove my innocence I'm going to have to part with some cherished keepsakes. I just couldn't give them up to that moron. Now there doesn't appear to be a chance I'll ever see them again unless it's in court and they're introduced as evidence. So I have nothing to lose by telling you about them."

"You've just met me, Mr. Little. Why do you think I'm any smarter than your trial attorney?"

"Because the firm of Reed, Briggs, Stephens, Stottlemeyer and Compton saw fit to hire you, and they don't employ idiots."

Brad sighed. "I appreciate the vote of confidence, but it may be too late for me to help you. I'm handling your appeal. An appeal is based on the record of the court below. We can't introduce new evidence in the Ninth Circuit."

"What if you could prove that I'm innocent? The authorities would listen to a lawyer from Reed, Briggs. If the police were convinced that I didn't kill Laurie Erickson the governor would pardon me, wouldn't he?"

"I really don't know. I'm good at research, which is why I was assigned your case, but I'm not really up on criminal law or procedure. There probably is some way to help you if you can give me a way to prove you didn't commit the murder."

Little was quiet for a moment. Brad could almost hear him weighing the pros and cons of confiding in his new attorney.

"All right, I'll take a chance. At this point, as you so aptly pointed out, I've got nothing to lose." Little leaned forward. "On the night Laurie Erickson was kidnapped and murdered I was with somebody."

"So you've said, but I need a name and a way to contact the witness."

"Her name is Peggy Farmer."

Brad wrote the name down on his legal pad. "Do you know how I can find her?" he asked.

"Yes, I do. She's in the Deschutes National Forest about five miles from the parking lot of the Reynolds Campgound. On the evening the police insist I was kidnapping Laurie Erickson I was disemboweling Peggy."

Brad's stomach shifted and he felt like he might throw up. Little noticed his discomfort and smiled.

"She was camping with her boyfriend. They were deep in the woods; a very athletic couple. I followed them, eliminated her friend while he was sleeping, and played with Peggy until I grew bored. The confusion arises because no one has discovered the bodies. They're listed as missing. There have been search parties, but I did a very good job of hiding them."

"Mr. Little," Brad said, trying very hard to keep his voice steady, "if Miss Farmer is dead how can she help your alibi defense?"

"You know about my pinkie collection?"

Brad nodded, not trusting himself to speak. Bile was already rising in his throat.

"If a forensic expert examined my collection he would find a pinkie belonging to Peggy, but he wouldn't find one belonging to Laurie Erickson."

An image of a Mason jar filled with pinkies flashed in Brad's mind and he felt faint.

"Peggy's roommate will tell you that Peggy and her boyfriend went camping Wednesday afternoon and were supposed to come home Friday night because they had a wedding to attend on Saturday. I worked Thursday and Friday. I called in sick on Wednesday. If I killed Peggy it would have to have been on Wednesday, and Laurie was snatched on Wednesday evening. I couldn't have been in two places at once."

This was way more than Brad had bargained for. He was supposed to be reviewing contracts and checking property records, not sitting inches away from a lunatic with a pinkie collection.

"I see this is a bit much for you," Little said kindly. "You can ask the guard for some water."

"I'll be fine," Brad insisted though he felt anything but.

"You don't have to be brave, Mr. Miller. We all fall apart if our situation proves to be too much for us. Believe me, I've seen it first-hand." Little got a wistful expression on his face. "Some of them cry and beg right away. Others curse and threaten. They try to be strong. But even the strong beg when the pain is too much."

"Okay," Brad said as he tried to maintain his dignity. "I'm going to leave now."

"I'm sorry if I upset you. But I must remind you that you are my lawyer and you have a duty to give me a vigorous defense. Anything less and you could be disbarred."

"Look, Mr. Little, this is the firm's case. I'm just working on it. I'll file a brief for you on the issues raised at your hearing but that's it."

"I don't think so. I've given you a way to prove my innocence. If you don't pursue it I'll file a bar complaint then I'll sue you and then I'll go to the press. I'll tell them you failed to help me because you were too frightened. How do you think that publicity will help your career?"

"You wouldn't get anywhere with a suit or a complaint."

"Maybe, but you'll be front-page news because I am. No one wants a coward for a lawyer. Think over what I just told you then get back in touch and I'll tell you how to find my lovely souvenirs."

Brad walked back to his car in a daze and had trouble concentrating on the road during the return trip to Portland. The visions in his head shifted back and forth between Clarence Little's collection of severed pinkies and Peggy Farmer's disemboweled corpse. His emotions swung between anger at Little for putting him in a bind, an irrational fear that the convict would escape from death row and torture him to death, and curiosity about the truth of his client's claims. Who better to frame for a murder than a serial killer? No one would take the protestations of a homicidal maniac seriously.

Halfway to Portland, Brad dialed his cell phone.

"Ginny Striker," the voice at the other end answered.

"Hey, it's Brad, Brad Miller."

"Hi, what's up?"

"Do you have time to meet me for coffee?"

"I'm kind of busy. Paul Rostoff gave me a rush job."

"This is important. I'm really desperate for some advice."

There was dead air for a moment and Brad held his breath. He'd called Ginny because she was very smart and had good judgment. Also, he couldn't think of anyone else at the firm in whom he could confide.

"I guess I can use a break."

"Can you meet me at the coffee shop on Broadway and Washington?"

"Brad, this is Portland. I can see at least a million places to get coffee from my window. Why don't we meet someplace closer to the office?"

"I don't want to risk running into anyone we know."

"What's going on, Brad?"

"I'll tell you in twenty-five minutes."

Ginny was nursing a caffe latte at a table at the back of the coffee shop when Brad walked in. He waved at her then ordered a black coffee and carried it to the table. He'd grown up drinking his coffee black and had yet to develop a craving for the lattes, cappuccinos, and other fancy coffee drinks to which Portlanders seemed addicted.

"I feel like Mata Hari," Ginny said when Brad sat down. "Why all the secrecy?"

Brad looked around to make sure that no one from the firm was in the shop.

"I'm going to tell you about a confidential communication I just received from a client. You're bound by the attorney-client confidence rules because we both work for Reed, Briggs, right?"

"Yeah, that's how I understand it."

"Because you can't talk about what I tell you to anyone."

Ginny ran her finger back and forth across her chest. "Cross my heart and hope to die," she said with a grin.

"This isn't funny."

"Sorry, but you're so serious. I thought I'd lighten things up."

"You won't be laughing when you hear what I have to say. I just got back from meeting Clarence Little at the state pen."

"What's he like?" Ginny asked eagerly.

"He's worse than I imagined," Brad answered. Then he told Ginny about his meeting. She wasn't smiling when he finished.

"Do you think he's telling the truth?" Ginny asked.

"I don't know. The guy's a freak. When he told me he'd disemboweled that poor girl he didn't show an ounce of emotion. I thought I was going to throw up. I'm sure he found my discomfort amusing. Little is sick and he's a sadist."

"But is he a liar?"

"I don't know, but if I had to bet I'd guess he was telling the truth. He seemed genuinely offended at being convicted for something he claims he didn't do, and he was adamant about proving his innocence, even though it won't do him a damn bit of good because he's going to be executed anyway."

"Why did you ask me here?" Ginny asked.

"I don't know what to do. My assignment is to research and file Little's appeal. It's not to prove he's not guilty. And, anyway, legally, his guilt or innocence doesn't mean anything in the Ninth Circuit. The court's only interested in whether his lawyer was incompetent. Even if I find the pinkies the court wouldn't consider the evidence."

"So don't do it. Just write the brief."

"Can I just do that? I am his lawyer. Wouldn't I be incompetent if Little gave me proof of his innocence and I didn't investigate? And what if I don't investigate and he goes to the press? How would that go over at the firm?"

"I can make an educated guess," Ginny said. "The partners loathe bad publicity. It discourages well-heeled clients from shoveling money into the Reed, Briggs vault. So I'd guess that you'd be thrown to the wolves."

"That's what I thought. But would they like it any better if I was responsible for the acquittal of the most fiendish killer in recent Oregon history?"

"Good point. At least they could argue that Reed, Briggs fights for its clients no matter how despicable they might be. That would endear them to the tobacco and oil companies."

"So you think I should try and find the pinkies?"

"It sounds a lot more interesting than trying to find the meaning of the section of the tax code they've got me studying. And there's something else you should think about. What if he is innocent and you could prove it? You'd be famous. You might get enough great PR to bring business into the firm and speed you on your path to a partnership. Then you'd be the one at five o'clock on Friday who hands out thousand-page files to the associates with weekend plans. Wouldn't that be great?"

Brad sighed. "Please get serious. This whole thing is giving me a splitting headache."

"I say you do it. Call Little's bluff. Ask him to tell you where he hid the pinkies. If he's screwing with you, you're off the hook."

"And if he's not?"

"You dig them up. I'll even come with you. I'll be your trusty sidekick."

Brad was suddenly suspicious. Ginny seemed a little too eager. He narrowed his eyes and studied her.

"What's going on? How come you're so anxious to get involved in my case?"

Ginny blushed, embarrassed. Brad thought it made her look adorable.

"I got interested in Laurie Erickson's murder after we talked," Ginny confessed. "Do you know Jeff Hastings?" she asked, naming another first-year associate.

"Sure. We've played tennis a few times."

"Jeff grew up in Portland and went to law school here, and his folks are loaded. They're members of all the right clubs and know everyone and are connected politically, so Jeff heard all the gossip about Christopher Farrington when he was governor."

"What gossip?"

Ginny leaned forward and lowered her voice. "There were rumors that Farrington was fooling around with Laurie Erickson."

"What! I don't believe that. She was just a kid."

"Do you know what a dirty old man is?" Ginny asked with a smirk.

Brad blushed. "I'm not an idiot, Ginny, but don't you think the media would have been all over this with Farrington running for president?"

"I asked Jeff the same thing. He said Farrington's dodged a bullet. There were rumors floating around about an affair but everyone clammed up after Erickson was murdered. One rumor was that Laurie's mother was paid off. Supposedly, a lot of money changed hands."

"I thought Farrington was poor. Where would he get enough cash to buy off a mother whose child was just murdered?"

"Farrington has wealthy backers, but the obvious source would be his wife. Claire Farrington's family is rich. The Meadows made money farming in Eastern Oregon. Then they diversified into Japanese car dealerships, and they provided the seed money for some successful high-tech companies. After they got engaged, Dr. Farrington's family financed Christopher's first run for state office. If it was necessary to save her husband's career, Claire could come up with the cash."

"Is there any evidence that Farrington was fooling around, anything concrete?"

"Jeff says no, but he also says that if Farrington was screwing Erickson it wouldn't be the first time he lusted after tender, young flesh."

Brad grimaced. "You've been reading too many Harlequin romances."

"Farrington may have been acting them out. Jeff says that a year or so before he ran for the state senate Farrington settled a PI case for a seventeen-year-old girl who was injured in a skiing accident. Supposedly, he brought over the settlement check in a chauffeur-driven limo stocked with champagne and who knows what else and celebrated with her in the backseat."

"Where did all this come from?"

"The chauffeur. Jeff says Farrington's driver was so disgusted that he went to the cops. Supposedly, the girl's parents wouldn't let her talk to the police, so no charges were brought. Everyone thinks they were paid off by Chuck Hawkins, Farrington's hatchet man."

Brad took a sip of coffee and mulled over the titillating information Ginny had just provided. The more he thought the more his brow furrowed.

"So," he said finally, "your theory is what, that the president of the United States killed his babysitter to shut her up about their affair."

"Hawkins could have done it for him. Jeff's met Hawkins a few times. He says the guy is scary. He was some special ops guy in the military and still wears his hair like a marine. He and Farrington are supposed to be very tight. The word is that there isn't anything Hawkins won't do to protect the president and the first lady."

"Okay. This just got way out of my league. I'm not going to accuse the president of murder. Not only would Reed, Briggs fire me but I'd never get another job as long as I lived."

"Who said you had to accuse the president of murder? Didn't you pay attention in crim law? When you're defending someone accused of a crime you don't have to prove who did it. You just have to show that there's a reasonable doubt about your client's guilt. The police will have the job of arresting Erickson's killer if you convince them that Little didn't murder her."

Brad hadn't paid very close attention in his criminal law class and he'd forgotten that his responsibility to Clarence Little wouldn't extend to finding the real killer the way the lawyers did on TV and in legal thrillers.

"You're right," Brad said, relieved. Then he looked serious. "Don't tell anyone else your theory about Farrington. It could get you in trouble."

"I'm not crazy, Brad. And I was just playing devil's advocate before. I have no idea who killed Laurie Erickson. But I still want to help you find out if there's anything to Little's claim of innocence."

"I don't know."

"Come on, pretty please. The stuff they've got me working on is boring. I want a case I can get excited about."

Brad frowned. "I need to think."

"By all means."

"I do appreciate your advice and the information you gave me."

"No problem."

"Give me a day or so to work this out."

"Take all the time you want. But remember one thing. If Little is innocent and you stand by and do nothing about it, you'll be helping the real killer get away with murder."

Part Three

The Ripper

Washington, D.C.

Chapter Eleven

Keith Evans was exhausted. As the agent-in-charge of the D.C. Ripper task force he was expected to set an example by outworking the FBI agents under him. Last night, he'd crawled into bed after midnight. Now it was 5 A.M. and he was up again, groggy, eyes raw, and with no time to shower before heading to the scene of the Ripper's latest atrocity, a Dumpster in the alley behind a Chinese restaurant in Bethesda, Maryland. The task force office had been notified as soon as the locals realized they had another victim of the Ripper. Evans was sorry that the Bethesda police were so competent; he could have used the extra sleep. At least the bastard had been considerate enough to leave the body only a few miles from Evans's house.

After finding a parking spot a block from the crime scene Evans took a swig from his thermos and grimaced. He'd been too rushed to put up a fresh pot, and the day-old coffee he'd reheated in his microwave was barely tolerable. As Evans trudged along the sidewalk the wind blew a page of newsprint toward him. He was so exhausted that the skittering sports page hypnotized him and it took an effort to pull his eyes away from it. Evans shook his head to clear it. The Ripper case was wearing him out. When he looked in the mirror he no longer saw the fresh-faced Omaha detective who'd broken a serial case that had stumped the FBI. The agent-in-charge of the FBI task force had been hunting the killer for three years and he was so impressed by Evans's spectacular detective work that he'd convinced the young man to apply for a spot in the Bureau.

When Evans started the course at Quantico he'd been twenty-nine, six two, and a rock hard 190. All of his hair was sandy blond, his skin was tight, and his blue eyes were piercing. Evans was almost forty now and he resembled that younger man only from a distance. There were gray hairs among the blond, and you could see black shadows under his eyes when he removed the glasses he needed for reading. He was carrying an extra ten pounds around his waist and his shoulders were slightly stooped. And the truth was that he'd never duplicated the intuitive leap that had led him to crack the case in Nebraska. There had been victories or he wouldn't be heading up the Ripper task force, but they'd been accomplished by dogged police work rather than brilliant deduction.

Along the way, Evans's long hours had ruined a decent marriage and worn him down; not the best state for dealing with an extremely bright murderer. And there was no denying that the Ripper was smart. He knew police procedure and he was great at covering his tracks and eliminating trace evidence. There were the usual theories about the killer being a cop or a cop wannabe, some disgruntled security guard who had not been able to qualify for the force and was taunting the police to prove they'd made a mistake in rejecting him. But anyone with half a brain could go online and learn all about crime scene investigation. The truth was that the task force had no idea who was behind the killings that were starting to freak out the good citizens of Washington, D.C., and its environs.

A barrier manned by a Bethesda police officer had been set up across the mouth of the alley to keep out curious civilians who, despite the early hour, were already straining to see the activity around the crime scene. Evans squeezed through them and stopped on the other side of the sawhorse to sign the security log that contained the names of everyone who entered the crime scene and the time they'd signed in and out. The alley was swarming with crime scene technicians, uniformed cops, and agents recognizable by their blue windbreakers with FBI stitched on the back in bright yellow letters. Evans pulled on a pair of latex gloves and donned a set of Tyvek paper booties even though he knew it probably didn't matter what he deposited at the crime scene now that it had been compromised by the cops, techs, and agents who'd been through the alley in the past few hours, not to mention any civilians who had wandered by since the killer had deposited his grisly package.

The Dumpster was halfway down the alley, and a body bag holding the victim lay next to it. At the other end of the alley was the van that would transport the corpse to the morgue for the autopsy. Standing next to the body bag was Arthur Standish, the county medical examiner, who was sipping coffee from a Starbucks cup. Evans trusted Standish, who had done a thorough job autopsying the second Ripper's victim before the Bureau got involved.

Evans started toward the body but was intercepted by a stocky officer with a salt-and-pepper crew cut.

"Ron Guthridge, Bethesda PD," the man said as he extended his hand. "I was in charge of the scene until your boys took over."

"Keith Evans. I'm lead on the FBI task force."

"I know," Guthridge said, grinning. "You're a TV celebrity."

"Thanks for calling so fast," Evans said, ignoring the dig. He was the public face of the FBI on this one. His fellow agents had been ribbing him about how bad he looked at his press conferences. Now he had to put up with kidding from the locals.

"Believe me I'm pleased as punch to turn this baby over to you."

"Do we have an ID?"

Guthridge nodded. "The victim is Charlotte Walsh, an AU student. We have an address for her apartment, too."

"And you know this because you found Walsh's ID in the Dumpster under her body."

Guthridge's eyebrows went up. "Yeah. How did you know that?"

"The Ripper always leaves his victim's ID under the body," Evans said, regretting that he'd had the urge to show off as soon as the words were out of his mouth. Exhaustion was eroding his IQ. "We haven't made the fact public," Evans added quickly.

"No one will learn it from me," Guthridge assured him.

"Has anyone visited her apartment?" Evans asked.

"No. As soon as we realized we might be dealing with the Ripper I put everything on hold so I wouldn't step on your toes."

"I appreciate the courtesy."

"Like I said, this is your baby and you're welcome to it."

"Great way to start the day," Dr. Standish said to Evans when he and Guthridge arrived at the Dumpster.

"I love the smell of garbage and dead bodies in the morning."

Standish chuckled and Evans flicked his head toward the body bag. "Why do you think we have another Ripper victim?"

Standish was suddenly serious. "The eyes are missing."

The authorities hadn't told the public that the Ripper removed his victims' eyes, either. It was always good to hold back certain facts to weed out false confessions.

"What about the substance we've been finding in their mouths?"

"I won't be able to tell until I've conducted the autopsy and sent a sample to the lab."

Minute traces of a substance had been discovered in the mouths of all four of the Ripper's victims but the FBI lab had not figured out what it was and why it was there.

"Hillerman, bring over the wallet," Guthridge yelled at the tall, thin African-American policeman who was in charge of logging in the crime scene evidence.

Hillerman brought over a plastic evidence bag containing, among other items, a black leather Prada wallet. Evans fished the wallet out of the bag and examined its contents. The driver's license belonged to Charlotte Walsh and listed an address a few miles from American University.

Evans squatted down and unzipped the body bag. He knew what

to expect but he was still appalled by the horrors one so-called human being could visit on another member of the human race. The Ripper dressed his victims before disposing of their bodies, but Evans could still see the black holes where the poor girl's eyes should shine and her throat, which looked like a wild animal had gotten at it. There was no question that the pretty girl in the driver's license photograph and the abused young woman in the body bag were the same person.

"Did anyone find a car belonging to Walsh nearby?" Evans asked Guthridge.

"No, but we've got an APB out," the sergeant answered.

Evans stood up and copied the address on the license into a notebook. Then he replaced the wallet in the evidence bag and handed it back to Hillerman.

"I really want to catch this son of a bitch," Evans muttered.

"I'll drink to that," Standish said before taking a sip of coffee.

Guthridge's cell phone rang. He stepped away and pressed it to his ear. After a brief conversation, the sergeant returned to the small group.

"They just found Walsh's car in a remote part of the lot at the Dulles Towne Center mall. The car won't start because someone disconnected the battery, and there's blood on the driver's seat."

"Is there a crowd around the car?" Evans asked.

"No. A security guard noticed the car sitting by itself before the mall opened and got suspicious. When he saw the blood he called it in."

"I'm going to send a forensic team out there. But we'll tow the car as soon as they give the okay. Play this down."

"I'm on it," Guthridge said.

Evans talked to one of the members of the forensic team before walking over to the Dumpster. He held his breath when he looked in so he wouldn't have to smell the odor of rotting food that permeated the area behind the restaurant.

"Where was she lying?" he asked.

Hillerman handed Evans a bag with crime scene photos that had been snapped before the body had been removed. The top shot showed Walsh's corpse splayed across several black garbage bags. He rifled through the other shots, which documented the place where the body had been found and the condition of the Dumpster after the body was removed. All of the other victims had been found in Dumpsters. Evans didn't have to be an English lit major to figure out the symbolism for which the Ripper was aiming.

"I can't do anything more here. You can take the body, Art."

Dr. Standish signaled to two men who were waiting to take away the corpse.

"I'm going to drive over to Walsh's apartment."

"I'll call you as soon as I have any results."

"Thanks," Evans said, feeling twice as tired now as he had when he'd entered the alley.

Charlotte Walsh lived on the fourth floor of an eight-story building, part of a shiny new complex that combined housing with trendy restaurants, upscale chains, and quaint boutiques. As soon as Evans found the address, he knew Walsh came from money. No starving student could afford to live in this apartment house, which was meant for young professionals earning six-figure salaries.

During the drive from the crime scene, Evans had called his partner, Maggie Sparks, and told her to meet him at Walsh's place. A slim, athletic woman in her early thirties dressed in a black pinstripe pants suit and a white, man-tailored shirt was pacing the sidewalk near the entrance to the building. Sparks's glossy ebony hair, high cheekbones, and dark complexion suggested Native American DNA. She did have some Cherokee blood but her ancestors had also been Spaniards, Romanians, Danes, and others of unknown origin, so she wasn't certain where she belonged in the genetic hodgepodge that had produced the human race.

"Sorry to roust you out of bed," Evans apologized.

"No you're not," Sparks answered with a smile. "Misery loves company."

Evans smiled back. He liked Sparks. She worked as hard as any of the task force members but was able to keep her sense of humor. They'd gone out for drinks a few times after work but he'd never gotten up the nerve to ask her to do more.

The lobby was marble, dark wood, and polished metal lit by Art Deco wall sconces. Colorful abstract art hung on the yellow pastel walls. Evans flashed his ID at the security guard who sat behind a desk in the lobby. The guard was dressed in a blue blazer and gray slacks and looked like he pumped iron. His black hair was slicked back, and he eyed Evans's credentials suspiciously.

"We need the apartment number for Charlotte Walsh, please," Evans said.

"I'm not certain I can give out that information, sir," the guard said as he squared up his shoulders and tried his best to look dangerous.

Evans read the black lettering on the guard's gold name tag.

"Miss Walsh was murdered this morning, Bob. I'm sure you don't want to impede a homicide investigation."

The guard's eyes grew wide. "Sorry," he said as he ran down the list of tenants, all traces of his tough guy persona gone. "That's seven-oh-nine."

"Does she live alone?"

"No, she's got a roommate, Bethany Kitces. She came in two hours ago."

"Thank you. We're going up. Don't tell Miss Kitces. Let us break the bad news."

"Yeah, of course." The guard shook his head sadly. "That's terrible. She was a sweet kid."

"You knew her?" Sparks asked.

"Just to say hello to. She was always friendly."

Evans briefed Sparks during the elevator ride to the seventh floor and the walk down a lushly carpeted hall lit by more wall sconces. Evans stopped in front of a black lacquered door with a decorative gold lion's head knocker and a doorbell. He opted for the doorbell and they waited patiently through three rings before a sleep-drugged voice ordered them to stop their racket. Evans told Maggie Sparks to hold her ID up to the peephole.

"Miss Kitces," Sparks said through the closed door, "I'm Special Agent Margaret Sparks. I'm with the FBI and I'd like to talk to you."

"About what?" Kitces asked. Evans could hear the suspicion in her tone.

"It concerns Charlotte Walsh, your roommate."

"Has anything happened to her?" Kitces asked, concerned now.

"I'd prefer to talk to you in your apartment where we'll have some privacy."

Evans heard locks snapping and the door was opened by a bare-foot woman who looked to be in her late teens. She was wearing pajama bottoms and an AU T-shirt and could not have been taller than five feet. Bethany Kitces's round face was framed by long, unkempt, curly blond hair, and she wore no makeup. It was obvious that she'd been roused from bed, but the presence of the FBI agents had acted like a cup of powerful espresso and her large blue eyes were wide open.

Evans found himself in a small foyer standing on a blond hardwood floor that was partially covered by a Persian throw rug. Beyond the vestibule was a large cluttered living room outfitted with ill-used but expensive furnishings. The agent noticed a state-of-the-art stereo system, a large plasma TV that hung from the wall like the abstract art in the lobby, a black leather couch, and a coffee table. Sweatpants were draped over an arm of the couch, and a bowl stained by melted ice cream stood on a coffee table next to an opened Coke can. The floor and two leather recliners were littered with other items of clothing, fashion and fan magazines, and CD holders with the names of pop groups Evans didn't recognize. A bookshelf held a mix of textbooks and trashy novels.

"This is Special Agent Keith Evans, Miss Kitces. He's working on Miss Walsh's case with me."

"What case? What's happened to Lotte?"

"Maybe you should sit down," Sparks suggested, walking past the wary young woman and heading toward the couch. Evans held back until Walsh's roommate was seated. The young woman looked nervous.

"We're sorry to wake you up," Sparks said. "I understand you just got in a few hours ago."

Kitces nodded.

"Were you out all evening?"

"Yes."

"When did you leave the apartment, last night?"

"A little after seven."

"Was Miss Walsh still here?"

"No, she left around four."

"Do you know where she went?"

"No. She just said that she had some stuff to do."

"Where did you go?"

"What's this about? Has something happened to Lotte?" Kitces asked again.

"I'll answer your questions in a moment," Sparks said, "but I need your answers first."

Sparks noticed that Kitces's shoulders were hunched and she'd clasped her hands tightly in her lap.

"I was with my boyfriend. We stayed at his apartment. I just got back around five."

"Why didn't you stay all night?" Sparks asked.

Kitces blushed. "We had a fight. I got angry and left."

"Can you tell us your boyfriend's name?"

"Barry Sachs. Now, can you please tell me what happened to Charlotte?"

"I'm afraid I have bad news, Bethany," Sparks said softly. "Your friend is dead. She was murdered last night."

Kitces looked stunned. "She's dead?"

"I'm afraid so."

Kitces stared for a second then she leaned forward and began to wail. Sparks moved next to her quickly and placed a comforting arm over her shoulder.

"It's okay," she said soothingly as the young woman wept. Evans went into the kitchen and filled a glass with water. Bethany was sobbing quietly when he returned.

Sparks took the glass from Evans and helped Bethany drink it down.

"I have some things I'd like to ask you," Sparks said when Kitces was calm enough to question.

"Okay," she answered, her voice so low Evans had to strain to hear her.

"Can you think of anyone who would want to hurt Miss Walsh?"

"No, everyone liked her."

"She didn't have any enemies, anyone she mentioned that she was afraid of?"

"We've been rooming together since the term started and we were in the dorm last year. I never heard her say anything like that and I never heard anyone say anything bad about Lotte."

"Have you noticed anyone suspicious lurking around here or on campus, or did Lotte mention anything like that?"

"No."

"Can you think of anything out of the ordinary that's happened recently?"

"I really can't. She just had fun, you know. We're in a sorority. Lotte was involved in campus politics. She dated."

"Any boyfriend problems?"

"No. She was going with this Alpha Sig, but they both decided it wasn't working. They're still . . . were still friends."

Kitces paused. "Gee, I can't get used to . . ." She choked up and managed a tearful, "You know."

The agents waited for Bethany to regain her composure. When she signaled that she was ready Sparks asked her next question.

"Can you tell us something about your friend? It will help us find the person who hurt her."

Kitces wiped her eyes and took another sip of water.

"She's from Kansas," Bethany said when she could speak without crying. "Her dad's an orthodontist and her mom is a lawyer in a big firm in Kansas City. Lotte is . . . was very smart. She had almost all A's her freshman year. She's poli-sci. She wanted to go to law school, then maybe politics. She worked on a congressman's campaign in high school and she was working for Senator Gaylord."

Bethany paused and frowned.

"Yes," Sparks prodded.

"You asked about anything odd. There was something. Lotte was working on President Farrington's election committee. Then she quit and started working for Senator Gaylord."

Evans's brow furrowed. "You're saying she switched her allegiance?"

"Yeah. What made it strange was she really liked the president, she was a huge fan, and she used to bad-mouth Gaylord all the time. When she started working for Gaylord she still didn't seem all that excited about her campaign or her positions. And, now that I think of it, what makes everything weirder is the way she acted when she came back from Chicago."

"What happened in Chicago?"

Kitces hesitated. "I promised her I wouldn't say anything."

"I can understand that you want to be loyal to your friend, but she's been murdered, Bethany. You wouldn't want to hold back information that might help catch her killer."

Bethany looked away. The agents let her think.

"Okay," she said when she turned back. "It was something to do with President Farrington. That's all she would tell me. One afternoon, I came home from class and found her packing an overnight case. This was when she was still volunteering at Farrington's campaign headquarters. I asked her what was up. Like I thought maybe she was meeting some boy and staying over, not that she did that a lot. She was pretty old-fashioned. She'd only stay with a guy she really liked and not right away, you know. Like not on the first date or even a second."

Bethany looked at Sparks to make sure she understood that her roommate wasn't a slut. Sparks nodded.

"So I teased her about her seeing some guy, and she said it wasn't like that. She said that the president was giving a speech in Chicago and she'd been invited to hear him and help out at the fund-raiser, but it was all hush-hush and she wasn't supposed to tell anyone. And that's when she swore me to secrecy."

"She didn't say why her trip was hush-hush?"

"No. I tried to get it out of her but she wouldn't give." Kitces looked down. "I feel bad about telling you. She didn't want me to say anything, and I promised."

"You're doing the right thing."

"I hope so."

"Was Lotte excited about this trip?"

"Yeah, but that changed when she came back. She stopped volunteering for Farrington and she was quiet and seemed nervous. Then, a week or so later, she started volunteering for Gaylord."

"Did she ever tell you why she switched?"

"No."

"You said that her mood changed after Chicago. What was the difference?" Sparks asked.

"Lotte was always upbeat. After Chicago she seemed to go up and down, quiet for a few days then excited and secretive then nervous and quiet again."

"And you don't know what was causing her to be like that?"

"No. I asked a few times if everything was okay. I thought it was a boy."

"And you're sure that wasn't it?"

"If she was seeing someone she'd have told me."

"Do you have a number for Lotte's parents?" Sparks asked.

The color drained from Bethany's face. "Oh my gosh, her parents. I'm not going to have to tell them, am I?"

"No, we'll take care of that."

"I guess I'll have to talk to them about the funeral and all. I want to be there."

"It seems like you were a good friend to her," Sparks said.

"It was easy," Bethany said. Then she sobbed, "She was the best."

"Could you show us Lotte's room?" she asked when Kitces had cried herself out.

Bethany wiped at the tears that streaked her cheeks as she led the agents down a short hall. Walsh's room was luxurious by the standards of most college students and much neater than a typical dorm room. The bed was made, there were no clothes on the floor, and the top of Walsh's dresser and desk were orderly. Evans guessed that Bethany was responsible for the mess in the living room. He wandered over to the desk while Sparks looked in the dresser and the closet. Several books about the United States Congress were stacked in a neat pile.

"She was working on a paper about the Senate majority leader for an honors program," Bethany explained.

"Thanks," Evans told her. He found a physics text and a few books about international politics on the other side of the desk. Evans frowned. Something was wrong, but he couldn't figure out what was bothering him. He opened the desk drawer and rummaged through it. He riffled through a checkbook but found nothing of interest. There were pens, Post-its, some paper clips, and a stapler. Another drawer contained letters from Walsh's parents. Something dawned on Evans. Walsh's parents might be old enough to communicate through snail mail but anyone closer to her age would be using e-mail. Evans searched the room but he didn't find what he was looking for.

"Where is Miss Walsh's computer?"

Bethany looked around the room too before answering. "If it's not here she must have had it with her. She had a laptop. She took it everywhere. She carried it in her backpack."

Evans took out his cell phone and dialed the agent who'd taken custody of the evidence from the Bethesda police at the crime scene. He asked if a backpack or a computer had been found in the alley. Then he asked if a laptop or a backpack had been found in Walsh's car. After a few minutes, Evans hung up.

"Bethany, if Miss Walsh didn't have the laptop with her where would it be?"

Bethany shook her head. "It wouldn't be anywhere. She never let it out of her sight. It had all her stuff on it: her papers, private stuff. It was either on the desk or in the backpack."

"She must have backed up her hard drive," Sparks said.

"Sure," Bethany said. "Everyone does. She kept her backup disks in a plastic box in her desk."

Evans started opening the drawers in Walsh's desk again but he couldn't find the box.

"Bethany," Evans asked, "I don't want to alarm you—and there may be a simple explanation for the missing laptop and backups—but can you check this room and the rest of the apartment to see if anything else is missing?"

Kitces looked scared. "Do you think someone broke in?"

"I don't know what your place usually looks like so I have no opinion. Did you notice anything unusual when you got home, this morning?"

"No, but I was pretty tired. I just went right to bed. I didn't look around."

Sparks and Evans helped Bethany search the apartment, but they didn't find the laptop or anything else that would help them in the investigation and Bethany couldn't point to anything else that was missing or out of place. When they were certain that there was nothing more to be done Sparks asked Bethany if she wanted them to call a friend to come over. Bethany said she'd call her boyfriend. Evans called police headquarters and asked to have a policeman come over to take Bethany's statement regarding the missing laptop and backup disks. As soon as the police officer arrived the agents thanked Bethany again, gave her their cards, and left.

"Do you think someone broke in, last night?" Sparks asked as they rode down in the elevator.

"I don't know."

"What do you think happened to the laptop?"

"If she had it with her, the Ripper might have kept it as a souvenir or he could have left it with the body and someone took it."

They walked side by side for a few moments then Sparks turned to Evans.

"We should have someone in the Kansas City office break the news to Walsh's folks."

Evans shuddered. He always felt so sorry for the parents. He could not imagine what it felt like to learn that your child was dead and then to learn that she'd died in pain and terror. He felt guilty that some other poor bastard would have the responsibility of visiting Charlotte's parents.

"When is this son of a bitch going to screw up?" he muttered angrily.

"He will, Keith. They always do."

Evans frowned. "This business with the campaigns is strange. I wish I knew what happened in Chicago."

"You can ask someone in Farrington's campaign headquarters. There's probably a simple explanation."

"I don't think so. You don't just switch sides like that. Something must have happened." Evans thought for a moment. "Maybe the Ripper works on Farrington's campaign. Maybe he hit on her and freaked her out."

"That would explain Walsh quitting Farrington's campaign, but it wouldn't explain why she went to work for Gaylord."

"True. I don't remember. Have we found any connections between the other victims and either campaign?"

"Not that I recall, but I'll have someone check it out. But I'm betting that whatever made Walsh switch her allegiance to Gaylord had nothing to do with our case."

Chapter Twelve

Dana drove random routes until she found the type of run-down motel that sits on the outskirts of small towns that have seen better days. The accommodations at the Traveler's Rest consisted of rustic cabins whose peeling paint had not been touched up since around the time we were fighting World War II. The only hints that the motel existed in the twenty-first century were the signs advertising FREE HBO AND INTERNET ACCESS. A little after five in the morning, Dana paid the clerk cash for a few days' lodging then drove Jake's Harley behind the fourth cabin from the office so it couldn't be seen from the road. About the only advantage she had was that no one knew what she was using for transportation, and she wanted to keep it that way.

Dana had used cash to pay for a toothbrush, toothpaste, and other basic toiletries plus a few days' supply of prepackaged sandwiches, taco chips, and bottled water in a gas station minimart hours away from the motel. She'd also made a stop at a Wal-Mart where she'd purchased a few changes of clothes and a duffle bag. After taking a quick shower and brushing her teeth, she caught a few hours of fitful sleep. When she woke up, she sat around in her T-shirt and panties, watching CNN while she ate half of a ham and cheese sandwich and drank a bottle of water.

The lead news story was about the D.C. Ripper, who had claimed a new victim. The police were withholding the name of the deceased until her parents were notified. There was nothing about the shooting at her apartment, but she wasn't expecting a story. The people who'd attacked her wouldn't want any publicity. They had probably sanitized the place and had someone with authority that could not be questioned silence the cops. If she could hide for a few days they might conclude she'd hightailed it for someplace far from Washington, D.C. That would give her a little breathing room. With no place to go and nothing to do, Dana killed the day watching old movies and periodically checking out the news.

A river flowed behind the motel. Sometime in the distant past, one of the owners had set up a picnic area with three tables in a copse of cottonwoods that grew near the bank. The sun was close to setting when Dana grew claustrophobic and left her room. It had been a warm day, and she went outside in a T-shirt that covered the gun she'd shoved into the waistband at the back of her jeans. Dana brought a sandwich and a bag of chips to one of the tables and washed them down with swigs from a water bottle. While she ate she thought over her options. There weren't many. She couldn't run forever without money, and the pictures of Walsh and Farrington were the only things of value she possessed. How to cash in, though? She couldn't drive up to the White House and demand to meet with the president.

The sun went down and a chill wind pushed away the warmth. Dana decided to go inside and research Christopher Farrington in the hopes that she would spot a way to get her demands to him. It turned out that the motel's boast of Internet access was a bit overblown. There wasn't a way to access the Internet from Dana's room but there was an old computer in a corner of the motel office that a guest could use. To do so, Dana had to pay for the use of the motel's password. This was fine with her, since her inquiries would show up as the motel's inquiry if she was on an agency hot list.

The owner's teenage daughter was manning the desk in the office.

Dana paid for the password. The young girl put the bills in the till before turning her attention back to the television that perched on a corner of the counter. Dana went online and typed in "Christopher Farrington." A dizzying number of references popped up on the screen, and she started shuffling through them, looking for something she could use.

Dana had lost her interest in current affairs during her stay in the mental hospital and had not rekindled it when she became an outpatient. She hadn't voted in any election for some time, so a lot of the information that was common knowledge to the average voter was news to her. Dana read about Farrington's rags-to-riches story and a biography of the first lady. After learning that Charles Hawkins had been with the president since his early days in Oregon politics she read his biography, too. The article about Hawkins contained a paragraph about his role as a witness in the trial of Clarence Little, who was accused of murdering the Farringtons' teenage babysitter when the president was the governor of Oregon. She was just starting to read an account of the case when she heard the name of another teenager on the television.

"Miss Walsh is believed to be the latest victim of the D.C. Ripper, who has been terrorizing women in the D.C. area for over a year," a newscaster was saying as the picture on the screen showed an alley filled with police personnel.

Dana was too stunned to work on the computer. As soon as she reentered her room she began pacing back and forth across the short strip of floor that ran between the bed and the dresser. She felt sick to her stomach and racked with guilt. Would Walsh still be alive if she had continued to follow her? Would she have been able to foil the attack by the Ripper?

When she was in the hospital, some of her fellow cops who visited had told her that they couldn't imagine what she'd been through. Dana didn't have to imagine what Charlotte Walsh had gone through. She'd been to the far side of terror and despair herself. The only difference between Walsh and herself was that Dana had survived the journey.

Another thought occurred to her, and she felt a chill. What if Walsh wasn't a victim of the D.C. Ripper? Dana trembled, and she sat on the bed. She thought about everything that had happened to her and to Walsh and decided that there was no way this was a simple coincidence. Dana wasn't buying Walsh as the *random* victim of a serial killer. Not when Dana had just escaped being the victim of a *random* burglary-rape-murder. Maybe the men in her apartment *had* been federal agents following orders from Farrington to get rid of anyone who knew about his affair. Not only did Dana know that the president had been with Walsh, but she also had photos that could prove it.

Dana took a deep breath and tried to calm down. The president couldn't kill her as long as she had the pictures, but she knew his agents would stop at nothing to get her—or anyone who was helping her—to tell them where they were. The pictures were her only way out of this mess, and she could think of only one person who could negotiate her safety with the president. Dale Perry had gotten her into this mess, and he was going to get her out of it.

Chapter Thirteen

The chambers of the United States Senate were impressive but they were also small because only one hundred citizens of the United States were entitled to hold the office. Maureen Gaylord was one of them. Everyone who watched her stride across the Senate floor toward the podium was impressed by her poise and air of command. This impression had not been left to chance. Gaylord's hairdresser had worked on her at home early this morning and a makeup artist had come to her office. The outrageously expensive suit she was wearing made her look businesslike but approachable. She knew this because this suit and several others had been paraded in front of a focus group earlier in the week, as had several versions of the speech she was about to deliver.

Senator Gaylord, a former Miss Ohio, was a wholesome-looking brunette who had used the scholarship money from several beauty pageants to finance a degree in business at Ohio State and a law degree from Penn. She'd grown up as trailer trash, which gave her credibility with the common folk, her years as an attorney for a major corporation worked for conservatives, and her Ivy League credentials played well with intellectuals. Gaylord was a political everywoman who was wily enough to avoid committing to the right or the left but duplicitous enough to make those who approached her believe she was on their side.

The president pro tempore of the Senate gaveled the chamber to order, and Maureen stared into the television cameras. There weren't many people in the gallery that hung over the Senate floor but there were plenty of media representatives in attendance, and that was all that counted.

"I am standing today in the most august deliberative chamber in the world thanks to the Federal Bureau of Investigation. Six months ago, a homegrown group of radical Islamists calling themselves the Army of the Holy Jihad conceived a despicable plan to attack the office buildings of the United States Senate with enough explosives to inflict massive casualties. One of the offices that would have been destroyed was mine. If it had not been for the brilliant work on the part of the Bureau these evil men might have succeeded. The fact that these deluded maniacs were willing to attempt such a brazen act highlights the absolute necessity of giving as much support as possible to the gallant men and women who risk their lives daily so that we may live our lives in freedom.

"I am proud to be a cosponsor of the American Protection Act, which will greatly add to the weapons the Bureau, Homeland Security, the CIA, and other groups on the frontlines of the war on terror presently possess. Some people have carped about various provisions of this act. One complaint I find especially galling is that which has to do with the profiling, investigation, and possible internment of Arabs living in or visiting the United States, including citizens of Arab descent. Those who complain about these important provisions of the act have let political correctness blind them to reality. With few exceptions the perpetrators worldwide of acts of atrocity have been Arabs, and some of these Arabs, like the Army of the Holy Jihad, have been the homegrown variety. They have reaped the benefits of democracy and capitalism while spitting in the face of those who educated and protected them and gave them opportunities few other countries give to their citizens.

"Yes, a few may suffer unjustly if this act is passed, but if we are going to protect our citizens, sacrifices must be made in this age of suicide bombers and terrorists unfettered by the laws of common decency. Our wonderful justice system can be counted on to correct most of these injustices, but our great American political and judicial systems must be protected so they may continue to help the United States remain the greatest country on Earth."

Senator Gaylord spoke about various sections of the bill for forty more minutes then held a press conference before walking back to the Russell Senate Office Building through one of the underground passages that connected the Capitol to her office. She could have taken the subway, whose small, open-top cars reminded her of a Disneyland ride, but Gaylord preferred to walk so she could have some quiet time. Some supplicant for some special interest took up almost every minute of her day, and her greatest gift to herself was her rare moments of solitude.

Gaylord knew that the American Protection Act had no chance of passing, but her defense of the act had solidified her support among the conservatives in her party. She was also certain that Christopher Farrington was going to condemn the bill, which would give her a chance to paint him as soft on terrorism. The president was so wishy-washy on so many issues that the label had a chance of sticking. Incumbent presidents were usually hard to defeat, but Farrington hadn't won his position. She didn't even think of him as a president. He was a political hack who was merely saving her place in the line of succession. Without the mantle of the presidency, Maureen knew that Farrington wouldn't stand a chance against her, and she was convinced that she could strip away the cloak that was concealing his true worth from his shoulders and expose his inadequacy to the world. By the time Senator Gaylord walked through the door of her office she was feeling righteous and self-confident and ready to do whatever was necessary to pound Christopher Farrington into dog meat.

"Good speech," Jack Bedford said from his seat on the couch. Her

chief of staff was a former political science professor with degrees
from Boise State and the Kennedy School at Harvard.

"I knew it would be. Any reaction yet from the press?"

"Fox loved it, and MSNBC vilified you. They brought up all that
World War II stuff about interning the Japanese."

"That's to be expected."

"But I'm not here to talk about your speech."

"Oh?"

"Something happened that I thought you should know about."

"And that is?" Gaylord asked disinterestedly as she took a brief
look through the stack of documents on her desk that her AA had
put in the priority pile.

"A girl named Charlotte Walsh, who worked at campaign headquarters, was murdered by the D.C. Ripper."

Gaylord stopped what she was doing and looked up. "That's horrible," she said with genuine emotion. "We'll send condolences to the
parents and order flowers for the funeral. Nothing cheap."

"Already done."

Gaylord looked upset. "I hope the Ripper isn't one of our staff or
volunteers."

"The FBI was questioning everyone at campaign headquarters but
Reggie Styles has everything under control. If the Ripper is involved
in your campaign there's no evidence to show it. He's probably some
deranged, Caucasian loner who lives with his mother. That's what the
profilers always say."

Gaylord grunted then she grew uncommonly quiet. Bedford sat
patiently. His boss always got like this when she had an idea.

"Do you think we can use the presence of a successful serial killer
in the D.C. area to paint Farrington as weak on the crime issue?"

"I've already written a line for you to use when you meet the press
about Walsh's death. 'If Farrington can't protect the people who live
in his city how can he protect an entire nation?' What do you
think?"

Gaylord smiled. "I like it."

Bedford grew serious. "There's something else. Walsh may have been a spy for Farrington."

"What!"

"As soon as we found out Walsh worked for you I sent someone to offer condolences and support to her roommate. It turns out that Walsh was a big Farrington supporter up until a week before she volunteered to work at our campaign headquarters. I mentioned this to Reggie. There's a kid from Georgetown who's volunteering. Seems he had dinner with Walsh the evening she died. He told Reggie she was pretty much alone in the office when she wasn't scheduled to be there and she jumped when he found her making copies of an economic report. Then, a few minutes later, he caught her in Reggie's office, and she jumped again. Reggie checked his office and nothing's missing, but he had a list of our secret contributors in a locked drawer in his desk."

"If Farrington planted a spy in our office we may be able to use that to our advantage."

"My thinking exactly, but we have to tread carefully, especially now that she's dead. We don't want to be seen as throwing mud on the victim of a terrible crime."

"Of course not. Why don't you look around a little more and see if you can come up with some solid evidence that implicates Farrington's people. Meanwhile, schedule a press conference for me. Maybe we can fly the parents in. That would be nice, don't you think?"

Chapter Fourteen

"Where the hell have you been?" Perry demanded angrily when his secretary put Dana's call through.

"I've been busy."

"You'd better have a damn good explanation for your behavior. My client says you quit in the middle of your assignment after leaving some insane message about attacking someone in the woods."

"It wasn't my message that was crazy, Dale. It was the assignment. And, quite frankly, I don't think your briefing was complete. You left out the part about the armed Secret Service agents and a few other tiny details."

"What Secret Service agents?" Perry blurted out. Cutler thought he sounded genuinely confused, but lawyers were trained to lie.

"We're going to meet tonight and have a long talk," Cutler said.

"The fuck we are. What you're going to do is bring the pictures you took and the cell phone I gave you to this office immediately."

"And if I don't, what are you going to do, sue me? I think Court TV will have a field day airing a trial that features a discussion of the goings-on at the president's fuck pad."

"What are you talking about?"

"President Christopher Farrington sent two men to kill me last night because I have pictures showing him in a bedroom with Charlotte Walsh shortly before she was supposedly killed by the D.C. Ripper. Guess what Mr. Family Values was doing in that bedroom with a girl who's young enough to be his daughter?"

"Jesus Christ, Cutler, not on the phone."

"It looks like I finally have your attention."

"How soon can you get to my office?"

"Do you think I'm a total idiot? I'm not going anywhere near your office. Tonight, after the sun sets, you're going to take a drive. Bring your cell phone. I'll tell you where to meet me as soon as I'm certain you haven't been followed. And don't think I'm alone. I'll have people watching you," she lied, "and you'll never know they're there. If they spot a tail, the pictures go to the press. Understand?"

"Do not even think about making those pictures public."

"That's completely in your control, Dale. I want money for them. Either the president pays or CNN pays. I don't care. I wasn't planning on voting for Farrington anyway."

For the meeting, Dana chose The 911, a bar in South-West D.C. that had two exits in addition to the front door. One was near the restroom and opened onto a side street, and the other was in the kitchen and opened onto a back alley. They would come in handy if she had to run. The bar was owned by Charlie Foster, a retired police sergeant she knew from the force. He'd put his life savings into it, and Dana had the impression he wasn't making much of a return. The 911 was dark and smelled of stale beer and sweat and the noise level was high and threatening. Best of all, for Dana's purposes, the customers were poor and black, and so was the neighborhood. If Farrington sent a Caucasian anywhere near The 911 he would stand out.

Meeting in a predominantly African-American neighborhood worked in Dana's favor for another reason. In the legal community, Dale Perry's reputation for viciousness rivaled that of Vlad the Impaler. Tales of Perry's hardball tactics were tossed around at bar conventions the way baseball fans traded tales of no-hitters. Dana had heard the stories and knew she needed an edge. Meeting at The 911 gave it to her. Dale Perry didn't like poor people and he feared blacks, whom he assumed all wanted to rob and kill him. Fear would keep Perry off balance during their negotiations.

Dana surveilled the area around The 911 for two hours before entering the tavern through the kitchen and mysteriously appearing on the seat across from the frazzled lawyer. She hadn't told Perry the type of establishment she'd chosen for the meet and he was still wearing a dark blue business suit, a silk shirt, and a Hermès tie, which made him as conspicuous in The 911 as someone dressed like Santa Claus.

"Enjoying the ambience, Dale?" she asked with a smirk.

"You're lucky I'm still here," Perry answered, trying to sound tough. It might have worked if it weren't for the sheen of sweat on his forehead and the way his eyes shifted nervously as he spoke.

"Here's the deal, Dale," Dana said. "What you paid me to follow Charlotte Walsh was more than fair for a simple surveillance assignment, but it didn't come close to compensating me for being hunted by armed Secret Service agents or being attacked by two men in my apartment who told me that they were going to rape me if I didn't give them the pictures I took of Farrington and Charlotte Walsh. You know my history, so you know how that kind of threat would affect me."

"I had nothing to do with any of that."

"As far as I'm concerned you're responsible for totally fucking up my life. I had to knock out a Secret Service agent when I was escaping from Farrington's love nest. Then I had to shoot a man claiming to be a federal agent to keep from being raped. So, not only am I running for my life, I'm facing serious federal charges. If I get arrested I'm not going to protect my employer, Dale. I'm going to cut any deal I can and I'll implicate anyone I have to in order to protect myself. Believe me, it's in your best interests and the best interests of your buddy, Christopher Farrington, to buy me off and shut this thing down."

"What do you want?"

"I want assurances that I am not being hunted and that I will never be charged or arrested for any possible crime growing out of this fiasco. Then I want a million dollars."

"You've got to be kidding."

"I lowballed the price, Dale. I could have asked for a lot more. But I figured a million is an amount your cronies can come up with quickly, and while it's a lot of money to me it's chump change for people in your circle. It's also fair pay for what I've gone through and a hell of a lot less than Farrington will have to pay a PR firm for spin control if I sell these pictures."

"Assuming I can come up with the money, how do you propose I call off a federal investigation?"

Dana shook her head in disgust. "Don't yank my chain if you want the pictures. You're on a first-name basis with every powerful politician in the administration, including the attorney general, and the president is his boss."

"What assurance do I have that you won't take the money and sell the pictures anyway?"

"Dale, my primary goal is not to get a million dollars; it's to live to spend it. The president can have me killed anytime the spirit moves him. I want Farrington to have a reason to forget about me. I'm keeping an insurance set of photos that will go to the media if I die under mysterious circumstances, but I have every reason to keep them a deep, dark secret if everyone plays fair."

Perry shook his head. "You are one crazy bitch, Cutler. I can't believe you have the balls to blackmail the president."

"It's not a question of courage, Dale. I'm scared to death. Those photographs are the only thing keeping me alive, and I'm going to use them any way I can so I can keep breathing."

Perry looked down at the table. When he raised his eyes he looked contrite.

"I'm sorry you're in this mess, and I'm very sorry about what happened in your apartment, especially because of what you went through when you were a cop. I really had no idea you'd get in so much trouble when I asked you to take the job. I thought the assignment would be easy money for you."

"Well it wasn't."

"I feel responsible for getting you into this fix and I'll do my best to get you out of it. Let's get out of here and I'll see what I can do."

"Thank you, Dale."

"Hey, I like you, Cutler. You're tough, and you've always done good work. You'll come out of this okay, trust me."

It was the "trust me" that did it. Dana had almost bought Perry's sudden change of heart until he said that. Something was going on, and Dana knew it wasn't going to be good. While she smiled "trustingly" at Perry her eyes worked the room. No one seemed out of place so the people working with Perry had to be outside.

"Why don't you give me a number where I can get in touch when I have news for you?" Perry said.

"It would be best if I called you."

"That's fine. Give me a day to work on the problem. I should know something soon."

"Great, and thanks, Dale."

"I'll walk you out," Perry said.

"I have to hit the powder room first. You don't have to wait."

"Okay. I'll talk to you soon."

Dana watched Perry leave. She kicked herself for not frisking the lawyer. She bet he was wired and broadcasting their conversation. If so, there were probably men waiting for her to walk out of the door near the restroom, so Dana headed in that direction before ducking into the kitchen. The kitchen staff was comprised of two short order cooks, who gaped at her as she stripped off her jeans and T-shirt and pulled the change of clothes Charlie Foster had left her out of a plastic garbage bag. She slipped a hairnet over her hair and pulled on a pair of baggy pants and several sweatshirts that made her look dumpy and heavier than she'd ever been. An apron, glasses with plain glass for the lenses, and a .45 completed the ensemble. When she was dressed, Dana filled one garbage bag with refuse and another with her clothes before opening the back door wide enough to peek into the alley. No one was waiting in front of the door, but she saw a shadow at one end near the street. There was probably someone at the other end, too.

She yelled as loud as she could in Spanish that they were bastards for making her haul this shit out all the time. "I'm a chef, I ain't no garbage man."

Dana slammed open the lid of the Dumpster and tossed in one bag. Then she stomped down the alley, muttering to herself. When the man stepped out of the shadows to check her out she tightened her grip on her sidearm and looked at him.

"What cho want, *pendajo*?" she asked belligerently.

"Sorry," the man said as he stepped back into the shadows.

Dana sucked in air and walked quickly along the escape route she had paced off hours before. As she walked she imagined eyes boring into her back and she waited for the sound of a shot, but the disguise had worked. In a few moments, she was astride the Harley and racing away from The 911.

Chapter Fifteen

Christopher Farrington had been in Iowa campaigning when the police identified Charlotte Walsh as the Ripper's latest victim. He ordered Charles Hawkins to fly to his next campaign stop then rushed back to the hotel from the fund-raiser he was attending as soon as he was notified that his aide was waiting for him.

Farrington was seething when he entered his hotel suite. After telling everyone else to leave, he confronted his friend.

"CNN reports that Charlotte was the Ripper's latest victim. That's some coincidence."

Hawkins shrugged. "You always were lucky, Chris."

Farrington glared at Hawkins. "What is wrong with you? The D.C. Ripper? What were you thinking? That's the most high-profile case in Washington since those snipers. We needed to stay under the radar and you've put us on national television."

"*We* are under the radar. It's the Ripper who's on the hot seat. Who's going to make a connection between a college sophomore and the president of the United States?"

"That fucking PI, that's who. Have you a line on her yet?"

"No. She set up a meeting with Dale Perry and we put a wire on him, but she got away."

"Damn it, Chuck, how did that happen? She's a low-rent snooper.

You've got special ops and the latest technology. Why didn't you track her with a satellite?"

"We didn't think we'd need to. We thought we had her trapped, but she's very resourceful."

"Why was she meeting with Dale?"

"She wants to sell the pictures for a million dollars and assurances that we'll let her alone."

"Then buy them."

"It's not that simple. She told Dale that she's going to keep an insurance set in case we renege on our bargain."

"Well we won't."

"Chris, if we pay her it will be in her best interest to sell another set to the media. We wouldn't dare kill her once the pictures are public knowledge. You'd be the prime suspect if she dies, even if it's from natural causes. There would be an uproar. Gaylord would claim you had the CIA take her out with some exotic, untraceable poison that mimics a heart attack. If we controlled Congress we could stop an investigation, but we don't. Even if you're eventually cleared, the investigation would last through the election and the bad publicity would kill you."

"What are you going to do about Cutler?"

"Try to find her. Once we've got her I can assure you she'll tell us anything we want to know."

"Then find her and do it quickly. I have a bad feeling about this."

"Well, don't. Everything is under control."

"It doesn't sound like it," Farrington answered. "Is there anything else I should know?"

Hawkins hesitated.

"What aren't you telling me?"

"There may be a few problems I didn't anticipate, but they're nothing you should worry about."

"What problems?"

"One of our people in Gaylord's camp says that she's going to use the Ripper murders against you by suggesting that you can't be trusted to protect America if you can't protect the people of the D.C. area against one murderer."

"That's ridiculous. I don't have anything to do with finding the Ripper. That's a local police matter."

"The FBI does have a task force that's running the investigation," Hawkins corrected.

"Right, but I have nothing to do with that. You get Hutchins to set the record straight," he ordered, referring to Clem Hutchins, his press secretary.

"We're working on it."

"Good. You said 'problems,' plural. What else has gone wrong?"

"My source also tells me that Gaylord's people suspect that Walsh was our spy."

"Can they prove it?" Farrington asked, concerned.

"I don't think so. They can prove she volunteered for us before she switched sides, but they can't prove she gave us copies of Gaylord's secret contributor list."

"If it ever gets out that we asked Charlotte to steal from Gaylord's campaign headquarters I'd be ruined. It would be Watergate all over again."

"You don't have to worry, Chris. Even if Gaylord could prove that Walsh was our spy, she can't use the information without making the list public knowledge. They'd be exposing their secret slush fund."

"That's right," Farrington answered with a smile of relief. Then he grew pensive.

"How close is the FBI to catching the Ripper?"

"My sources in the Bureau tell me that they have no idea who he is."

"That's good. Maybe they'll never catch him. That would be the best scenario for us."

"I agree. But if he is caught he'll probably take credit for killing

Walsh just to up his body count. And, if he says he didn't kill Walsh, who'll believe him?"

Farrington sighed. "You're right. Okay, concentrate on the PI. I want her found and neutralized. Do whatever it takes. Once she's dealt with we should be home free."

Farrington was suddenly lost in thought. When he spoke he looked sad.

"She was a good kid," he said softly.

Hawkins wanted to tell his friend that he should have thought of the consequences of his actions before he decided to bang the young volunteer, but he held his tongue.

Chapter Sixteen

Keith Evans had no social life, so spending the weekend at work required no sacrifice. Six months ago, when his last girlfriend broke up with him, she told the agent that she'd come to believe that the only way she'd get to see him was by committing a federal crime. Evans did like football, but the Super Bowl had been played months ago, he wasn't into basketball or baseball, and he'd never developed an interest in golf. When he started to feel sorry for himself he just plunged more deeply into his work. Keeping a lid on his personal problems got harder when his workload was low or, as now, when he was spinning his wheels.

This weekend Evans had reread every piece of paper in the Ripper cases, hoping for a new insight, and all he'd gotten was eyestrain. Now it was late Monday morning and he couldn't think of a thing to do, since he'd exhausted his efforts on the case Saturday and Sunday. It seemed that his only hope was that the Ripper would screw up at some point, which was not unlikely.

Sociopaths or psychopaths or antisocial personalities (or whatever the current term was) were able to kill so easily because they had no empathy for their victims. Evans thought that this was because they had never been fully socialized like normal people. He believed that all children were sociopaths who thought only of themselves and their needs. Parents were supposed to teach their children to think about the effect of their actions on others. Serial killers never successfully completed the course, so they never developed a conscience. The reason that Evans was certain that the Ripper would make a fatal mistake was because most serial killers, like most little children, saw themselves as the center of the universe and believed they were infallible. If they did screw up they usually blamed their failures on others—the victim, their lawyer, or any person or institution that was convenient. The big problem with this theory was that serial killers frequently had above average intelligence, so the big mistake might take a while to manifest itself. Meanwhile, more women would die.

Just before noon, while finishing a deli sandwich, Evans picked up a report on the first Ripper murder and realized that he'd read it an hour before. He couldn't think of another way to occupy his time so he stood up and headed for the coffeepot. He was halfway there when his phone rang.

"Evans," he answered.

"I've got a Dr. Standish on two," the receptionist said.

Evans punched the button and was greeted by Standish's cheery voice.

"I've completed Charlotte Walsh's autopsy and we should talk."

Standish had insisted on meeting Evans at an Italian restaurant a few blocks from the coroner's office. The agent found the medical examiner sitting in the back of the restaurant. Standish had chosen to eat there out of consideration for the sensibilities of the other patrons, whose meals would be ruined if they overheard the graphic anatomical descriptions that often accompanied any discussion of an autopsy report. While Standish took for granted the blood and gore in which he waded each day, he was aware that the vast majority of Americans did not. That point had been brought home during one of the first trials in which he'd testified, when a thirty-two-year-old appliance salesman on the jury had fainted during his description of a death by chain saw in the trial of a mean-spirited drug dealer.

"Hey, Art," Evans said, sliding into the booth just as the waiter walked up to their table.

"Try the veal scaloppini," the medical examiner suggested as he dug into his side dish of spaghetti in marinara sauce.

"I ate already," he told Standish. "Just coffee, please," he said to the waiter.

"So, what have you got for me?" Evans asked as soon as the waiter was out of earshot.

"Some strange shit," Standish replied when his mouth was empty.

"Oh?"

The medical examiner picked up a sheaf of papers that had been lying on the vinyl beside him and tossed it to Evans.

"First off, cause of death. The eyes were missing and there were many stab wounds identical to the type of wounds we've found in the other Ripper murders. The torso and genital area were a mess, and there were a large number of slashing wounds all around the neck. In fact, the whole neck was pretty hacked up."

"That sounds like the other killings."

"Right, except the other victims were mutilated before they died. Most of Walsh's wounds were postmortem. I could tell that because I didn't find the quantity of blood you'd expect when a person is stabbed and the heart is still beating."

"So, what killed Walsh?"

"That's interesting. When I took out the brain I found a wound that indicated to me that a sharp instrument had been thrust into the base of the back of the neck between the skull and the first cervical vertebra. This severed the spinal cord and caused instant death but hardly any bleeding."

"So the stab wound to the spine killed Walsh, but the Ripper still went after her as if she was alive."

"That's one way to look at it."

"Maybe he was upset that the first thrust killed her and he inflicted the other damage in a rage."

"That's possible, too," Standish agreed before shoveling some more veal into his mouth. Evans sipped some coffee and thought while he waited for the medical examiner to swallow.

"We've got some other anomalies," Standish said, pointing his red-stained fork at the FBI agent. "I didn't find evidence of forced intercourse as I found with the other victim I examined. The autopsies you sent me on the other women listed bruising around the genitals and other indications of rape, but there was no indication of this with Walsh."

Evans spread his hands and shrugged. "He may not have been in the mood if she was dead."

"True."

"And the other anomalies?"

"You know the substance that's been found in the victims' mouths?"

"The one we can't identify?"

"Right. You found it in every victim's mouth, right?"

Evans nodded.

"Well, it wasn't present in Walsh's mouth."

Evans frowned. "Are you suggesting that we're dealing with a copycat?"

"I'm not suggesting anything. I'm just the sawbones. You're the detective."

"How similar to the wounds in the other cases are the wounds in this one?"

"Oh, the MO is almost identical except for the extensive damage to the neck."

"Is it possible that the postmortem neck wounds were inflicted to draw attention away from the real cause of death?"

Standish shrugged. "Anything's possible. I will say that creating that much carnage was effective. I wouldn't have stumbled across the fatal wound if I hadn't decided to remove the brain myself."

Evans was quiet for a while, and Standish took the opportunity to finish off his lunch.

"If we have a copycat who is able to duplicate the MO so closely, he'd have to have seen the other bodies at the crime scenes, or crime scene and autopsy photos, or he'd have to have read the autopsy or crime scene reports," Evans mused.

"I'd say so," the doctor agreed. "Unless the newspapers gave a very detailed description of the injuries that each victim suffered."

"No, there was nothing like that in the press or on TV. Tell me, Art, could the Ripper have killed Walsh by accident? That would support the idea that he mutilated her postmortem in a rage. You know, he's all set to work on her then she has the audacity to die on him. That could have set him off."

"As I said, anything is possible, but I don't really see the killing being committed by mistake. It's like a rapist who claims he slipped and his dick accidentally penetrated the victim. This was a pretty precise thrust."

Evans scowled then shook his head. "Thanks for ruining my day."

"Hey, don't blame me. I just work here."

"As if I didn't have enough to do, now I may have to find two killers."

"You'll solve the case, Keith. Remember, neither snow nor rain nor heat nor gloom of night stays these . . . Oh, wait, that's the postmen. What do you boys do when it snows and rains?"

"We go after the bad guys. Some days, though, are easier than others."

Part Four

Rotting Corpses and Severed Digits

Oregon

Chapter Seventeen

On Saturday morning, Brad Miller drove to Salem for his second meeting with Clarence Little. Ginny Striker was riding shotgun, and he was grateful for the company. He usually didn't have any on a weekend. He also enjoyed discussing strategy with the attractive associate. In fact, he liked everything about Ginny. The only good thing to come out of Tuchman's assignment was the opportunity it gave Brad to spend time with her. When he was with Ginny he felt none of the anxiety and sexual tension he always felt when he'd been dating Bridget Malloy, who seemed to go out of her way to keep him on edge. Ginny seemed genuinely nice, and the only friction between them arose when he refused to let her meet Clarence Little.

"Are you nuts?" Brad had replied when Ginny broached the subject. "I don't want you within a mile of Little."

"I'll be perfectly safe," Ginny insisted. "You told me there was concrete and shatterproof glass between you. How is he going to get to me?"

"That's not the point. I don't want him knowing you exist. What if he gets out somehow?"

"I don't think freedom is in Mr. Little's future, Brad. He's serving three death sentences."

"I don't want to take any chances."

"That's sweet," Ginny answered in a voice dripping with sarcasm, "but your chivalrous attitude is a bit outdated. I helped subdue paranoid bikers on speed when I was working the emergency room. I know how to take care of myself. If Clarence busts through the glass I'll protect you."

Out of desperation, Brad played his trump card. "Look, Ginny, I know you're tough. You're probably a lot tougher than me. But the truth is, you'd be a distraction."

Ginny opened her mouth, but Brad held up a hand. "Hear me out. This guy loves to play games. He's doing it with me, right now. I wouldn't be surprised if this whole deal with the pinkie collection is a sick practical joke that will have us running all over Oregon on a wild goose chase. God knows what he'll want you to do if you show up with me. Little's idea of a good time is torturing women. If he can't get his hands on you, he'll figure out a way to play mind games with you and that will complicate our job of figuring out if he's telling the truth about his alibi."

Ginny folded her arms across her chest and stared through the windshield. Her silence was a good sign. It meant she was thinking about what he'd said. Irrational as it might be, he was worried about what might happen if Clarence Little met Ginny Striker.

On Brad's second trip to the prison there were different visitors in the waiting room, but they had the same look of tired desperation and fake joy as the women he'd waited with the first time he'd visited Clarence Little. When his name was called he felt like an old hand as he navigated the metal detector, walked down the ramp to the visitors' area, and arrived in the noncontact room reserved for visitors to death row inmates. He should have been thinking about his meeting while he waited for the guards to bring his client. Instead, Ginny occupied his thoughts. She was still mad at him for refusing to let her go into the prison, but she'd grudgingly conceded that putting her in close proximity to a man with very odd ideas about male-female relationships might interfere with their goal of discovering the truth behind Little's protestations of innocence. As he waited for Little, Ginny was waiting for him in a coffee shop near the penitentiary, working away on her laptop at her assignments from the partners.

The door opened and the guards escorted Little into the cramped space on the other side of the glass. When Little saw Brad he smiled. The smile might have simply been the inmate's way of greeting a visitor, but Brad suspected that it signified Little's satisfaction with his victory in their battle of wills.

Little and Brad picked up their phones as soon as the guards disappeared.

"Thank you for visiting again," Little said. "You have no idea how boring it is sitting in my cell all day with nothing to do. Every break in my routine is a wonderful gift."

"I'm glad I've brightened your day, Mr. Little," Brad answered brusquely. "But I'm here to find out where you hid the pinkies so I can try to clear your name in the Laurie Erickson case."

Little's smile widened. "I knew I was right to trust you."

"Yes, so, where are they?" Brad asked, anxious to get the meeting over with as quickly as possible.

"Before I tell you where I've hidden my keepsakes, why don't you tell me a little about yourself."

Brad rolled his eyes. "This isn't going to be like *Silence of the Lambs* is it? You're not expecting me to trade intimate details about my life for clues to the whereabouts of the pinkies?"

Little laughed. "Not at all. I'm just not in a rush to go back to my cell, and I think I'm entitled to know a bit more about the qualifications of someone to whom I'm entrusting my life."

"Okay. What do you want to know?"

"Your accent suggests that you grew up on the East Coast."

"New York. Long Island, actually."

"And did you go to college in New York?"

"Hofstra."

"What was your major?"

"English."

"That's not a very practical major. Why not something in the sciences or engineering?"

"I'm not very good at math or science and I like to read."

"A good choice then. Where did you go to law school?"

"Fordham."

"Didn't you have the grades to get into Columbia or NYU?"

"My grades were fine, but I don't do well on standardized tests. Look can we get back to the pinkies?"

"I see your patience is running thin. Impatience is not an admirable trait. I used to take a lot of time with my female friends. Here's a tip, Brad. Never kill them quickly. It spoils the fun."

"Okay, I've had enough. I don't think there is a pinkie collection. I think you're having fun at my expense."

"If there's no pinkie collection what happened to them?"

"You know, Mr. Little, I don't care. I'm going now. I'll do my best on your brief and I'll argue your appeal, but I'm not going to waste my time and the time of my firm playing bullshit mind games with you."

Brad stood up and Little started to laugh.

"Sit down. I'm fucking with you. I liked *Silence of the Lambs,* although it's totally unrealistic. All those serial killer movies are ridiculous. I can't sit through most of that shit. Watching them is like a busman's holiday anyway."

Brad stared through the glass, unsure of how to respond.

"Sit down, please. I wanted to see just how long I could string you along with this act. I don't even talk like this. I even comb my hair differently when I'm not meeting with you. I was just doing my best Hannibal Lecter impersonation."

"Your best . . ." Brad shook his head, thoroughly confused. "What's going on here?"

"I thought you'd expect someone a little weird and I didn't want to disappoint you. It was just harmless fun. I really am sorry I jerked you around."

"I don't appreciate being a mental hacky sack."

"I said I'm sorry. It's just that it really is boring sitting on death row all day with nothing to do. This was just a way of killing time."

"So the pinkie thing was bullshit?"

Little sobered immediately. "No, no, that's real. Get someone to fingerprint the pinkies and you'll see I'm one hundred percent innocent of killing that babysitter. And I'm very serious about getting the bastard who had the audacity to frame me."

Brad sat down. "No more nonsense. Where are the pinkies?"

"They'll be a little difficult to find. Tell me, are you fond of the outdoors?"

"Not particularly. I'm basically a city boy."

"Well, I'm a country boy, and I love to hike and hunt and shoot the rapids. There are so many wonderful wilderness areas in Oregon. You'll thank me for introducing you to one of them."

Oh, shit, thought Brad, whose idea of a wilderness adventure was a walk through Central Park.

"You buried the pinkies in the woods?"

Little nodded. "I was bringing them a new companion when I stumbled across Peggy and her friend." He looked sheepish. "I hadn't planned to kill her, but I couldn't let the opportunity pass."

"The fingers are buried near the bodies?"

"You're definitely much faster on the uptake than my trial attorney. I'm certain you would have won my case had you been representing me. Then we wouldn't have to be going through all this trouble to prove my innocence."

"Is this treasure hunt going to involve an overnight stay in the woods?" asked Brad, who was starting to worry about bears and mountain lions.

"No, nothing like that. I told you, Peggy left Portland on Wednesday and had made camp when I found her. The trailhead is a few hours from Portland, and I've buried my cache near a waterfall about five miles in on a side trail. The bodies are very close by. Say hello for me, won't you?"

"You know I might have to give the authorities the location of the bodies and turn over the pinkies to the police?"

"I authorize you to do whatever is necessary to catch the son of a bitch who framed me." Suddenly a dreamy look suffused Little's face. "Wouldn't it be interesting if he ended up on death row, say in the cell next to mine. That would create some fascinating possibilities."

Chapter Eighteen

Sunday morning, Brad and Ginny drove down I-5, past the prison, and turned onto a state highway heading east toward the Cascade Mountains. The outlet malls, motels, and gas stations that passed for scenery on the interstate gave way to farmland then forest in almost no time. The pace of work at Reed, Briggs had been so intense that Brad hadn't had a chance to explore Oregon, and he was surprised by the rapid disappearance of anything remotely resembling the crowded, tightly packed urban and suburban areas he'd grown up with on the East Coast. The population of the towns they drove through was often listed in three or four digits, and the road ran parallel to rivers and dense forest instead of strip malls and tract homes. Every once in a while the course of the two-lane highway would veer and without warning the snowcapped peak of a huge mountain would loom over the vast expanse of green foothills, only to disappear when the road changed direction again.

"Does this look anything like the Midwest?" Brad joked.

"Are you kidding? A five-story building passes for a mountain where I come from. This is awesome."

"Long Island's flat as a pancake, too. It's where the glaciers stopped. When they retreated they turned the whole place into a parking lot. And I can't remember seeing this much green outside of Saint Patrick's Day."

Ginny smiled. Then she took another look at the MapQuest directions she'd gotten from the Internet. It was almost an hour and a half since they'd turned off I-5.

"Start looking for signs for the Reynolds Campground. It should be on our left."

Ginny was wearing a T-shirt and shorts, and Brad caught himself casting surreptitious glances at her legs. He'd donned a T-shirt, jeans, and sneakers, the only items in his wardrobe that seemed appropriate for a hike in the woods, something he'd only done at summer camp when he was ten.

"There it is," she said, pointing to a highway sign that was posted just in front of a gravel road.

Brad made the turn. A quarter mile later they found themselves in a primitive parking lot. A wooden sign pointed them toward a dirt path that served as the trailhead for part of the Pacific Crest Trail that wound through the Mount Jefferson Wilderness on its way from Mexico to Canada. Little had instructed Brad to follow the Pacific Crest Trail for a half mile before turning off onto another trail that would eventually take them—if Brad's client was to be believed—to two decomposing bodies and a Mason jar filled with pinkies.

Brad and Ginny had purchased some collapsible digging tools at an outdoor store. They put them in their backpacks along with a few cans of soda, some bottled water, and a few sandwiches. Ginny claimed to have an excellent sense of direction and insisted that she lead the way. They set off after Brad gave her the directions Little had dictated in the prison.

The day was perfect for hiking. When they'd left Portland it had been warm and unusually muggy, but they were almost three thousand feet above sea level and the air was cooler. As soon as they were in the forest the shadows cast by the leafy canopy lowered the temperature some more. Even so, Brad's lack of exercise began to tell after they'd walked only a mile and he began sweating and taking swigs of bottled water.

"How much farther?" he asked a little while later.

"You asked me that same question ten minutes ago. I feel like I'm stuck in a station wagon with an eight-year-old. 'Are we there yet, Mommy?'"

"Give me a break. I'm not used to jungle treks."

"Well, Jane, I'd guess we've got another thirty minutes before we get to the side trail to the waterfall. Think you can make it, or do I have to have the apes carry you?"

"Very funny," Brad muttered as he forged on.

The area around the waterfall was idyllic. Most of the sun's rays were blocked by the trees that stood on the crest of the high cliff where the water began to tumble down, leaving the ground in shadow. Green clumps of iridescent moss clung to the shiny black rock face, and a mist formed where the cascading water splashed into the pool at the bottom. They ate their lunch sitting on a log with their feet dangling in space as they watched the swirling stream formed by the falling water rush by with a soft shushing sound.

Brad wasn't so certain that it was a good idea to eat so soon before digging up a moldering corpse, but he was starving and too exhausted to pass up food. He decided that he'd deal with a queasy stomach when the time came. He still wasn't completely convinced that they would find anything anyway and he occasionally flashed on a chuckling Clarence Little brightening the days of his fellow death row residents with his hilarious tale of the gullible lawyer and the phantom pinkies.

"Have you thought about what we're going to do if we find the bodies or the pinkies?" Ginny asked.

"What do you mean?"

"Do we have to tell the police where they are?"

"I guess Susan Tuchman will make that decision. We'll have to tell her what Little's told us if we find anything that supports his story. But I did do some research, so I can advise her if she asks me what we should do.

"There's a split of opinion about whether we have to call the cops. If we take possession of the pinkies we'll probably have to tell the police about them eventually, but we should have a reasonable amount of time to have a private forensic expert print them. I'm not sure about the bodies. We'll know where they are, but we won't be in possession of them."

"Damn straight," Ginny said. "I'm not carrying them out."

"I hadn't planned on dragging a rotting corpse down the trail, either. But some legal experts think we have to tell the police the location of the bodies and others don't think a lawyer who just sees the corpse has any obligation to reveal the location to the cops."

"What about attorney-client confidentiality?" Ginny asked.

"That just extends to what the client says to you and not to physical evidence. We can't be forced to tell the authorities how we knew where to find the bodies or the pinkies but we may not be able to keep them a secret."

"It won't take a genius to figure out that you got the information from Clarence."

"True. All they'll have to do is check the visitors' list at the prison to find out who I visited or look up the records to see the list of my criminal cases—all one of them. But there won't be a big battle over this. Little wants me to give the pinkies to the police so he can prove he's innocent of the Erickson murder and he doesn't seem to care if they nail him for Farmer."

Ginny shook her head. "Your client sure has a twisted set of principles."

"That could be one of the great understatements of all time."

Ginny stood up and stretched. Her T-shirt rode up her flat belly. Brad looked away, embarrassed, and concentrated on picking up his trash.

"According to Little's instructions, the bodies should be two miles in," Ginny said.

"I can't wait," Brad answered with a shudder.

As it turned out, he could have waited—forever. That's what Brad told himself as soon as he'd used a napkin Ginny handed him to wipe his mouth after throwing up in a bush a few steps from Peggy Farmer's corpse.

"Sorry," he mumbled.

"Don't mention it," Ginny said as she placed the soiled napkin in the bag they'd brought for their trash before handing Brad a bottle of water so he could wash out his mouth. "I did the same thing the first time they brought a really bad accident victim into Emergency while I was training to be a nurse. This guy's stomach was ripped open and his intestines—"

"Please," Brad begged weakly as he bent over, eyes squeezed shut, and fought to keep from tossing his cookies again.

"Oops, sorry," Ginny said sheepishly.

Little had told Brad that he'd buried Peggy Farmer and her boyfriend a few yards into the forest from a fallen tree. The tree was supposed to be an eighth of a mile off the trail that led past the waterfall. Ginny used an odometer to pace off the distance, and they found the thick capsized trunk exactly where Little had said it would be. So were the bodies, although there was a lot less of them than there had been when they were buried years before.

Scavengers had uncovered the shallow grave, and there was very little flesh left on the skeletal remains. Even so, the sight of a real dead body disoriented Brad even more than seeing Laurie Erickson's autopsy photos. Ginny helped him sit with his back against a tree in a position where he couldn't see the corpses. While he recovered his equilibrium, Ginny returned to the fallen tree and started digging under the trunk where Little said he'd buried his collection of severed fingers.

"I've got them," she told Brad. "There's no reason to look if you think it will upset you. I can just put the jar in my backpack."

"No, I should look at them," Brad said as he pushed himself to his feet. "I'll have to at some point, and you've already seen me make a fool of myself."

Brad took a deep breath and forced himself to walk over to the Mason jar Ginny had placed on top of the tree trunk. Brad was surprised that he didn't have the same visceral reaction to seeing the fingers he'd had when they'd unearthed the bodies. Maybe between seeing Laurie Erickson's autopsy photos and the dead bodies he'd exhausted his capacity for horror. Brad studied the fingers. They forced him to see his client with a clarity he'd been unable to achieve before. Clarence Little wasn't weird or clever. Clarence Little was pure evil. Brad's duty to do everything in his power to clear Little of Laurie Erickson's murder made Brad feel worse than he had when he'd discovered Peggy Farmer's body.

Chapter Nineteen

"Sit, sit," Susan Tuchman said when her secretary showed Brad Miller into her office, first thing Monday morning. "How's your project coming?"

"That's what I wanted to talk to you about," Brad answered nervously. "There have been a few developments."

"Good. Tell me about them."

"I went to Salem like you suggested, to the penitentiary."

"I bet that was quite an experience."

"Yes, it was very . . . interesting. Anyway, I talked to Mr. Little about his case. He says he's innocent."

Tuchman smiled knowingly. "I had dinner with the attorney general the last time I was in Washington. He told me he felt terrible because every person he sent to prison when he was a district attorney in Arkansas claimed he was innocent. He said he wished he could have convicted at least one guilty person."

Tuchman laughed. Brad smiled dutifully.

"Little may actually be innocent," he said.

Tuchman stopped smiling. "Why do you say that?"

Her tone was not friendly, and Brad guessed that she was sensing that his pro bono assignment might take more time than it was supposed to, which meant it would cut down on Brad's billable hours.

"Uh, well, I did read the transcript of his trial and there was only circumstantial evidence connecting him to the crime."

"Most murderers are convicted with circumstantial evidence, since any eyewitness is usually dead."

"Still, looking at the case objectively, the key evidence against Mr. Little concerned other murders, which—by the way—he doesn't deny committing. If the modus operandi of those cases didn't match the MO in Laurie Erickson's case the judge would probably have dismissed the case when the defense lawyer moved for a judgment of acquittal."

"But it did match."

"Well, yes."

"So there you are."

"Someone could have killed Laurie Erickson and copied Little's MO."

Tuchman sighed. She looked disappointed. Brad was glad Tuchman didn't know about Ginny's part in his investigation.

"You're young, Brad, and I'm glad to see you're still idealistic, but you've also got to be realistic. There are copycat killers in the movies and in legal thrillers. In real life one sick bastard does all the dirty work by himself.

"You're also losing focus. This whole discussion is irrelevant to your assignment. You're handling a case in which the only issue is whether Little's trial attorney was incompetent. The guilt or innocence of Clarence Little is not your concern."

"That's a good point, except I've found evidence that could prove our client's claim of actual innocence."

"Evidence?"

"Yes. Mr. Little told me his alibi for the night Laurie Erickson was murdered. He claims that he was murdering another victim named Peggy Farmer in the Deschutes National Forest. He said it was impossible for him to have kidnapped Laurie Erickson from the governor's mansion because he was too far away from Salem when Erickson was kidnapped. I checked. He's right. If he killed Farmer he couldn't have killed Erickson and vice versa."

"I'm confused here, Brad. He confessed to another murder in the forest?"

"Yes. The police don't know about it. That was his alibi, but he didn't tell his trial attorney because he didn't trust him."

"How do we even know there was such a murder?"

"Uh, well I know because I dug up the corpse."

"You what!!!"

"Actually, there was more than one. Mr. Little killed Farmer's boyfriend, too. He told me where to find the bodies and his collection of pinkies, which was buried under a fallen tree near the corpses."

"What pinkies?"

"Mr. Little took the pinkies of his victims as souvenirs. The police could never find them."

Tuchman looked stunned. Her mouth was open and she was staring at Brad. He pushed on.

"Mr. Little says Farmer's pinkie is in the jar, but Erickson's pinkie isn't. I have the pinkies, or rather Paul Baylor, a private forensic expert, has them. I didn't know how to preserve them. I didn't want the fingers to fall apart anymore than they have already or we won't be able to test them for fingerprints. Mr. Baylor is a respected expert and he knows how to preserve, uh, body parts."

"Oh. My God, Mr. Miller. What have you done? That's tampering with evidence and I don't know what else. How could you go off on your own like that without my permission?"

"I went down to the penitentiary on Saturday and I dug up the bodies on Sunday. I didn't want to disturb you on a weekend when I didn't know if Mr. Little was telling me the truth. And then when I did it . . . I just decided it would be better to tell you when you were well rested."

"I don't believe this."

Tuchman took a deep breath and regained her composure. "Okay, here is what we are going to do. I'm going to get Richard Fuentes in here. He was a deputy district attorney and an AUSA before he joined the firm. You're going to tell him what you've done and he's going to figure out whether you or our firm have any criminal liability because of your impetuous actions. Then we're going to give those fingers and the location of the bodies to the authorities. When that's all done I'll figure out what to do about you."

Part Five

Copycat

Washington, D.C.

Chapter Twenty

"There's a call on two," the receptionist told Keith Evans.

"Who is it?"

"He won't give a name. He says he has information about the Charlotte Walsh case. He asked for you."

That didn't carry much weight with Evans, since he was on TV whenever the Bureau felt the need to hold a press conference about the case. He was tempted to shuffle the call to someone else but the investigation was stalled and you never knew.

"Evans here. To whom am I speaking?"

"I'm not going to give my name over the phone. All you need to know is that I'm a cop and I know something that may help you with the Walsh murder."

"A cop? Look—"

"You look. I'm taking a chance here, so we do this my way. Walk over to the Mall. Go into it between the Indian museum and the Botanical Garden."

Evans started to say something but the line was dead.

The Mall was mobbed with tourists and Evans never spotted his caller until a man wearing a lightweight jacket and tan slacks appeared at his side. He was medium height and stocky with the beginning of a beer belly. His face was flat and pockmarked and he'd compensated for his receding black hair by growing a bushy mustache.

"Officer . . . ?" Evans started.

"Not until I get some assurances," the man interrupted. "Then you get my name and what I know."

"What kind of assurances?"

"That nothing happens to me if I tell you what I know."

"Why do you need that kind of assurance?"

"It's nothing really bad. I just bent the rules for someone and now I find out . . . Look, what I did was no big deal, but it could get me in trouble on the job so I want my ass protected."

"I can't make any promises if I don't know what we're talking about."

"Okay. I'll give you a hypothetical. Let's say someone who wasn't a cop called a cop and asked this cop to trace some license plates. How bad is that?"

"Not very."

"So, what would you do for this hypothetical cop if he could give you information that might help you in a murder case?"

"I'd promise that the Bureau wouldn't go to his boss and I'd list him as a confidential reliable informant in my reports so I wouldn't have to use his name."

"What if his boss found out what he'd done?"

"You understand I have no direct influence with the D.C. cops?"

The man nodded.

"The best I can promise is that I'd go to bat for him and I'd go as high up as I could in the Bureau for backing."

"Okay, I can live with that."

"Do you want to tell me your name?"

"It's Victor Perez."

"Thanks, Victor. So, tell me why we're meeting."

"There's this ex-cop I know, Andy Zipay. He's a PI now. We used to play poker once a month. One night, we were in a big pot and I did something stupid. I had this really good hand and I flipped an IOU into the pot I couldn't cover. So I owed him the money but I didn't have it."

"What's this got to do with Charlotte Walsh?"

"That's what I'm about to tell you. This guy could have been a prick about the money, but he cut a deal with me instead. Every once in a while he needs information he can't get, now that he's private, so he calls me up and I work off the debt. The night Walsh was murdered I got a call from Zipay asking me to run some license plates. There were three of them."

Perez handed a list with the numbers to Evans and waited while the agent scanned them.

"One is for a car registered to Charlotte Walsh," the policeman said. "The next day it's all over the news that Walsh was murdered by the Ripper. I wasn't going to say anything at first. Then I started thinking, what if it's important? So I called."

"You did the right thing."

Perez nodded.

"You said Zipay asked you to run three plates," Evans said.

"Yeah, one car was registered to an electrical contracting company, but the other is used by the Secret Service."

Evans frowned. "What does the Secret Service have to do with this?"

"That's what I asked. Andy said he didn't know, he was asking for someone else. He sounded surprised about the Secret Service. If I had to bet I'd say he didn't know I was going to say the Secret Service used one of the cars. Then again I'm not that great a gambler."

Chapter Twenty-one

Andy Zipay's office was on the third floor of an older office building that had seen better days but was still a respectable address. Keith Evans guessed that he was doing all right but hadn't struck it rich yet. The small waiting area was manned by a plump, pleasant-looking woman in her midforties who was typing away at a word processor when Evans walked in. He flashed his ID and asked to talk to her boss.

Two minutes later, Evans was seated across the desk from Zipay, a slender man a shade over six feet, whose dark suit contrasted sharply with pale skin that looked like it rarely saw the sun. A narrow mustache separated a hooked nose from a pair of thin lips, and there was a touch of gray in his black hair. The austere suit and the mustache made Zipay look a little like the private dicks in black-and-white movies from the 1940s.

"How can I help you, Agent Evans?"

"I'm in charge of the D.C. Ripper case and you can help me by telling me why you're interested in a car belonging to Charlotte Walsh—his latest victim—and another car that's the property of the United States Secret Service."

Zipay steepled his hands in front of his chin and studied the FBI agent for a moment before answering.

"If I were interested in that information it would probably be on behalf of a client. If that client was an attorney who was acting on behalf of a client I would be an agent of that attorney and prevented by the attorney-client privilege from discussing the matter."

Evans smiled. "Andy, you may be an agent of an attorney but I checked with some friends on the D.C. police force before coming over, and they say you're also an ex-cop on the take who was lucky to avoid some real unpleasantness. These people would be ready, willing, and able to bust your balls if they found out *how* you learned the Secret Service and Miss Walsh owned those cars. So don't go all legal on me and I won't go all legal on you."

Zipay flushed but he held his temper. "I didn't know it was standard procedure for FBI agents to insult people when they want their cooperation."

"I wasn't being insulting. I was stating facts. Now I have no interest in busting your balls. All I want is information. If I get it I'll probably forget the source unless you turn out to be an essential witness in the Ripper murders."

Zipay mulled over the agent's proposition. Evans could see that the PI was upset, which surprised him. Finally, Zipay took a deep breath. He looked very uncomfortable.

"Okay, I'll help, but I don't know much and the person who does . . . I don't want her hassled. It wouldn't be right."

"Why is that?'

"She was a cop and she's gone through some really bad times. She was in a mental hospital for a year."

"What happened?"

"Nobody I've talked to knows the whole story. I was off the force by then so I don't have a lot of the details—and I've never asked her for them—but what I know is pretty awful. She was undercover and she got friendly with a meth cook. These were bikers. Very violent guys, but she worked her way in. They had a secret lab. No one could figure out where they were cooking. She was going to lead the cops to the lab when the bikers got on to her." Zipay looked down. He shook his head. "They had her for three days before they found her."

Zipay looked up and straight into Evans's eyes. "You know I left the cops because I got into trouble. Almost everybody turned their back on me, but she didn't. When I went private she fed me jobs, helped me out when she could. She has some kind of pension but it's not much. Whenever I can I return the favor by hiring her to do odd jobs. This deal with the licenses was one of them."

"Why did she want to know the registered owner?"

"She wouldn't tell me. She said I should forget about the conversation. I will say that she sounded surprised about the Secret Service. I don't think she was expecting me to say that one of the cars was registered to them."

Maggie Sparks rapped her knuckles on the door to Dana Cutler's apartment. When no one answered she knocked again, louder.

"Miss Cutler, this is the FBI. We'd like to talk to you."

"What now?" Sparks asked Evans after they'd waited long enough for a response. He was about to answer when the door across the hall opened a crack.

"Are you really the FBI?" a woman asked in an accent that placed her origins somewhere in Eastern Europe.

"Yes, ma'am," Evans replied.

"Show me some identification."

Sparks and Evans held up their ID in the narrow space where a chain spread between the door and the jamb. A second later, the chain was detached and the agents found themselves face to face with an elderly woman in a pink house dress.

"She's not in," the woman said. "She hasn't been there since the commotion."

"What commotion?" Evans asked.

"It was a few nights ago. I called the police as soon as I heard the gunshot."

"Why don't you start from the beginning, Mrs. . . . . ?"

"Miss, young man. Miss Alma Goetz."

"Miss Goetz, please tell us what happened."

"These walls are paper thin. When I heard the shot I opened my door a crack to see what was happening. There wasn't anyone in the hall and the shot sounded close by. That's when I called 911. Then I heard her slam the door across the hall open."

"Her?" Evans asked.

"Dana Cutler, the woman from across the hall."

"How do you know it was Miss Cutler?" Evans asked.

"I saw her running toward the stairs."

"Did the police come?" Sparks asked.

"Yes, there were two of them, but they were very rude."

"Oh?" Evans said.

"You'd think they would be polite, since I risked my life to make the call. I could have been shot, you know?"

"Yes, ma'am," Sparks said. "What you did was very brave."

"I'm glad you think so because the police officer was very short with me. He told me to go inside and he didn't even ask me any questions."

"He didn't take a report?" Evans asked, surprised.

"When I tried to talk to him he said that everything was under control and he ordered me to shut my door. He said this was police business and I could get arrested for obstruction of justice if I continued to 'butt in.' Those were his exact words, 'butt in.'"

"So you didn't see or hear anything else?" Evans asked.

"Oh, no, I heard plenty. Like I told you, these walls are very thin."

"What did you hear?" Sparks asked.

"I heard screams before Miss Cutler ran out. That was after the shot."

"Go ahead," Evans urged.

"The police went into the apartment. They had their guns out. A man yelled out, 'Don't shoot, we're federal agents.' Then the policemen went inside and shut the door."

"Did you see anything else?"

"I certainly did. About fifteen minutes after the policemen came, two men left the apartment. One of the men was supporting the other man. He looked like he was in pain. Ten minutes later, the police left. Fifteen minutes after that three other men went into the apartment."

"Were they with the police?"

"I don't know. They didn't have uniforms."

"How long were these men in the apartment?"

"An hour or so. When they left they were carrying black trash bags."

"Did Miss Cutler ever come back to her apartment after the excitement died down?" Sparks asked.

"I never heard anyone go in or out, but I guess she could have come back while I was sleeping or out shopping."

"Thank you very much, Miss Goetz. You've been a big help." Evans handed her his card. "If you think of anything else, please call me."

"I will. And you're much nicer than those policemen."

"Thank you, ma'am."

"I guess they teach you manners in the FBI."

"Can you tell me where the super lives? We'd like to get inside Miss Cutler's apartment."

Miss Goetz gave them the apartment number and Sparks talked with Cutler's neighbor while Evans went downstairs. He returned ten minutes later with the key.

Cutler's bedroom was so messy it was hard to tell if it had been searched or not, and the tiny living room had the same lived-in feel, but someone had scrubbed down every surface in the hall and the kitchen.

"What do you think?" Evans asked.

"If you believe Miss Goetz, Cutler shot someone who may be a federal agent."

"There's no evidence anyone was shot."

"There's plenty of evidence that someone cleaned up. Just compare the hall and kitchen to the bedroom and living room. And you said that your informant ran plates that belonged to the Secret Service. If we're talking about people in this town with enough clout to shut down a police investigation they'd be near the top of my list."

"We don't know that the investigation was shut down. There may be a police report, 911 tapes, medical records. We should check. This could just be a domestic dispute. Maybe Cutler was dating someone who works for a federal agency and she went off."

"You don't believe that, do you?" Sparks asked

"Not really."

"What do we know? We've got a PI who writes down some license numbers. Why would she do that?"

"She's on a case; we're talking about car licenses, so she's tailing someone," Evans answered.

"Charlotte Walsh?"

"That's my guess. She asked my informant to run Walsh's plate and she was surprised when he told her that another plate was registered to the Secret Service. She wouldn't be surprised if she was tailing a Secret Service agent."

"So, somewhere, Walsh crosses paths with the Secret Service," Sparks said.

Evans walked to the door to the bedroom and looked it over again.

"They were searching the apartment. Cutler came back and caught them," he said.

"She shoots a federal agent then runs," Sparks said. "Either she shot him thinking she'd surprised an intruder or she shot in self-defense."

"She's an ex-cop. If she found a burglar she'd hold him for the police whether she shot him or not."

"She shot a person she thought was a burglar, learned she'd shot a Fed, and ran because she was scared," Sparks said.

"What if it was self-defense? What if they were searching for something they thought Cutler had? She comes home and they try to force her to tell where it is and somehow she gets the drop on them."

"What were they looking for?"

"If the intruders were Secret Service, it has to be something that connects Walsh to . . . Jesus, Maggie, Walsh worked for Farrington's campaign, and the Secret Service guards the president."

"PIs take pictures of people they're following," Sparks said.

Evans was quiet for a moment. "If Cutler was hiding pictures in this place they'd have found them. It's too small."

"Unless Cutler interrupted the search before they got them."

"Or Cutler has them someplace else."

Evans's cell phone rang and he snapped it open. While he was talking, Sparks looked around more carefully than she had the first time they'd gone through the apartment. She noticed that all of the trash baskets had been emptied and there were no scraps of paper with writing on them anywhere in sight. She pulled open the drawers of a desk in the living room and found them empty. And she didn't see a computer. Whoever had gone through the apartment after the police left had been very thorough.

"I had someone run Cutler's phone records for her cell and home phones," Evans said when he finished the call. "Fredricks looked them over and came up with something interesting. Does the name Dale Perry ring a bell?"

Sparks thought for a moment before shaking her head.

"He's an attorney with a lot of political contacts, including several in the White House."

"There's the Secret Service connection again," Sparks said.

"Cutler's called him a few times this year and twice the week before Walsh was murdered. Some of the calls were to Perry's private line at his office or his cell phone."

"Why would a small-time PI be calling a big shot lawyer with ties to the White House?"

"Let's ask him."

"One other interesting thing," Evans said. "I asked Fredricks to get me Cutler's file from the cops."

"What's it say?"

"That's what I'd like to know; it's classified."

"I bet this place is bigger than my apartment," Maggie Sparks said as she looked around the reception area of Kendall, Barrett and Van Kirk.

"I bet they pay more rent than you do, too," Evans said.

"I bet I could retire on what they pay in rent for a year."

Their ruminations on the reception area of Dale Perry's law firm ended abruptly when a stunning blonde with a deep tan walked into reception dressed in a fire-engine red dress and sporting a lot of gold jewelry.

"Agents Sparks and Evans?" she asked, flashing a radiant smile that would have lit up the room in a blackout.

"I'm Keith Evans, and this is Margaret Sparks."

"I'm Irene Miles, Mr. Perry's personal secretary."

I'll bet you are, Maggie Sparks thought. Out loud she said, "Pleased to meet you, Ms. Miles. We'd like to speak with Mr. Perry."

"He's waiting for you," Miles said. "Would you like some coffee or tea? I can also bring you a caffe latte or a cappuccino."

The agents passed on the refreshments then followed Miles down a carpeted hallway where they found Dale Perry waiting in a large corner office decorated tastefully with antiques. Before leaving, Miles motioned the agents to a place on a couch under an exquisite oil painting of a French country village that looked a lot like a Cezanne Evans had seen in the National Gallery. The window behind Perry's desk had a view of the White House. Evans wondered if Perry and the president flashed coded messages back and forth when the lawyer was lobbying for one of his clients.

"Thanks for taking the time to see us, Mr. Perry."

The lawyer smiled. "When the receptionist told me who was in the waiting room I got curious. It's not every day I get a visit from the FBI."

Evans smiled back. "Let me put you at ease. We're not here to arrest you. Your name popped up in an investigation, and we're hoping you can help us."

"I will if I'm able."

"Thanks. Do you know a woman named Dana Cutler?" Evans asked.

Perry's smile stayed on his lips but he shifted in his seat. "She's a private investigator."

"Does she work for your firm?"

"She's not employed by Kendall, Barrett, but I have contracted with her on occasion when I needed help on a project."

"Has she worked for any of the other partners?"

"I don't know."

Perry definitely looked uncomfortable.

"Doesn't Kendall, Barrett have in-house investigators?" Maggie asked.

"We do."

"Then why would you need Miss Cutler?"

Perry wasn't smiling anymore. "If I answered that question I would have to violate the confidences of my clients. That would be unethical."

"I can understand your concern," Evans said, "but we're worried about Miss Cutler. Her name came up in connection with a murder investigation. We tried to interview her, but she's missing. We're concerned for her safety."

"Who was murdered?"

"A young woman named Charlotte Walsh. We have reason to believe that Miss Cutler was following her. Was she tailing Miss Walsh on your instructions?"

"I just explained that I can't discuss the firm's business."

"Then she was working for the firm on this case?"

Perry looked annoyed. "I didn't say that. I am forbidden by the rules of conduct that govern my profession to either confirm or deny any involvement Miss Cutler may or may not have had with this Walsh individual."

"Would you be willing to tell me the last time you spoke to Miss Cutler?"

"No."

"Don't you want to help us find her? She may be in danger."

"I'll help any way I can as long as it doesn't involve discussing the business of Kendall, Barrett. In my opinion, your inquiry is doing just that."

Evans frowned. "How can the business of your firm possibly be affected by you telling me the last time you spoke to Dana Cutler?"

"Are you aware that I am a personal friend of the attorney general and the director of the FBI?"

"No, sir, I'm not."

"I feel your questions are verging on harassment. I've taken time from my day to talk to you, but I am very busy and this interview is terminated."

Evans stared directly at Perry for a moment. Then he stood up.

"Thank you for your time, sir."

"I'm sorry I wasn't able to provide more assistance."

Evans smiled. "Don't worry, sir. I thought this meeting was very informative."

Perry must have pressed a button under his desk because Irene Miles opened the door and held it in a way that suggested she expected them to leave. Sparks and Evans didn't say a word until they were standing at the elevator bank.

"I think we just got the bum's rush," Maggie said.

"That we did, but Perry told us more than he wanted to."

"He's worried about something."

"That's for certain, and it concerns Charlotte Walsh."

Evans was about to follow up on his thought when his cell phone rang. He looked at the readout.

"We've got to go back to headquarters," he said as soon as he broke the connection. "That was Kyle. They've figured out how to find the Ripper."

Chapter Twenty-two

Half an hour after leaving Dale Perry's law office, Keith Evans walked into the conference room that had been assigned to the Ripper Task Force. The energy in the room would have run the lights in the city for a year. Everyone was in motion, talking excitedly on their phones, pacing with purpose, or energetically punching computer keys.

"What's up, people?" Evans asked, and everyone started talking at once about polyvinyl siloxane, also known as PVS, the substance that had been found in the mouths of every Ripper victim with the exception of Charlotte Walsh.

"It's the impression material a dentist uses when he's going to have a crown or a bridge made for a patient," explained Kyle Hernandez, a former soccer star at UCLA with a chemistry degree. "It's soft when the dentist places it over a patient's teeth. After it sets it's removed from the mouth, and die stone, which is like a very hard plaster, is poured into the impression. Then the PVS, which is very elastic, is lifted off. The die stone model is scanned using a computer, and a robot mills the crown from porcelain or a technician makes a bridge or crown using a lost wax technique. We think we found minute traces of PVS in the victims' mouths because someone used it for a model. When the PVS was removed from the mouth small traces remained."

"How does this help us find the Ripper?" Evans asked.

"Dentists work closely with the technician who's going to use the model. Sometimes they have the tech come to their office while the patient is there. Sometimes they'll send a full-face photograph to the tech."

"Do these technicians have access to personal information about the patient like an address or phone number?"

Hernandez grinned and nodded. "They could. Say they're standing next to the dentist while they're examining the patient and the patient's file is sitting on a table. All the tech would have to do is take a peek. Or it could be something as simple as the dentist introducing the patient to the technician."

Now Evans was as excited as everyone else. "Did all of the victims have dental appointments shortly before they were killed?"

"Bingo!" Hernandez answered as his grin widened. "But they all went to different dentists . . ."

". . . who used the same lab," Evans said, finishing the agent's sentence with a flourish.

"Sally Braman is at the lab now talking with the owner, and Bob Conaway from the U.S. attorney's office is ready to draft a search warrant application as soon as we give him an affidavit laying out probable cause."

Evans smiled. "Good work people. Let's hope this is the end of the line."

"He's two blocks away in a tan Toyota van, turning onto King Road . . . now," the agent tailing Eric Loomis's van reported.

Evans, Sparks, and two other agents were across the street from Loomis's house in an unmarked car. A SWAT team was hiding behind Loomis's detached garage and would seize him as soon as Evans told them Loomis was out of the van. He tried to calm down, but he felt like he'd been injected with methamphetamine. His hands were shaking, his palms were damp, and the way his heart was racing he was certain he'd flunk his yearly physical. He shut his eyes and pictured a clear mountain lake surrounded by green meadows and domed by a blue sky dotted with white, puffy clouds. The meditation technique failed miserably as soon as the agent tailing Loomis announced that the lab technician was turning onto Humboldt Street and would be pulling into his driveway momentarily.

Loomis's house was a Dutch Colonial that had been built on a quarter-acre lot. There were two floors above ground and a basement, which was entered from a mudroom on the side of the house opposite the garage. A narrow alley separated the garage from the house. Doors on the side of the garage and the house opened into the alley. This meant that Loomis could park in the garage and carry his victims into the basement with little risk that he would be seen.

The van slowed down as it approached the house. Loomis used a remote to raise the garage door, and moments later he was inside.

"Now," Evans said the moment Loomis shut the van's door behind him. Four agents in SWAT black rushed inside the garage, and the tailing car swung in front of the van to block an escape attempt.

"FBI, FBI!" Evans heard the SWAT team shout as he sprinted across the street. The men who'd come through the front of the garage trapped Loomis against the van just as the side door to the garage jerked open. Evans lost sight of Loomis as more agents surrounded him. By the time he entered the garage Loomis was flattened against the side of the van and his hands were cuffed behind him.

The SWAT members parted leaving him face to face with his prisoner. Evans had checked for a criminal record and found two traffic tickets. Loomis's record was as unexciting as his appearance. If he had to use one word to describe the prisoner it would be "soft." The lab technician was five ten and flabby. His hair looked limp, and he wore thick glasses with a black plastic frame. An unimpressive mustache graced his upper lip and a scraggy goatee hid a weak chin.

"Eric Loomis?" Evans asked.

Loomis looked dazed. "What . . . what is this?" he stuttered.

"Are you Eric Loomis?" Evans repeated.

"Yes, but . . ."

"Mr. Loomis, I have a search warrant for your home. With your permission, one of my men will use your keys to open your door."

"What are you talking about?"

"If you don't help us by letting us use your keys and telling us the combination for your alarm, we'll have to break, in and that could cause damage to your door."

"Wait a second. What's going on? Why do you want to search my house?" Loomis asked, his voice rising.

"Will you give us permission to use your keys?"

Loomis was sweating and looked panicky. His head jerked around. Everywhere were men in black with menacing countenances.

"I don't know," he managed.

"Very well, Mr. Loomis, since you're unwilling to cooperate I'll have one of my men break the window in your side door."

"Wait, don't. The keys are in my pocket. Don't break anything."

Evans nodded, and Maggie Sparks stepped forward. When Loomis saw that an attractive woman was going to search him, he flushed and looked even more anxious. When Sparks fished in his pocket for his set of keys Loomis grew rigid.

"The combination, please," Evans commanded.

Sparks opened the door and shut off the alarm, and Loomis was herded into the living room and placed in an armchair. The prisoner was docile, head down, eyes on the floor. Evans left two agents with him then organized a search of the house. As soon as the search teams dispersed, Evans and Sparks headed for the basement. The first thing that hit them when they opened the door was the smell of rotting meat. Evans slipped on a surgical mask, Tyvek booties, and latex gloves. Then he turned on the light at the top of the stairs and walked down cautiously with his weapon drawn. Everyone assumed that the Ripper was a loner, but you never knew.

The first thing Evans noticed was the soundproofing. Loomis had made sure that the neighbors would not hear his victims scream. The next thing he noticed was the shelf against the wall. Arrayed across it were four glass jars. In each jar was a model of a set of teeth. Evans froze on the stairs when he saw the teeth and so did Sparks. In the silence they heard labored breathing.

The basement had the feel of an operating room. Bloodstains covered the floor, and a table covered with surgical tools stood to one side. But it wasn't these implements that drew the eye, nor was it the two large dog cages that stood against one of the walls. What stunned Evans and Sparks was the dental chair that was positioned in the center of the room and the naked, gagged woman who was manacled to it.

Jessica Vasquez was hungry and dehydrated but she appeared to be unharmed with the exception of some bruises she'd received when Loomis kidnapped her from a mall parking lot several days earlier. Evans and Sparks talked to Vasquez while they waited for the ambulance to take her to the hospital. She told them that Loomis had kept her in one of the dog cages without food or water for two days and never spoke to her during her ordeal. One evening, he'd drugged her and taken impressions of her teeth before returning her to the cage. This morning, he had manacled her to the chair and fitted her with a leather S&M mask with a ball gag before he went to the lab.

"I know I should feel elated, but I just feel sick and exhausted," Evans told Maggie as they watched the ambulance carrying Vasquez disappear around the corner.

"Hey, get a grip. We saved Jessica Vasquez's life and captured a truly evil man. You should feel proud of what we accomplished."

"But I don't. I just feel sad because of what those other poor souls went through."

Sparks laid a hand on his forearm. "You'll never save everybody, Keith. Think of all the women who are going to be safe because Loomis will be behind bars."

"Good point, but I still feel sick about what we saw in that basement."

"You can take a shower tonight. And I'll buy you a drink or two after we interrogate Loomis."

"I don't know, Maggie . . ."

"Well I do. You're too damn maudlin for someone whose team just cracked one of the biggest serial cases in D.C. history."

"Agent Evans."

Evans turned to find one of the lab techs approaching. He was holding a jar like those that had been found in the basement. In it was another model of a set of teeth.

"We found this. Ted Balske thought you'd like to know."

"Where was it?"

"Hidden in the rear of Loomis's van under a blanket."

Evans and Sparks took a close look at the model.

"How many of these models do we have now?" Evans asked the forensic expert.

"There were four in the basement. This makes five."

"Thanks."

The forensic expert left to log in the model, and Evans frowned.

"What's wrong?" Sparks asked.

"Loomis made models of the teeth of his victims for trophies."

"Right. That's where the PVS comes in."

"There should be six sets of teeth, but there are only five."

"You're right," Sparks said. She looked as troubled as did Evans.

"The medical examiner didn't find any PVS in Walsh's mouth," Evans said. "What if none of the false teeth match Walsh?"

"What are you getting at?" Sparks asked, afraid she knew what Keith was going to say.

"We could have a copycat murder. Someone who killed Walsh then faked the Ripper's MO. Think about it. We just figured out what the substance in the victim's mouths is, so Walsh's killer wouldn't know how to fake that part of Loomis's MO. And there's no way he could plant a set of false teeth in Loomis's basement because we just figured out that he's the Ripper. We have to find out if the dental work matches every victim except Walsh."

"The MO for Walsh's murder was almost identical to the MO Loomis used when he killed the other victims, including evidence we held back from the press and the public," Sparks said. "The copycat would have to have access to the case file."

"A federal agency would have access," Evans said, "and some federal agencies employ people who can sanitize the scene of a shooting."

"You're talking about Cutler's apartment."

Evans nodded.

"You're beginning to sound like a Web site for conspiracy nuts."

"I am, but sometimes there really are conspiracies. While I'm talking to Eric Loomis, why don't you see if you can find a police report detailing what happened at Cutler's apartment?"

Chapter Twenty-three

There was nothing friendly about the surroundings in which Eric Loomis found himself. The dull brown walls were stained, the fluorescent lighting flickered at odd moments, and the bridge chair on which he sat was cold and hard. Keith Evans wanted badly to break Loomis but he waited patiently, observing the prisoner for forty-five minutes through a two-way mirror before going into the interrogation room. The lab technician's legs were secured to a bolt in the floor limiting his range of motion. He sat quietly at first before shifting his position more and more frequently, failing in his attempts to get comfortable and growing more agitated as the seconds ticked away.

When Evans finally entered the room the manacled prisoner looked up. The FBI agent sat on a comfortable chair on the other side of a scarred wooden table and worked hard to mask his distaste. Loomis wore an orange jail-issue jumpsuit, which was intentionally a size too small and cut into the rolls of fat at his waist and thighs. His limp, uncombed hair was oily, there were pimples on his forehead, cheeks, and chin, and the prisoner exuded an odor that reminded Evans of stale cheese. The agent wondered if his reaction to Loomis would still have been revulsion if he was meeting him for the first time under different circumstances and didn't know what the lab technician had done in the basement of his house.

"Good evening, Mr. Loomis."

Loomis didn't answer.

"Do you mind if I record our conversation?" Evans asked as he placed a tape recorder on the table between them.

"I don't care what you do."

"Well you should. You're in a lot of trouble."

"We'll see," Loomis answered with an enigmatic smile.

"Before we talk, I'm going to give you the Miranda warnings. You probably think you know them from television or the movies but you should listen carefully anyway."

Loomis folded his arms across his chest and looked away while Evans recited the warnings.

"Do you understand your rights, Mr. Loomis?" Evans asked when he finished.

"Do I look stupid? Of course I understand them. I have a degree in chemistry."

"I didn't mean to imply that you're stupid, Mr. Loomis. I'm required to ask everyone I question if they understand their rights. Not everyone has an IQ as high as yours."

Loomis raised his head slowly until he was staring into Evans's eyes. Then he smirked.

"What number interrogation technique is that?"

"I'm sorry?"

" 'Flatter the prisoner and gain his confidence. Make him feel that you're on his side,' " Loomis said in a mock instructor's voice.

Evans laughed. "That actually was a heartfelt statement. You are smart and you had us going. If you hadn't made one small mistake we might never have caught you."

Loomis looked down. Evans knew the prisoner was dying to know how he'd been tripped up, but he was smart enough not to take the bait.

"Before we go any further, I need to know if you want to be represented by a lawyer."

Evans wanted to continue questioning Loomis, but Loomis's answers would be inadmissible in court if he didn't waive his right to counsel.

"I plan on representing myself, Agent Evans."

"Are you sure you want to do that? Virginia and Maryland have the death penalty. What you did will qualify you for it."

Loomis smiled. "Another clever interrogation technique. If I say anything suggesting that I know I qualify for the death penalty you can use my words as an admission."

"I hadn't thought of that. I just want you to understand the seriousness of your situation. Trying a death penalty case is a specialty. The government will provide you with a lawyer experienced in capital cases if you can't afford an attorney. Even someone as intelligent as you would have trouble learning everything you'd need to know if you decide to represent yourself."

Loomis smirked again. "I'll take my chances."

"If you're sure you don't want a lawyer?" Evans repeated so there wouldn't be any questions later if Loomis challenged his interrogation.

"Okay," Evans said when Loomis didn't answer, "Mr. Loomis has waived his right to an attorney and is choosing to represent himself. So, Eric . . . Can I call you Eric?"

"Sure, Keith," Loomis answered sarcastically.

Evans laughed. "You're okay. Not many people in your position can keep their sense of humor. What I can't figure out is why someone with a chemistry degree and a good job would kidnap and kill those women."

Loomis smiled again and shook his head. "You aren't very good at this, Keith. From your question I take it that I'm supposed to believe that an FBI agent working the biggest serial murder case in the history of the D.C. area has not been schooled by the VICAP experts at

Quantico in the psychological profile of the serial killer he's hunting. Try again."

"Okay, Eric. Why'd you do it?"

"Do what?"

Evans shrugged. "Let's start with Jessica Vasquez. Why did you kidnap her?"

"I didn't."

Evans looked perplexed. "You're saying she somehow found her way into your basement then decided to strip off her clothes, put on an S&M mask and strap herself to a dentist chair? That's pretty weird behavior."

"I have no idea how that woman ended up in my basement. But I suspect the FBI may have had something to do with planting her there along with the other so-called evidence you claim to have found."

Now it was Evans's turn to smile. "So you're the victim of a government conspiracy?"

"That's one possible explanation."

Evans asked the question he'd been waiting to drop into the conversation.

"Do you think the FBI was so anxious to make an arrest that we murdered Charlotte Walsh and dropped her in a Dumpster, or did the *real* D.C. Ripper do that?"

Loomis sprang upright and strained against the chain that manacled his legs to the floor.

"I did not kill that bitch. That is totally bogus. That is a complete frame-up."

"That's hard to believe, seeing as how the MO in Charlotte Walsh's case is identical to the other Ripper murders."

"Not if the FBI committed the murder to frame me. You'd know how to duplicate the Ripper's MO. You think you're clever but I'm a lot smarter than you and I'll—"

Loomis stopped. He seemed to realize that he'd lost control. Rage showed on his face for a moment more. Then he slumped down on his chair and stared at the tabletop. Evans tried to continue the conversation, but Loomis refused to speak from that point on.

Maggie Sparks found D.C. police officer Peter Brassos and his partner, Jermaine Collins, sitting at a table in Starbucks, where she'd had their supervisor tell them to meet her. Brassos was thick and heavy muscled and Sparks pegged him for a gym rat. Collins was a lanky, light-skinned African-American. There were no coffee cups on the table and neither man looked pleased to see her.

"Thanks for meeting me," Sparks said after flashing her credentials. "Can I get you a coffee?"

"What's this about?" Brassos demanded curtly, ignoring her offer.

"I'm working on the D.C. Ripper task force."

"I heard you got him," Collins said.

"We think we have, but there are always loose ends to tie up."

Brassos looked confused. "We haven't had anything to do with the Ripper murders."

Sparks nodded. "This is probably a wild goose chase, and I know you're anxious to get back to work, so let me get to the point. A few nights ago, you two responded to a 911 call about a shooting at an apartment house on Wisconsin Avenue."

Both men stiffened as soon as she mentioned the address.

"What about it?" Brassos asked, keeping his tone neutral.

Maggie took out a copy of the police report Brassos had written after the incident. She pretended to check something in it.

"You talked to an Alma Goetz?"

Brassos forced a laugh. "The crazy neighbor. Yeah, I talked to her."

"You think she's crazy?" Maggie asked.

"Not crazy but a real busybody, a snoop. Lives alone, wants attention, that type. We run into them from time to time."

"She said she heard a shot from the apartment of Dana Cutler, the neighbor across the hall."

Collins's brow furrowed. "Pardon me, Agent Sparks, but what does this have to do with the Ripper case?"

Sparks flashed a friendly smile. "Cutler's name came up during the investigation. So, what about the shot?"

"There wasn't one," Brassos said. "We went across the hall. The door was unlocked. We knocked. No one answered, so we went in to see if there was an injured person inside. There wasn't."

"You looked through the apartment?"

"Yeah, the whole place."

"Did you see anything that struck you as odd?"

"Nah, it was just an apartment."

"Why do you think Ms. Goetz was so certain she heard a shot?"

"It was the door," Brassos said. "She told me she was inside her apartment and heard the so-called shot through the walls. I told you the door to Cutler's apartment was unlocked. I think Goetz heard the door slam. She's pretty old. Her hearing probably isn't great."

Maggie nodded. "That's one explanation. I talked to her, and she said she heard someone inside the apartment tell you not to shoot because he was a federal agent."

Brassos threw his head back and laughed. Maggie thought the laugh sounded forced.

"I told you, the apartment was empty. Goetz is dingy."

"Yeah, she struck us as unreliable, but what about the wounded man? Where did he come from?"

"What are you talking about?"

"Miss Goetz saw a man being helped out of the apartment by a second man."

"I told you, there wasn't anyone in the apartment," Brassos said.

"Was someone else in the apartment house hurt at the same time?"

"You know, I'm talking to you as a courtesy," Brassos said. "This sounds like an interrogation to me." He stood up. "If you got a beef with us about our report, file it. I got work to do. Come on, Jerry."

Collins stood, too. Sparks did nothing to stop them. If it became necessary, she could always subpoena the officers.

"I'm sorry if I upset you," she apologized as she got to her feet.

"I don't think you are," Brassos said, and the officers walked out.

While he'd been interrogating Eric Loomis, Evans was so focused that he forgot he was exhausted, but his fatigue flooded over him as soon as he was done questioning the serial murderer. Evans had turned off his cell phone during the interrogation so he wouldn't be distracted. When he checked for messages he found one from Maggie Sparks asking him to call as soon as he was able. Evans arranged to meet her at a bar near Dupont Circle and he was washing down the bite he'd taken out of his cheeseburger when Maggie walked in. She scanned the bar and smiled when she saw Keith's upraised hand.

"How did the interrogation go?" she asked as she slid into the booth opposite Evans.

"Not well, but we don't need a confession with all the evidence we have. He's representing himself, by the way. Loomis thinks he's going to outsmart us."

"Sounds like he's a true megalomaniac."

"A classic case."

"That should make things easier for the prosecution. Did he offer any explanation for the presence of a naked woman in his basement and all those false teeth?"

"Of course. We planted them to frame him."

"Oh, yeah, I forgot."

Sparks signaled the waiter and ordered her own beer and burger.

"What did he say when you brought up Walsh?" she asked when the waiter left.

"That's interesting. He was very calm, very superior, during the questioning, like it amused him. He played mind games with me as soon as I started. But he went ballistic when I mentioned Walsh."

"What's your impression?"

"I don't think he killed her."

"Whether he did or not, something is going on. I asked for the police reports for the Cutler incident. There is one. Officer Peter Brassos wrote it. He says he and his partner, Jermaine Collins, went to the apartment in response to a 911 report of shots fired. There's an account of an interview with Miss Goetz that jibes with her version of what happened, but Brassos wrote that he didn't find any evidence of a shooting in the apartment and there's no mention of a wounded man being helped out of the apartment.

"I had Brassos's supervisor set up a meeting. Collins and Brassos told me the door to Cutler's apartment was unlocked, but there was no one inside and no sign of a shot being fired."

"What did they say about the wounded man?"

"They told me there wasn't one."

"Do you believe them?"

"No. They were nervous all the time I was questioning them. I'm certain they're covering up something, but I don't know how we can prove it. There isn't any evidence that anyone was shot in Cutler's apartment. I went back and talked to some of the other neighbors. No one admitted that they heard a shot or saw a man being helped out of the place. So what do we do now, boss?"

"I'd like to go to sleep but I've been thinking about Dale Perry all afternoon. That fucking gnome pissed me off with that name-dropping bullshit."

"It's probably not bullshit. I bet he has tea and crumpets with the AG and our boss every day at four. Guys like that move in circles we can't even dream about."

"They also put their pants on one leg at a time, Maggie. I still be-lieve we're in America where an asshole like Perry is subject to sub-poenas and can be perp walked with enough probable cause. So, I'm thinking we pay him a visit and see if we can shake him up a bit. What do you say?"

If you went strictly by mileage Dale Perry's mansion in McLean, Virginia, wasn't that far from Keith Evans's apartment in Bethesda, Maryland. In the real world, the two communities were light-years apart. As far as Evans knew, no Supreme Court justices, members of the Kennedy clan, or former secretaries of defense lived on his block, and none of the homes in Evans's neighborhood were surrounded by a stone wall and sat on several acres with a view of the Potomac River.

"Old Dale is doing well," Maggie commented.

"I don't think we'll find him begging for handouts anytime soon."

"Unless the handouts are in the billion-dollar range and ear-marked for Boeing or Halliburton."

"True."

The trip that started at the Chain Bridge ended at the spear-tipped wrought-iron gate that blocked the driveway to Perry's house.

"You call on the intercom," Evans said. "I don't think he likes me, and you're young and sexy."

"That's two strikes. Ask me to bring you coffee and I'm slapping you with a sexual harassment suit."

Evans smiled and Sparks leaned out of her window and spoke into a metal box affixed to the wall. They waited, but there was no answer. Sparks noticed a small gap between the two edges of the gate. Out of curiosity, she got out of the car and pushed. The gate eased backward. Sparks pushed harder, and the gate opened enough for Evans to drive through.

"What do you think is going on?" Sparks asked when she was back in the car.

"I don't know, but the gate shouldn't open like that, and someone should have answered the intercom."

Evans experienced a nervous tingle in his gut when Perry's house came into view. Most of the three-story brick Colonial was dark.

"This doesn't feel right," Sparks said.

A driveway curved in front of a portico supported by white columns that contrasted pleasantly with the red brick walls. When Evans got out of the car, it was so quiet he could hear the river flowing behind the estate and the wind pushing through the heavy-leafed trees.

Evans walked under the portico and pressed the doorbell. The agents could hear the bell echo through the house but no one came to the door. Evans leaned forward and tried the doorknob. The door opened. He looked at Sparks, and the agents took out their guns.

Even in shadow the entryway of Perry's house was impressive. A crystal chandelier hung over a floor laid out in a checkerboard pattern of black and white marble. A polished oak banister curved upward to the second floor along marble stairs. Evans imagined the elegance of the foyer when it was bombarded by the refracted light that would pour from the massive light fixture.

"Mr. Perry," Evans called loudly. No one answered.

"There," Sparks said, aiming her weapon down a hall that ran to the right of the staircase. Evans took the point and the agents moved cautiously down a narrow hall toward the light coming from a room at the end. Evans motioned Sparks to one side of the door. When the door was almost open, Evans slid into the room with his gun leading the way, but he knew instantly that the weapon wasn't necessary. Dale Perry, the room's only occupant, sat at his desk, his head back and his sightless eyes staring at the ceiling. His right arm hung straight down, and the fingers of his right hand almost touched the smooth side of a .38 Special. An ugly bloodstained wound at his temple was an advertisement for the cause of his death. Evans felt Perry's neck for a pulse. Then he straightened up and holstered his weapon.

"Call 911." He sighed. "Tell them we've discovered an apparent suicide."

Chapter Twenty-four

It was the third item on the eleven o'clock news after the lead story about the arrest of the Ripper and a discussion of Claire Farrington's pregnancy. Dana Cutler heard it while she was sitting on the bed in her motel room with her back against the headboard eating another ham and cheese sandwich. She lost her appetite when the anchorwoman announced the suicide of prominent D.C. attorney Dale Perry.

According to the news report, Perry had worked until 6 P.M. then driven home. His butler said that it was unusual for his employer to come home before eight, and Perry's chef said that he hadn't prepared dinner because he had been told that Perry was eating with a client and would be home late. Perry had given his staff the night off with no explanation. Although there would be no official determination of the cause of death until the autopsy was complete, an unidentified source had told a reporter for the station that the death looked like a suicide.

A few things occurred to Dana as she considered the implications of Perry's death. According to the stories about Walsh's murder, unidentified sources had told the press that the coed had been abducted from her car in the parking lot of the Dulles Towne Center mall. If Walsh was a Ripper victim that was one thing, but if the Ripper hadn't killed her, Dana wondered how the killer knew Walsh had parked at the mall and where she was parked. Dale Perry's mysterious client knew. Dana had phoned the client with the information. With Perry dead it would be impossible to learn the client's identity.

Dana was certain that Dale Perry was no suicide and that she would die as soon as she was found by the men who'd killed Perry. Dana had been counting on selling her pictures to the president in exchange for money and a guarantee of safety, but with the president undertaking a scorched earth policy it looked like that option was off the table. What to do? Only one other option occurred to her.

The offices of *Exposed*, Washington, D.C.'s largest circulation supermarket tabloid, occupied two floors of a remodeled warehouse within sight of the Capitol dome in a section of the city that teetered between decay and gentrification. The inflated prices paid by upwardly mobile young professionals for rehabilitated row houses had sent rents soaring and the old established neighborhood businesses scurrying. As a result, trendy new restaurants and boutiques were interspersed with lots filled with construction equipment and abandoned storefronts.

Patrick Gorman, the owner and editor of *Exposed*, was a grossly obese man with heavy jowls, a massive stomach, and the permanent crimson complexion of an alcoholic. He had purchased the warehouse for a song when his only neighbors were junkies and the homeless. If he chose to sell he could make a fortune, but he had too much fun peddling phony news stories to people who needed to believe in miracles, the existence of legendary creatures, and the idea that the rich and famous led lives more unhappy and tumultuous than their own. Real news was about death and destruction. *Exposed* reported on a world filled with wonder.

Gorman was in high spirits when he left the *Exposed* building a little after eight at night. Headlines touting Elvis sightings always sold, but the lead story in this week's paper had Elvis boarding a UFO, a one-two punch that was guaranteed to boost circulation. There was a small parking lot in the rear of the building. The security guard opened the door for

Gorman and watched him waddle over to his car. Though most of the neighborhood's unsavory characters had fled there were still some vagrants who were too lazy to go elsewhere, so you could never be too careful. Gorman struggled into the front seat of his Cadillac. As soon as his door was locked he waved at the guard, who waved back before returning to his desk in the lobby to watch Gorman leave on one of his monitors. Gorman was thinking about the profits he anticipated from next week's sales when he felt the muzzle of a gun press into his right temple.

"Don't be frightened, Mr. Gorman," said a voice from the backseat.

"Don't hurt me," Gorman begged.

"Don't worry," Dana said as she shucked off the blanket that had concealed her. "My name is Dana Cutler and I'm here to help you win a Pulitzer Prize."

Oh, great, Gorman thought. I'm being held captive by a lunatic. Out loud, he said, "Winning a Pulitzer has always been one of my fondest wishes."

"Good. Now drive out of the lot before the security guard gets suspicious and pull into the first side street so we can talk."

"What do you want to talk about?" Gorman said as he made odd faces in hopes that the security guard would realize something was wrong.

"I can see what you're doing in the rearview mirror. Cut it out and drive. I told you, I'm not here to hurt you. I have a business proposition. Take me up on it and you'll be famous."

Gorman was certain his captor was delusional and he decided that he couldn't risk upsetting her. He drove out of the lot and turned into the first street, which made up one side of a construction site for more upscale condos. Dana told him to park in the shadows between two streetlights.

"Okay, Ms. Cutler, what do you want?"

"Have you been following the Ripper case?"

"Of course. We've carried a story about it in every issue since he was identified as a serial killer."

Gorman almost added "It was great while it lasted," but thought better of it.

"The police think the Ripper had six victims," Dana said.

"Right."

"I think there were five. Charlotte Walsh was murdered by a copy-cat killer, and I know the killer's identity."

"That's an interesting theory."

"It's more than a theory. I can prove it."

"And you want to sell me the proof?" he guessed.

"Exactly. So tell me, how much you think it would be worth to get your hands on proof that the president of the United States was having an affair with Charlotte Walsh and was with her on the evening she was murdered?"

The president! She was definitely nuts, Gorman thought.

"A lot of money," Gorman said out loud to humor Dana.

"See, we agree on something. How much is a lot?"

"Uh, I don't know, fifty thousand dollars."

"I'd say more like one hundred and fifty thousand."

"That sounds fair. Why don't I drop you someplace and I'll start getting the money together?"

Dana laughed. "I know you think I'm crazy, but it's insulting that you also think I'm stupid."

"I didn't—"

"It's okay. I know how crazy I sound. So it's time to show you the proof."

Dana handed Gorman an envelope filled with the best shots from the farmhouse and some other photographs of Charlotte Walsh.

"I'm a private detective," Dana explained. "A few days before she was murdered, I was given an assignment to follow Walsh and report to a client on everything she did. And don't ask me for the client's identity. I don't know it.

"The night she was murdered I followed Walsh to the Dulles Towne Center mall. A car arrived and she got in. I followed Walsh into the

Virginia countryside to a farmhouse. There were armed guards patrolling the grounds and a car registered to the Secret Service parked outside. I have shots of the license plate of the car used by the Secret Service. I'd advise you to run the plate yourself. Some of these shots also show the weapons the guards were carrying. Check out the weapons carried by the Secret Service and you'll find they're the same type.

"Walsh went upstairs. She was with a man. The lights in the room went off long enough for them to have sex. When the lights came back on, Walsh was angry. She stormed out of the house and yelled at someone inside. I have a clear picture of the man. It's Christopher Farrington."

Gorman had been shuffling through the photographs in the envelope during Dana's narration. He froze when he came to the photograph of the president staring after the car that was returning Walsh to the mall. Dana saw the reaction and smiled. She knew she had him.

"These pictures have a date and time on them. Walsh left before midnight of the day her body was discovered in the Dumpster. The Ripper could have killed her, I guess, but think about it. Farrington is running an election campaign, his wife's pregnant, and his mistress—a teenager—is upset with him. Then the one person who could destroy his election chances just happens to be the random victim of a serial killer. That would certainly be a piece of good fortune, would it not?"

Gorman stared at the time and date stamp.

"So, Pat, are you ready to do business?"

"*Why me*? The *Washington Post* can pay a lot more, and they'd print your proof immediately. I publish a weekly."

"You'll put out a special edition if we do business. That's one of my conditions."

"Okay, but you still haven't explained why you want to do business with *Exposed*. Our credibility isn't the best. Aren't you afraid the White House will just claim this is a hoax?"

"You know who Dale Perry is?"

"The lawyer who committed suicide."

"Only I don't think he did. Dale is the man who hired me to follow Walsh for his client. I was spotted when I took these pictures. A few hours after I took the shots, two men attacked me in my apartment and demanded the pictures. I shot one of them and escaped."

"You're kidding?"

"I wish I was. Several nights later, I met Dale at a bar to arrange for the sale of the photos to the president. More men were waiting for me when I left, but I managed to slip by them. The fact that Dale is dead tells me that the president isn't buying. I need money fast so I can go on the run. You're the owner of *Exposed*. If I talk to the *Post* it will take time to get the money. For the amount I want, a *Post* reporter would have to talk to his editor, who would have to get permission from the board of directors. Then they wouldn't pay until they'd investigated. The longer I wait, the greater the chance Farrington's men will find me. I need those pictures published fast. Once they're front-page news the president won't have any reason—other than revenge—to want me dead. And he'd be the prime suspect if I die. My only hope of staying alive is that the scandal will make Farrington forget about me."

"How do I know these are real? It's easy to fake digital pictures."

"You publish stories about Bigfoot and alien abductions, Gorman. Why do you care if they're real?"

"Because this story isn't about Bigfoot. You don't call the president of the United States a murderer without unimpeachable proof."

"Fair enough, Pat. Check the clothing."

Gorman looked puzzled.

"The pictures of Walsh show the clothes she was wearing when she went to the farmhouse. The Ripper's victims were all found fully clothed. Find out if the clothes on the corpse are the same as the clothing in my photographs."

Gorman was quiet for a moment. Then he turned in his seat so he was facing Dana.

"I'm not going to print these pictures if this is hoax, but if they're real I'll go after this story with everything I have."

Part Six

Exposed

Oregon/Washington, D.C.

Chapter Twenty-five

Claire had finished reading this evening's installment of *Peter Pan* to Patrick when the president walked into his son's bedroom.

"Do you think I could fly, Dad?" Patrick asked.

Chris saw the book they were reading. "Definitely," he said, "if you were sprinkled with pixie dust."

"Can you get some pixie dust?" Patrick asked hopefully.

Chris walked over to the bed and ruffled his son's hair. "I'll get the Department of Defense right on it. Now, hit the hay. I've got something I have to talk over with your mom."

Claire tucked Patrick in and followed her husband into a sitting room near Patrick's bedroom. The president shut the door. For the first time, Claire noticed that her husband was holding a rolled-up newspaper.

"We have a problem and I wanted to be the one to tell you."

Christopher held the paper out to her. The bright red headline in *Exposed* read:

PRESIDENT'S LOVE TRYST WITH TEENAGE MURDER VICTIM *EXPOSED*.

Under the headline was a photograph of Charlotte Walsh yelling at someone who was half exposed in the doorway of a house and a second photograph of the president standing in front of the house.

Claire stared dumbstruck at the headline and the photographs.

"I don't understand," she said.

Christopher looked at the floor, unable to meet his wife's uncomprehending gaze.

"I fucked up, Claire. I know I promised you I wouldn't do this again, and I feel awful about betraying you but . . ."

"Someone photographed you?" Claire asked incredulously as she stared at him wide-eyed. "It wasn't enough that you cheated on me? You had to make sure the world found out?"

The president continued to look at his shoes. "I . . . I don't know what to say."

"There's nothing you can say, you dumb bastard."

Claire read the story beneath the photographs. Then she threw the paper onto the polished wood coffee table so hard it bounced.

"You have made me look ridiculous. You have disgraced me and your son. I'm an adult. I can survive this—God knows I survived your other affairs—but Patrick is a child."

Chris was smart enough to stifle any urge to respond. Claire paced back and forth, her eyes blazing. Then she picked up the paper and threw it in her husband's face. He made no move to protect himself and the tabloid fell to the floor.

Claire stood inches from him. "You fix this, you hear. You get this fixed. If you lose this election I will leave you. Do you understand me. You'll be back in Portland chasing ambulances, and Patrick and I won't be with you."

Claire turned on her heel and walked out of the room. Just before she slammed the door, Christopher heard her say, "I hope she was worth it."

Chapter Twenty-six

Brad smiled as soon as Ginny walked into the bar at the Shanghai Clipper. They had started meeting at the restaurant after work, and these get-togethers had become the best thing about his day. The worst part of his day was his job, which had gotten a lot tougher since his disastrous meeting the week before with Susan Tuchman. Brad thought that he might be unemployed if Richard Fuentes hadn't told the Dragon Lady that Brad had done the right thing when he pursued their client's claim of actual innocence and turned over the pinkies to Paul Baylor, the private forensic expert, instead of the police. But Fuentes wasn't any happier than Tuchman that Brad had dug up the corpses and moved the pinkies before consulting with the partner who was supervising him.

"Sorry I'm late," Ginny said as she dropped onto a chair across from Brad and grabbed a piece of a California roll.

"Not a problem," said Brad, who was working on his second beer. Ginny noticed.

"Another bad day?"

"I swear Tuchman has ordered everyone to double my workload so I'll quit."

"Well don't. You're the only person in the firm who keeps me sane."

"We should both quit."

"I'll be out the door as soon as you find me a sugar daddy to pay off my student loans."

Brad sighed. "I do feel like an indentured servant sometimes."

"Any word on the pinkies? Has Paul Baylor printed them?"

"I don't know. Tuchman took me off the brief and assigned it to another associate. She wouldn't even tell me who it is and she said I'll be fired if she finds out I've done anything connected to Little's case, including calling Baylor's lab."

"Boy is she a bitch."

Brad shrugged. "It doesn't matter anymore what she is. In the near future I'm probably not going to be working for her or anyone else in the firm. I figure I'm done for as soon as the partners conduct the next performance review."

"Wait," Ginny said as her attention was drawn suddenly to the television set above the bar.

"What?"

"Shush," she commanded, holding up her hand for silence.

Brad turned toward the TV where a newscaster was talking about a story in a special edition of *Exposed*.

"... The photographs published in the supermarket tabloid show Miss Walsh arguing with President Farrington shortly before the medical examiner estimates she was killed. The American University coed is wearing the same clothes she had on when her body was discovered in a Dumpster in the rear of a suburban Maryland restaurant.

"The young woman was originally believed to be the victim of the D.C. Ripper, a serial killer who has been terrorizing the District of Columbia and the surrounding area for several months. A suspect in the Ripper case has been arrested but confidential sources have informed this station that there are reasons to believe that Charlotte Walsh was the victim of a copycat killer.

"*Exposed* claims that the meeting between Walsh and President Farrington took place on a farm in rural Virginia that the CIA uses as a safe house. The president has not commented on the newspaper article, leaving the public in the dark about why he was meeting a teenage college student at a CIA safe house and why he and Miss Walsh were arguing shortly before she was murdered."

"Holy shit," Ginny said.

"What?"

Ginny leaned toward Brad and lowered her voice. "Don't you see it?"

"See what?"

"Charlotte Walsh, a teenager, has a relationship with Christopher Farrington and she's murdered. Laurie Erickson, another teenage girl whom the president knew when he was the governor of Oregon, is murdered. In both cases the killer copies the MO of a notorious serial killer. That's a pretty big coincidence, amigo."

"Wait a minute, Ginny. I know you like playing detective, but we don't know if any of what we just heard is true. The reporter said that *Exposed* is a supermarket tabloid. Those rags have *real* photographs of UFOs and Bigfoot. They probably phonied up the whole thing."

"Bigfoot is one thing. Accusing the president of murder is something else."

"Yeah, a way to sell a lot of newspapers, and they didn't accuse Farrington of anything. They just said he had an argument with the student on the evening she was killed. You're jumping to the conclusion that the Ripper didn't kill her. The police haven't said anything about that. Besides, what would we do if there is something to the story? The murder took place three thousand miles away."

"But the two cases could be related. Remember I told you about the rumors that Farrington was having sex with Erickson?"

"Yeah, but that's all they are, rumors."

"Let's suppose they're true and he was sleeping with her. She threatens to go public, and Farrington decides to shut her up. The last person to see Erickson alive was Charles Hawkins, Farrington's right-hand man and an ex-Ranger. Those guys are killing machines.

"The only reason Little was convicted for murdering Erickson was that MO evidence. The governor would want to be kept up-to-date on a serial murder case that was big news in Oregon. I bet Hawkins had access to the police reports, which means he'd know how to fake Little's MO."

"This is total speculation, Ginny, and how could we prove it's true? Are you going to fly to Washington and give Hawkins the third degree? You wouldn't even be able to get into the White House. Besides, if I start investigating this case again I'll be fired. Solving murders is the job of the police."

"The police are convinced that Clarence Little killed Laurie Erickson. They'd look bad if it turned out it was someone else, so they're not going to give us the time of day. And can you just see the reaction if we marched into Central Precinct and demanded that a detective investigate the president of the United States for murder? No one is going to listen to us without rock solid proof."

"That's what I've been saying."

"So we have to get some," Ginny said.

"Hey, I hear there's a sale on rock solid proof at Wal-Mart. Let's head over."

Ginny's eyes narrowed and she looked angry. "Witty remarks are not your strong suit, Brad."

"I'm just being realistic. I know you're all excited about proving Little didn't kill Laurie Erickson, but we'd become laughingstocks if we told anyone that we suspect Christopher Farrington is a serial killer."

Ginny's scowl disappeared. "You're right. But there's got to be something we can do."

They both fell silent. Ginny popped another piece of sushi in her mouth and Brad sipped his beer thoughtfully.

"We could try to find Laurie Erickson's mother and ask her if she was bought off by Farrington," Brad said after a while.

Ginny's face lit up. "You're a genius."

Brad relaxed, pleased that Ginny wasn't angry at him anymore.

"That's exactly what we'll do," Ginny said. "If Mrs. Erickson confirms the rumors that Farrington was sleeping with her daughter we're halfway home. And we can try to find the teenager he was supposed to have had sex with when he was practicing law. If we can show that Farrington has a thing for teenage girls it would boost our credibility."

Ginny's excitement was contagious, and Brad felt his depression lift. Then he thought of something and he deflated.

"I can't let you work with me on this, Ginny. I'll have to see Mrs. Erickson alone."

"What are you talking about?"

"Tuchman doesn't know you helped me find the bodies and the pinkies. She thinks I'm the only one involved in Little's case. It's my job that's hanging by a thread. I don't want her angry at you, too."

Ginny reached across the table and placed her hand over Brad's. "That's sweet, but I am involved. If we turn out to be right what can Tuchman do? We'll be heroes. We'd be famous. Remember what happened to Woodward and Bernstein when they brought down Nixon."

"I'm not so certain about the way people would react, Ginny. Have you ever been in Tuchman's office? She has a wall decorated with pictures of her and Farrington and other big political figures. If we bring down Farrington we'd also be bringing down his party and turning over the presidency to Maureen Gaylord. That won't win us any friends at the firm. And I'm not so certain that I want to be friends with the people who run Gaylord's party."

Ginny frowned. "You have a point."

"I'll follow up. I've got nothing to lose. With the way Tuchman feels about me I'll never make partner even if the firm doesn't fire me right away. I'd feel awful if I got you in trouble."

Ginny's hand was still on his. She looked across the table and into Brad's eyes. Brad felt his cheeks get hot but he didn't look away.

"How do you think I'd feel if you were fired and I kept my job? I say we're in this together, pardner. Think *Titanic*. I'm Kate Winslet and you're Leonardo DiCaprio. If we go down, we go down together."

"Uh, I don't think you picked the right movie. Kate lived and Leonardo drowned."

"Oh. Well I never was any good with movie trivia."

"That's okay. I get the point."

Ginny tilted her head to one side and studied Brad. She still hadn't removed her hand, and he hoped she never would.

"I think it's your turn to pay the bill," she said. "Then I think we should go to my apartment and talk about this some more . . . or not."

Brad wished he could think of some witty repartee that would show Ginny how cool he was in situations like this, but Ginny had been right when she pointed out that witty remarks were not his strong point. Besides, he was too excited to think straight. He just signaled for the check.

Chapter Twenty-seven

Exposed was under siege. Arrayed behind barriers erected by the D.C. police were representatives of every branch of the media, foreign and domestic, screaming questions at anyone unfortunate enough to enter or leave the building. As Keith Evans drove by at a crawl to avoid running over some of the more ambitious correspondents he had a vision of a medieval siege in which catapults hurled fanatic reporters in feverish pursuit of a scoop through the *Exposed* building's windows and brick walls.

A manned barricade stretched across the entrance to the newspaper's parking lot. Evans flashed his credentials at the bored officer who leaned in his window. The policeman had been told to expect Evans. He pulled back the sawhorse and waved him through moments before a group of journalists surged forward like a school of piranhas lured by the scent of blood.

"I wish I had some raw steak to toss at them," Maggie said as they got out of their car.

Gorman and another man were waiting in Gorman's office on the second floor of the converted warehouse. The office walls were decorated with framed front pages displaying *Exposed*'s most outrageous headlines. Gorman stayed seated when the FBI agents were shown in, but his companion walked over and shook hands. He was a distinguished, white-haired gentleman in his midsixties. If his black pinstripe Ermenegildo Zegna suit and gold Patek Philippe watch were any indication, he was doing quite well.

"I'm Harvey Lang, Mr. Gorman's attorney."

"Keith Evans and Margaret Sparks. Pleased to meet you, Mr. Lang." He nodded toward the newspaper owner. "Mr. Gorman. Thanks for taking the time to see us."

"Did I have a choice?"

"Actually, yes. You could have refused. But then we'd have to come to your house in the middle of the night and make you disappear into one of our secret prisons."

Gorman's eyes grew wide, and Evans laughed.

"That was just a little FBI humor. Actually, my partner and I left our rubber truncheons and cattle prods in the car. This whole conversation is off the record. You have enough people bugging you. I just want a minute of your time. Then we're out of here."

"What exactly do you want?" Lang asked.

"The name of the person who gave you the photographs you printed in your story about Charlotte Walsh and President Farrington," Evans said, directing his answer at *Exposed*'s owner.

"I'm sorry. Those photographs were provided by a confidential source," Lang said. "I'm sure you're aware that such information is protected by the Freedom of the Press provision of the First Amendment."

"What I'm aware of are the reporters who were sentenced to jail for contempt for taking that position, but I don't think we have to resort to mortal combat for both of us to get what we want. I'm almost certain I know who took those pictures and I think she's in great danger."

Gorman's features flickered from blank regard to concern and back in a heartbeat.

"None of us want to see this person hurt," Evans continued, "so I have a plan that will let everyone get what they want."

"Let's hear it," Lang said.

Evans focused on Patrick Gorman. "I'll tell you the name of the person I think took the pictures. All I want you to do is confirm the name if I get it right. I also need to know where she might be. I wasn't kidding when I said she's in danger. I think someone may already have tried to kill her for those pictures."

"What does Mr. Gorman get if he helps you?" Lang asked.

"Peace and quiet. No subpoenas, no grand jury, no time in a cold, damp cell while you run up your billable hours debating the First Amendment with an assistant United States attorney. What do you say?"

"I'd have to advise my client to refuse to cooperate in order to protect his source."

Evans smiled at Gorman. "Why play games? I'm certain Dana Cutler gave you those photographs." Gorman's eyes shifted. "She was following Charlotte Walsh for Dale Perry, a lawyer who *allegedly* committed suicide a few days ago. We think someone attacked Cutler in her apartment on the evening she took the shots. The people who are after her don't fool around. If you know anything that will help us find her, tell me. You don't want her death on your conscience."

"We met twice."

"Pat—" Lang started, but Gorman held up his hand.

"They know already, Harvey, and I don't want her hurt."

"Amen to that," Evans said.

"The first time we met she showed me some of the pictures. When I realized how big the story would be I agreed to her price.

"The next time we met I paid her for her story and the photographs. She told me she thought President Farrington was trying to kill her to get the pictures back. She hoped he'd stop once I published them."

"Why did she think the president was behind the attempt on her life?"

"Two men were hiding in her apartment the night she took the

206 *Phillip Margolin*

pictures. They attacked her and demanded the photographs. She shot one of them and escaped. Only the president, Dale Perry, and his client knew about the pictures, and she couldn't think of any reason why Perry or the client would try to kill her when they were expecting her to hand them over.

"When Miss Cutler learned that Charlotte Walsh had been murdered she met with Perry. She wanted him to negotiate a sale of the photographs to the president. She wanted money and assurances that she wouldn't be killed. When she left the meeting with Perry there were men waiting for her but she got away."

"Did she tell you the name of the person Perry was representing?"

"No. Perry never told her, and Cutler told me that she never discovered the identity of the client."

"Where is Miss Cutler, Mr. Gorman?"

"I don't know. She had no reason to tell me where she was going and I had no reason to ask."

"Did we accomplish anything?" Sparks asked when they were back in their car.

"We're filling in the blank spaces. Gorman confirmed that Cutler took the pictures of Walsh with Farrington and she told Gorman that the people who were in her apartment were after the pictures. The only people who would know about the existence of the pictures would be Perry and his client, who were expecting Cutler to give them to Perry, and the president. That's pretty strong evidence that Farrington sent the people who attacked Cutler."

"Cutler's the key. We have to find her."

Chapter Twenty-eight

When Charles Hawkins drove through the east gate of the White House, Travis "Jailbreak" Holliday was under a blanket, lying on the floor in the back of Hawkins's car. This wasn't easy. The Texas attorney was six four and weighed thirty pounds more than the 254 he'd packed on his big-boned frame when he'd starred at linebacker for the Longhorns.

Holliday had been given his nickname by a columnist for the *Dallas Morning News*, who had written a story claiming that hiring Holliday was like drawing a "Get Out of Jail Free" card in Monopoly. The columnist was upset that the defense attorney had just gained an acquittal for a wealthy rancher charged with killing his wife after branding her. Word was that Holliday's closing argument was so confusing that a team at the Institute for Advanced Studies at Princeton was still trying to figure it out.

Earlier in the evening, the lawyer had flown his private jet to Andrews Air Force Base in Maryland, where Air Force One is housed. Hawkins had been waiting in a drab Chevrolet, a make not used by the White House staff or the Secret Service and so less likely to be noticed. The guards at the east gate had been warned about the unorthodox method Hawkins was going to use to get the criminal defense attorney to his meeting with the president, so getting by them was easy. It was the reporters camped outside the west gate who worried Hawkins. In some circles, hiring Travis "Jailbreak" Holliday was the equivalent of an admission of guilt. News that Holliday had entered the White House would generate more bad press than an actual indictment.

After the guards at the east gate waved him through, Hawkins rode along the horseshoe-shaped driveway until the Rose Garden and the Oval Office came into sight. He parked in back of the mansion and helped Holliday out of the car. Then he directed the lawyer through a door that stood between the Oval Office and the State Dining Room and up a flight of stairs to a study in the private residence, where Christopher Farrington was waiting.

Holliday had not worn his trademark string tie, Stetson hat, and snakeskin boots for the White House meeting. He'd chosen a plain business suit to avoid attracting any more attention than his height and bulk usually did.

"Mr. President," Holliday said, "it's an honor."

Hawkins noted that "Jailbreak" had lost a lot of the Texas twang that dominated his courtroom speech.

"Thank you for coming," Farrington said as he crossed the room. "I apologize for the dramatics."

"Not a problem," Holliday answered with a wide smile. "Made me feel like I was in a James Bond movie."

"Well, I'm pleased I could add a little excitement to your life. Mine has certainly been an adventure for the past few days. In case you didn't hear the news, Senator Preston, one of Maureen Gaylord's toadies, is demanding the appointment of an independent counsel to look into my connection to the murder of that poor young woman. Of course, Maureen is pretending to stand above the fray, saying that no one should rush to judgment. But her tone implies I'm another Ted Bundy, and there's enough innuendo in every word she speaks to fill an edition of that rag *Exposed*."

"I'm sorry you have to go through this, sir. Especially seeing as how you're in the middle of an election and with everything else you have on your plate."

"Thank you. Has Chuck gone over the business side of our relationship?"

"Yes, sir. The retainer was mighty generous, so let's you and me forget about everything except how I'm going to help you out of the unfortunate situation in which you find yourself. And before we start talking, I'm going to ask Mr. Hawkins to leave us alone."

He turned toward the president's aide. "Anything the president tells me as my client is confidential, but he can lose the attorney-client privilege if a third party is sitting in on our conversation."

"That's not a problem," Hawkins said. He started to leave but Farrington stopped him.

"I'm being a poor host," the president said to Holliday. "You must be starving. Can I offer you something to eat?"

"A medium-rare steak, a side of fries, and a Johnnie Walker Black Label on the rocks would be mighty nice."

"Chuck, ask the kitchen what they can do," Farrington said.

"Can you tell me what I'm facing?" Farrington asked as soon as the door closed behind his friend.

"Well, sir, I did a little reading up on this independent counsel thing. It seems that until 1978, your predecessors appointed special prosecutors to look into scandals in their administrations. Grant started it in 1875 when he had General John B. Henderson investigate the so-called Whiskey Ring. Then you had Garfield, Teddy Roosevelt, Truman, and Nixon appointing special prosecutors. Trouble was if the president appointed the fellow, he could also unappoint him, like Nixon did when he fired Archibald Cox in the Saturday Night Massacre. So, in 1978, Congress passed the Ethics in Government Act and left the selection of the independent counsel up to the Special Division of the U.S. Court of Appeals for the District of Columbia, a panel of three circuit court judges created specially to handle independent counsel matters. This independent counsel is charged with investigating and prosecuting certain designated high-ranking executive branch officials, including you.

"The Act is triggered when the attorney general receives information of possible criminal conduct by a covered person. The AG conducts a preliminary investigation. If credible evidence of criminal conduct is found or if it's determined that the AG has a conflict of interest an application is filed with the court asking for appointment of an independent counsel."

"I hired you to take care of this problem. Do you think you'll be able to do it?"

"I usually can, Mr. President, I usually can."

"God damn it, Chuck, the situation is getting out of hand," the president complained two hours later when Hawkins walked into the third-floor study after making sure that Travis Holliday would be returned to Andrews Air Force Base without being seen.

"Didn't you hit it off with Holliday?"

"No, no, Holiday is fine. That's not what concerns me. The latest polls show I'm dropping like a rock. Holliday says the investigation by the independent counsel can drag on for years. That means it will be front-page news with no clear resolution long after the election. We've got to get the FBI to clear me of killing Walsh or hiring someone to do it."

"There's still the Ripper."

"He was arraigned. Every channel covered it. He made a point of claiming that someone was trying to frame him for Charlotte's murder."

"What about Cutler?"

"What about her?"

"You've read her file. She's an ex-mental patient. She was following Walsh. She knew where she was parked."

"What possible motive would she have for killing Charlotte?"

Hawkins shrugged. "That's for the FBI and the independent counsel to figure out. Don't forget, Cutler is on the run. That's what guilty people do."

"No, no, Chuck. We can't send an innocent person to prison."

"We've done it before."

"Clarence Little is a mass murderer."

Hawkins leaned forward and stared directly into his friend's eyes. "Your son and unborn child need you. Claire needs you. This country needs you. If Cutler has to be sacrificed it's a small price to pay."

"I don't know, Chuck."

"I do. You run a strong campaign and steer this country to greatness. Let me handle this."

The president found the first lady in the sitting room that adjoined their bedroom sipping a cup of tea while she read a novel. When he entered the room, Claire placed her book next to the tea service that rested on the small walnut end table at her elbow.

"How did everything go?" Claire asked. She was calm, and none of the fury that had greeted his confession of infidelity was in evidence.

Christopher sank onto a chair on the other side of the end table.

"We'll be okay," he said as he poured himself a cup of tea. "Holliday is smart and he knows what he's doing. He had all sorts of ideas."

"Good. Maureen is behind this scandal. The voters will see she's trying to smear you, and her plan will backfire."

"I certainly hope so. My God, the press is calling the investigation *MurderGate*. Every time I try to talk about my platform all I get are questions about Charlotte Walsh."

"Are you and Clem working on your speech?"

"Yeah. It sounds pretty good. God willing, I'll nail Maureen at the press conference and we can put this inquisition behind us."

Claire reached across the small table, and Chris held her hand.

"I love you," Claire said. "I have complete faith in you. You will crush Maureen Gaylord. On the day after the election, you will still be the president of the United States and our baby will be born in the White House."

"I hope you're right," Christopher said in a voice that lacked conviction.

Claire squeezed his hand hard. "I know I am," she said.

Chapter Twenty-nine

"Jake Teeny?" Keith Evans asked the suntanned man in the T-shirt and jeans who answered the door of the suburban ranch house.

"Yes?" Teeny answered, eyeing the agent suspiciously. The photo-journalist was five nine with wavy brown hair and hard brown eyes. Evans judged him to be in his midthirties, but he still had the thick chest and narrow waist of someone who stayed in top shape, and his skin had the rugged, leathery look that comes from being baked by harsh suns and blasted dry by cruel winds.

Evans flashed his credentials. "I'm with the FBI, Mr. Teeny, and I'd like your help in an investigation I'm conducting."

Teeny looked confused. Evans smiled.

"Don't worry. You're not involved as far as we know, but your name came up and—like I said—I'd appreciate your help. May I come in?"

"Sure," Teeny answered as he stepped aside to clear a path for the agent. "Excuse the mess. I've been out of the country on assignment and I just got in twenty minutes ago."

Camera equipment and traveling bags were strewn around the entryway. Evans walked around them and followed Teeny into the living room.

"So, what's this investigation about?" Teeny asked when they were seated.

"Have you heard of the D.C. Ripper?"

"Sure."

"And do you know Dana Cutler?"

"Dana? What does she have to do with the Ripper?"

"We came across her name in connection with one of the Ripper's victims. We've tried to find her, but we've been unsuccessful. One thing we did get was her phone records, and we found numerous calls to your number."

"Dana and I are good friends. We call each other frequently."

"And she stays over?"

"Yeah, on occasion. How did you know that?"

"Her car is parked two houses down. I thought she might be here."

"She might, but I just got in so I can't say one way or the other."

"Could you look through the house to see if she's staying here?"

"Look, Dana is a good friend. What do you think she's done? I'm not going to help you if it's going to get her in trouble."

"Have you read the article in *Exposed*?"

Teeny smiled. "They don't sell *Exposed* in Afghanistan."

"Is that where you just were?"

Teeny nodded.

"Okay. Well, I'll fill you in. A young woman named Charlotte Walsh was murdered by the D.C. Ripper. Miss Cutler works as a private investigator on occasion, doesn't she?"

Teeny nodded.

"We think she may have been following Miss Walsh around the time she was killed. We know she took photographs of her with President Farrington shortly before Charlotte Walsh died."

"The president?"

"The story has been front-page news. We want to know what Miss Cutler saw, but we can't find her. Can you please look around and see if she's been staying here?"

Teeny led Evans to the bedroom first. "She was supposed to housesit for me while I was away and it looks like she did," he said, pointing to the women's undergarments and clothing strewn around the room. Teeny smiled. "Dana isn't the neatest person. I'm always after her to straighten up."

In the bathroom, Teeny pointed out Dana's toiletries.

"She's probably coming back because her toothbrush and hairbrush are here."

"Does Miss Cutler have more than one means of transportation?"

"You mean besides her car?"

"Right."

Teeny suddenly remembered something. "I have a Harley. I let her borrow it the night I went away."

"So she might be riding the Harley."

"That would be my guess if her car's outside."

"Can you give me the license number of your bike and check to see if it's here?"

Teeny rattled off the number while he led Evans to the garage. The bike was gone. Teeny had just finished describing the Harley when Evans's cell phone rang.

"I've got to take this," he apologized. Then he opened the phone and went outside so Teeny couldn't hear him. Roman Hipple, his supervisor, was calling.

"How soon can you get back to headquarters?" Hipple asked.

"Half hour, maybe less."

"Well get back here. Justice Roy Kineer has been appointed as the independent counsel in this Charlotte Walsh thing, and he wants you seconded to him because you know all about the Ripper case."

Evans returned to the garage, thanked Teeny for his cooperation, and promised the worried boyfriend that he would do his best to find Cutler. As soon as he was in his car Evans put out an APB on the Harley.

Roy Kineer looked more like the fifth Marx Brother than a towering legal genius or one of the most powerful men in the United States, which he'd been when he was the chief justice of the Supreme Court. He was partially bald with a fringe of long gray-flecked black hair that always looked uncombed. His Coke bottle glasses and overbite gave him a goofy appearance, and he was always grinning, as if he'd figured out a joke no one else could understand. All in all, Kineer was not someone who was taken seriously unless you knew his biography.

The judge had been born in Cleveland to working-class parents who had been slow to recognize their son's genius. In fact, they suspected Roy was not too bright, because he was poorly coordinated and didn't speak until he was three. Once he did speak there was no denying that their child was special. Roy had been first in his class in high school and first in his class at MIT, where he'd majored in physics. After a year at Oxford, Kineer chose law over the sciences and finished a predictable first in his class at Harvard, where he was the editor of the *Law Review.* After a clerkship at the United States Supreme Court, Kineer surprised everyone by going to work for an organization that handled death penalty cases in the Deep South. Kineer argued three successful appeals before the court in which he'd clerked before joining the faculty at Yale Law School.

Never one to sit on the sidelines, Kineer became actively involved in politics as the legal advisor to Randall Spaulding, the United States senator from Connecticut who went on to become the attorney general of the United States. As soon as he was appointed attorney general, Spaulding asked Kineer to be his solicitor general and argue the position of the United States before the Supreme Court. When the justice for whom Kineer had clerked resigned, the president appointed Kineer, the finest legal mind in the country, to take his place.

The ex-justice's professional credentials were perfect, and his personal life was without blemish. He was a grandfather of four, father of two and happily married for thirty-five years. No scandal had ever touched him. In other words, he was the perfect person to investigate a president of the United States who was suspected of being a murderer.

"Come in. Have a seat," Kineer said enthusiastically when Keith Evans walked into the small, windowless conference room at FBI headquarters that Kineer had chosen for their meeting.

"Mr. Chief Justice," Evans answered nervously as he shook the legend's hand.

"It's Roy. We're going to file the honorifics away for the duration."

"Yes, sir."

Kineer laughed. "No 'sirs' either. Please sit down."

Evans had expected a meeting with a lot of people, but he and the judge were alone in the room and there wasn't a scrap of paper on the conference table. This didn't surprise Evans, who knew Kineer was supposed to have a photographic memory.

"Do you know why I'm meeting with you before I meet with anyone else, Keith? You don't mind if I call you Keith instead of Agent Evans, do you?"

"I guess I can do away with the title if you can."

Kineer grinned. "Good. So, do you know why you're the first person I selected for this project?"

"No."

"I've been told that you know more about the Ripper investigation than anyone in D.C."

"That's probably true."

Kineer nodded. Then he leaned back and fixed his eyes on the FBI agent.

"Is Christopher Farrington a murderer?"

Evans thought for a moment before answering. "If President Farrington was a plumber or a doctor, no one would raise an eyebrow if we considered him a suspect. He and Walsh argued shortly before she was murdered. If they were sleeping together we have the mother of all motives. Have you seen the polls?"

Kineer nodded.

"An angry teenage mistress and a popular pregnant wife equal a politician's worst nightmare. Of course, I don't think Farrington did the deed himself. But I don't doubt that he could find someone to do it for him."

Evans paused to compose his thoughts, and Kineer waited patiently.

"What I've just told you is what anyone who has read *Exposed* would know, but I was looking into the president's involvement with Charlotte Walsh before *Exposed* broke their story."

Kineer's eyebrows rose and he looked at Evans with new respect. The respect increased as Evans told him about the tip that led him to Andy Zipay, the cover-up of the shooting at Dana Cutler's apartment, and his belief that Eric Loomis—the man he'd arrested for the Ripper killings—had not murdered Charlotte Walsh. Then he told Kineer about the connection between Dale Perry and Dana Cutler.

"Now that's interesting," Kineer said when Evans was done. "What do you think we should do next?"

"I'd like to talk to the Secret Service agents who were with President Farrington when Walsh visited the safe house so we can eliminate the president's direct involvement in the murder. I also want to eliminate Eric Loomis as Walsh's killer if I can. I've put out an APB on the motorcycle I think Cutler is riding. Cutler may be the key here. She told Patrick Gorman that there have been two attempts on her life since she photographed Farrington with Walsh. I want to know what Cutler saw that makes her so dangerous to someone."

"You said that Agent Sparks has been working with you?"

"Yes."

"Is she a good investigator?"

"I think so."

"Then I'll have her assigned to my office. Put what you've told me in writing then set up interviews with the Secret Service agents. If you need a subpoena, or anything else for that matter, see me."

"There is one thing. I've tried to get Dana Cutler's file from the

D.C. police, but it's classified, and they're making me jump through all sorts of hoops."

"I'll see if I can expedite the process."

"Thanks."

"This will be an exciting project, Keith. If we conclude that the president was involved with Charlotte Walsh's murder we're going to be part of history, and people will be reading about our exploits long after we're gone."

Chapter Thirty

Brad Miller had not had a chance to carry on his clandestine inquiry into the *Little* case because Susan Tuchman had kept him buried under case files. He knew she was trying to make him quit, but he was determined that he would not give her the satisfaction. He was equally determined not to give her an excuse to fire him. His insane workload meant he was staying at the office long after everyone else had gone home, including Ginny. If one thing was going to break his resolve it would be that his work was keeping him from her.

The night they'd gone to her place from the Shanghai Clipper they had fallen into each other's arms before the door to her apartment had closed. Brad had been nervous when they were finally in bed, but Ginny had been so kind and patient that the sex had ended up being great. Or maybe it was being with Ginny that was great.

Brad decided that it was too early to compare sex with Ginny and sex with Bridget Malloy, since he'd only slept with Ginny once. He remembered that the sex had also been great the first time he and Bridget made love. In fact—for a while—sex with Bridget had been a mind-blowing whirlwind of discovery. That was when he was besotted and—he decided later—she was interested enough to give it her all. As Bridget's interest cooled so did the frequency and the experimental nature of their intercourse. They'd pretty much settled into very fast missionary couplings before Bridget broke up with him the first time.

When they made love again after the second incarnation of their relationship Brad thought the sex was still pretty good. Then Bridget started making excuses for avoiding his bed. This, she finally confessed as they approached their second breakup, was because she was sleeping with an artist who lived in Chelsea. Bridget claimed that she was cheating because of her fear of commitment.

The third time they started seeing each other the sex had come to feel like an obligation.

Being with Ginny had helped Brad see that he'd been fooling himself about his feelings for Bridget during most of their relationship, and he was finally able to accept the fact that he'd been obsessed with a Bridget who had never really existed. He was lucky that Bridget had called off their wedding, which would have been the start of a marriage that was doomed to failure.

While spacing out during an assessment of a tax-avoidance scheme a partner had dreamed up for a wealthy client, Brad decided that the major difference between Ginny and Bridget was that Bridget was self-absorbed while Ginny was just plain nice. He arrived at this conclusion at 2:13 in the afternoon and was about to return to the tax code when an annoying clang signaled the arrival of e-mail on his computer. Brad brought up the message and smiled when he saw it was from Ginny. The message read: COFFEE NOW! OUR FAVORITE PLACE.

Brad found Ginny in the rear of the coffee shop at Broadway and Washington where they'd gotten together after his first meeting with Clarence Little. She was sipping a caffe latte, and Brad waved to her as he started toward the counter to order. Ginny smiled and pointed at the cup of black coffee she'd bought for him. Brad tried to remember if Bridget had ever done something so inconsequential yet so considerate during all of the time they'd been together and came up blank.

"I was beginning to think I'd never see you again with the hours I'm putting in," Brad said when he arrived at the table.

"This too shall pass. Tuchman will find another associate to torture, and she'll lose interest in you. Just hang in there."

"I'm beginning to wonder if it's worth it. I'd start hunting for another job but I don't have time with my workload. So, do you have a reason for this secret rendezvous or do you just miss me?"

"I do miss you but that's not the only reason I dragged you to our favorite caffeine salon. Guess what I discovered?"

"This doesn't have anything to do with Clarence, does it?" Brad asked, alarmed.

"It does, but don't worry. I figured a lot of it out online. And I didn't use a computer at the office."

"Figured what out?"

"What happened to the teenage client Farrington was rumored to have been sleeping with. You know what the *Portland Clarion* is, right?"

"The alternative newspaper?"

Ginny nodded. "When Farrington ran for governor the *Clarion* printed an article about the rumors of sexual impropriety. The client's name was Rhonda Pulaski, and she was injured in a skiing accident on Mount Hood. Farrington sued the ski lodge operator, claiming they'd incorrectly marked a trail that Pulaski wasn't skilled enough to ski down. The case was settled out of court for a sum in the high six figures.

"The day he received the check for the settlement Farrington rented a Town Car and picked up Pulaski at her high school. On the way, he showed the check to the chauffeur, Tim Houston, and bragged about the settlement. Houston told the paper that Farrington had been drinking and brought a bottle of champagne to Pulaski's school. Houston thought that was really inappropriate.

"Instead of taking Pulaski straight home, Farrington had the chauffeur cruise around. There was an opaque window between the backseat and the driver's seat, so Houston couldn't see what happened between Pulaski and Farrington, but he claims to have heard them having sex."

"What did Pulaski say?"

"Her parents wouldn't let the police or the paper talk to her, and no charges were brought. Farrington threatened to sue the newspaper. The *Clarion* runs on a shoestring and defending a lawsuit would have bankrupted it, so they printed a retraction. I called the paper. The reporter who wrote the piece isn't there anymore, but Frieda Bancroft, the editor, is still around. I wanted to talk to Houston, but she said he disappeared. No one knows where he is."

"What about Pulaski?"

Ginny lowered her voice and leaned forward. "Are you ready for this? She's dead. The victim of a hit-and-run driver who was never found. The car was though. It had been stolen. The cops think the thief was joyriding, but the car had been thoroughly cleaned so there were no prints, hairs, fibers, nothing to use to trace the driver. So Pulaski is dead and the only other witness is gone, maybe permanently."

"I get less interested in pursuing this every minute," Brad said nervously.

"Don't be a sissy."

"You're confusing cowardice and prudence. If we're right, Farrington is responsible for the deaths of three teenage girls and a chauffeur. I don't want to add two associates to his total."

"Farrington doesn't even know we exist."

"Yet. If we keep poking around, eventually we'll appear on his radar."

"Brad, this is too important to drop. Do you really want a murderer running America? If he's responsible for all these killings we have to do something. Once we go to the authorities Farrington won't have any reason to come after us. We'll turn over everything we know to the police. We're not witnesses. Killing us wouldn't help his defense."

"You forget revenge, which has always been a pretty strong motive for murder."

"Farrington is too busy to bother with us. We're the smallest of fry. He's already worrying about the independent counsel's investigation of the Walsh murder. If he has to worry about the Erickson and Pulaski cases he won't have time to think about us."

"You're probably right, but do you want to take a chance that you're wrong when the consequences could be that we end up dead?"

"As I see it, the only thing we're going to do is try to find Laurie Erickson's mother. If she doesn't talk to us, that's that. If she implicates Farrington, we go to the cops or the FBI and they'll take it from there."

"*We* aren't doing anything. I told you I'd talk to Mrs. Erickson myself so you wouldn't get in trouble with Tuchman."

"Then you'll do it?"

Brad nodded. "You're right about how important this is. But talking to Erickson is all we're going to do, right? After that we forget about the Clarence Little case, agreed?"

Brad stuck out his hand, and Ginny shook it. Brad held on and looked her in the eye. Ginny looked back and didn't blink. Brad still thought she was lying.

Chapter Thirty-one

Unlike an incoming attorney general of the United States who starts his tenure with an existing office, staff, and equipment, an independent counsel starts with nothing but the piece of paper appointing him. On an independent counsel's first day on the job he does not have computers or telephones or desks on which to put them. He has to locate and lease office space then fill it with furniture, equipment, investigators, books, and lawyers. This explained why Keith Evans was using a room in an inexpensive motel on the outskirts of Washington, D.C., to conduct his interview with Irving Lasker, the head of the Secret Service detail that guarded President Farrington at the farmhouse in Virginia.

Lasker was a wiry, stern-looking, middle-aged man with tight skin, sunken cheeks, and bright blue eyes that Evans half-believed could beam death rays. From his crew cut and the way he held himself, Evans guessed the Secret Service agent was ex-military.

Lasker sat stiff backed on a chair with gold casters that was upholstered in imitation red leather. Evans sat on a similar chair. The two men were separated by a round wooden table over which hung a cheap brass light fixture. Cars sped by on a freeway through the window on Keith's left. To his right were a queen-size bed and an armoire containing a television that showed in-room movies. The room was dark and depressing and smelled of cleaning fluid.

"Sorry about the accommodations," Evans said, using the apology as an icebreaker. "Justice Kineer's out house hunting as we speak and we don't have a big enough budget to rent at the Willard."

"Understood," Lasker answered tersely. Keith hoped the interview wouldn't be as difficult as Lasker's demeanor suggested.

"Thanks for bringing the log," Evans said.

"The log was mentioned in the subpoena."

"Yes, but you could have given us a hard time."

"That's not in my job description, Agent Evans. Ask me your questions and I'll answer them truthfully, as long as they don't concern protection procedures or security arrangements."

Evans scanned the log on which were recorded the times and identities of the people who had entered and left the safe house.

"It says here that you brought the president to the farm at eight P.M."

"That's right. He was in the car with me."

"No one else arrived until Walsh showed up?"

Lasker nodded.

"Then Walsh arrives at nine and leaves at nine-thirty-six."

"That seems right."

"Who drove her?"

"Sam Harcourt."

"Is Agent Harcourt here?"

"He's waiting in the lobby."

"After Miss Walsh got out of the car did you hear anything that the president said to her or she said to him?"

"Not when she arrived. I was outside. When she left, I heard her yell at President Farrington."

"What did she say?"

"Threats. He thought he could use her then toss her away. He'd be sorry. Stuff like that. I don't remember the exact words."

"What, if anything, did the president say?"

"He didn't get emotional. I think he told her to calm down. Again, I can't remember the exact words."

"Okay, then Walsh is driven away?"

"By Agent Harcourt. He picked her up from the Dulles Towne Center mall and returned her to her car."

"Did the president say anything after Miss Walsh left the farm?"

"Not about her, or, at least, not to me."

"Tell me about the woman in the woods."

"Okay. Right about the time Miss Walsh left, Bruno Culbertson spotted a woman in the woods taking pictures. He chased her, and she hid and hit him from behind. Richard Sanborne and I chased her and Sanborne wrote down what he believed to be the woman's license plate number."

"Did you discover who owned the car?"

"If Agent Sanborne wrote down the number correctly the car that drove away from the farm is registered to a Dana Cutler."

"Did you or anyone to your knowledge follow up on the possibility that Miss Cutler was the person who took the pictures?"

"Mr. Hawkins told us that he'd be following up."

"That's Charles Hawkins, the president's aide?"

"Yes."

"Wouldn't the Secret Service normally follow up on potential threats to the president?"

"Yes, but President Farrington instructed us to leave the investigation to his aide."

"President Farrington told you this himself?"

Lasker nodded. Evans thought that this was very unusual and that it might be a key piece of evidence in the investigation.

"Has an arrest warrant been issued for Dana Cutler for assaulting a federal officer?"

"The Secret Service hasn't requested one."

"Why not?"

"We don't know for certain that Cutler struck Bruno. He didn't get a good look at the woman he was chasing, and he didn't see who hit him. Rich Sanborne isn't certain about the license number. Then Mr. Hawkins told us to drop the matter."

"So Cutler's not a fugitive?"

"Not as far as I know."

"The log says that Mr. Hawkins arrived at the farm at eleven-fifteen P.M."

"That sounds right," Lasker said.

"Did he drive himself or was someone with him?"

"He was alone."

"Did you hear any part of his conversation with the president?"

"No. President Farrington was in the library. Mr. Hawkins joined him. I was outside the house."

"The log says that Mr. Hawkins left the farm at eleven-fifty."

"That sounds right."

"When did you leave the farm to drive the president back to the White House?"

"Shortly after midnight."

"When did you arrive at the White House?"

"Somewhere around one in the morning."

"Was President Farrington in your presence from the time he arrived at the farm until he returned to the White House?"

"If you're asking whether he could have murdered the Walsh girl between eight and one, the answer is no."

Secret Service Agent Sam Harcourt was forty-two. There was gray mixed into his jet-black hair, lines on his face, and his eyes were as alert as those of the other Secret Service agents with whom Evans had come in contact. It seemed to him that these men and women were on the alert for any trouble no matter what situation they were in. He wondered if they ever relaxed.

"You were the agent assigned to pick up Charlotte Walsh at the Dulles Towne Center mall and return her there?"

"Yes."

Evans had the distinct impression that something was bothering Harcourt.

"You seem . . . I don't know, upset," Evans said.

Harcourt stiffened. "Of course I'm upset. She was a nice kid and she was tortured to death."

"So, you liked her?"

"I really didn't get a chance to know her. I guess I should have said that she seemed like a nice kid. We were only together during the trips to and from the mall and she didn't talk much, especially on the trip back."

"Her mood was different going to the farm and coming back?"

"Definitely. She was excited on the way to the farm. Not that she talked much, but I could see her in the rearview mirror."

"When she did talk, what did she say?"

"Nothing important. Where are we going, how much longer, that kind of thing. I was instructed not to talk to her, so I never initiated a conversation."

"Who told you not to talk to Walsh?"

"Agent Lasker. He headed up the detail. He said the president didn't want me to chat with Walsh, so I didn't."

Once again, Evans sensed that Harcourt was angry about something.

"Was Miss Walsh's mood different on the return trip?"

"Definitely. She was very upset. I could see her crying for part of the ride."

"Did she explain why she was upset?"

"No, and I didn't ask because of my orders."

"Did you have any conversation with her?"

"I remember asking if she was okay and if she wanted some water, but she said she was fine and she turned down the water."

"Agent Harcourt, did you hear or see anything that would lead you to believe that Miss Walsh had engaged in sexual relations with the president?"

Harcourt hesitated.

"If you know something about this you have to tell us. The independent counsel is charged with determining if the president had any involvement in Miss Walsh's death. If they were intimate and she was angry at him, the president would have a motive."

Harcourt took a deep breath. "When Walsh came out of the house she was very angry. I could hear what she said because she was standing right next to the driver's door. She yelled at the president. She said, 'You can't just fuck me then toss me away like a used tissue.' That's a direct quote."

Evans studied the agent, whose face was flushed. "You seem more upset than I'd expect. You seem angry. Is there something else you know that's made you critical of President Farrington that concerns Miss Walsh?"

Harcourt nodded. Then he looked directly at Evans. "I was on the president's detail when he went to Chicago for a fund-raiser. I can't remember the exact date but it wasn't that long ago. I saw Charles Hawkins smuggle Walsh into the president's suite. She was in there about an hour when Hawkins showed up again to collect her. They went up and down by a service elevator that goes to the kitchen."

"Do you know if they had sex?"

"No. I never went into the suite while she was inside."

"Is there anything else?"

Harcourt shook his head. "It's just not right. I'm a Christian and I don't hold with this behavior. He's a married man and Miss Walsh was very young."

"I understand why you'd be upset. Tell me, when you got back to her car did you see anything suspicious?"

"No, and I've thought about that a lot. I was worried that there might have been something I could have done to save her."

"What do you think now?"

"Honestly, I can't say I saw anything that would help your investigation. I dropped her off, I waited until she was in her car, then I left."

"So you didn't see anyone lurking around?"

"No, but there were cars parked in the vicinity of her car. Someone could have been hiding in one of them or behind one of them and I wouldn't have known."

"Did you see Miss Walsh drive off?"

Harcourt's brow furrowed. "I didn't, and now that I think about it, I didn't see her headlights come on."

"If she was upset she may have been sitting in her car trying to calm down before she drove off."

"Maybe. I don't know. All I do know is that it's a damn shame that a nice kid like that is dead."

Evans pressed for more evidence about the president's infidelities but Harcourt didn't have any further useful information.

When he was finished interviewing the last Secret Service agent Evans checked his cell phone for messages. There was one from Sparks asking him to call her.

"Hey, Maggie, what's up?" Evans asked when Sparks picked up.

"Did you put out an APB on a Harley?"

"Yeah."

"A cop just called in from Webster's Corner, West Virginia. The bike's been spotted at the Traveler's Rest Motel."

Chapter Thirty-two

When Keith Evans and Maggie Sparks followed the Webster's Corner cop around the side of the Traveler's Rest, Dana Cutler was sitting at a picnic table finishing off her evening meal. Until then, Dana had been at peace. The sun was just starting to set, and a gentle breeze was rustling the surface of the river that ran behind the motel. There was birdsong in the air and a quarter mile to the east, a speedboat was stirring up the blue-green water.

Dana cursed herself for not sensing that something was wrong earlier in the day when she saw the same cop stop at the motel office after cruising by twice. The Harley was parked a twenty-five-yard dash away, and the money belt with the cash Gorman had paid her was cinched around her waist. Dana stood so she could make a break for it if they gave her a chance.

"Miss Cutler?" Evans asked pleasantly.

"Who wants to know?" Dana asked. Her instincts told her to go for her gun but the cop's hand was hovering over his sidearm and she figured the odds were against her. She might have tried to shoot her way out anyway, but Evans and Sparks didn't scare her the way she'd been scared by the men in her apartment and the men in the alley behind The 911. Dana decided that the two suits weren't going to kill her with the cop as a witness.

"I'm Keith Evans. I'm with the FBI." Evans handed Cutler his card. "This is Margaret Sparks, my partner. We'd like to talk to you."

"About what?"

Evans smiled. "Conking a Secret Service agent on the skull, for starters."

"I don't know what you're talking about."

"It's okay. We aren't here to arrest you. No one has filed a complaint. I've been assigned to assist the independent counsel in his investigation of the president's possible involvement in the murder of Charlotte Walsh. We're here to offer our protection. From what I hear, there have been two attempts on your life already. You've been lucky so far, but the men who've tried to kill you will find you if we did."

"I still don't know what you're talking about and you're interrupting my dinner."

"Watch your lip," the cop said. "That bike you're riding isn't registered to a woman. If I get the word, you'll be in the lockup until we find out if you're riding a stolen vehicle."

"Thank you for your assistance, Officer Boudreaux," Evans said, "but there's no need to play hardball with Miss Cutler. We just want to talk to her. In fact, we'll take it from here."

"I just don't like her attitude, is all," the policeman insisted sullenly.

While Evans was talking to the officer, Dana's eyes were drawn to the two men in the speedboat. There was something familiar about them. One man was steering the boat and the other man was scanning the shoreline with binoculars. The binoculars turned toward her and fixed in that position for a moment. Then the man spoke into some object that could have been a cell phone or a walkie-talkie.

The boat drew close enough for Dana to hear the hum of its motor at the same time the rumble of other engines pulled her attention toward the highway. The policeman was walking back the way he'd come when two motorcycles tore around the corner. Dana drew three conclusions simultaneously: the man in the speedboat with the binoculars looked very much like the blond, long-haired man who'd threatened her in her apartment; the man steering the boat looked like the man she'd shot in her apartment; and the men on the bikes were armed.

"Get down," Dana screamed just as the gunman on the lead bike shot the policeman through the eye.

Evans and Sparks were slow to react because their backs were to the bikes but Dana dropped to the ground, drew her gun from its place at the small of her back, and drilled the second gunman just as he was drawing a bead on Evans. His bike flipped in the air, wheels spinning, then skidded on its side across the grass. Dana aimed at the other rider. The bike roared by. Dana's shot went wide. She started to roll onto her stomach to take a second shot when a corner of the table exploded. A splinter from the table stabbed Sparks in the cheek and she fell to the ground.

"The boat!" Evans screamed as he dragged Sparks behind the table. Dana glanced toward the river and saw the blond take aim with a high-powered rifle. Evans squatted, grabbed the edge of the table, and heaved it over so that the top was shielding them. A second bullet tore through the wood just missing him but Dana paid no attention because the gunman on the motorcycle was making another pass. He was hunched over his handlebars to present as small a target as possible as he aimed his weapon. Dana fired until her gun was empty. One of the shots hit the motorcycle's rear wheel and the bike pitched forward, sending the shooter into space. He crashed to the ground and tried to sit up. Dana grabbed her ankle gun and ran at him, firing nonstop. Two rounds caught the killer in the face. He collapsed onto his back just as a round from the rifle whizzed by Dana's ear. She hit the ground and rolled back to the table next to Evans. Sparks writhed on the ground beside them, gritted her teeth, and pressed her hand to the right side of her face, which was covered with blood. The boat was close now. Evans took careful aim and shot at the man at the wheel. The shot missed but it shattered the windshield.

The driver ducked and the boat swung back and forth. The blond lost his balance and tilted sideways, almost dropping the rifle. The driver wrenched the boat around and headed upriver. Evans collapsed on his backside and sucked air.

"Call for backup and an ambulance for your partner," Dana ordered as she ran to the policeman.

"The cop is dead," she shouted at Evans, who was speaking into his cell phone.

"So are the shooters," Dana said after checking the two riders. "How's your partner?"

"I'm okay," Sparks said between clenched teeth. "This just hurts like hell."

"The ambulance is on its way," Evans said.

"Good. I'm out of here," Dana said.

"Wait," Evans said as he aimed his gun at Dana.

"You're going to have to shoot me because I'm not waiting for more of Farrington's killers to take me out."

Evans lowered his gun. "We'll put you in the witness protection program."

"Which is run by the Justice Department, which is part of the executive branch whose boss is Christopher Farrington? No thanks."

Dana turned and ran to her Harley. She wheeled it toward the front of her room so she could grab her gear.

"Are you letting her go?" Sparks asked.

"The alternative was shooting her, and she did save our lives."

"You saved mine," Sparks said.

Evans blushed. "Nah, I was trying to use you as a human shield but I couldn't boost you up in time."

Sparks tried to smile but a spasm of pain made her grit her teeth. Keith heard sirens in the distance.

"Here comes the cavalry," he said.

Chapter Thirty-three

In junior high school, Brad had erased a file with a term paper on it. After that, he'd been a fanatic about backing up important files and taking the disc wherever he went in case a fire, theft, tsunami, earthquake, or other disaster deprived him of his hard drive. Susan Tuchman had ordered Brad to turn over the *Little* file along with the file on his computer that contained his notes, but Tuchman had never asked Brad if he had a backup disc. Brad was certain the disc contained a recent address for Marsha Erickson, Laurie's mother, he had found in the trial lawyer's file. He was right but there was no phone number. When he tried to get a number from directory assistance he was told that it was unlisted. That was why he was using precious time on a Sunday driving down a narrow dirt road located halfway between Portland and the coast instead of working or, better yet, watching the Yankees play Boston.

Oregon oaks created a leafy canopy over the dirt track, casting it in shadow. Through the trees Brad could see low-lying hills and a clear blue sky. Below the hills were cultivated fields divided into fire-blackened squares, where field burning had been used to enrich the soil, and other squares of wheat yellow and jade green. Brad wished he could share the gorgeous scenery with Ginny, but he knew he had to conduct his interview alone to protect her job.

An unspectacular ranch-style house was waiting for Brad at the end of the road. The yard did not look like it had been tended recently, and the paint on the house was peeling. Brad parked in the gravel driveway and rang the doorbell. He could hear the chimes echo in the interior of the house. When there was no answer he rang the bell again. Moments later, he saw a shape moving toward him through the frosted glass on one side of the door.

"Who are you?" a woman asked. It was only one in the afternoon but her speech was slurred.

"I'm Brad Miller, ma'am. I'm an associate with the Reed, Briggs law firm in Portland."

Erickson had worked as a legal secretary for Christopher Farrington, so Brad hoped that the firm's name would impress her. A moment after he'd said the magic words the front door opened. In a photograph of Marsha Erickson taken shortly after her daughter's murder she looked a little heavy but nothing like the grossly overweight woman in the red-, yellow-, and blue-flower print muumuu who stood before him. Rings of fat circled her neck, she had a double chin, and her eyes, which were almost hidden beneath fleshy folds, were bloodshot.

"What does Reed, Briggs want with me?" she asked belligerently. Her breath left no doubt about why she was swaying and why her words ran together.

"Reed, Briggs is a very successful law firm but we don't want the public to see us as simply a money machine," Brad answered, remembering the pep talk Susan Tuchman had given before dumping the *Little* case on him. "In order to give back to the people of Oregon we take on pro bono projects, and I've been assigned to one."

"Are you going to get to the point?" Erickson asked impatiently.

"Yes, well, could we step inside? It's a little hot out here."

"No, we can not. I'm not letting you in until you tell me why you're here."

"It's Clarence Little, ma'am. I was assigned his appeal in the Ninth Circuit from a denial of habeas corpus."

The blood drained from Erickson's face.

"We have reason to believe that Mr. Little may not have been responsible for your daughter's death," Brad blurted out, afraid that Erickson was going to shut the door in his face.

"Who sent you?" Erickson asked, her voice trembling.

"Reed, Briggs," Brad said as he handed her his card. "I just have a few questions I wanted to ask you about your daughter's relationship with President Farrington."

Erickson's head jerked up at the mention of the president. "No, no. You have to leave."

"But—"

"Leave or I'll call the police."

"Mrs. Erickson, did Christopher Farrington bother your daughter sexually?"

Marsha Erickson stared at Brad. She looked terrified. "You have to go," she said as she stepped back into the house.

"But Mrs. Erickson—"

"You have to go."

Erickson slammed the door shut, leaving Brad alone.

Ginny and Brad were sitting side by side on secondhand lawn chairs on the tiny balcony outside Ginny's living room window. Three stories below people strolled along the sidewalks of Portland's fashionable Pearl District where savvy developers had converted warehouses into expensive condos and apartments and lured in upscale eateries, art galleries, and chic boutiques. Ginny justified the high rent she paid for her small one-bedroom by pointing to the money she saved on gas by walking or taking the trolley to work.

"It doesn't sound like you learned much," Ginny said when Brad finished filling her in on his visit to Marsha Erickson.

"I learned that Marsha Erickson is scared to death of Christopher Farrington," Brad answered. "I bet he paid her off and she's smart enough to know that you don't double-cross the president of the United States."

"I bet you would have learned a lot more if I'd been along. She would have related better to a woman."

"I don't think so. I'm not kidding when I say she was scared. As soon as I mentioned Farrington she panicked."

"Damn."

"I tried."

Ginny took hold of his hand. "I know you did, and you're probably right about her not talking to me, either." She sighed. "Without Erickson's mother we have nothing."

"We tried our best. Now all we can do is hope that Paul Baylor proves that Laurie Erickson's pinkie isn't in the Mason jar and whoever Tuchman's got working on the case goes to the police."

"There's not much chance of that with the Dragon Lady supervising. You said yourself that she's Farrington's big buddy."

"If I tell you something will you promise not to get mad at me?" Brad asked Ginny.

"That would depend on what you tell me."

"I'm relieved that Mrs. Erickson wouldn't talk to me and that we have no further leads. I don't like Clarence Little one bit. He's a sick bastard who deserves to be on death row. This case is probably going to cost me my job, and it might have put your position with the firm in jeopardy if Tuchman learned you've been helping me, so I'm glad it's over for us. There, I've said my piece. If you want to hate me, go right ahead."

Ginny squeezed Brad's hand. "I don't hate you and I'm sorry the case has caused you so much trouble. It's just that . . . Damn it, I believe in our system of justice. If it's going to mean anything at all it's got to work for scum like Little as well as for the decent people who get in trouble. But you're right, enough is enough. I won't get on you anymore about the case. I'll even take some of your workload off your hands so you can catch up."

"You don't have to do that."

"I know, but two of the partners I work with are on vacation, so I've got some free time. And I want you to have some free time because I'm horny."

"Right now?"

"Yes."

"Damn, I was hoping to catch a few innings of the Yankee game."

Ginny stood up and put her hands on her hips. "Who would you rather sleep with, me or George Steinbrenner?"

"How long do I have to make up my mind?" Brad asked with a grin.

Ginny grabbed Brad by the ear and pulled him to his feet. "Get in the bedroom, Bradford Miller, before I really get mad."

Chapter Thirty-four

Dana Cutler drove aimlessly to give the adrenaline in her system time to subside. Then she gassed up and headed for Pennsylvania. She spent the night sleeping in a farmer's field then drove through Ohio on back roads, spending the next night in an abandoned ware-house outside of Columbus. Dana was in the middle of a meal at a fast-food place in Des Moines, Iowa, when she decided that she couldn't keep running. She had a lot of money, but it would be gone eventually, and the forces hunting her were much better at finding people than she was at escaping detection. She knew that for a fact after what had happened at the Traveler's Rest. If she was going to survive, she was going to have to fight back, but how?

Dana abandoned Jake's bike in the rear of the restaurant. She felt bad about ditching the Harley, but she couldn't risk riding it any-more. She vowed to buy Jake a new one if this one wasn't returned to him and if she wasn't dead or in prison.

After dyeing her auburn hair jet-black in the bathroom of a gas station, Dana put on the glasses she'd saved from her escape from The 911 and changed into a plain, loose-fitting print dress that made her look poor and pathetic. Then she walked a mile to the public li-brary on Grand Avenue, intent on learning as much as she could about Christopher Farrington in the hope that the key to her survival lay somewhere in Farrington's past.

Any president has access to scores of trained killers. He is, after all, the commander in chief of the armed forces of the United States. But there's a difference between sending an army to fight a country's enemies and murdering a college coed. Dana didn't doubt that Farrington had access to people who would obey the order of a president to kill a helpless civilian, but where would he have found such a person on short notice? Unless Farrington had planned to kill Charlotte Walsh before he asked her to come to the farm, the decision had been made after she left the farm and before she returned to her car in the mall parking lot. That suggested that the killer was someone very close to the president.

Dana followed a young couple inside and wandered through the library until she located an open computer. She logged on with the password from the motel and started to Google "Christopher Farrington," but she stopped in midstroke. At the motel, she'd been reading something when the TV news report of Charlotte Walsh's death interrupted her. What was it? Dana shut her eyes and tried to remember. A murder! That was it. Charles Hawkins had been a witness in a murder case in Oregon, something to do with a teenage babysitter.

Dana's fingers flew over the keyboard. In a few moments she had the case name. Seconds later, she had a number of hits by using the name "Clarence Little." The more she learned about the murder of Laurie Erickson the more confident she was that Charles Hawkins and the president had copied Little's modus operandi in Oregon and Eric Loomis's in D.C. to cover up the murders of two teenagers who had become threats to Farrington. A newspaper story informed her that Clarence Little was challenging his conviction for the murder of Laurie Erickson by claiming an alibi for the time of Erickson's death. Eric Loomis was denying that he was culpable for Charlotte Walsh's death. Dana saw a pattern starting to develop. Later that evening, she got on a bus headed for Portland, Oregon, where Brad Miller, the attorney of record for Clarence Little, was practicing law.

Chapter Thirty-five

Keith Evans stayed at the hospital with Maggie Sparks while the doctors stitched up her cheek. The wound was nasty but the damage was all cosmetic. Maggie joked that the scar would make her look tough. Evans drove her home after she was discharged and offered to stay with her, but she said she'd be fine. When Evans finally got to sleep it was three in the morning and he didn't get up until eight.

At the office, Evans was bombarded with questions as soon as he stepped out of the elevator. He assured everyone that he and Maggie were okay. He had almost reached his office when Justice Kineer's secretary grabbed him and led him to the justice's office for a private, detailed account of the motel shoot-out.

Evans finally made it to his office at ten-thirty. The first thing he noticed was a thick folder sitting squarely in the center of his desk. He sat down and read the tab. It was Dana Cutler's classified file. Evans opened it and blinked. He found himself looking at photographs that documented a scene so gruesome that it took a while for his brain to process it.

Three men were sprawled on the floor in different parts of a rec room. There was a pool table in the middle of the scene, and Evans noticed a pool cue on the floor next to the right arm of one of the victims, a burly, bearded man wearing jeans and a black T-shirt. When he looked closer, Evans realized that the man's right hand was not connected to the arm. He also noticed several deep, slashing wounds on the man's face, neck, chest, and legs. The body was drenched in blood.

Evans shuffled through the stack of photographs. The other men had also been hacked to pieces. Evans tried to remember if he'd ever seen such carnage and the closest he could come to it was an act of Russian Mafia vengeance that had wiped out an entire family. But those murders had been carried out unemotionally in an orderly manner because the executioners had been interested in sending a message. These killings suggested pure savagery.

A second set of photographs portrayed a fourth victim who had been discovered in the basement. A chain that ended in an open manacle lay near his body. A close-up of the victim's face showed a jagged piece of glass protruding from the man's left eye and several bullet holes in his face.

There was an audiocassette of Dana Cutler's statement in the file and a transcript of the tape. Before listening to the tape, Evans read through the police reports. A squad of D.C. narcotics detectives had responded to a call from Dana that directed them to a house in a rural area near the Maryland shore. The narcotics officers had lost contact with her three days before when the meth cook she was traveling with gave them the slip. The reporting officer noted that Dana spoke in a monotone and could barely be heard. She refused to discuss what had happened when asked and restricted her conversation to directions that would bring the police to her.

When the police arrived at the house they found Dana sitting in the rec room near the phone staring into space. She was naked and covered in gore. A blood-soaked ax lay at her feet next to two .357 Magnum handguns. The dead men all had lengthy police records and had been arrested for or charged with multiple assaults, rapes, and murders. A report written after talking to the physician who had treated Dana at the hospital informed Evans that she had suffered several savage beatings over every part of her body and had been raped repeatedly. She had been transferred to a psychiatric hospital as soon as her physical problems had been treated.

Evans put the cassette in a tape recorder and pressed the play button. He had to turn the volume up because Dana spoke in a voice that was barely audible and she slurred her words, giving the impression that she was drugged or exhausted. The interview was conducted by Detective Aubrey Carmichael, who asked Dana what had happened after she arrived at the meth lab.

"They hit me," Dana answered.

"Hit you how?" Aubrey asked.

"On the head. I don't remember much. When I came to I was chained by the leg to the wall in the basement."

"What happened after you woke up?"

"They beat me and they raped me. I was naked. They kept me naked."

Evans heard sobs on the tape. Aubrey offered Dana water. There was no sound on the tape for a while. Then the conversation resumed.

"How did you escape?" the detective asked.

"Brady was drinking beer while he waited to rape me."

"Brady is the cook?"

"Yes. He put the bottle down. It was empty. He forgot to take it with him. He came down later to rape me again. He was alone. He . . . he was in me. His eyes were closed. When he opened them I . . ."

"It's okay. We can fill in the details when you're better."

"I won't be better. Not ever."

Evans lost contact with his surroundings as he listened to Dana Cutler describe her walk up the cellar steps with Brady's Magnum in one hand and an ax in the other. She had taken the other gang members by surprise while they were playing pool and shot them in their legs and shoulders, disabling them. Then she'd taken the ax to each of them. Dana's account was sketchy because she didn't remember a lot of what she'd done.

Reports from the mental hospital characterized her as suffering post-traumatic stress disorder and extreme depression. Dana experienced recurring nightmares and flashbacks. She had become an outpatient almost a year after being admitted.

"Jesus Christ," Evans muttered when he finished the file. He could not begin to imagine what Dana had felt during her ordeal and he felt an overwhelming need to find her and protect her.

Chapter Thirty-six

"We have problems," Charles Hawkins told President Farrington.

"I don't want to hear about any problems now, Chuck. I've got to go on television in ten minutes and try to save my campaign."

"You need to hear this. Cutler escaped again."

Farrington gaped at his friend. "What's wrong with you? She's one woman."

"She's very resourceful."

"You've got to eliminate her. She can blow the story I'm going to tell the American people to pieces. I need Cutler dead."

"Calm down. We'll get her."

Farrington fumed silently for a moment. Then he noticed that Hawkins looked like he had more to say.

"Out with it. What else happened?"

"Two of our men were killed, a cop was killed, too, and an FBI agent was wounded."

"She was involved in the shoot-out in West Virginia?"

Hawkins nodded.

"That's been the lead on every news show. With a dead cop and a wounded FBI agent the investigation will be massive."

"Don't worry. I'm on top of it."

"You'd better be." Farrington shook his head. "A dead cop and a wounded FBI agent. How could this happen?"

"Look, it's too bad about the cop and the agent, but they're collateral damage. The important thing is that there's nothing pointing toward the White House and there won't be. Our men can't be traced. They don't carry ID on a mission, and their prints have been erased from the system."

"Is there any more bad news?"

"There is one other minor problem. Marsha Erickson was told to call Dale Perry if there was ever any trouble. She didn't know he was dead and she called him. Mort Rickstein handled the call. She told him that Brad Miller, an associate with the Reed, Briggs firm in Oregon, tried to pump her for information about you and Laurie Erickson."

"What did she tell Miller?" Farrington asked, alarmed.

"Nothing. She refused to talk to him just like we told her to do if anyone ever asked about her daughter. And we don't have to worry about the associate. Mort is a friend of Susan Tuchman. She's been supervising this kid. She promised to read him the riot act."

Farrington smiled. "Poor bastard. If Sue is on his case we won't have to worry."

"Too true, but I am concerned about Erickson. She's a lush. She won't be able to deal with the pressure if her daughter's case gets reopened."

A bead of sweat marred Farrington's makeup, which had been carefully applied just before Hawkins had come in and banished the makeup artist.

"My God! If anyone links Laurie's murder to Charlotte's . . ."

"They won't. I'll take care of it like I always do. So don't worry. Concentrate on your speech. While you're winning over the public I'll be taking care of the loose ends."

Hawkins spent a few more minutes calming his friend. Then he left him and used a secure White House line to make a call.

"Hey," he said to the man who answered. "Remember that potential problem we discussed? Why don't you take care of it? And do not fuck up this time."

* * *

When Christopher Farrington stared into the lens of the television camera he felt certain that he looked humble and contrite because his press secretary, Clem Hutchins, had secretly flown in one of the best acting coaches in New York to train him to look humble and contrite on cue. Standing at Farrington's shoulder was Claire Meadows Farrington, obviously with child and the very model of the loving and supportive wife.

"My fellow Americans, several days ago a Washington, D.C., newspaper published a story that implied that I'd had an extramarital affair with a young woman named Charlotte Walsh. What made this story so sad was the tragic fact that Miss Walsh's life was snuffed out by a degenerate criminal, who, fortunately, has been captured, due to the brilliant work of an FBI task force.

"I could stonewall the newspaper's allegations but that would mean stonewalling you, the American public, the very people I am asking to trust me with shepherding our country through the next four years. How can I ask you to trust me with your vote if I'm not willing to discuss these accusations with you openly and honestly?"

Farrington bowed his head, as he'd been instructed to do. Then he took a breath, as if he was composing himself, and once again addressed his audience.

"I met Miss Walsh briefly at my campaign headquarters where she was a volunteer. Without my knowledge, she told my assistant, Charles Hawkins, that she wanted to help our campaign by pretending to be a supporter of Senator Maureen Gaylord and infiltrating her headquarters. Mr. Hawkins told her that it would be unethical to spy on Senator Gaylord, and he rejected the offer. Unfortunately, Miss Walsh volunteered at Senator Gaylord's headquarters despite Mr. Hawkins's stern warning that she should not do so.

"The newspaper story appeared in *Exposed*, a weekly supermarket tabloid that is not known for honesty in reporting. The so-called facts behind the story were credited to an unnamed source, and no effort was made to check on the truth of the allegations before the story was printed.

"The story in *Exposed* featured photographs that showed me and Miss Walsh together. On the evening that the photographs were taken, Miss Walsh phoned Mr. Hawkins and told him—without revealing how she had obtained them—that she had copies of documents that proved that Senator Gaylord had a secret slush fund that clearly violated the campaign financing laws. She offered to bring these documents to him. Mr. Hawkins was supposed to accompany me to a farm where I was to take part in a meeting involving matters of state security, the details of which I cannot discuss tonight. He arranged to have Miss Walsh driven to the farm where the pictures were taken.

"Unexpected events conspired to create the situation in which I find myself. First, I asked my wife to represent me at a fund-raiser at which I was supposed to speak. Just before I left for my meeting, Claire told me she was pregnant. I was overjoyed but I was also concerned about her speaking in public in her delicate condition."

Farrington smiled warmly. "Those of you who know the first lady know that she is as tough as nails. You don't get to be an all-American and a medical doctor if you can't handle pressure. Claire assured me that she would be fine, but I insisted that Mr. Hawkins accompany her. Chuck is one of our oldest and dearest friends and I wanted to make certain that he would be with Claire should anything go wrong."

At this strategic moment, Claire, as instructed, gazed lovingly at her husband and took his hand. The president returned her adoring gaze with one of his own. Then he returned to his audience.

"When I arrived at the farm I learned that the people I was supposed to meet had been forced to cancel at the last minute. Then Miss Walsh arrived. Mr. Hawkins had briefed me about his conversation with her, but I had forgotten about Miss Walsh because of the excitement over Claire's pregnancy and my preparations for the meeting.

"Miss Walsh and I went upstairs to discuss the documents she had brought. As soon as we were alone, Miss Walsh gave me what she claimed was a list of secret contributors to Senator Gaylord's campaign. Then she told me that she had posed as a volunteer to infiltrate Senator Gaylord's campaign headquarters and had stolen the list from the desk of Reginald Styles, Senator Gaylord's campaign manager. As soon as I learned what she had done I told her that I could not accept the list because it was stolen property. At that point Miss Walsh began to make sexual advances toward me.

"Presidents are also human beings, and Miss Walsh was very attractive. I admit to you that I was tempted, but I swear to you that I fought the temptation to betray my wife. I told her to stop what she was doing. I explained that I had just learned that my wife was expecting our second child and that I loved her very much and would never cheat on her. I told Miss Walsh that her behavior was very inappropriate and I reiterated that stealing from Senator Gaylord was illegal. Then I asked her to leave.

"At this point, Miss Walsh started yelling at me. I left the room, and Miss Walsh continued her tirade as she descended the stairs. She implied she had just slept with me and stormed out of the house, shouting. This was extremely embarrassing, but in light of what we have discovered since the incident, I believe I can offer an explanation for her behavior. I believe that Miss Walsh planned to help my opponent's campaign all along.

"When Miss Walsh left the upstairs room she also left the alleged slush fund document. An analysis of the document has led us to conclude that the list is a fake. Had we gone public with this list my campaign would have been embarrassed. I do not know if Senator Gaylord or people working for her used Miss Walsh to try and create a scandal that would assist the senator in winning the presidency or if this plan was solely of Miss Walsh's devising. I do know that very few people knew where Miss Walsh was supposed to meet Mr. Hawkins, yet a photographer conveniently appeared at the farm and took pictures which made it appear that Miss Walsh and I were having a lover's spat. Then these pictures conveniently appeared in *Exposed*."

The president squeezed Claire's hand and looked directly into the camera lens.

"One mistake that those behind this scheme made was to believe that I would cheat to win an election. They also erred when they decided that I would violate my marriage vows. Finally, they miscalculated when they concluded that you, the American public, would believe this smear.

"Claire Farrington is the most important person in my life; she is my life. I would never disgrace her, my son, Patrick, or the child Claire is carrying by engaging in the disgraceful conduct that the story that appeared in *Exposed* suggested. This is what I swear to you, my fellow Americans, and I trust you to judge if I am sincere, I trust you to see through the veil of lies that *someone* has woven. Thank you."

Farrington nodded to the camera and exited, holding Claire's hand. As soon as they were off camera, Claire turned to her husband.

"You were magnificent."

"Clem and Chuck wrote the speech," Chris said, blushing.

"But you delivered it. I can't wait to see the polls."

Charles Hawkins hung around listening to the reporters long enough to get a sense for how well the speech had gone over. There was a lot of skepticism but there were a significant number of media members who seemed to have bought what Farrington had been selling and others who weren't certain where the truth lay. Hawkins believed that the American public was much more gullible than the press, who were by and large professional skeptics. The chances were good that the story would fly with the voters if a substantial portion of the press corps was buying it. The only fly in the ointment was Dana Cutler, who had seen the lights go out in the bedroom of the farmhouse and knew how long they'd been out, which was something you couldn't tell from the pictures that *Exposed* had published. Another problem Cutler presented was that she could testify that she'd been hired by Dale Perry and not by someone working for Senator Gaylord.

Hawkins left the press room and started toward his office when a large man with sandy hair stepped into his path.

"Mr. Hawkins," Keith Evans said as he displayed his credentials, "can I have a few minutes of your time?"

"I'm really very busy. What's this about?"

"My name is Keith Evans and I'm the FBI agent-in-charge of the Ripper Task Force."

"Oh, yes. That was good work."

"Thanks. I hope we've been doing a good job of keeping the White House up-to-date on the Ripper case. I tried to make sure you had a complete set of our investigative reports."

"The president appreciates the excellent job you've done. So, what did you want to see me about? Is there some way we can help with the Ripper?"

"I'm not here to talk about Eric Loomis. I'm on temporary assignment to Justice Kineer, the independent counsel."

Hawkins's friendly smile disappeared. "You mean the grand inquisitor, don't you? What makes you think I'd cooperate with Maureen Gaylord's witch hunt?"

Evans laughed. "We like to think of our investigation as an official inquiry authorized by an act of Congress. And I only have a few general questions for you."

"Such as?"

"In his speech, the president said that you invited Charlotte Walsh to the safe house."

"That's what the president said."

"Then President Farrington asked you to accompany his wife to the fund-raiser."

"You know all this from the speech."

"Right. What I don't know is what you and the president talked about when you got to the farmhouse."

Hawkins flashed a cold smile. "I'm sure you appreciate that I can't discuss conversations I've had with the president of the United States."

"You're not an attorney or a priest, are you?"

"No."

"Then you don't have any privilege that makes your conversations confidential."

"What's your next question?"

"I can get a subpoena."

"Do what you have to do, Agent Evans."

Evans could see that Hawkins wasn't going to cave in, so he moved on.

"Where did you go after you left the safe house?"

"You know, you should be looking at Senator Gaylord and her people."

"For what reason?"

"I'm not an idiot, Agent Evans. Our little exchange before you told me you were working for Kineer revealed that I knew about the Ripper's MO and would be able to fake a copycat killing, as suggested by the story in *Exposed*. I'm guessing that Gaylord's people had the same information and an excellent motive to get rid of Walsh to keep her from testifying that Gaylord put her up to her stunt at the farm."

"That's interesting. I hadn't thought of that. Thank you."

"Now, if there's nothing else . . ."

"Actually I did have one more thing I wanted to ask you about."

"What's that?"

"Chicago."

"What about Chicago?" Hawkins asked cautiously.

"Did you bring Charlotte Walsh to see the president in Chicago or was it another member of your staff?"

All emotion vanished from Hawkins's features. One moment Evans had been talking to a human being and the next moment he was standing opposite a machine.

"It's been nice talking to you," Hawkins said. "Tell the members of the Ripper Task Force that they did a great job and the president appreciates it."

Hawkins turned his back on the agent and walked away. Evans watched him disappear before strolling over to the members of the press corps who were still around. He'd spotted Harold Whitehead earlier. Whitehead worked for the *Washington Post*, and they'd run into each other several times since Evans moved to D.C. The reporter was in his early sixties, and he'd been working in the newspaper business before the big corporations and twenty-four-hour news channels had converted the news from information to entertainment, as he constantly reminded people. Early in his career, he'd reported from war zones and visited the scenes of disasters, but a bad hip and a serious heart attack had ended his globe-trotting days and landed him on the political beat.

"I hear you're working with Kineer at the independent counsel," Harry said.

"You hear correctly," Evans answered as the men shook hands.

"So, did Farrington off the coed?"

"As soon as I find out, you'll be the first to know. Are you up for a beer?"

"Always," Whitehead said as he eyed Evans suspiciously. Reporters sought out heads of serial killer task forces and the right-hand men of independent counsels, not vice versa.

"You know The Schooner in Adams Morgan?" Evans asked.

"Sure."

"See you there."

During the drive from the White House to the bar, Evans thought about Maggie Sparks. While he'd waited with her for the ambulance, Evans realized that she meant a lot to him. He'd thought about all the reasons he'd given himself for not trying to get to know her better and he'd decided that none of them made sense. He vowed that he would find out how she felt about him when he had some time to breathe.

The Adams Morgan section of Washington was funky and crowded with jazz nightclubs, pizza parlors, Ethiopian restaurants, and bars. While many of the local bars catered to young professionals or college kids, the clientele of The Schooner were laborers, firefighters, cops, and gentlemen who were between jobs. Evans arrived at the bar at ten past two. Harold had beaten him by twelve minutes, and the agent found the reporter nursing a beer in a booth in the back.

"Okay, Keith, what's this about?"

"Can't a guy buy another guy a beer without a hidden agenda?"

"You're an underpaid government employee, Evans, and you've got alimony payments. You don't make enough money to treat me to a beer."

"Sad but true."

"So?"

"We're off the record or you don't get your beer."

"Prick."

"Well?"

"Yeah, yeah," Whitehead answered grudgingly.

"It's Charles Hawkins. I want to know as much as you can tell me about him."

"What's your interest in the Farringtons' attack dog?"

"We're trying to figure out what happened on the evening Charlotte

Walsh was killed. I asked Hawkins about it and I got nowhere. We know he was at the farmhouse after Walsh left, but he won't tell me anything. I want to know who I'm dealing with."

"A very dangerous guy, according to the rumors. A former army Ranger with combat experience."

"You called him 'the Farringtons' attack dog.'"

Whitehead nodded. "Hawkins is completely dedicated to the Farringtons. There's nothing he won't do for them. He's like those knights of the Round Table, totally devoted to the king and queen. Hawkins could have turned his relationship with the president to his advantage, but I've never heard a hint that he's made a penny off of it. I think he would consider it dishonorable."

"Now that you mention it, he doesn't dress for success like some of the other movers and shakers I've met."

"His relationship with the Farringtons makes Hawkins one of the most influential men in Washington, but you'd never guess the power he wields by looking at him. He buys his suits off the rack, doesn't wear a Rolex like every other Washington player, and still drives a Volvo he bought before Farrington became governor of Oregon."

"How did Hawkins and the president meet?"

"They both went to Oregon State. The president was the star of a basketball team that made it to the Sweet Sixteen. Hawkins played, too, but he rode the bench most of the time. They both excelled in the classroom, but, from what I hear, Hawkins was a plodder while academics came naturally to Farrington. The biggest difference between the two was self-confidence, which Farrington had in spades and Hawkins lacked. The people who knew them at OSU told me that Farrington had a clear vision of his future, but Hawkins had no idea what he wanted to do with his life, so he enlisted in the army."

"I remember reading somewhere that Claire Farrington went to OSU, too."

"Hawkins met her there. She was a star on the volleyball team. They started dating their senior year. Claire had met the president when she and Chuck double-dated with him. She and Farrington lost touch after college. During his second year in law school, Farrington ran into Claire at a party hosted by an intern at the medical school where she was studying. By the time Hawkins left the army, Claire and Christopher were an item."

"Was he angry when he learned that Farrington had stolen his girl?"

"Hawkins had bigger problems when he left the military. He was wounded in action, and he returned to Portland depressed and hooked on painkillers. The only people who cared about him were Claire and Christopher. Claire got him into rehab and helped him recover. Christopher represented him for free when he had legal problems with the VA. When Hawkins got out of rehab, Farrington asked him to work on his state senate campaign and to be his best man. From what I hear, Hawkins wasn't bitter that Farrington ended up with his girl."

"Did Hawkins ever marry?"

"No. You see him with women from time to time at fund-raisers or parties but the rumors are that Claire was the love of his life."

"Sounds a little sad, don't you think?"

"Don't waste your time feeling sorry for Hawkins. He's got no morals where the Farringtons are concerned. The guy's got a screw loose if you ask me."

Chapter Thirty-seven

"Good morning, Brad," Susan Tuchman said.

"Good morning," Brad answered nervously as he took a seat opposite his nemesis. The Dragon Lady was dressed in a black pants suit and black turtleneck and looked the way a supervillain in a comic book would look if her secret identity was a senior partner in a really big law firm.

"I'm getting very good reports about your work," Tuchman told him with a smile that was intended to lull Brad into a false sense of security. "I hear you're burning the midnight oil and producing high-quality research."

"Thank you," Brad answered as he waited for the other shoe to drop.

Tuchman leaned forward and smiled brightly. "I hope you don't feel that we're overworking you."

"No. I expected to work hard when I was hired." Brad forced a smile. "That's what associates are supposed to do, isn't it?"

"Yes indeed. That's why you get the big bucks right out of school when you really don't know anything about the practice of law. But it looks like you're earning your pay. I hear that you're working so hard that you caught up with your caseload."

"I wouldn't say I've caught up," Brad said, terrified that Tuchman was about to assign him another huge project. "I've just made a dent in it."

"Enough of a dent to spend Sunday in the countryside," Tuchman said calmly. "My memory isn't what it used to be, Brad. Remind me; didn't I specifically order you to have no further involvement in the Clarence Little case?"

"Yes."

Tuchman leaned back and examined Brad like a bug collector trying to figure out the best place to stick the next pin into a truly pathetic specimen.

"Have you heard of Kendall, Barrett and Van Kirk?"

"It's a big firm in Washington, D.C., isn't it?"

"Yes it is. I received a disturbing call from Morton Rickstein. He's a senior partner at Kendall, Barrett and a good friend. We defended an antitrust suit several years back and got to know each other very well. Anyway, Mort called me this morning. It seems a client of the firm called him. A Marsha Erickson. Do you know who she is?"

"Yes," Brad answered as his heart dropped into his shoe.

"Correct me if I'm wrong, but isn't she the mother of the young woman Clarence Little was convicted of killing?"

"Yes."

"She was a witness in the case, wasn't she?"

Brad was tired of being the victim in Tuchman's game of cat and mouse, so he just nodded.

"According to Mort, Mrs. Erickson was very upset, Brad. No, let me be accurate here. Mort said she was *very, very* upset. It seems an associate from this law firm came to her house and harassed her Sunday afternoon."

"I didn't harass her. I just asked her a few questions. I didn't know she'd get so excited."

Tuchman looked confused. "Let me make sure I understand your position. You don't think that dredging up the memory of a murdered child on a Sunday morning—just showing up unannounced, out of the blue, and reminding Mrs. Erickson that her lovely daughter was horribly tortured to death—you didn't think that would upset her?"

"Well I knew it was possible, but I—"

Tuchman held up her hand. She wasn't smiling now. "So you admit that you are the associate who caused Mrs. Erickson so much pain that she called her attorney in Washington, D.C., to complain?"

"I went out there, but—"

"Stop. I don't need to know any more. You were under specific orders from me to cease and desist from any involvement in the *Little* case. By your own admission you questioned a witness in the case this Sunday. I am very disappointed in you, Brad, and, as much as it grieves me, I will be forced to discuss this matter at the next partners' meeting."

"Ms. Tuchman, you can fire me if you want to, but you should know why I've been pursuing the *Little* case even after you told me to stop. If you're going to complain about me to the partners you should know all of the facts."

Tuchman leaned back and made a steeple of her fingers. "Why don't you enlighten me?"

"Okay, well, this is going to sound crazy—well, not crazy but hard to believe—but I'm convinced there's something to it."

"You might want to get to the point, Mr. Miller. I've got a conference call in five minutes."

"Okay, right. I don't think Clarence Little killed Laurie Erickson. I think the killer used his MO to make everyone think Little murdered her. I also think the same murderer pulled the same stunt in Washington, D.C. There was a murder there recently. You probably know about it. It's all over the news. Charlotte Walsh was having an affair with President Farrington and the police think the D.C. Ripper murdered her shortly after Miss Walsh had sex with—"

"Stop right there," Tuchman said angrily. "You're repeating unfounded rumors spread by a supermarket scandal sheet about someone who is a close personal friend."

Brad figured he had nothing to lose so he took a deep breath and jumped in with both feet.

"I know he's your friend, but President Farrington may be involved with two murders. I think he was having sex with Laurie Erickson, and Mrs. Erickson was paid off to keep quiet about it. I think someone working for President Farrington murdered Laurie Erickson and Charlotte Walsh and used the MOs of local serial killers to throw the police off the track."

Tuchman didn't look angry anymore. She looked dumbfounded.

"I know you're insubordinate, Mr. Miller, but I never suspected that you were also . . . Well, you've left me speechless. I don't really know how to categorize your bizarre behavior."

"What about the independent counsel? The Congress thinks the president may have been involved in Walsh's death."

"Correction, Mr. Miller, one of the two *parties* in Congress is accusing our president of immoral conduct, and that *party* doesn't believe that Chris is guilty of anything. *It* believes that this witch hunt will help Maureen Gaylord win the presidency."

Tuchman's face looked like a storm front had just crossed it. If she'd seen anything funny in Brad's theories a moment ago she'd lost her sense of humor.

"Now get this straight," she said, leaning forward and jabbing a finger in Brad's direction. "Your time with this firm is probably over, but you are not to spend what's left of it spreading gossip about a great man. This firm will not aid and abet Maureen Gaylord's shameless ploy. Do you hear me?"

"I—"

"I've wasted enough time. I have work to do. Our meeting is over. I will be in touch with you soon concerning your future with Reed, Briggs."

"What are you going to do?" Ginny asked.

Brad shrugged. He'd walked to Ginny's office as soon as he left Tuchman, and they were sitting in it with the door closed.

"I've made some friends at other firms. Two of them helped me set up interviews, but I don't know if anyone will hire me after they read the letters from Reed, Briggs about my job performance that Tuchman is going to write."

"Your job performance is excellent. Your problem is Susan Tuchman. She's a narrow-minded bully."

"She's also one of the most respected lawyers in Portland. I may have to give serious thought about going into some other profession, like shining shoes or running a supermarket checkout."

"You'll be fine. Anyone who's interviewing you will understand why you got a raw deal. You were fired for representing a client too zealously."

"By accusing the president of the United States of murder. You can bet that Tuchman will share that tidbit with any possible future employer who asks for a reference."

"You know, getting fired from Reed, Briggs might not be all that bad. You really don't fit in here. You're too nice. And you're smart enough to get another job. I've made some friends, too. I'll give them a call."

"Thanks." Brad stood up. "I'm going back to my office and try to clear my desk so I can go home."

"You can stay with me tonight. I don't want you to be alone."

"Let me think about that. I'll buzz you when I'm ready to leave."

Brad trudged down the hall to his office with his shoulders hunched and his head down, as if he was expecting a blow. Rumors traveled fast at Reed, Briggs and he imagined that everyone he passed was waiting to whisper behind his back as soon as he was out of earshot.

"Brad," his secretary said as soon as she saw him.

"Yeah, Sally?"

"A woman has been calling. She says she wants to talk to you, but she won't leave her name or a number."

"Did she say what it was about?"

"No, she just said she'd call back."

"I don't want to talk to anyone. In fact, hold all my calls."

Brad closed the door to his office, slumped on his chair, and looked at the mountain of work on his blotter. He knew it was his imagination, but the pile seemed higher than he remembered it being when he went to meet Susan Tuchman. Could files reproduce like rabbits? They certainly seemed to. He knew there was no end to them. Legal work spewed from the bowels of Reed, Briggs like rotten fruit from an evil horn of plenty. The only good thing about his situation was the strong odds that he would not be harvesting this paper crop for long. Maybe Ginny was right. Maybe moving on was not a bad thing. He sighed. Good or bad, moving on was definitely in his future. For now, he had to get back to the fields if he wanted to keep getting the paychecks he needed for food and shelter.

Brad walked home from the office because it was the only way he could get any exercise. His vow to work out several times a week had gone unfulfilled, buried under the Everest of paperwork Susan Tuchman had dumped on him. He wished he was walking to Ginny's place, but he'd taken a rain check. He was so tired when he called it quits at the office that he didn't have the energy for anything except sleep.

Brad opened the door to his apartment, switched on the light, and dragged himself into the kitchen to prepare a snack. He paused for a moment in front of the refrigerator to watch a tanker churn its way down the Willamette River toward Swan Island. Brad loved his view, night or day. When sunset made Mount Hood and the Willamette disappear, the glow on the east side of the city and the lights on the slow-moving river traffic brought Brad a feeling of peace. This feeling suddenly changed to unease. Something was wrong. Brad squinted at the darkened living room and realized that part of the view was obscured by the silhouette of a head. He jumped back and grabbed a knife from the wooden holder on the kitchen counter.

A black shape rose from the couch. "Please put down the knife, Mr. Miller. My weapon is bigger than yours."

The shape morphed into a woman holding a gun. Brad's heart skipped a beat, and he found it hard to breathe. The woman was tall and athletic. She wore tight jeans and a black and red TRAILBLAZER T-shirt under a black satin TRAILBLAZER jacket. Her piercing green eyes and the grim set to her mouth gave Brad the immediate impression that she was not someone to mess with.

"You can relax. My name is Dana Cutler, and I just want to talk to you, not kill you."

"What's this about?"

"The knife," Dana said, gesturing with her gun at Brad's hand. He looked down, surprised to see he was still gripping the shaft.

"Let's continue this conversation in the living room," Dana said as she switched on the lights and motioned Brad into an armchair. She ordered him to keep his hands, palm down, on the armrests and sat facing him on the couch.

"No sudden moves. I'd hate to shoot you."

Brad eyed Dana's gun nervously. "How did you get in?"

"Easily. You don't have an alarm, and the lock was child's play."

"If you're a burglar, I don't have anything worth stealing. If you want to hire a lawyer, I don't handle criminal cases."

"You're handling one, Clarence Little."

Brad hid his surprise. "Actually, I'm not," he said. "I was taken off the case. If you want to talk to someone about that case, you've got the wrong guy."

"When were you taken off the case?"

"A few days ago."

"Why?"

"My supervising attorney felt I was getting too involved."

"Involved how?"

"I can't really discuss that. I'd have to reveal attorney-client confidences."

"Are we in court, Brad? Do you think the rules of evidence apply when the person asking you a question is aiming a loaded gun at your balls?"

"Good point," Brad answered nervously.

"I'm glad you agree. Now tell me what you were doing that got you canned."

"I decided that Clarence Little may not have murdered Laurie Erickson and I was gathering evidence of his innocence."

"Why don't you think Little is guilty?" Dana asked, intrigued by the direction their conversation was going.

"First off, he says he didn't do it."

"He's on death row. What did you expect him to say?"

"Yeah, but he had proof."

Brad explained about finding the bodies in the woods and the pinkie collection. He was careful to keep Ginny's name out of his narrative.

"Has the forensic expert printed the fingers yet?"

"I don't know. I'm under strict orders to stay away from the case. I'm probably going to be fired because of it."

"Am I missing something? How can they fire you for trying to prove your client is innocent?"

"There's a little more to it."

Dana Cutler listened intently to Brad as he explained his theory that Christopher Farrington had ordered Charles Hawkins to use Clarence Little's MO to frame the serial killer for the murder of Laurie Erickson and his belief that Hawkins had replicated the plan by using the Ripper MO when he murdered Charlotte Walsh.

"Fascinating," Dana said when Brad finished. "I've come to the same conclusion."

"You have?"

"I came at the problem from a different direction, but I think it's significant that we both arrived at the same place."

Curiosity replaced fear as Brad's dominant emotion. "Why the melodrama?" he asked. "Breaking and entering, and holding me at gunpoint."

"There have been several attempts on my life, so meeting in public places during the day is out. This seemed like the best bet for privacy."

"Who are you?"

"Have you been following MurderGate?" Dana asked, using the name the press had given to the scandal.

Brad nodded.

"I'm the photographer who took the pictures of Farrington and Walsh that *Exposed* printed, and I'm certain that Charles Hawkins killed Walsh and Erickson under orders from the president."

"Hawkins is the logical suspect, but we don't have any proof."

"It has to be him," Dana insisted. "Farrington couldn't have killed either woman. He was at the library fund-raiser in Salem when Erickson disappeared, and he was at the farm or with the Secret Service or his wife when Walsh was murdered."

"I don't think the Secret Service would lie to cover up a murder, but Farrington's wife might."

"The timing doesn't work. Credible witnesses vouch for Farrington until he goes up to his room at the White House. If Claire Farrington lied when she said her husband was in bed with her, he would still have to get out of the White House without being seen. Then it would take at least forty-five minutes to get to the mall. That's way past the time when Walsh was killed. No, I think we can rule out the president as the person who actually murdered Walsh."

"So you're going with Hawkins?" Brad asked.

"Hawkins came back to the governor's mansion to get the information for Farrington's speech. He was alone with Erickson. He came

in the back door, which is next to the basement door, and the basement is where the laundry chute empties out. He gets the paper for
the speech, murders Erickson, and puts her down the chute. Then he
backs up his car to the basement door and puts her in the trunk."

"What about Walsh?" Brad asked. "Hawkins went from the hotel
to the farm and met with the president. Assuming that Farrington
ordered him to kill Walsh, did he have time enough to do it?"

"Her car was disabled. She couldn't drive off."

"But Walsh had to have been killed soon after she returned to the
mall. The news reports said that Walsh had Triple A but she never
called them or anyone else to help her or pick her up."

"Hawkins could have called someone from the farm and sent
them to kill Walsh," Cutler said. "The night Walsh was murdered two
men tried to kill me for the pictures I took, and there have been other
attempts on my life. So we know the president and Hawkins have access to assassins, and that's the clincher."

Brad looked confused. "I don't get it."

"Hawkins and the president have access to the CIA, Special Forces,
and Defense intelligence operatives *now*, but they didn't have access
to those people when Erickson was murdered. Farrington was only
the governor of Oregon then."

"Hawkins was an army Ranger. He could have buddies from the
military he could call on."

"True, but no one but Hawkins was seen going into the governor's
mansion. He's the one who claims to have been the last person to see
Erickson alive. Erickson was tiny. She wouldn't have been able to put
up much of a fight against someone like Hawkins. If he was with her he
wouldn't have needed help. If Farrington wanted Erickson killed on
the evening of the library fund-raiser, my bet is that Hawkins did it."

"Do you know that there may have been a third murder?"

"What!"

Brad filled in Dana on the hit-and-run killing of Rhonda Pulaski
and the disappearance of Tim Houston.

"Unfortunately, this is all speculation," he said. "We don't have any concrete evidence that Hawkins killed anyone. We don't even have evidence that Farrington and Erickson were having sex. The only person who might be able to help us is Erickson's mother, Marsha, and she refused to talk to me."

"Tell me about that."

As soon as Brad finished telling her about his visit to Marsha Erickson, Dana stood up.

"Get your coat," she said.

"Where are we going?"

"To visit Mrs. Erickson."

"It's too late to go out there tonight. She lives in the country. She'll probably be asleep."

"She'll wake up very quickly when she sees this," Dana said as she hefted the gun. "She may have refused to talk to you, but I assure you she's going to talk to me."

Brad turned onto the road to Marsha Erickson's house shortly before eleven-thirty. Dana ordered Brad to kill his lights, and they drove by moonlight until the house came into view.

"Stop here," Dana commanded just before they reached the place where the road became the driveway.

"Did you see that car when you were here before?" Dana asked, pointing at a black SUV that was parked in front of the garage, facing back toward the road.

"No, but it could have been in the garage."

"Then why isn't it in the garage now, and why is it positioned for a getaway? Pull into those trees," Dana told him.

When they were hidden Dana took her ankle gun out of the holster and held it out to Brad.

"What's that for?" he asked, making no move to touch the weapon.

"Do you know how to shoot?"

"No. I've never even held a gun."

"If you have to use this, aim at the chest and keep shooting."

"I'm not shooting anyone," Brad answered, alarmed.

"Brad, I hope to heaven that the SUV belongs to Marsha Erickson because the people who are after me will not hesitate to kill you. So you'd better lose the knee-jerk liberal attitude about gun control fast."

Brad stared at the weapon for a moment before grasping it with the same enthusiasm he would have shown if Dana had handed him a dead animal. She got out of Brad's car.

"If you hear shots, call 911, report a break-in, then get out of here. Do not follow me inside under any circumstances. Do you understand?"

"Yes, but—"

"No buts. If you hear shots, take off fast."

Dana shut the door and jogged toward the back of Marsha Erickson's house. As she turned the corner she heard a high-pitched scream. There was a sliding door in the living room that opened onto a back patio. The lock had been jimmied and the door was open wide enough to admit her. The living room was dark, but light bled into it from a short hall.

"Bring her into the living room," Dana heard a man say. The voice sounded familiar, but she didn't have time to think about where she'd heard it. She dashed behind a large armchair and crouched down. Seconds later, a thick-set man dragged Marsha Erickson toward the living room. Erickson's hands and ankles were secured by plastic handcuffs, but she was fighting him and the man had to brace himself to move her along the carpet. The blond man from her apartment who had shot at Dana from the speedboat followed Erickson into the living room.

"Help me with this bitch. She weighs a fucking ton," Erickson's tormentor complained.

The blond man hit Erickson in the stomach and she stopped struggling as she was forced to gasp for air. The blond grabbed her legs and helped his partner get their victim onto the living room rug. Then he knelt by her head and spoke to her in the calm tone you would use with a recalcitrant child.

"You behave, Fatty, and we'll make this painless. Give us any shit and you'll take a long time to die. Understand?"

Erickson had gotten her wind back and she croaked out a yes.

"Good," the blond said. Then he smashed a gloved fist into Erickson's nose. Dana heard cartilage crack and blood gushed out.

"That's for giving us a hard time."

The blond turned to his companion. "Smash up some stuff. Make it look like a burglary."

The thick-set man started toward the television. Dana stood up and shot him. He was falling when the blond dove behind the sofa. Her second shot went wide and blasted a vase to pieces. The blond fired back, and Dana's left shoulder felt like it had been smashed by a ball-peen hammer. She fell on her back and her gun flew out of her hand.

"You!" the blond said as he walked toward her.

"I should have killed you when I had the chance," Dana said, grimacing with pain.

"Woulda, shoulda, coulda." The man laughed. "Hey, we all have regrets. I regret not fucking you when I had the chance. Now the opportunity presents itself again and you're all bloody, which—believe me—is a big turnoff. So, I guess I'll just have to kill you instead."

Over the blond's shoulder, Dana saw Brad creeping across the patio. She pulled her legs up and curled into a fetal position.

"Please, don't kill me," she begged as she slid her hand toward her ankle.

"Uh, uh, babe. You know that old saw about 'Fool me once . . .'? That ankle gun thing was great the first time, but it's not going to work again. So very slowly lift up your pant leg and toss the piece over here."

"I don't have the gun."

"Pardon me if I don't believe you."

Dana raised her pants cuff slowly. "Where is it?" the man demanded.

"Put up your hands," Brad said, his voice shaking so badly he could barely get the words out.

"Don't talk! Kill him!" Dana yelled at Brad, who was holding the ankle gun in both hands, trying to keep it steady.

The blond whirled and fired. A bullet whizzed by Brad's ear and the glass in the sliding door exploded. Brad closed his eyes and squeezed the trigger again and again until it clicked on an empty chamber. When he opened his eyes there was no one standing in front of him. He looked down and his knees buckled. The blond man was stretched out on the floor, facedown, moaning.

"Oh, my God! I shot him," Brad said. He dropped the gun and groped for the wall so he wouldn't collapse.

"Don't flatter yourself," Dana said between clenched teeth. "All of your shots missed, which is pretty amazing from less than ten feet. You were a good diversion, though. While he was focused on you, I got my gun back."

Brad looked disappointed. Dana rolled her eyes. "Will you get this asshole's gun and call 911, like I told you to do before? And get an ambulance for me and Mrs. Erickson."

Dana dragged herself into a sitting position and braced her back against the sofa so she could keep an eye on the blond as Brad inched cautiously toward the wounded man.

"I shot him six times, for Christ's sake," Dana said. "Just get the gun."

"Sorry, but I've never been in a shoot-out. I'm a little shaken."

"What you are is an idiot. Didn't I tell you to get the hell out of here if you heard shots?"

"I am an idiot," Brad said as he grabbed the wounded man's gun, "but it worked out okay, didn't it?"

Dana sighed. "Yeah. I owe you. Now call the ambulance."

Brad dialed 911 on his cell. He felt light-headed and a little nause-ated, but he was able to hold it together while he talked to the dispatcher. As soon as he was through with the call, he knelt down to work on the plastic cuffs that bound Mrs. Erickson.

"Are you okay?" he asked.

Marsha Erickson's face was a mass of blood, and she had trouble focusing. Brad felt awful. He was certain that his first visit had triggered the chain of events that had led to the beating. When Erickson recognized him her eyes widened.

"You!"

"I'm really sorry about this."

"What have you done to me?"

"I haven't done anything. Christopher Farrington sent those men to kill you. You'd be dead if we hadn't come by."

"No one would have come here if you hadn't shown up in the first place."

"That's bullshit," Dana said. "You're a loose end that Christopher Farrington needed to tie up. He'd have tried to kill you even if Miller had never visited you. If you want to stay alive you'd better think about telling what you know about your daughter and the president."

Pain was making Dana woozy, and she was having difficulty keeping her gun trained on the blond. She knew she might pass out, which meant that Brad Miller would have to handle the situation. She didn't have much faith in his ability to do that. If the wounded man was in any condition to fight, he'd eat Brad for lunch.

Then there was the problem of the police. The locals would never believe that the president had sent the men she'd shot. They would consider this a burglary gone bad. If Mrs. Erickson turned on them the police might even arrest her and Brad. Dana decided to take a chance. She fished out her wallet and tossed it to Brad.

"There's a card in there with the number of Keith Evans, an FBI agent who's working for the independent counsel. Call him, then give me the phone. If I black out, tell him that we have the man who shot at him from the speedboat. Tell him to get someone down here fast to take over from the local police if he wants witnesses who can tie the president to Charlotte Walsh's murder."

Brad dialed the number. Evans answered after three rings. Brad handed Dana the phone. She laid the gun by her side and took it.

"Agent Evans, this is Dana Cutler. Brad Miller, an associate with a Portland law firm, is with me. I just shot two men who were trying to kill Marsha Erickson, a witness who can prove the president was involved in a murder in Oregon when he was governor."

"That's not true," Marsha Erickson yelled.

Dana covered the cell phone. "One more peep and I'll have my friend tape your mouth shut."

Dana uncovered the mouthpiece. "I want you to send some agents here fast because the local police are on the way. Brad will tell you the hospital they're taking me and Marsha Erickson to. Get guards on our rooms and the room where they're taking the survivor. He's the guy who shot at us from the speedboat."

"Where are you?"

Dana gave him the address and how to get to it. Then she had Brad read her Erickson's home phone number. She repeated it to Evans.

"I'm ready to cooperate," Dana said. "I want protection for me, Miller, and the witness."

"Are you okay?" Evans asked. "You sound funny."

"No, I'm bleeding from a shoulder wound and I might pass out. But I hear sirens and I think I'll be okay. Now stop talking and get some agents here fast. And make certain that you can trust them, because, at best, the president is going to try and take control. At worst, he's going to try and kill us all."

Chapter Thirty-eight

Brad was pacing the fifth-floor corridor of the St. Francis Medical Center waiting to learn how Dana Cutler's surgery had gone when the elevator doors opened and Susan Tuchman stormed out. Her eyes lasered in on Brad, and he could almost see the red dot marking the spot on his heart where Tuchman was going to shoot her death ray.

"What did I tell you would happen if I caught you mucking around in the *Little* case?" Tuchman said as she bore down on him.

Brad faced the onslaught with utter calm. Until this moment, Brad's encounters with Susan Tuchman had either unnerved or depressed him. But the verbal bullets of the furious attorney lacked the power to frighten someone who had just survived a shoot-out featuring live ammunition.

"Did you hear my question, Mr. Miller?" Tuchman asked as she halted inches from him.

"Why are you here?"

"Instead of worrying about why I'm here, you should be worrying about where you're going to be working tomorrow. So let me put your mind at ease. You don't have to worry about your tenure at Reed, Briggs anymore. As of this moment, you are no longer our employee. You're fired."

"Good," Brad said coolly. "I don't think working at your sweatshop is that great."

Tuchman blinked. This was hardly the reaction she'd expected.

"I'd still like an answer to my question," Brad persisted. "Why have you suddenly appeared in this hospital in the middle of the night?"

"That is none of your business, Mr. Miller."

"Did your buddy at Kendall, Barrett tell you to shut down Marsha Erickson?"

"This conversation is over," Tuchman said as she walked by him.

"Mrs. Erickson would be dead if I'd paid any attention to your unethical order to ignore the possible innocence of a Reed, Briggs client," Brad yelled after her, but Tuchman paid no attention and kept walking toward the nurses' station.

Brad wished he had the power to make Tuchman answer, but he didn't. His job was gone along with his salary and any prestige that being an associate at Reed, Briggs might have conferred. He'd been fired, which could have an impact on his future as an attorney. Brad didn't care. He had his dignity and his integrity, and truth be told, he was relieved that he would not have to toil fourteen hours a day solving boring problems for unappreciative egomaniacs.

The elevator doors opened again to reveal a large man with thinning sandy hair who matched the description of Keith Evans that Dana Cutler had given him. A very attractive woman sporting wicked-looking stitches on her right cheek accompanied him.

"Agent Evans?" Brad asked.

The man stopped. "Brad Miller?"

"Yes."

"Pleased to meet you. This is my partner, Margaret Sparks. We flew out as fast as we could. How is Dana Cutler doing?"

"She's in surgery. She was shot in the shoulder. The doctor told me that she lost a lot of blood but she'll recover. He just doesn't know how badly her shoulder was injured."

"Can you fill me in on what's been going on out here?"

"That can wait until we head off Susan Tuchman. She's a very powerful attorney who works for Reed, Briggs, the state's biggest law firm. I'm certain she's going to Marsha Erickson's room to try to get her to stonewall you."

Evans smiled. "She may have a problem."

When they arrived at Marsha Erickson's room, an irate Susan Tuchman was berating a solid young man who stood in front of the patient's door.

"I do understand that you're an attorney, ma'am, but my orders are to admit no one except medical personnel," Erickson's guard said.

"Give me the name of your superior," Tuchman demanded.

"Hi. I'm Keith Evans, and I ordered the guard for Mrs. Erickson. What's the problem?"

Tuchman's anger turned to confusion when she saw Brad standing beside Evans, but she recovered quickly.

"I am Susan Tuchman, Mrs. Erickson's attorney, and I have a right to speak to her."

"You might, if she was under arrest, but she's a victim, so she doesn't need a lawyer."

"I'll be the judge of that," Tuchman said.

Evans smiled patiently. "Not in this case, Ms. Tuchman. A real judge will have to decide whether you can see Mrs. Erickson. But I'm curious. Have you represented Mrs. Erickson in the past?"

"No."

"Then why do you think you're Mrs. Erickson's lawyer?"

"I'm afraid that's privileged."

Evans nodded. "I respect that. But I'm still confused. I've been in contact with the police, the agents I sent to Mrs. Erickson's house, and the hospital. According to my information, Mrs. Erickson hasn't phoned anyone tonight. If you've never represented her and she didn't ask you to come here, why should we let you see her?"

Tuchman looked unsure of herself for the first time since Brad had met her. She didn't appear to know what to say. Evans smiled again.

"I'm sorry you had to lose sleep, Ms. Tuchman, but there's not much you can do here."

"I was contacted by Morton Rickstein of Kendall, Barrett, a Washington, D.C., law firm. Perhaps you've heard of it."

"I certainly have," Evans said.

"Kendall, Barrett represents Mrs. Erickson, and Mr. Rickstein asked me to stand in for him until he arrives. I hope that satisfies you, Agent Evans. Now, please let me speak to my client."

"We still have a problem. If Mrs. Erickson didn't phone for help, she didn't ask Mr. Rickstein to represent her either. So, we're back to square one. Now, if you'll excuse me, I have business to attend to."

Tuchman looked furious, but she was smart enough to know when to back down.

"I will be in touch with your superiors, Agent Evans. Good night."

"It looks like you're not going to get your way, for once," Brad said.

Tuchman glared at him then stomped off without saying another word. Evans turned to Brad.

"Before I talk to Mrs. Erickson, I think it would be a good idea if you told me why you think President Farrington was involved with the murder of her daughter."

Marsha Erickson was a mess. Her broken nose was bandaged, her right cheek had been stitched, and her bruised and bloodshot eyes followed the agents warily when Evans and Sparks walked into her room.

"Good evening, Mrs. Erickson. How are you feeling?" Evans said.

"Who are you?" she asked.

Evans heard the tremor in her voice and smiled to calm her. He was certain that she'd been crying.

"We're not anyone you have to fear. I'm Keith Evans, an FBI agent assigned to the independent counsel's office. This is my partner, Margaret Sparks. We're here to guard you from the people who are trying to kill you. I've made sure that agents will be posted outside your door as long as you're in the hospital, and I'm here to offer you protection when you're discharged."

"What do I have to do to get protected?" Erickson asked, her suspicions edging aside her fear.

"Mrs. Erickson, the United States Congress has charged our office with the task of determining President Farrington's involvement—if any—in the murder of a young woman named Charlotte Walsh. I assume you're aware of the matter, since it's been front-page news."

Erickson nodded warily.

"You know about the D.C. Ripper, the serial killer?"

Erickson nodded again.

"At first, we thought that Miss Walsh was a victim of the Ripper. Now we think that the person who killed her copied the MO of the Ripper to throw us off the track. We also have evidence that suggests that President Farrington may have been having an affair with Miss Walsh."

"What does this have to do with me?"

"A serial killer named Clarence Little was convicted of kidnapping and murdering your daughter while she was babysitting for Christopher Farrington when he was the governor of Oregon. We have evidence that suggests that someone else killed Laurie and copied Mr. Little's MO in the same way that someone may have copied the MO of the D.C. Ripper in the Walsh case.

"I know you've been through hell. You've had to deal with the death of a child and this vicious attack. I don't want to cause you any more pain, but I have to ask. Do you have any reason to believe that President Farrington was intimate with your daughter?"

"I can't talk about that."

"I'm afraid you'll have to, for several reasons, the most important being that telling us the truth will keep you alive. I know what happened at your house. You'd be dead if Dana Cutler and Brad Miller hadn't saved you. If you continue to protect Christopher Farrington, and he's behind this attack, it won't help you stay alive. He'll always be better off with you dead. Then you can never tell what you know.

"And you won't be able to keep your secret anyway. The independent counsel has subpoena powers. I can always take you in front of a grand jury. If you don't answer questions there, you could be sent to jail for contempt. I really don't want to resort to that option because I feel very sorry about all you've gone through. It would be cruel to punish you that way. But I am prepared to do what I must to learn what you know.

"If you think about it, your interests and our interests are the same. We both want you alive. And here's something to think about. Once we know what you know, the president won't have any reason to kill you because the cat will be out of the bag. So, what do you say?"

Erickson looked down at her blanket, and Evans let her think. When she looked up, her eyes were filled with tears.

"I don't know what to do. He was so good to me and he said he didn't do those things. He said he was paying me the money because I was always a good secretary and because he felt bad that Laurie was kidnapped from his house."

"But you had reason to disbelieve him, didn't you?" Evans asked gently.

Erickson bit her lip. Then she nodded.

"Why didn't you believe Farrington was telling the truth?"

Erickson tried to speak, but she was too choked up. There was a glass of water on her nightstand. Sparks handed it to her. She took a sip. Then she squeezed her eyes shut and wept.

"She was all I had, and she was so good. When she told me . . ." Erickson shook her head. "I feel so guilty. I wouldn't believe her. I told her she was a liar and I promised to punish her if she ever said anything like that again. But she'd never lied to me before. Not about anything important. I should have believed her."

"What did she tell you, Mrs. Erickson?" Evans asked.

"She told me ... She said Chris—the governor—had bothered her."

"When was this?"

"Months before—I don't remember exactly—but months before she was ..."

"Take your time."

Erickson sipped some more water.

"Can you tell us exactly what your daughter told you? Did she describe how Governor Farrington was bothering her?"

Erickson nodded. "She said that he was touching her in places, her breasts. Sometimes he would put his arm around her shoulder and pull her close. She said he tried to kiss her once."

"Did she say she resisted?"

"Yes, she told me she didn't like it."

"How did she react when you told her you thought she was lying?"

"She was very upset. She cried and she ... she swore at me."

"Did you ever bring up the subject again?"

"No."

"Did she?"

"No." Erickson shook her head and took more water. Tears glistened in her eyes. "I should have believed her, but I was afraid. And, at first, I didn't believe her. Chris had been so good to me—to us. When my husband left me he made sure I'd be okay financially. He handled the divorce for free. He was good to Laurie, too. He bought her nice presents for her birthday and ..."

Erickson stopped. She seemed exhausted.

"Did you notice any changes in your daughter between the time she made the complaint and the time of her death?"

"Yes. She grew distant, cold. She started wearing makeup and dressing differently, more grown-up."

"What do you mean?"

"Provocatively."

"Sexy?" Sparks asked.

"Yes. And she was, I don't know, more adult. I was upset by the way she was acting. I spoke to her about it, but that always led to arguments."

"Did she ever mention the governor again? Did she complain about him?"

Erickson shook her head.

"Mrs. Erickson," Evans said, "I've heard rumors about another girl Mr. Farrington may have molested, a Rhonda Pulaski. Do you know anything about that?"

Erickson wouldn't look Evans in the eye. "I heard some things when I was his secretary at the law firm and the case was in the office. There was gossip, but I didn't believe that either."

"Don't get down on yourself," Evans said. "It's always hard to believe the worst about someone you know well."

Erickson didn't respond.

"Mrs. Erickson, you said that Mr. Farrington paid you money after your daughter died."

"Yes."

"Were there any conditions attached to receiving the money?"

"I had to promise that I would never tell that he was paying me and I had to promise that I would never discuss anything about Laurie and the governor with anyone. If I did, the payments would stop. That's why I was frightened when the lawyer showed up."

"Brad Miller?"

"Yes. That money is all I have. And the house. President Farrington owns my house. I'd lose that, too."

"Who sent you the money?"

"Dale Perry. He was a lawyer with the Kendall, Barrett law firm in Washington, D.C. They told me he died."

"That's true."

"He was from Oregon. He knew Chris in college. He told me that the governor was doing this from the heart, that he didn't have to. It was to help me."

"Did you sign an agreement when you received the money?"

"Yes."

"There was an actual paper you signed?"

"Yes."

"Do you have a copy?"

"Mr. Perry said he would send it to me, but he never did."

"Did you ask for it?"

"What with the funeral and all, I forgot for a while. Then the money came each month and I didn't think I needed the paper."

Evans hid his excitement. He would subpoena the document to prove that Farrington had bought Erickson's silence and he would subpoena bank records to document the payments. He was about to continue questioning Mrs. Erickson when the door opened and a thick-necked agent stuck his head into the room.

"We have a problem. The John Doe lawyered up."

"How did he do that?" Evans asked. "I left strict instructions that he was not allowed to call out."

"He didn't. He's still out from the operation. This guy just showed up. He says his name is Joseph Aiello and he claims 'Doe' retained him."

"This is like that stunt in the circus," Sparks said, "but instead of clowns coming out of the little car, we have lawyers."

Evans's brow furrowed. Sparks was right. Too many lawyers were showing up on too short notice. How did Rickstein, who was three thousand miles away, know about a shoot-out in the boonies in Oregon? Why would someone tell him about it in the wee hours of the morning? The person who sent "John Doe" to kill Marsha Erickson would know something had happened when "John" didn't report in, and he could have learned that "Doe" had been shot and was at St. Francis Medical Center if he was monitoring the police bands. Which meant . . .

Evans turned to the agent. "If you're here, who's guarding 'John Doe'?"

The agent looked flustered. "I told him he couldn't go in."

"Shit. Maggie, you stay here and I'll take care of this."

Evans followed the agent down the corridor.

"That's him," the agent said, pointing at a bald, heavyset man dressed in an expensive, three-piece suit and wearing wire-rimmed glasses who was limping away from "John Doe's" room. As soon as the agent spoke, Aiello spun toward them and fired. Evans dove behind a cart stacked with towels and drew his gun. He hadn't heard a shot but the agent was down and blood was oozing from a ragged hole between his eyes.

A silencer, Evans thought. That meant he was dealing with a professional, and that also meant "John Doe" was probably dead.

Evans peeked around the cart and saw Aiello limp around a corner. He raced after him. Just as he rounded the corner, Aiello collided with a nurse. She fell back and Aiello tried to open an exit door. Evans fired. His shots echoed through the corridor seconds before the nurse screamed and Aiello fell to the floor. Evans closed in on the hit man seconds before Maggie Sparks raced around the corner.

Chapter Thirty-nine

At the crime scene, as best he could remember, Brad had told his tale to representatives of the state police and two police officers, a detective, and a deputy district attorney from the county where the shooting had occurred. At the hospital, in addition to Agents Evans and Sparks, he remembered being questioned by an assistant United States attorney, but he was certain he'd forgotten somebody. By the time Brad finished telling the last interested representative of a law enforcement agency what had happened at Marsha Erickson's house he was running on fumes.

Between interviews, Brad called Ginny to tell her enough about what had happened to upset her. He'd assured her that he was okay and he promised to come by as soon as he could, which is why Brad drove to Ginny's apartment when Evans told him he could go home. Even though it was 3:30 A.M., Ginny opened the door before Brad finished knocking. She threw her arms around his neck and they clung together.

"Hey, I'm okay. Not a scratch," he assured her.

"I never thought I might get you killed when I insisted we look into Little's claim. I'm so glad this is over."

"It is, and in more ways than one. I had a run-in with Susan Tuchman at the hospital."

"What was she doing there?"

"Rickstein, the lawyer from the D.C. firm, sent her to represent Marsha Erickson, but the FBI wouldn't let Tuchman see her. She was really pissed when she left."

"I'll bet."

"I was the first person she saw when she walked out of the elevator. Tuchman may be a lot of things but dumb isn't one of them. She knew right away that I'd disobeyed her order to stay away from the *Little* case, so she canned me."

"Oh, Brad. I'm so sorry."

"Don't be. I'm not. It was inevitable. I'm actually happy I'm out of Reed, Briggs. I never fit in. I'm just worried that Tuchman will bad-mouth me and I won't be able to find another job as a lawyer. I guess I can always hang out a shingle."

"Don't worry about a job. From what you told me on the phone, you saved Marsha Erickson's life. You're a hero. People will admire you for what you did. You proved you'll go the distance for a client."

Brad flashed a rueful smile. "I hope I don't have to promise to shoot it out with opposing counsel to get a job. One gunfight is enough for a lifetime."

Ginny touched his cheek. "You're going to come out on top. You'll see."

"I'll worry about employment tomorrow. Right now I'm famished."

"I can take care of that. Let's go into the kitchen."

Brad watched her walk away from him, and he smiled. Ginny was sexy and nice and everything a man could want in a woman. He decided that this was a perfect time to tell her.

"You know, there was a moment there when I thought I was going to die. It made me very sad because that would mean not seeing you again, and I want to see a lot of you in the future."

"That's not a double entendre, is it?"

Brad laughed. "Have I ever told you you're a pervert? Here I'm trying to be romantic and you're making lewd jokes."

"Sorry," Ginny said, flashing a wicked smile. "I promise that I'll never bring up the subject of sex again."

"You don't have to go that far, but I hope I won't insult you if I say that my interests right now lie solely in the area of food and sleep."

"I'll get you some food, but you don't get to sleep until you tell me everything that happened tonight."

The sun was starting to come up, and Keith Evans's energy level was way down. He was jet-lagged from his cross-country flight in the FBI jet and he had sustained himself on doughnuts, a wretched tuna fish sandwich, and foul coffee. Evans had insisted that Maggie go to their hotel for some much needed rest. He envied her. He was ready to trade all of his worldly possessions for a decent meal, a shower, and eight hours of sleep. Unfortunately, there was work to be done.

On balance, if he discounted his personal state of well-being, things had gone well. Marsha Erickson was cooperating, and Dana Cutler's wound wasn't serious. They had lost "John Doe," but they had the man who'd killed him, a swap Evans hoped would work in their favor.

"What's Aiello's condition?" Evans asked the agent who was guarding the killer's room.

"The last doctor I spoke to said he'd be coming out of the anesthesia soon. That was half an hour ago. The doctor said he was lucky. None of the bullets hit a major organ."

We're lucky, too, Evans thought ruefully. If I was any kind of shot we wouldn't have a witness.

Evans opened the door. Aiello watched him with a pair of dull, blue eyes as he crossed the room and stood beside his bed. Evans guessed he would be a tough guy. How tough remained to be seen.

"I'm Keith Evans with the independent counsel's office. How are you feeling?"

The man didn't answer.

"I have good news and bad news, Joe." Evans paused. "You don't mind if I call you Joe or Aiello, do you? I'm certain they're not your real names, but it's the best I can do before we get a report on your prints."

The prisoner still didn't answer.

"Okay, have it your own way. So, what would you like to hear first, the good news or the bad news?"

Evans waited a beat. "Since you won't make up your mind, I'll give you the good news. The doctors say you're going to pull through. That's also the bad news, because you'll be standing trial in federal court for murdering an FBI agent and in Oregon for murdering our witness. That means you're a candidate for the death penalty. But there's more good news. Now, you're the witness. If you're smart you can avoid a lethal injection."

"You think you're funny, don't you," the man managed. His words were slurred from the residual effects of the anesthetic.

"You're right. I can be a wiseguy at times. I should cut the humor and get serious. So, seriously, Joe, I would love to watch you die for killing a decent young man whose shoes you aren't fit to shine, but I have to ignore my personal desires and do my job. Professionally, I'm much more interested in the people who sent you to kill our witness than I am in sending you away. Tell me everything you know and we'll deal. Clam up and you die."

"We'll see," the man said. His dry lips cracked into a smile that told the agent Aiello thought Evans was incredibly naive.

"You think your friends will protect you but they won't," Evans said. "Facing a death sentence is a big motivation to talk, so you've become a problem. Think about the way your boss has been solving problems. Cutler was a witness who could hurt him. What did he do? He sent you and the man you just murdered to kill Cutler."

Aiello's eyes shifted, and Evans noticed.

"Yeah, Joe, we showed Dana Cutler your photo and she says you're definitely the guy she shot in her apartment and one of the people who attacked her in West Virginia from the speedboat. The doctors say you have a recent scar on your thigh that's consistent with a bullet wound. Coincidentally, it's right where Cutler says she shot you."

Aiello remained quiet.

"You can clam up, but do some thinking, too. Think about what happened when your buddy was arrested. You were sent to kill him because your boss can't afford to leave witnesses alive. Now, you're the witness, which means you've become a huge liability. As soon as he learns you're alive, he'll send more men to silence you. He has to. He can't afford to let you talk."

The smile stayed on the killer's lips but it shrunk in size as Evans's words registered.

"There are only two ways you can go, lawyer up or cooperate. If you choose door number one, you die. If you aren't killed awaiting trial, they'll take you out in prison after a conviction or you'll be murdered in the free world if you're acquitted. Cooperate and we'll try to put away the men who want you dead, and we'll work very hard to keep you alive. What do you say?"

"Fuck you."

"Hey, Joe, I'm way too exhausted to fuck right now. What I do plan to do is take a shower, get some rest, then eat a hearty breakfast. After that, I'll be back to talk some more. While I'm gone, I suggest you think about what I said."

Chapter Forty

A week after the West Coast shoot-outs at the hospital and Marsha Erickson's house, Erickson and Dana Cutler were tucked away in separate safe houses near Washington, D.C., and Keith Evans was swimming, once again, in the humid, ninety-degree heat of the nation's capital. At nine o'clock Friday morning, fortified by a breakfast of bacon, eggs, biscuits, grits, and black coffee, Evans seated himself across from Charles Hawkins and his attorney, Gary Bischoff, in a conference room at the office of the independent counsel. With Evans were a court reporter, Maggie Sparks, and Gordon Buss, an assistant United States attorney.

Bischoff was a lanky man with curly, salt-and-pepper hair. He ran marathons for a hobby, and his cheeks were as hollow and his eye sockets as deep set as the victim of an African famine. Bischoff was dressed in an expensive suit that was tailor made to fit his skeletal frame, but Hawkins, true to form, was attired in a cheap mismatched jacket and slacks. Evans thought the president's advisor looked less self-confident than he had when they'd spoken at his boss's press conference.

"Would you like to tell us why you've summoned my client to this meeting?" Bischoff asked when the introductions were completed.

"Sure," Evans replied. "We think he's responsible for a couple of murders and attempted murders in Virginia, Maryland, the District of Columbia, West Virginia, and Oregon."

Evans paused and counted on his fingers. When he was satisfied, he nodded.

"Yeah, those are the jurisdictions to which he can expect to be extradited. I don't think I missed any. If I did, they'll come after him, so you'll find out where they are.

"Now, there are also some assaults in there and a burglary or two, and I'm certain I've forgotten a few more charges. Mr. Buss is the criminal lawyer. He can tell you all of the possible crimes Mr. Hawkins will be charged with committing, or you can talk to the DAs who'll be filing the indictments."

Bischoff had been practicing criminal law at the highest levels for thirty years, so he'd been around the block. Evans amused him and he laughed.

"You obviously haven't seen Mr. Hawkins's schedule. I don't think he's got time to brush his teeth, let alone run around the country killing people."

"I didn't say he committed all of these crimes himself." Evans shifted his gaze to Hawkins. "He had help. For instance, he sent a fellow who posed as a lawyer and used the alias 'Joseph Aiello' to St. Francis Medical Center in Portland, Oregon, to murder one of his hit men, who we were lucky enough to capture. 'Aiello' killed our witness, but he didn't get away. Now he's spilling his guts, and he has a lot of interesting things to say about Mr. Hawkins."

"A man facing the death penalty will say a lot of things," Bischoff offered.

"True, but here's something for your client to think about. Aiello's real name is Oscar Tierney. Oscar's prints aren't on file. If he hadn't given us his real name we wouldn't have been able to figure it out, so you know he's talking to us. He also says that he and the fellow he killed at the hospital are part of a black ops squad that operates out of the CIA. One of his assignments was to kill Dana Cutler, who he'd been led to believe was a spy for the Chinese. He claims that your client told him that Cutler was going to use the photos of Farrington and Walsh to blackmail the president into making decisions that would not have been in the national interest. I'll give you Tierney's statement by and by and you can learn how your client is able to commit mass murder while helping run the country."

Bischoff smiled patiently. "That sounds like the type of story someone would concoct if they were caught in the act and had no defense."

"Yeah, it would be far-fetched if Dana Cutler, the first person Tierney was sent to kill, hadn't told us that Tierney wanted her to give him the photos she'd taken of the president in flagrante delicto. This was less than three hours after Cutler took the pictures, and it was around two in the morning. The only people who knew about those photos at that time were Cutler, who took them, the president, the Secret Service agents who were guarding the president, and your client. Cutler doesn't have a suicide wish, so she didn't send Tierney to her apartment. That sort of narrows the suspects, don't you think?"

"I hope you didn't ask Mr. Hawkins here expecting him to confess to these outrageous accusations."

"That would save me a lot of time and effort. It might also help Mr. Hawkins avoid the death penalty if he confesses *and* clarifies President Farrington's role in his criminal enterprises."

"Do you have any other evidence that leads you to believe that Mr. Hawkins is a modern-day Al Capone?"

"You bet, and I'll give him a preview of our case so he can make a reasoned decision about cooperating. Of course, the investigation is ongoing, so we'll get more evidence soon, but here's some of what we have right now."

"We're all ears."

Evans directed his words at Hawkins, who listened without expression.

"When Mr. Hawkins got out of the army, President Farrington was practicing law and having sex with a high school girl named Rhonda Pulaski. Pulaski was not only underage, she was also a client. If any of that ever came out you can imagine what would have happened to our commander in chief. He'd face prison and disbarment, not to mention a big fat civil suit. And those possibilities were looming on the horizon because Farrington had screwed Miss Pulaski in the back of a limousine driven by Tim Houston, a man who was so appalled by the president's behavior that he went to the police

"Mr. Hawkins owed the Farringtons a lot and he was extremely loyal. We think he made the problem go away by buying off the Pulaski family and killing Rhonda Pulaski and Houston."

"Can you prove any of this?" Bischoff asked.

"We're working on it."

The lawyer returned the smile. "Why don't you tell us about something you can prove?"

Evans ignored the taunt. "When Farrington was practicing law he had a secretary named Marsha Erickson, who had a daughter named Laurie. Farrington brought Marsha with him to the governor's mansion when he was elected governor of Oregon. Laurie was in high school and was about the same age as Rhonda Pulaski. Farrington started noticing her, and not in a good way. Soon, he was coming on to her. Are you starting to see a pattern, Gary?"

"Go on," Bischoff answered blandly.

"My pleasure. Eventually, Farrington had sex with Laurie. That's when she became a threat to Farrington's political future. One evening, the governor was scheduled to attend a fund-raiser at the Salem Library. Laurie was babysitting the governor's son. Your client returned to the governor's mansion on the pretext of getting some notes for the governor's speech and murdered Laurie Erickson.

"A serial killer named Clarence Little was killing women in the Salem area at this time. Your client had access to police reports that detailed Little's MO, and he made the murder look like Little's work.

Little was convicted of murdering Laurie and sentenced to death. We now have forensic and other evidence that strongly suggests that Little did not kill Laurie Erickson.

"Mr. Hawkins testified at Little's trial that he was with Laurie around the time she went missing. By his own admission, he's the last person who saw her alive. No one else was seen entering the grounds of the mansion after Mr. Hawkins left."

"Is this man Little still on death row because of the Erickson case?" Bischoff asked.

"He is."

"So, you have no proof that my client murdered Pulaski, and a jury found Little guilty of killing Erickson," the attorney summed up.

"Yup."

"You know, this would make a great movie—*Mission Impossible XII* say—but I'm more interested in hearing the type of evidence that would be admissible at a trial."

"Okay, I'll talk about a case I'm sure you're familiar with. It's the reason an independent counsel was created. Charlotte Walsh was a student at American University who was very attractive and about the same age as Laurie Erickson and Rhonda Pulaski were when Farrington was involved with them. Walsh was majoring in poli-sci, and she went to work at Farrington's campaign headquarters. We think Farrington had your client bring Walsh to Chicago to convince her to become a spy in Senator Maureen Gaylord's campaign. We think that the president had sex with Walsh in Chicago, but we know she quit the Farrington campaign when she came back to D.C. and promptly volunteered at Maureen Gaylord's headquarters.

"On the night she was murdered, Walsh stole documents from Gaylord's campaign headquarters and arranged to give them to the president at a farm in Virginia that the CIA uses as a safe house. Walsh was instructed to park in the lot at the Dulles Towne Center mall. A Secret Service agent picked her up and took her to the farm.

"Farrington was supposed to appear at a campaign fund-raiser in the Theodore Roosevelt Hotel, but he talked his wife into going in his place. Just before he was leaving the White House, the first lady told him she was pregnant. Farrington told Mr. Hawkins to go to the event with Dr. Farrington."

Evans looked directly at Hawkins, who met his eye without flinching.

"You know Dale Perry, don't you, Mr. Hawkins?"

Bischoff held up his hand and addressed his client. "Don't answer that, Chuck.

"Mr. Evans, I instruct you to desist from asking Charles Hawkins, my client, any questions," the lawyer said, making certain that the stenographer got the prohibition on the record. "If you want him to answer a question, please direct it to me first and I'll advise him whether he should answer it."

"That's okay with me," Evans answered, "but it doesn't matter what your client says about his relationship with Perry. They were in the same class at Oregon State University. We have several witnesses who'll confirm that Perry, Christopher Farrington, and your client were friends. After college, Mr. Hawkins went into the army and President Farrington went to law school in Oregon. Mr. Perry went to law school at the University of Chicago. After law school, he went to work for the Kendall, Barrett law firm.

"A client hired Dale Perry to make arrangements to have Miss Walsh followed. By hiring a lawyer, the client could use the attorney-client privilege to shield his identity. Perry hired Dana Cutler, who is a PI, to tail Walsh but didn't tell her who she was working for. The client wanted pictures of everyone Walsh met, and he wanted Cutler to give him a running report when Walsh went somewhere or did something. To facilitate the reporting Perry bought two cell phones. He gave one to the client and one to Cutler. Cutler was ordered to leave voice messages when she had something to report.

"On the evening that Walsh was murdered, Cutler followed her to the Dulles Towne Center parking lot and reported the position of

Walsh's car in the lot. That means that the client was one of a small group of people who knew the exact location where Walsh would be after she left the farm. Cutler followed the Secret Service agent and Walsh to the farm where she met President Farrington. Cutler reported to the client when Walsh left the farm to return to the mall, but a guard spotted Cutler, and she couldn't continue following Walsh.

"Dana Cutler hung on to the cell phone Dale Perry gave her. She also gave us the number she called to leave the voice mail messages for the client and she gave us the date and time she called the client with the information about the location of Walsh's car. Once we had the client's number we were able to identify the cell phone provider. The cell phone provider stored the voice mail messages from Ms. Cutler on a backup computer and gave them to us along with the time they were retrieved.

"When a person wants to retrieve voice mail messages that have been left on his cell phone he dials a remote voice mail retrieval number for the provider's voice mail system from his cell phone. The system will ask the caller for a password. After the person punches in the password he's given his messages. The cell phone provider was able to give us the mystery client's remote voice mail retrieval number, but the provider did not have a record of telephone calls to the client's voice mail system between the time Cutler left the message explaining where Walsh was parked and the time she was murdered. They had no record because there was bad reception that night. Bad reception is common, and it can be intermittent. In this case, the client couldn't use his cell phone to call for his messages and he was forced to use a landline to retrieve them.

"As soon as we suspected that Mr. Hawkins was the mystery client we tried to learn where he was when Cutler left the message with the location of Walsh's car. We learned that he was at the Theodore Roosevelt Hotel. One of the Secret Service agents remembers him getting a call on his cell phone around nine-forty. The agent also remembers Mr. Hawkins complaining about the reception and leaving to try to get a clear signal.

"The hotel confirmed that Mr. Hawkins reserved a suite for Dr. Farrington so the first lady could rest if her pregnancy fatigued her. He also reserved an adjoining suite for security purposes. Several Secret Service agents remember Mr. Hawkins coming out of one of the two suites he reserved shortly after complaining about the poor reception on his cell phone.

"We went to the phone company and asked for a record of all calls to the cell phone company voice mail retrieval system telephone number in the D.C. area on the date and time in question. There were thousands of calls because everyone using the cell phone provider would call that number to get their voice mail, but only a few calls were made from the Theodore Roosevelt Hotel. Once we'd confirmed that calls had been made from the hotel we got the hotel records to see from what rooms the calls had been made. One room was in the suite adjoining Dr. Farrington's suite."

Evans stopped talking. Bischoff waited until it became obvious that the agent was finished presenting as much of his case as he was going to reveal.

"That's it?" the lawyer asked.

"I think I've given Mr. Hawkins enough to think about for the time being."

"You're going to indict Chuck based on the word of a man facing multiple death sentences and a cell phone call?"

"We have other evidence that I'm not prepared to reveal at this time," Evans bluffed.

The lawyer stood. "This has been very entertaining, but Mr. Hawkins and I have busy schedules."

"I understand, but you should understand this. I really want Mr. Hawkins. The only reason I would even think of cutting a deal with him is my belief that the president may be involved. If he is, the only way your client is going to come out of this alive is by cooperating, and I'm not going to wait very long for your call."

"I'll let you know Mr. Hawkins's position as soon as we've had a chance to confer," Bischoff said as he ushered his client out of the office.

"What do you think?" Evans asked Maggie Sparks and Gordon Buss as soon as the door closed.

"I wouldn't wait by the phone," the AUSA answered. "You've got as much of a chance of cutting a deal with Hawkins as I do with Osama bin Laden."

"Do you agree, Maggie?" Evans asked.

"I think the next time you talk to Hawkins he'll be sitting in the witness box in a federal court."

Evans sighed. "You're probably right. I knew it was a long shot, but I had to try."

Roy Kineer wasn't in, so Evans couldn't report on his meeting with Hawkins and Bischoff right away. Instead he went back to his office and read over a report he'd received from Oregon that morning. Clarence Little's pinkie collection had been printed. Laurie Erickson's pinkie was not a part of it, but Peggy Farmer's was. The report concluded that it was highly improbable that Little would have been able to kill Farmer and her boyfriend in Central Oregon and return to Salem in time to kill Laurie Erickson. The report cheered up Evans, who felt that the interview with Hawkins had been a complete bust.

Shortly before noon, Kineer's secretary told Evans that Justice Kineer was back and wanted to be briefed about the meeting. Evans spent an hour with the judge before his boss left to have lunch with several members of the House Judiciary Committee.

Evans had his secretary pick up a sandwich for him, which he ate at his desk. He was halfway through it when the receptionist buzzed to tell him that Gary Bischoff was on the phone. Evans was surprised.

"What's up, Gary?"

"Are you busy?" Bischoff asked. Evans thought he sounded upset.

"No, why?"

"We need to talk. Can you come to my office?"

"When?"

"Right now. Hawkins wants to cut a deal."

Evans was stunned. "Okay," he said, trying to sound nonchalant.

"And come alone. This is between the three of us."

"I'll be there."

Bischoff hung up without saying good-bye. Evans stared out the window, but he didn't see a thing. He had to believe that Hawkins was thinking of pleading guilty against the advice of his counsel, but he couldn't think of what he'd said that would have frightened a man as powerful as Hawkins into negotiating a guilty plea.

Chapter Forty-one

Gary Bischoff's law office occupied part of the first floor of an elegant red brick Federalist-style house on a quiet, tree-lined street in George-town. The stately home had been built in 1826 by a wealthy merchant, but Keith Evans was too preoccupied to pay any attention to the antiques, oil paintings, and period furniture that Bischoff used to furnish the place.

Bischoff's secretary showed the agent into an office in the back that looked out through leaded windows on a beautifully maintained garden where a very attractive woman was sunbathing in a lime bikini. Evans remembered reading that some years ago Bischoff and his first wife had been involved in a bloody divorce. He guessed that the woman in the backyard was Bischoff's trophy wife, which would explain Bischoff's rigorous exercise routine. She was at least fifteen years younger than the lawyer, who appeared to have aged since the morning meeting.

"I want you to understand that I've advised Mr. Hawkins against this course of action," Bischoff said, straining to maintain a professional demeanor, "but he's the client and he makes the ultimate decision on how he'll proceed."

"Okay, Gary, I understand."

Evans studied Hawkins, who was sitting in a high-backed

armchair, one leg crossed over the other, looking calm to the same degree that his attorney was agitated.

"Can I speak directly to Mr. Hawkins?"

Bischoff waved a hand at Evans, signaling that he wanted nothing to do with what was going to occur.

"Mr. Hawkins, may I record this conversation?" Evans asked as he took a cassette recorder out of his jacket pocket.

Hawkins nodded. Evans stated the date, the time, the place where the interview was being conducted, and the names of all present. Then he gave Hawkins his Miranda warnings.

"Mr. Hawkins, why are we here?" Evans asked as soon as Hawkins acknowledged the warnings.

"I want to plead guilty to the charges."

"All of them?" Evans asked, unable to hide his surprise.

"I'll have to see the indictments before I can answer that. But I'm prepared to accept responsibility for the crimes I committed."

"You understand that conviction for some of these crimes can carry a death sentence?"

"Yes."

"Gary says that he's advised you that this meeting is not in your best interest. Is that true?"

"He told me that you don't have much of a case. It's his opinion that it would be very difficult for a prosecutor to get a conviction."

"So why do you want to confess?"

"I'm Catholic. I have a conscience. I've done terrible things, and I want to atone for them."

Evans didn't buy the religious angle, but he wasn't going to stop Hawkins if he wanted to confess.

"I don't want to put words in your mouth," the agent said, "so why don't you tell me what crimes you believe you've committed?"

"Chuck, don't do this," Bischoff begged. "At least let me try to negotiate some concessions from the government."

"I appreciate your concern, Gary, but I know what I'm doing. If the authorities want to show me mercy, they will. I'm in God's hands now and I'm prepared to accept whatever He sees fit to give me."

Evans got the impression that the attorney and his client had debated Hawkins's position many times before his arrival, with Bischoff losing the argument every time.

"You were right about everything," Hawkins told Evans. "I killed Rhonda Pulaski, Tim Houston—"

"That's the chauffeur who saw President Farrington having sex with Pulaski?"

Hawkins's features tightened. When he spoke his tone was as cold as his eyes.

"Let's get one thing straight. I'm guilty of many things, but disloyalty to Christopher Farrington is not one of them. He's not responsible for my actions and I will not discuss him. If you insist on asking about the president of the United States this meeting will end."

"Okay, I accept that. Go ahead."

"I killed Mr. Houston. I also murdered Laurie Erickson and Charlotte Walsh."

"Why did you kill Erickson?"

"She was going to make false accusations against the president. She demanded money. Even though the accusations were false his career would have been ruined."

"How did you kill Erickson?"

"I left the papers for Chris's speech in my office in the mansion on purpose to give me an excuse to return. She was very slender. I knocked her out, wrapped her in sheets, and sent her down the laundry chute. I bound and gagged her in the basement, smuggled her out the basement door, put her in the trunk of my car, and returned to the fund-raiser. I'd read the police reports of Clarence Little's crimes. Later that night, I duplicated his modus operandi."

"Was Laurie Erickson alive during the fund-raiser?"

Hawkins nodded, and the image of the terrified girl, bound and gagged in suffocating darkness, made it difficult for Evans to maintain his composure.

"What about Charlotte Walsh?"

"Cutler sent me a voice mail telling me where she'd parked. I disabled her car and waited until she came back to the lot. Then I knocked her out, bound and gagged her, put her in my trunk, and drove to the farm to meet with the president."

"Was Walsh in your trunk while you were at the farm?"

Hawkins nodded.

"She was alive?"

Hawkins nodded again. "As soon as I could get away I killed her, duplicating the Ripper's MO. Then I left her in the Dumpster."

"Why did you have Dale Perry hire Cutler?"

"I didn't trust Walsh. I knew what had happened with Pulaski and Erickson. Those girls were a threat to the president's career. He's a great man. The country needs him. I couldn't let those whores bring him down."

For the first time, Hawkins's voice trembled with emotion. Evans might have some questions about Farrington's involvement, but he had no doubt about the depth of Hawkins's commitment to the president.

"If you already felt that Walsh was a threat, why did you need to have her followed?"

"I don't think you need to know that."

Evans could see that there were problems with Hawkins's story, but he decided that he wouldn't pressure Hawkins now. He'd let him talk himself out, put him behind bars, and hit him again when he'd had a nice taste of jail.

"Did Dale Perry commit suicide, did you kill him, or did you order Oscar Tierney or someone else to go after Cutler?"

"I don't want to discuss Dale Perry's death."

"We're going to cut Tierney a deal, so it won't hurt him."

"I may not have made myself clear, Agent Evans. I will tell you what I did but I will not implicate anyone else in a crime. I'm pre-pared to die for what I've done, but I won't take anyone down with me. And don't waste your time trying to persuade me to change my mind. I'm going to be executed, so there really isn't anything you can use to threaten me."

Evans saw nothing that convinced him that the president's aide could be moved.

"Mr. Hawkins, based on what you've told me I'm going to place you under arrest on kidnapping charges for taking Charlotte Walsh across state lines. We'll sort out all of the charges and the jurisdic-tional disputes later. Would you please stand and place your hands behind your back."

Hawkins did as he was told, and Evans snapped on a pair of cuffs.

"Maggie," Evans said into his cell phone, "I'm at Gary Bischoff's office. I need you and Gordon down here. Charles Hawkins has con-fessed to several murders."

Evans paused while Sparks said something.

"I'll go into it later. We need to book Hawkins, and I have to brief Justice Kineer. Can you get him back to headquarters for a meet-ing?"

Evans hung up and turned his attention back to the president's aide.

"I appreciate your honesty, Mr. Hawkins, but I think your loyalty to the president is misplaced. Your loyalty shouldn't be to the man but to the office and to the country Christopher Farrington swore to serve. If the president conspired with you to commit the crimes to which you've confessed he has betrayed his oath and he has betrayed the American people."

Justice Kineer had deserted his congressional lunch companions in the middle of their meal after telling Maggie Sparks to have a war council assembled by the time he returned to the office. When Keith Evans, Gordon Buss, and Maggie Sparks returned from booking Hawkins into jail they found the conference room packed with lawyers and investigators waiting to hear what had happened.

"Give me your best shot about what's going on here," Kineer asked Evans when the agent finished his summary of his meeting with Hawkins and Bischoff.

"It's pretty obvious, isn't it? Hawkins is falling on his sword to protect the president."

"Convicting Hawkins will be a hollow victory if Farrington is involved in the death of those girls and he skates. Can we do anything to prevent that from happening?" Kineer asked.

"Hawkins is the key," Evans said. "I can't think of anyone who can nail Farrington if Hawkins clams up, and believe me I've been thinking of nothing else since Hawkins told me he wouldn't talk about Farrington."

Kineer looked around the conference room. "Ladies and gentlemen, I suggest we all give this our undivided attention because our mission is to determine what involvement, if any, President Farrington has in these murders. If he's innocent, so be it. If he's guilty, we have to prove it. We need to decide if we can do that without Hawkins's cooperation. Does anyone have any bright ideas?"

After forty-five minutes of unproductive discussion Kineer shooed everyone but Evans out of the room.

"I notice you didn't have much to add to our discussion," the judge said.

"I couldn't think of anything to say."

"Is Farrington guilty, Keith?"

The excitement Keith had felt when Hawkins confessed had died away and the agent looked depressed.

"My gut tells me he is, but I don't think we can touch him if Hawkins won't talk."

"Can he be made to talk?"

"It's going to be tough. Hawkins is fanatically loyal. He's idolized Farrington since his college days, and he feels that he owes him his life. He has no family. He has acquaintances but no friends except for the Farringtons. Everything in his life revolves around the president and it has for a long time. I think he's going to say that he committed all of these crimes on his own. Everyone will believe him because he'll come off looking like a crazed killer who deluded himself into believing that the murders were necessary.

"But say he changes his story and implicates Farrington. The president's lawyer will crucify Hawkins by reading back all of the statements in which he exonerates Farrington. I think he's got us, judge."

Part Seven

The Queen of Hearts

Washington, D.C.

Chapter Forty-two

Brad got back to his apartment just before three after spending the morning and early afternoon at a law firm interviewing for a job. As soon as he checked for phone messages and e-mail, he changed into running gear. Now that all he had was free time, he was finally able to keep his resolution to exercise.

Working out hadn't been easy right after the shoot-out. Every time he left his apartment he had to run a gauntlet of reporters who wanted to know what had happened at the Erickson house. Television vans crowded the parking lot at his apartment complex and reporters tied up his phone lines at all hours. Brad wanted to tell everybody what he knew about the Clarence Little case, but Keith Evans had explained that the independent counsel's investigation could be compromised if he talked to the press, so Brad had been forced to stick to "no comment."

Shortly after the last reporter called him about the shoot-out, a reporter from the *Portland Clarion*, Portland's alternative newspaper, phoned to ask Brad to comment on Paul Baylor's report, which had concluded that Peggy Farmer's pinkie was in with the rest of the fingers, but Laurie Erickson's was nowhere to be found. Brad knew about the report because Ginny had used her feminine wiles to get information out of the associate Tuchman had assigned to take over Little's appeal, but he had no idea how the reporter had learned about the pinkies. When the reporter said that a confidential source had given him the information Brad suspected immediately that the leak originated with Ginny. His suspicions grew stronger when the reporter told him that the anonymous caller had suggested that Brad had been fired for pursuing the *Little* case too vigorously because of Susan Tuchman's ties to the president.

A few days later, a scathing editorial in the *Clarion* condemned Tuchman for firing an associate who'd gone above and beyond the call of duty to try to prove that a client had been unjustly convicted of murder. The editorial pointed out that Brad had put principle above public opinion by risking his life to see justice done even though his client was detestable.

Brad showered when he finished his run. Then he called Ginny to discuss their plans for the evening.

"Reed, Briggs, Stephens, Stottlemeyer and Compton."

"Ginny Striker, please."

"Whom shall I say is calling?"

"Jeremy Reid of Penzler Electronics."

"One moment, please."

Brad waited for Ginny to answer.

"Hey," he said.

"Thank goodness you were smart enough to use an alias. You have no idea how persona non grata you are around here since the *Clarion* published that editorial."

"Tuchman deserves everything she gets."

"I couldn't agree more, but it would mean my job if anyone found out we were dating."

"Is that what we're doing? I thought I was bartering food for sex."

"Pig. So, how was the interview?"

"Good. I'll tell you about it tonight. Will you want to go to the movie straight from work or will you have enough time to go home, change, and come back downtown."

"I'm not certain I'll have time for a movie and dinner. I'll call you when I've got a handle on my workload. Are you going to be at home?"

"That's where I am now. I'll be here for the rest of the afternoon."

"Okay. Let me try to clear my desk. I'll see you soon."

Brad felt a little guilty that Ginny had to work while he spent his days as he pleased. Besides running, he'd hiked in the mountains and at the coast and had gone to an occasional movie. Then there were the pleasant afternoons sitting on his deck reading a book and sipping a cool drink. The life of leisure sure beat toiling away in the bowels of Reed, Briggs, but Brad knew those days were numbered. He'd have to get a job soon if he wanted to feed himself and keep a roof over his head.

Ginny joined him on the weekends when work permitted and he'd been spending his nights at her place when she wasn't too tired. Brad was a fair chef. On two occasions he'd spent an afternoon working up an elaborate menu for their evening meal. Ginny had paid him back with some of the best sex ever and all the office gossip she could dig up.

Another way Brad spent his time when he wasn't hiking, cooking, or looking for work was by keeping up with the independent counsel's investigation. He'd absorbed every piece of information about it in *Exposed*, the *New York Times*, and other media outlets. He knew more about the case than most. While they were driving to Marsha Erickson's house Dana Cutler had told him what had happened after Dale Perry hired her to tail Charlotte Walsh. Most of that information had been in *Exposed*, but Brad had learned about the shoot-out at the motel, which had happened after she'd given Patrick Gorman the story.

Keith Evans checked in on Brad from time to time because Brad was a witness. When they talked, Brad pumped the FBI agent for news, but Evans was tight-lipped and Brad rarely got any information that the media didn't have.

To kill time until Ginny called, Brad read about new evidence against Charles Hawkins that the *New York Times* had unearthed. A photographer had snapped a shot in the meeting room at the Theodore Roosevelt Hotel. The photograph showed Hawkins off to one side answering his cell phone as the first lady finished posing with the last contributor in front of President Roosevelt's clock. The clock read 9:37, which was around the time Dana Cutler said she'd phoned her mystery client with the news that Charlotte Walsh was returning to the Dulles Towne Center lot from the farm.

Something about the photo bothered Brad, but he couldn't figure out what it was. He wandered into the kitchen, poured a cup of coffee, and carried it out on the deck. While he watched the traffic on the river he sipped from his cup and worried the problem, but nothing came to him. He was still stumped when Ginny called.

Brad was lost in a swamp, fighting his way through mud that sucked at his shoes and vines so thick that he could barely see where he was going. The heat was unbearable—a heavy blanket that wrapped around him, making it hard to move or breathe. From somewhere in the swamp two women begged him for help and he despaired that there wasn't time to rescue both of them. He wanted to give up but he couldn't.

In the dream, Ginny stood next to him. Instead of offering encouragement, she calmly informed him, "It just can't be done. There isn't enough time to go one place then get to the other."

Brad shot up in bed, his heart pounding. He knew what had bothered him the day before. When he spoke to Ginny after returning from his run Brad had asked if she had enough time to go home and change before coming downtown or if she was just going to go to the movie straight from work. Ginny had told him that she might not have time to go to a movie and eat dinner.

Brad groped for the light on his nightstand and turned it on. He was bathed in sweat, and his breathing was labored. He swung his legs over the side of the bed and tried to calm down. The important thing was to hold on to the dream. In it Brad was panicky because there wasn't enough time to be in two places at one time. His subconscious was trying to point out that on the evening of Charlotte Walsh's murder Charles Hawkins had been faced with the same predicament. Had everyone been going at this case the wrong way?

The clock on Brad's nightstand said it was 5:58. He knew there was no way he could get back to sleep, so he went into the bathroom and prepared to face the day. While he brushed his teeth, Brad made a plan of action. He would eat breakfast then reread everything that bore on the time element. Just as he ducked under the medium hot spray in the shower a sudden thought distracted him. He paused, the bar of soap in his hand and water cascading down his face and chest. There had been something in Laurie Erickson's autopsy report that had made no impression on him when he read it. Now the memory triggered a really scary idea.

After finishing in the bathroom, Brad put up coffee and toasted a bagel. As soon as he was done with breakfast, he started reviewing the file in Clarence Little's case and the articles about the Erickson and Walsh murders he had collected. It was almost eight when he finished reading the item he'd intentionally saved for last, Laurie Erickson's autopsy report. Brad sat back and stared at the wall across from the couch. A colorful print he'd purchased from a street artist in Greenwich Village hung over the fireplace, but he didn't see it. His thoughts were elsewhere.

When he'd worked the problem through, Brad went into his bedroom and got his appointment book. A few weeks ago, one of the partners had ordered him to call a doctor at home in the evening after court had recessed in a medical malpractice trial. He'd written the number in his book. The witness was the only doctor he knew in Portland. When the doctor picked up the phone, Brad asked him a question. When the doctor answered it, Brad felt sick. He hung up and sat quietly for a few moments. Then he found Keith Evans's card and dialed his cell phone. The agent answered after a few rings.

"This is Brad Miller. I'm calling from Portland."

"What's up, Brad?"

"I had an idea."

"Yes," Evans prodded when Brad hesitated.

"It's kind of crazy."

"Let's hear it."

"Can you answer a question about the autopsy report in Charlotte Walsh's case first?"

"I will if I can."

"Is there any evidence that Walsh received a stab wound to her brainstem?"

Evans was silent for a moment while he tried to recall the details of the report.

"Yes, I think there was something about that in the report," he answered. "Why?"

"You're not going to like what I have to say but I think you have a problem."

Chapter Forty-three

The events that followed Brad's call to Keith Evans would have been very exciting if Brad wasn't scared to death. First there was the black car filled with very serious FBI agents that spirited him away from his apartment less than an hour after Evans ended their call. Then there was the nonstop flight on the FBI jet to a military airfield somewhere near Washington, D.C., followed by the drive from the airfield to the safe house where Dana Cutler was living and the warning to stay inside and away from the windows so snipers would not have a good shot. And then there was the most terrifying part of the whole affair for someone who was a good but not great attorney—explaining his theory to retired United States Supreme Court Justice Roy Kineer, one of the greatest minds in jurisprudential history.

Brad guessed that Justice Kineer had a lot of practice greeting awestruck neophyte attorneys because Kineer did everything he could to put Brad at ease when Keith Evans ushered him and Dana Cutler into the conference room at the offices of the independent counsel.

"Mr. Miller, thank you so much for coming," the judge said as he extended his hand and flashed a big smile. "Agent Evans was effusive in his praise for your deductive abilities, and I'm very anxious to hear your theory."

Brad couldn't think of anything to say so he flashed a nervous smile.

"Can I get you something to drink?" Kineer asked. "We have coffee, tea, and soft drinks, and we might even be able to rustle up a
latte, or whatever is popular in your neck of the woods? I hear there's
a Starbucks not far from here."

"Actually, New York is my neck of the woods. I just moved to
Portland. So black coffee would be great, if it's no trouble?"

Kineer's smile shifted to Dana. "I'm also very pleased to finally
meet you, Miss Cutler. Can I get you something?"

"I'm fine."

"No thanks to Charles Hawkins from what I hear. It seems that
you've had several close calls."

The judge sent a young assistant to get Brad's coffee. Then he
turned to the nervous attorney.

"Let's get down to business, Brad. Can you sit by me? I'm a little
hard of hearing."

Kineer went to the head of a small conference table. Evans sat at
the other end with Cutler beside him. A middle-aged man and a
woman in her early thirties sat across from Brad. The man had a
notepad in front of him. The woman looked intense. Kineer introduced them as staff attorneys.

"So, what do you have for us?" he asked Brad, who suddenly
doubted every clever deduction he'd made. It had been one thing to
speculate about the case in his apartment and another to explain it to
Roy Kineer.

"I could be way off base on this," Brad hedged.

"Mr. Miller, I respect people who think outside the box. You can
get A's on law school exams by having a good memory, but you can't
ace a real case without exercising a little creativity. So let's have it.
The worst thing that will happen is that you'll be wrong." Kineer
smiled. "If you are I promise it will not go on your permanent record.
And if you're right—and Agent Evans thinks you may be—then you'll
have saved us all from looking like fools."

"Okay. We know that President Farrington couldn't have personally killed Charlotte Walsh."

"Agreed," Kineer said.

"Well, Mr. Hawkins couldn't have done it either. It takes about forty-five minutes to go from the Theodore Roosevelt Hotel to the Dulles Towne Center mall, about an hour to go from the mall to the safe house, and roughly an hour to go from the hotel to the CIA safe house. The picture in the *New York Times* proves that Hawkins was still at the hotel at nine-thirty-seven.

"We know that Charlotte Walsh was dropped off at the mall around eleven and the Secret Service logged Hawkins in at the farm at eleven-fifteen. If Hawkins got to the mall around ten-thirty and waited to kill Walsh at eleven, there's no way he could have gotten to the safe house at eleven-fifteen. If he went from the hotel to the farm and arrived at eleven-fifteen, there's no way he could have killed Walsh after she returned to her car."

"We've already worked that out," the judge said, "but it's encouraging to see that you know enough about the case to come to the same conclusion."

"Okay, well, Hawkins has men who are willing to commit murder for him. He sent them to Dana's apartment, Marsha Erickson's house, the hospital, and the motel in West Virginia. So Hawkins could still be guilty of Walsh's murder as an aider and abettor. But there's a problem with this theory. The earliest Hawkins could have learned about the location of Walsh's car in the mall was eight, when Cutler phoned in her report, but there's no record of anyone phoning to retrieve voice messages from any spot in the Theodore Roosevelt Hotel that's connected to Hawkins until the call that was made from the suite adjoining the first lady's suite around nine-forty-five. If Hawkins didn't learn the location of Walsh's car until then, he would have had to find Tierney and organize the hit fast enough to get Tierney to the mall before eleven. I guess that's possible, but it would be hard.

"Also, Tierney denies that he or any of his team killed Walsh. He could be lying, but seeing that he's already admitted to several murders it wouldn't make much sense to deny killing Walsh."

"We're with you so far, Brad," Kineer said.

"Once I realized that President Farrington and Hawkins couldn't have murdered Walsh personally and it was improbable that men working for Hawkins or the president had committed the murder I started to wonder if everyone wasn't approaching the case from the wrong direction. We've been assuming that Rhonda Pulaski, Laurie Erickson, and Charlotte Walsh were murdered because they were a threat to Christopher Farrington's political career, but they all have something else in common. Farrington was cheating on his wife with each of them, and that gave Claire Farrington one of the oldest motives in the book to kill them. When that thought occurred to me I remembered something I'd read in Laurie Erickson's autopsy report.

"According to the medical examiner, Erickson was almost decapitated when Clarence Little hacked away at every inch of her neck with a sharp object, tearing the skin to ribbons. The report also said that Little had sliced off several body parts *after* Erickson was dead. The only point about which the medical examiner had any question was the discovery of a subdural hemorrhage over the brainstem for which he could find no source.

"I asked a doctor in Portland about the subdural hemorrhage. He said that sticking a sharp object into the base of the back of the neck between the skull and the first cervical vertebra would sever the spinal cord and cause instant death without much bleeding. If the medical examiner didn't remove the brain, the only evidence of the cause of death would be a subdural hemorrhage.

"The ME in Oregon was sloppy and had his pathology assistant remove the brain. That's why he didn't look at the injury in situ. He couldn't see the entry wound for the sharp object because the neck had been hacked to pieces, and he didn't find a source for the subdural hemorrhage because he was so certain that Little murdered Erickson that he didn't pay attention to the spinal cord injury.

"I asked Agent Evans about the Walsh autopsy report. He told me that there were a large number of slashing wounds all around the neck, which is similar to what was done to Laurie Erickson's neck. He also told me about a difference between the way Walsh was assaulted and the assaults on the other Ripper victims. The other victims were mutilated *before* they died, but most of Walsh's wounds were post-mortem.

"Now, here's the crucial piece of information from Walsh's autopsy: she died because a sharp instrument was thrust into the base of the back of her neck between the skull and the first cervical vertebra, just as in the Erickson case. This severed Walsh's spinal cord and caused instant death but hardly any bleeding. The doctor who conducted the Walsh autopsy found the wound when he took out the brain.

"I asked the doctor in Portland if a scalpel could have been used to kill Laurie Erickson. He said it would do the trick. Claire Farrington is a medical doctor. She'd have a scalpel and would know how to use it to kill someone in the manner in which Erickson and Walsh died. Dr. Claire Farrington had the means and motive to kill both women."

"Didn't Mr. Hawkins see Erickson alive when Dr. Farrington was at the library fund-raiser?" Kineer asked.

"We only have Hawkins's word that Erickson was alive when he saw her. What if Dr. Farrington dosed her son so he would sleep all night then killed Laurie just before she left for the library, wrapped her in bedsheets, and dropped her down the laundry chute? At the fund-raiser, she tells Hawkins what she's done. Hawkins rushes back to the governor's mansion on the pretext of retrieving his notes, gets rid of the body, and makes the murder look like the work of Clarence Little."

"Why would Hawkins do that?" Kineer asked.

"Three reasons. One, he's been in love with Dr. Farrington since college; two, he's fanatically loyal to the Farringtons; and three"—Brad paused—"he'd done it before.

"Judge, I have no evidence to prove this—not one iota of proof—but the police never figured out who killed Rhonda Pulaski. What if Claire Farrington ran her down and told Charles Hawkins? What if Hawkins sanitized the hit-and-run car to protect Claire then got rid of the chauffeur?"

"That's an interesting idea, but, as you just said, there's no evidence to support your theory. Hawkins is taking full responsibility for the Pulaski and Houston murders."

"True, but President Farrington wouldn't have had the money to pay off the Pulaski family to keep them from going to the authorities after they learned that he was sexually involved with their daughter. He'd have had to turn to his wife, who was from a wealthy family. If he did, you can bet that Dr. Farrington knew what was going on."

"You can't get an indictment with guesses so why don't we move on to Charlotte Walsh. Assuming you're right about Dr. Farrington killing Laurie Erickson, how did she murder Charlotte Walsh when she was asleep in her suite at the Theodore Roosevelt?"

"Agent Evans told me that Claire Farrington went into her suite around ten and left a little after one. No one checked on her during that time. Dr. Farrington asked Hawkins to reserve adjoining suites. What if she suspected that her husband was having an affair with Charlotte Walsh? Maybe someone saw them together in Chicago. She could have been the person who asked Dale Perry to hire someone to follow Walsh and report to her."

"You're saying that Claire Farrington was Dale Perry's mystery client?"

"Yes. We know that President Farrington called Hawkins from the farm as soon as Charlotte Walsh stormed out. I think that was the call he took at nine-thirty-seven, when Dr. Farrington was posing with the contributors in front of the clock. Hawkins had bad reception. The Secret Service later saw him come out of the suite adjoining Dr. Farrington's suite. I think he ended up using the landline in that suite to find out about the president's call.

"I think Claire Farrington tried to check her voice messages on her cell phone once she was alone in her suite and found that she couldn't connect because of the bad reception. She could have used the phone in the adjoining suite so it would not appear that calls were made from her suite and learned where Walsh parked her car. She could have arranged for someone who knew about the adjoining suites, like Dale Perry, to leave a change of clothes in the suite and a vehicle somewhere on the street. Dr. Farrington could have gone through the adjoining suite, out the door, and down the stairwell. She would have been able to get to the mall just before Walsh arrived and would have had time to disable Walsh's car, kill her with the scalpel, and call on Hawkins again to get rid of the body. Then she could tell Hawkins that Dale Perry knew too much and Hawkins could have arranged to have him killed in a way that looked like a suicide."

"'That's a lot of 'ifs,'" Kineer said.

Brad had grown more confident as he spoke, more certain that he was right.

"What are the odds of two women who live a continent apart and have connections to Christopher Farrington being stabbed with a scalpel in the space between the skull and first cervical vertebra before having their necks mutilated to hide the entrance wound?" Brad asked the judge. "What are the odds that two different murderers a continent apart would make their killings of these two women look like the work of an active serial killer?

"What's more, if the killers wanted the police to think that Little and Loomis killed Erickson and Walsh why use a method to murder them that was totally alien to their MOs? On the other hand, it makes perfect sense if the victims were intentionally killed with the strike to the brainstem and the decisions to mimic Little and Loomis were made after the victims were dead."

"Point taken, but we're still dealing with a lot of speculation. What do you think, Keith?"

"I think there's a lot to what Brad's said. We've checked the phone records of the Theodore Roosevelt Hotel. Two calls were made from the suite adjoining the suite where Claire Farrington took her nap. They were made around ten in the evening, but they were made within five minutes of each other. Unfortunately, we can't pinpoint the time that the Secret Service agents saw Hawkins leave the adjoining suite so we can't prove that he didn't make both calls, but the time interval suggests two different callers.

"And we've also come up with this," Evans said as he handed copies of two grainy, black-and-white photographs to Justice Kineer. In one picture a person in jeans and wearing gloves and a hooded sweatshirt was going up a flight of stairs. In the other, the same person was going down.

"These were taken by a surveillance camera in the stairwell leading down to the lobby of the Theodore Roosevelt shortly after ten. I've had an agent make a trial run for me. A person leaving at this time and driving at night when the traffic would be minimal could get to the spot in the mall where Walsh parked in enough time to disable Walsh's vehicle and hide herself."

"Is there any way to determine if this person is a man or a woman?" Kineer asked. "I can't tell."

Evans shook his head. "We can't determine the sex."

Kineer looked around the room. "Any suggestions on what to do next?"

When no one answered Kineer smiled. "Do I have any volunteers who want to accuse a pregnant first lady of being a serial murderer?"

Chapter Forty-four

Keith Evans had survived gunfights and gone one-on-one with hardened psychopaths, but he still felt insecure as he followed the Secret Service agent up the stairs to the family quarters of the White House. The agent tried to convince himself that this would be like any other witness interview, but he failed miserably. He and Justice Kineer were not going to be grilling some two-bit drug dealer. They were going to be interrogating the first lady of the United States, an expectant mother who was married to the most powerful man in the world. Evans knew his career could go swirling down the toilet if he screwed up.

The Secret Service agent opened a door for Kineer and Evans, and they stepped into a cozy sitting room. The upholstered furniture sported a bright floral pattern that matched the drapes surrounding several floor-to-ceiling windows. Along the walls were a cherrywood writing desk and tall cupboards displaying pewter mugs and dinnerware from colonial times. Pastoral landscapes in gilt frames added to the feeling that the visitors were going to conduct their interview in the country home of an eighteenth-century American.

A man of average size, dressed in a dark blue business suit and sporting a trim, salt-and-pepper beard and wire-rimmed glasses was waiting at the door.

"Good afternoon, Mort," Roy Kineer said to Morton Rickstein.

"Good afternoon, Judge," Rickstein replied. The dapper lawyer and the former justice weren't friends, but they'd bumped into each other often enough at social and legal functions to call themselves acquaintances.

"Do you know Dr. Farrington?" Rickstein asked.

"We've met on a few occasions," Kineer answered, turning toward the woman seated in front of a tall window through which the sun shone. Claire Farrington's back was straight and a smile of mild amusement played on her lips as she studied her visitors the way a queen might regard a supplicant from an outlying part of her realm.

Kineer had forgotten how large and powerful Claire Farrington looked. The first signs of motherhood did nothing to diminish his feeling that it would have been easy for her to overpower girls like Charlotte Walsh and Laurie Erickson.

"This is Keith Evans, Dr. Farrington," Kineer said. "He's with the FBI, but I had him seconded to me because he was the lead investigator in the D.C. Ripper case."

"I'm pleased to meet you, Agent Evans," Farrington said. "You did fine work apprehending Eric Loomis."

"Thanks," Evans said, noting that she hadn't complimented him for arresting Charles Hawkins.

Kineer and Evans found a seat on a couch that was catty-corner to Claire Farrington's high-backed chair. Evans placed his attaché case on the floor next to a coffee table made of dark polished wood.

"Why do you feel it's necessary to interview Dr. Farrington?" Rickstein asked when Evans and the judge were comfortable.

"She's a close personal friend of Charles Hawkins," Justice Kineer answered.

"You don't intend to call her as a witness, do you?"

"I can't guarantee that. Dr. Farrington was with Mr. Hawkins on the evening of Charlotte Walsh's murder and may have evidence relevant to the case."

"I understood that Mr. Hawkins has confessed and plans to plead guilty. If there's not going to be a trial why would you need Dr. Farrington?"

"It's not sufficient to obtain a confession," Kineer said to the attorney before changing his focus from Rickstein to the first lady. "We have to be certain that Mr. Hawkins committed the crimes to which he's confessing. Sometimes people confess to a crime they didn't commit because they're mentally ill or they want publicity or they're covering up for the real perpetrator."

Farrington's expression and demeanor didn't alter.

"Do you have any reason to doubt Mr. Hawkins's confession?" Rickstein asked.

"There are parts of it that are causing us some concern so, unfortunately, we have to keep pressing our investigation."

"What parts?" Rickstein asked.

Kineer smiled. "I'm afraid I can't go into that at this time. Confidentiality and all that. You understand, Mort."

"Sure. Why don't we get on with this. You ask your questions and Dr. Farrington will answer them unless I tell her not to or she doesn't want to."

"Fair enough," Kineer said. He turned to Evans. "Keith knows more about the cases so he'll be asking the questions. Keith?"

"Thank you for taking the time to talk to us. I know you're really busy," Evans said.

"Chuck is a dear friend. I can't believe what's happening to him."

Evans nodded sympathetically. "Where did you two meet?"

"We were all in the same year at OSU."

"Oregon State University?"

"Yes. And we were all athletes. He and Chris were on the basketball team, and I played volleyball."

"I hear you were very good."

"Yes, I was," Claire answered without hesitation.

"Was Mr. Hawkins very good?"

"Not particularly. He wasn't a starter like Chris. He had some good games but most of the time he rode the bench."

"I understand you and Mr. Hawkins dated in college."

"Yes."

"Did you go out with the president at OSU?"

"We double-dated, Chuck and me and Chris with whoever he was dating."

"So the president and Mr. Hawkins were close?"

"Yes."

"Did the president have a steady girlfriend in college?"

A look of distaste changed the first lady's features for a second and then it was gone.

Claire answered stiffly. "Chris was the big man on campus and found it easy to attract women."

"When did you start going out with the president?" Evans asked.

"Isn't this getting a bit far afield?" Rickstein asked. "Dr. Farrington has a busy schedule, and she's been gracious enough to set aside this time for you, but we'll be here forever if you go over information that's readily available in every magazine and newspaper that's been covering the campaign."

"Good point," Evans conceded. "Dr. Farrington, would you say that Mr. Hawkins is intensely loyal to you and the president?"

"We helped him through some very tough times after he got out of the military and he's always been grateful."

"So he would do anything for you and Mr. Farrington?"

"I can't speak for Chuck."

"He wouldn't hesitate to help you if you were in trouble?"

"Again, I can't speak for Mr. Hawkins."

"Has he helped you or the president with personal problems?"

"What do you mean?"

"Mr. Hawkins has confessed to murdering Rhonda Pulaski and Tim Houston."

The first lady stiffened. "What has that got to do with me?"

"The Pulaskis were paid to keep quiet about your husband's sexual relationship with their teenage daughter . . ."

"My husband represented Miss Pulaski in a lawsuit, a *successful* lawsuit. She got greedy and tried to blackmail him with an outrageous allegation. No one was paid off."

"The Pulaskis say they were paid to keep quiet."

"Then they're lying."

"Agent Evans," Rickstein interrupted, "Mr. Hawkins confessed to the murders. I don't see what the first lady had to do with it."

"Dr. Farrington, did you give your husband money to pay off the Pulaskis?" Evans asked.

"I'm not going to answer any more questions about those people."

"I think we can move on, Keith," Kineer said amiably.

"Did you notice anything unusual in Mr. Hawkins's demeanor on the evening of the fund-raiser at the Theodore Roosevelt Hotel?"

"No, but I was preoccupied with my speech and I wasn't feeling well. I had a bad bout of morning sickness."

"So I understand. In fact, you'd reserved a suite at the hotel for just this contingency, hadn't you?"

"Yes."

"On the day of the fund-raiser."

"Yes."

"Two suites, actually? Adjoining suites?"

"That's correct. We needed to make certain that no one was next door for security reasons."

"I understand that Mr. Hawkins made the arrangements."

"Yes."

"The Secret Service told us that you stopped to use the ladies' room on your way to your photo op because you weren't feeling well."

"That's correct."

"Did you happen to check your cell phone for messages when you were in the ladies' room?"

The first lady hesitated and eyed Evans suspiciously before responding with a terse, "No."

Evans pulled two black-and-white photographs out of his attaché case and held them up so Dr. Farrington and Mort Rickstein could see them. In one picture a person in jeans and wearing gloves and a hooded sweatshirt was going up a flight of stairs. In the other, the same person was going down.

"Do you have an idea who this person is?" the agent asked.

Dr. Farrington leaned forward and studied the photograph for a few seconds. Then she shook her head.

"I'm sorry but I don't recognize this man."

"We're not one hundred percent certain it is a man," Evans said. "It could be a tall woman."

"What does this have to do with Mr. Hawkins?" Mort Rickstein asked.

"We're not certain it has anything to do with him."

"Then why are you showing these pictures to me?" Dr. Farrington asked.

"The pictures were recorded by a security camera in the stairwell of the Theodore Roosevelt Hotel shortly after ten on the evening of the fund-raiser you attended. There's a door to the stairwell opposite the suite adjoining the one in which you were resting. Dale Perry drew away the Secret Service agent who was watching the stairwell exit on two occasions that evening. If someone wanted to sneak in or out of the hotel by using the stairwell they would have had an opportunity when the guard wasn't watching the stairwell door."

"Why would that matter to me? I was asleep from ten to shortly before one."

"Did you ever go into the adjoining suite to use the phone?"

"No, why would I? There was a phone on the nightstand in the suite where I was taking my nap. I would have used that phone if I wanted to make a call."

Rickstein looked suspicious. "What's going on here?"

"Two calls were made from the suite adjoining the suite where Dr. Farrington was taking her nap. Mr. Hawkins made one of the calls around ten. We're trying to figure out if he made both calls," Keith said.

Rickstein frowned. "I thought this interview was going to be about Chuck Hawkins but I'm beginning to suspect that you have another agenda, Roy."

"Certain facts have come to light that have led us to believe that Dr. Farrington may be involved in the Pulaski, Erickson, and Walsh cases."

Rickstein looked astonished. "Involved how?"

"I'm afraid I can't be more specific," Kineer answered.

"Then I'm afraid I'm going to have to terminate this meeting."

Evans had been watching Claire Farrington closely during this exchange. She had said nothing, but she had stared hard at Roy Kineer with a look that Evans interpreted as pure hate.

"Good afternoon, Dr. Farrington," Justice Kineer said. "Thank you for taking time to meet with us."

Farrington didn't answer. A moment after the FBI agent and the judge walked out of the sitting room, the door opened and Mort Rickstein stepped out.

"Hold up, Roy," he called out.

Kineer and Evans turned around.

"What's going on?" Rickstein demanded when he caught up to them.

"Just what I said."

"You don't really suspect Claire of having some kind of direct involvement in these killings?"

"We have some evidence that points that way."

For a moment, Rickstein looked dumbfounded. The he got control of himself.

"There's an old saying about not missing when you aim at a king. That goes for a queen, too. If I were you, I wouldn't breathe a word of your suspicions to anyone unless you've got one hundred percent proof of wrongdoing."

"Don't worry, Mort. I take my position very seriously. I won't aim at your client until I'm certain that I can't miss."

Rickstein stared hard at the jurist. Then he shook his head and walked back toward the sitting room.

"What do you think?" Kineer asked when the lawyer was out of earshot.

"I think it's first lady, a hundred; independent counsel, zero."

"I agree. I also think she's in this up to her neck, but we may not be able to prove it."

"At least we know why Hawkins flipped so quickly," Evans said. "It was the phone calls. He didn't want us thinking about the possibility that Dr. Farrington had used the phone in the adjoining suite to retrieve Cutler's voice messages."

"Hawkins is the only person who can nail Claire Farrington," Kineer said. "Do you think we can turn him?"

"This guy is a samurai, Judge. He's going to die for his emperor and empress."

"So, what do we do?"

Evans shook his head. "I have no idea."

The president had a meeting with the Joint Chiefs of Staff, but he hurried up to his living quarters as soon as it was over to find out why Justice Kineer had met with his wife that afternoon. Claire was waiting in their bedroom.

"What happened?" he asked anxiously.

"I think they know," Claire said calmly.

Farrington dropped heavily into an armchair. He looked stricken.

Claire smiled. "They know, but they can't prove a thing, Chris. You don't have to worry. We'll be fine."

Farrington looked up. "What if they . . . ?"

"They won't. Be strong. Look where we are," she said, moving her hand across the expanse of the room. "I knew we'd be here one day. No one is going to take this away from us."

Claire's features closed up like a steel door sealing in the contents of a safe. When she was like this, his wife frightened him.

"No one," she repeated in a voice so cold that there was no doubt about the lengths she would go to keep him in the White House and to keep any woman from interfering with her marriage.

Chapter Forty-five

Dana Cutler and Brad Miller were watching CNN's coverage of Charles Hawkins's guilty plea when Keith Evans walked into the living room of the safe house. Hawkins had insisted on pleading immediately in Maryland state court to the murder of Charlotte Walsh. Gary Bischoff had refused to represent Hawkins, so he'd retained a new lawyer whose smile when he faced the television cameras suggested that he wasn't the least bit troubled by pleading a client who might be innocent to a capital murder charge.

"Why aren't you at the courthouse?" Brad asked.

"I couldn't do it. It's too depressing. Hawkins is taking the heat for the Farringtons, and he's probably going to spend the rest of his life in prison or be executed for crimes he didn't commit."

"It's not like he's completely innocent, Keith," Brad said. "He probably murdered Houston, the chauffeur, and he sent those men to kill Dana. At minimum he covered up for Claire Farrington when she killed Rhonda Pulaski, leaving her free to kill Erickson and Walsh."

"Murders she'll never pay for because of Hawkins," Evans answered bitterly.

"In life, unlike the movies, there are often untidy endings," Dana Cutler said.

"You're not giving up, are you?" Brad asked.

"No, and neither is Justice Kineer. We're forging on with our investigation. We're just not doing very well. But enough of this discouraging news." Evans smiled. "I'm here to tell you that you'll be going back to your lives this afternoon. With Hawkins pleading, we don't think you're in danger anymore. Brad, you've got a first-class ticket back to Portland. Dana, you'll have to settle for me driving you back to your apartment in my heap."

"I'm so anxious to get out of house arrest I'd ride a tricycle home," Dana said.

"It's been a privilege knowing both of you," the agent told them. "I'm just sorry your efforts didn't result in the Farringtons paying for their crimes."

"Yet," Brad said.

"From your lips to God's ears," Evans said.

Brad and Dana went upstairs to pack. Dana came down first, and she and Evans engaged in small talk while they waited for Brad to return. The trio traded good-byes, then Brad got into a car and disappeared in the direction of the airport.

"Ready?" Evans asked Dana.

She tossed the duffel bag with her clothes into the backseat of Evans's car and got in beside him.

"What are your plans?" Evans asked when they'd been driving for a while.

"The same plans I had before I became entangled with the powerful and famous; stay below the radar and earn enough to feed myself and pay my rent."

"I wish you luck. I guess you've had enough excitement for a lifetime."

"I had my full quota of excitement long before Dale Perry hired me," Dana answered grimly.

Evans focused on the road, ashamed that he had forgotten what Dana Cutler had gone through. If Cutler was upset with him she didn't show it, and she seemed lost in thought during the rest of the drive.

"Do you happen to have copies of the photos showing the mystery person in the stairwell of the Theodore Roosevelt Hotel?" Dana asked when Evans parked in front of her apartment.

"Why?"

"I'd prefer not to say. But I'd appreciate getting copies of the photos and a complete set of the police reports detailing the crime scene at the Dulles Towne Center mall."

Evans studied the private detective. Dana's features revealed nothing.

"I'll see what I can do," Evans said.

Dana nodded. Then she was out of the car and inside her building. As soon as she closed her apartment door behind her Dana pulled out her cell phone.

"Jake, it's me, Dana," she said as soon as Teeny picked up.

"Where the hell have you been?"

Dana was pleased that he sounded worried.

"It's a long story and I want to tell it to you, but my car is parked down the street from your house and I don't have any wheels."

"Where's my Harley?"

"That's another long story."

"Do you know that the FBI questioned me? What have you gotten yourself into?"

"Come over and I'll tell you. We'll go out for dinner, my treat. Believe me, the story is worth the trip. Oh, and please bring the envelope I left on the desk in your study with the DVD."

Jake hung up and Dana carried her duffel bag into the bedroom. She was glad that she had someone like Jake to turn to, and it didn't hurt that he was a genius at anything to do with photography. As she sorted through her clothes she mulled over the idea that had been brewing since Keith Evans told her that Claire Farrington was going to get away with murder. Dana's heart went out to Rhonda Pulaski, Laurie Erickson, and Charlotte Walsh. They had all been good kids, and they'd died way too young. Dana was outraged that Claire

Farrington had taken their lives and she felt white-hot anger every time she realized how close she'd come to joining the first lady's collection of corpses.

There weren't many good things that had come out of her hideous experience in the basement of the meth lab, but being so close to dying that you said good-bye to life did free you of the fear of death. That didn't mean that you wanted to die, and Dana vowed to make Claire Farrington pay for taking her right to live so lightly.

Chapter Forty-six

Morton Rickstein was exhausted. It was 9:30 P.M. and he'd been in his office since 7:30 A.M. preparing for a deposition. Normally Rickstein dressed impeccably, but he was so tired that he didn't bother to roll down his shirtsleeves when he put on his jacket, and he left his tie at half-mast before grabbing his briefcase and trudging to the elevator that would take him to the parking garage. On the ride down Rickstein thought about how good it would feel to sit in his den with a scotch on the rocks.

The elevator doors opened, and Rickstein walked into the garage. He worked late frequently but he'd never gotten use to the eerie quiet of the underground lot at this time of night. Most of the cars were gone and much of the garage was in shadow. Rickstein imagined things unholy hiding in the pitch-black recesses and caught himself glancing furtively at the thick, concrete pillars that supported the roof. A killer could hide behind them, completely unseen, until an unsuspecting victim passed by.

There were three pillars between the elevator and his car and the lawyer tensed as he passed each one. Rickstein fished his electronic key out of his pocket and used the remote to unlock his car doors so he could get inside as quickly as possible. He heard the reassuring beep and hurried his step. When he arrived at his Lexus unharmed, he let out a breath and bent down to open the driver's door.

"Mr. Rickstein."

The lawyer swung around, his heart seizing in his chest. A woman had appeared out of nowhere. She looked like a hard case in her black jeans and motorcycle jacket.

"Sorry if I frightened you. My name is Dana Cutler. I'm a private investigator, and I've worked for your firm. I did most of my work for Dale Perry."

It took a second for Rickstein to recognize the name and connect it to the client of Dale Perry who had called to complain about being harassed by a Reed, Briggs associate. Dana Cutler was the woman who'd been involved in the shoot-out at Marsha Erickson's house in Oregon.

"Look, Miss Cutler, I've had a long day. Call my secretary tomorrow and make an appointment if you have something to discuss with me."

"This can't wait. My business concerns another Kendall, Barrett client, Claire Farrington."

Dana extended her hand toward Rickstein. In it was a manila envelope.

"I want you to give this to the first lady. There is a photograph and a cell phone in the package. You're free to have the cell phone examined to make sure it's not a bomb, but I'd advise you against looking at the photograph. You're better off not knowing what it shows. It might interfere with your ability to represent your client.

"When you give the envelope to Dr. Farrington tell her that I lied to the police when I said I didn't go back to the parking lot at the Dulles Towne Center mall. I wasn't planning on going back when I left her the voice message, but I got curious. Tell her I took several very interesting photographs that aren't in the envelope. I'll call her on the cell phone and tell her how she can get the pictures."

"I don't know what you're up to, but I'm not going to involve myself in it."

"I can't think of any other way to communicate with Dr.

Farrington. People like me can't just ring the doorbell at the White House and ask to meet with the first lady."

"What you're suggesting sounds like blackmail and I will not assist you. Furthermore, if I hear you're persisting in this scheme I'll go to the police and let them deal with you."

"You really don't want to do that, Mr. Rickstein. Not if you're concerned about the best interests of your client. Remember the photographs in *Exposed* that caused President Farrington's problems? I took them, and I tried to be fair. Before I went anywhere else I met with Mr. Perry and offered to sell the photos to the president. Dale and the president double-crossed me, so I sold them to *Exposed*. The stories in *Exposed* are probably going to cost Farrington the election. The picture in that envelope could cost your client her life. So you decide what to do, but make it fast. If you turn me down I'll call Patrick Gorman at *Exposed*. He gave me the number of his home phone after the success he had with my first batch of candid snapshots."

The morning after her meeting with Rickstein, Dana called the lawyer at his office to find out when he was going to meet with Claire Farrington. Dana figured that Rickstein would hand over the envelope in the first ten minutes of the meeting along with her message. Once Dr. Farrington got a glimpse of the photograph she would ask Rickstein to leave because she wouldn't want to risk the lawyer seeing it or overhearing her conversation with Dana. Dana calculated that the first lady would begin studying the picture about fifteen minutes after Rickstein's arrival. That's when she placed the call. She wanted Farrington to see the picture, but she didn't want to give her a lot of time to think before making her demands.

The first lady answered the phone after two rings.

"Dr. Farrington?"

"Who else would have this phone?" Farrington asked angrily.

"Getting upset won't solve your problem. This is strictly a

business proposition for me. I tried to explain that to Dale Perry and your husband but they decided it would be better to kill me than meet my very reasonable demands. Look where that got them. Dale's dead, and your husband is probably going to be out of a job come November. I can guarantee he'll lose the election and you'll go to prison by selling the photos of you at the Dulles Towne Center lot to *Exposed*, but they don't pay nearly as well as you will."

"What do you want?"

"Three million dollars wired today to the account number you'll find in the envelope. If the money is safely in my account you get the pictures."

"I have no idea what you think these photographs have to do with me. They just show someone in a sweatshirt opening a car door. You can't see the person's face. I can't even tell if it's a man or a woman."

Dana laughed. "I can see you're worried that I'm taping this conversation. I'm not. But if it makes you feel better I won't ask you to say anything incriminating.

"Getting back to the reasons you'll pay, there's no question that the person in my pictures is identical to the figure in the stairwell at the Theodore Roosevelt Hotel. More important, there is a very nice photograph I didn't give you for fear that Mort Rickstein's curiosity would get the better of him. In this photograph, the hood is back just enough to see you staring menacingly into Charlotte Walsh's car. Enlarge that baby and you're assured of a date with the executioner."

"I don't believe you have pictures that would affect me in the least. But even if I wanted to purchase your pictures, there's no way I can get three million dollars together today. And I certainly wouldn't pay a blackmailer a red cent without seeing these pictures you claim are so incriminating."

"If you want to see the pictures before paying I'll meet you tonight at midnight in the Dulles Towne Center lot at the spot where Charlotte Walsh parked. It's wide open at night, and I'll be able to make sure that you're alone."

"It would be extraordinarily difficult for me to get to you without a Secret Service escort."

"Tell them you don't want an escort."

"It's not that simple. The Secret Service won't follow my orders if I might be in danger. An agent will have to come with me."

"All right, you can have an agent drive you, but if you're planning to arrest me or have me killed, think twice. I know this is a horrible cliché, but I really did give a second set of pictures to a lawyer who'll send them to *Exposed* if I meet with an untimely death."

"Your demands are ridiculous. If I was concerned about your insane accusations I would also be concerned that you'd ask for more money as soon as I paid you. Blackmailers never stop their demands once they've got you hooked."

"Good point, but you have no choice but to trust me. I don't think you'd enjoy being perp-walked out of the White House on national television. And if you're still pissed off, think of our transaction this way: the three million is for the mental distress I've suffered from trying to stay alive these past weeks. I'm sure a jury would award me more than that if I sued you. But a lawsuit would take years. I prefer one fast transaction.

"And you really don't have to worry about me coming back for more. If you've been briefed on my background you know why I quit the police force. Pay me and I'm out of your life. All I want is to be left alone. Three million dollars will set me up for life."

Claire Farrington held the cell phone in her hands for several seconds after Dana Cutler ended their call. Then she laid it down next to her on the couch and stared at the photograph of the hooded person standing next to Charlotte Walsh's car. The photo looked as if it had been taken from a distance from the driver's side of Walsh's car. It showed a hooded figure standing next to the driver's door. Something about the picture bothered her. She didn't see it for a few seconds. Then she realized that the hooded figure in the photograph was identical to the hooded figure in the surveillance photo taken in the stairwell of the Theodore Roosevelt Hotel.

Claire stared intently at the picture for a few more moments. She smiled. Now she was certain that the picture was as phony as Dana Cutler's story. The hooded figure was standing so that her right hand appeared to be on the door handle. That was wrong. When she killed Walsh she had grabbed the handle with her left hand so she could pull the door past her left side. If she'd opened the door with her right hand it would have been between her and Walsh.

In Cutler's last voicemail message she'd said that she was finished following Walsh. That had been the truth. Cutler had not been in the lot when she killed Walsh. The first lady breathed a sigh of relief. She didn't know how Cutler had faked the picture, but she knew the picture wasn't real. Claire buzzed Irving Lasker.

A few minutes later, Lasker was seated next to Farrington.

"Irv, do you know how to fake a photograph or do you know someone who does?"

"I know a little bit about it."

Farrington handed Lasker the photograph. "How would you make the person in the hood look like he was standing next to this car if he really wasn't?" she asked.

"You'd use Photoshop software. First you'd scan the photo of the car and the photo of the man in the hood into your computer. Then you'd use a technique called feathering to manipulate the pixels on either side of the images. Feathering will make an image blurry at the line where the images are being pasted together. You take one or two pixels on either side of the image and feather them together. The image will look real."

"Is there a way to tell if feathering has been used to join the hooded person to the scene with the car in this picture?"

"Sure. You just magnify it. If the picture was created with

feathering, the pixels won't look clear and crisp like they would in a real photo."

"Please have someone check this photograph and get back to me. And I need this done immediately."

As soon as Lasker left the room, the first lady smiled. Ignoring Dana Cutler was the wise course of action, but Dana had crushed Chris's chances of keeping the presidency when she went to *Exposed*. She had to pay for that. If the photograph turned out to be a fake—and Claire was certain it would—she would meet Dana at midnight. But the meeting would definitely not go the way Miss Cutler thought it would.

Chapter Forty-seven

By midnight there were no cars in the remote section of the mall parking lot where Charlotte Walsh had been murdered. Dana waited in the shadows behind a light several rows from the spot where she'd told Claire Farrington to meet her. An hour and a quarter after Dana began her surveillance a car pulled in near the spot where Charlotte Walsh had parked her car. Irving Lasker got out. The first lady waited in the car while the Secret Service agent scoped out the area. When he gave the okay she got out and walked to the spot where Charlotte Walsh had parked. Farrington was dressed in jeans and a lightweight tan jacket. A baseball cap with the brim pulled down covered her hair. Dana waited a few beats then walked over to them with her hands held out from her sides.

"I assume you want to search me for weapons," she said. Lasker nodded then searched her thoroughly. When he was certain that Dana was unarmed he stepped away from the investigator.

"We need some privacy, Irv," Farrington said.

Lasker joined the driver, who was standing next to the car and scanning the lot.

"Let's see the photograph," Farrington said without preamble when she was sure that her escorts couldn't hear her.

Dana took an envelope out of her jacket pocket and handed it to the first lady. Farrington took a photograph out of the envelope and studied it. Someone had pasted a picture of her face into the hood of the sweatshirt. This job wasn't as well executed as the first and the fakery was even more obvious.

Farrington held up the photograph and looked over her shoulder at Lasker.

"Can you hold this, please," she asked, using the signal they'd agreed on earlier in the evening. Lasker and the other agent walked over casually. When he was a few steps from Farrington Lasker drew his gun, and the first lady stepped behind the other agent.

"You're under arrest, Miss Cutler, for extortion."

A triumphant smile lit up Claire Farrington's face. "You must think I'm awfully stupid. I didn't murder Charlotte Walsh, so I knew that the pictures you sent me were fakes. An expert has confirmed this."

Farrington was about to continue when three cars appeared at the side of the mall and headed their way.

"Get in the car," Lasker told his charge.

"You don't have to worry about the first lady," Dana said. "That's the FBI. I arranged for them to be here."

Farrington looked confused. Lasker ordered her to get into the car again and she obeyed, but her eyes never left the cars, which stopped moments later. Keith Evans got out and held up his identification.

"Hey, Agent Lasker, remember me?"

"What are you doing here, Evans?"

"Before I answer that, I have a few questions I need to ask you," Evans said in a tone low enough so Farrington could not hear him. "How did you know where to go tonight?"

"The first lady told me."

"What did she tell you?"

"She wanted to go to this mall."

"What did she say or do when you got to the mall?"

"She directed us to a spot in the parking lot."

"What were her exact words?"

"I don't remember her exact words, but as best I can recall, she told us to drive around the corner of the mall and go to this row. Then she had us stop near this parking space."

"She gave you specific directions?"

"Yes. Now what's going on?"

"I'm afraid the first lady is in a lot of trouble," Evans said.

"Hey, wait," Lasker said as Evans and Sparks walked to the back of Farrington's car.

"Please don't interfere, Agent Lasker," Evans said. The FBI agents from the other cars moved in on Lasker and the driver, and the Secret Service agents realized they were outnumbered.

Claire had lowered her window in an attempt to hear what was being said.

"Good evening, Dr. Farrington," Evans said.

"Good evening, Agent Evans. We've just arrested Dana Cutler for trying to extort three million dollars from me for a set of photographs allegedly showing me murdering Charlotte Walsh. Unfortunately for her, I knew the photographs couldn't be real and I had them examined by an expert."

Evans smiled. "The photos are faked and we know Miss Cutler asked you to pay three million dollars for them, but she wasn't extorting money from you. She was helping us prove that you murdered Charlotte Walsh."

Farrington looked amused. "How would a set of phony photographs do that?"

"Oh, the photographs wouldn't. We would never introduce them at a trial as direct evidence. On the other hand, they did lure you to this parking lot. Agent Lasker just told me that you knew the exact spot where Charlotte Walsh parked, the spot where she was murdered. Mind telling us how you learned that information?"

Farrington started to say something but she caught herself.

"That's okay," Evans said. "You don't have to talk to me. In fact, you have a right to remain silent because anything you say can and will be used in court to convict you. You also have a right to an attorney. If you can't afford a lawyer, the court will appoint one to represent you."

"This is ridiculous."

"Is it? Charlotte Walsh's body was found in a Dumpster behind a restaurant in Maryland. As far as the public knows that was where she was murdered. There were rumors that she was killed here, but we were very hush-hush about the location in the lot. We towed the car without the press learning where it was discovered. In fact, very few people knew the exact spot where she was killed."

"Charles Hawkins . . ."

"Confessed to a crime he could not have committed. We can prove it was impossible for him to do it. He didn't have time to go from the hotel to the farm, meet the president at eleven-fifteen, and murder Miss Walsh in this lot at eleven. But you had time to sneak out of the hotel after Dale Perry diverted the guard at the stairwell, come here, kill Miss Walsh, and return to the hotel before one."

"This conversation is over," Farrington told the agents before calling to Lasker.

"Irv, please take me back to the White House."

"Sorry, Dr. Farrington, that's not going to happen right now," Keith Evans said. "I'm placing you under arrest. We'll do this quietly. I've already arranged to have a judge available, and Mort Rickstein will be meeting you at the federal courthouse. Given who you are, I bet he'll be able to get you released immediately. Everyone in this country will be fascinated to find out what happens after that."

Chapter Forty-eight

Dana finished giving a detailed statement to the FBI at three in the morning. She should have been exhausted but she drove away from the office of the independent counsel on a high that acted like a triple shot of espresso. Charlotte Walsh, Laurie Erickson, and Rhonda Pulaski had been avenged. Their spirits could rest easily because she had nailed Claire Farrington.

Dana was still too excited for sleep when she parked in Jake Teeny's driveway. Jake opened the front door before she could get out her key.

"Are you okay?" he asked, his concern obvious in his voice and on his face.

Dana pulled Jake to her and kissed him. Jake tightened, surprised by the ferocity of the kiss. Then he wrapped his arms around her and hugged her. "I love you," Dana said. "I've loved you for a long time but I've been too fucked-up to tell you."

Jake pushed Dana to arm's length. He stared at her, as if uncertain that he'd heard her correctly. Dana's high disappeared in an instant. She'd spoken without thinking, and she knew that when she'd said she loved him, she'd just messed up whatever it was that she and Jake had together.

"I'm sorry," she said. "I shouldn't have . . ."

"No, I love you, too. I've just . . . With all that happened to you . . ."

Dana's heart began to beat again. She felt lighter than air. It was going to be all right. She put a hand on Jake's cheek.

"You're my rock, Jake, my anchor. You kept me going when I wanted to give up, when I didn't care what happened to me. But you cared."

"It's easy to care for you. You're very special."

"Shit," Dana said, wiping away a tear that had suddenly strayed down her cheek. Jake kissed her hand then he kissed the spot where the tear had appeared.

"I'm no good at this mushy stuff," Dana said.

"Then don't talk," Jake told her as he took her hand and led her inside. For once Dana Cutler surrendered without a fight.

The next morning, Dana awoke with the sun. Jake was sound asleep and she crept out of bed, dressed quietly, and left a note on the kitchen table so Jake wouldn't worry. With the help of Keith Evans and the FBI, Jake's Harley had been retrieved. Dana pushed it onto the street and didn't start it until she was certain the noise wouldn't disturb her lover's slumber. As soon as she could, Dana opened it up and sped toward her destination.

The meth cook had brought Dana to the farmhouse after sundown and she had been rescued before dawn, so she'd only seen the place where she'd been brutalized at night. It was less frightening in the strong light of the sun—an abandoned, dilapidated structure punished by neglect, separated from a field of high and wild grass by a desolate dirt yard.

The steps up which Dana climbed to the front porch creaked underfoot and the cold fall wind blew the remaining scraps of crime scene tape out and away where they stuck to the front door. Dana tried the handle and the door opened. Her heart was beating wildly and she could feel the heat of panic when she walked into the front room. A floorboard creaked underfoot, the sunlight illuminated spiderwebs and dust devils that spun across the floor in the wake of the cold, fast-moving air.

Dana took a deep breath and forced herself to walk into the kitchen. She stood in front of the door to the basement, staring at it. It was just a door, she told herself, and the basement was just a basement, a place of concrete and cheap shelving. There would be ghosts down there only if she allowed them to exist.

Dana grabbed the knob and opened the door. The electricity had been turned off, but she'd brought a flashlight. The beam illuminated the steps. Some light filtered through the narrow, grime-covered windows. Dana stopped at the bottom of the stairs and shined her light on the space where she'd lain, naked and terrified, for three days while she had been raped and beaten. She felt sick so she squeezed her eyes tight and breathed in slowly and deeply. While her eyes were still closed, she conjured up Jake's face. She made her vision smile and she remembered how good it felt to nestle in his arms. He'd made her feel safe.

Dana opened her eyes, and she smiled. She felt safe now. There were no ghosts, just dust, spiderwebs, and concrete, nothing that could hurt her. Dana was filled with a sense of peace. Last night she had set free the restless spirits of the three girls Claire Farrington had murdered. Today she had set her own spirit free from the fears that had tried to make her dead inside.

Chapter Forty-nine

Brad Miller wrapped his arm around Ginny Striker's shoulders, and they huddled together as they struggled through the election night crowd mobbing the lobby of the Benson Hotel in downtown Portland and walked outside into the light rain that had been falling all evening. There had been no suspense in Maureen Gaylord's win. It had been a sure thing after the first lady's arrest. And the situation had gotten worse for the president when the Pulaskis and Marsha Erickson had appeared on every television show that would have them to tell how they'd been paid off by Christopher Farrington to keep quiet about his sexual involvement with their daughters.

"I guess the American people don't want a serial murderer and a sex pervert in the White House," Ginny had said when NBC declared Ohio firmly in Gaylord's camp, wrapping up the electoral vote for the senator. Even Oregon had voted overwhelmingly against the only native son to lead the nation.

"I only hope they both end up in prison," Brad said.

"I'll believe that when I see it."

"It's what they deserve."

"The rich and powerful seem to be able to commit crimes with impunity," Ginny said as they worked their way free of the rowdy crowd in front of the hotel.

"Some of the legal analysts think the case against Claire Farrington is too weak to win a conviction," Brad said. He sounded disheartened.

Ginny gripped his biceps tightly and squeezed. "That's not our problem anymore. I'm just glad this is over. I'm looking forward to a fresh start."

"I hope you like your job at your D.C. firm better than your tenure at Reed, Briggs," Brad said.

"I probably won't, but I still have loans to pay off and rent to pay and I can't count on you for much."

Brad grinned. It was true. Brad's clerkship at the United States Supreme Court was not going to pay anywhere near what Ginny would earn, but it would open the door to every legal job in the country when he was through.

"Do you mind that I'm marrying you for your money?" Brad asked.

"I thought you were only interested in my body."

"There's that, too. Now if you could only cook, you'd be perfect."

"For a kept man you're pretty picky. You should be satisfied with what you've got."

"I guess you'll do until a rich, sexy woman with a degree from Cordon Bleu comes along."

Ginny swatted him on the head, and he kissed her. Life was pretty good and his only real worry was that he would let down Justice Kineer, who'd obtained the position at the Court for him. He knew that the other clerks would be editors in chief from law reviews at Harvard, Penn, NYU, and other super law schools, and he was a little nervous about his place in this pantheon of intellect. But every time he worried about his ability to perform his job he remembered Justice Kineer's assurance that he would have chosen someone who'd successfully faced down assassins, brought down a first lady, and proved that the former chief justice of the United States had his head up his butt over any academic nerd.

*   *   *

During the drive to Brad's apartment the rainstorm got worse. The couple rushed from Brad's parking spot to his front door, crouching to escape the downpour. Brad flipped on the light in his entryway as soon as they were inside.

"I'm going to the powder room to dry my hair," Ginny said.

"I'll put up the water for tea."

Brad took off his raincoat and hung it on a hook. He was about to go into the kitchen when he spotted a slender white envelope lying on the entryway floor. He stooped down and picked it up. His name and address were handwritten, and there was no return address. There was also no stamp, so the letter had been hand delivered and slipped under his door. Inside the envelope was a single sheet of lined, yellow legal paper. Brad read what was written on it and felt a chill that had nothing to do with the weather.

> *Dear Brad,*
> *I knew I was right to trust you. I've just learned that my convic-*
> *tion for the murder of the Erickson girl is going to be set aside*
> *and that's all due to your hard work. I'll still be executed but I*
> *can live with that, if you'll pardon the pun. I'd invite you to the*
> *execution but I know you're squeamish. My only regret is that I*
> *didn't get to go to court to overturn the conviction. I might*
> *have seen my lovely pinkie collection one last time. Oh well,*
> *one can't have everything. Good luck on your new job and on*
> *your marriage to the lovely Ginny. She's a sweetheart. Too bad*
> *I won't get a chance to know her.*
> *Your Friend, Clarence*

Brad crumpled the envelope and the letter and hurried to the garbage pail in the kitchen. He pushed them under the other trash to make certain that Ginny would never see Clarence Little's letter.

"Hey, you're shivering," Ginny said when she walked into the kitchen. "Let me do something about that."

Ginny wrapped her arms around Brad and snuggled against him. Usually, Ginny made him believe that everything was going to be all right, but her hug couldn't dispel the feeling of dread created by Little's letter. How did he know about Ginny? Who had delivered the letter? Anger replaced dread as Brad realized that Clarence was bored and was playing mind games with him again. He would expect Brad to rush to Salem to discuss the letter. Well, he wasn't going to go. He would let Clarence sit in his cell alone, waiting for his day of execution. No more fun and games for Mr. Little. Not at Brad's expense, anyway.

Brad pressed Ginny to him. Then he kissed her ferociously.

"Whoa, mister, what's gotten into you?"

"It's what's not in me anymore, Ginny. You've chased my demons away. Bridget Malloy, Clarence Little, Susan Tuchman, they've all moved on to bother someone else. From now on, it's just you and me, kid."

Ginny smiled and kissed Brad. He smiled back. Life was good, and he had a feeling it was going to get better.

Epilogue

Christopher Farrington sat by himself in his mansion in Portland's West Hills, staring out of the window in his study. The nanny had put Patrick to bed and the house was very quiet. A fire in the deep, stone fireplace helped to combat the chill created by the constant rain. February was damp, cold, and dark in Oregon, like the thoughts he could not escape.

Events had not been kind to the Farringtons since Claire's arrest. Despite "Jailbreak" Holliday's best efforts, Claire had not been granted bail. The sheer number of the murder charges and her wealth had worked against her when the prosecutor had pointed out her motivation and ability to flee to a jurisdiction without an extradition treaty. Christopher's only visit to Claire in jail had been a nightmare. After he ran a gauntlet of paparazzi, he'd been forced to listen to Claire's insane ravings. She blamed him for everything, accusing him of causing her to kill to protect their marriage and hinting at the revenge she would take on him when she got out.

Then there was his own plight. He was not in retirement, he was in exile, ostracized by all but a crazed media that pursued him like a pack of jackals. When the din of the constant questions from the press was absent a cold silence was his only companion. No one visited, no one called except the attorneys who came to discuss Claire's case and the civil suits that had been filed against them.

It wasn't fair. All he'd done was fool around a bit. Other presidents had done that. Hell, Kennedy had sex with Mafia whores, and Eisenhower was supposed to have had a mistress. He wouldn't even start with Clinton. What was so wrong? Why couldn't Claire see how harmless it had all been? Why had she overreacted to a few flings he'd forgotten as soon as the act was over?

Farrington guessed that his mistake was admitting what he'd done with Rhonda Pulaski in the back of the limousine when he'd given her the settlement check. He'd needed Claire's money to pay off the family, and she refused to talk to her father until she knew every little detail. He'd been so contrite he was certain she'd forgiven him, and she hadn't said anything that would lead him to believe that she would react so violently.

It was Chuck who'd told him about the hit-and-run and the necessity of his providing an alibi for Claire if it ever came to that. It hadn't, thank God, because Chuck had cleaned up Claire's mess, but murder . . . My God, he'd never thought her capable of murder.

Then she'd done it again. Farrington could not even imagine what would have happened to his career if Chuck hadn't raced back to the governor's mansion and disposed of the body before someone found it.

Farrington paused. Of course he could imagine what would have happened. It was happening now. But he wasn't to blame for any of it. It was Claire. She'd killed the girls. All he'd done was suggest to Chuck that he help his wife. There was no culpability there, was there?

Before he could confront that moral tangle, headlights in his driveway distracted Farrington from his dreary thoughts. He walked to the window and saw a Town Car parked in front of his door. A member of his Secret Service detail was speaking to the driver. Moments later, the chauffeur opened the rear door, and Susan Tuchman got out and ducked under the portico.

Farrington hurried into the entrance hall to greet her. He hoped she had good news. Claire's family had cut off any financial support when they learned of his adultery; there had been none of the highly paid invitations to speak that other former presidents received; and a lucrative book deal was on hold while his attorney researched the viability of claims that might be filed against his advance and future royalties by the families of Claire's victims.

"Susan," Chris said, forcing a warm smile as soon as the attorney walked into the house.

"Chris," Susan answered tersely. He noticed that she did not return his smile.

"Come into the study. I've got a fire going. Can I get you something to drink?"

"No thanks. I can't stay long. I've got a meeting with some foreign investors who are considering a partnership with one of our clients."

"Don't you ever slow down?" Chris asked, trying to keep the conversation light. Tuchman didn't answer.

"So, what's up?" Chris asked when they were seated.

"Nothing good, I'm afraid," Tuchman answered. "The partners considered your proposal that you become 'Of Counsel' with the firm. We've decided, in light of your current situation, that it wouldn't be advisable at this time."

Farrington wanted to ask why his old friends were deserting him but he knew that the answer would only humiliate him.

"There's another reason why I'm here. A very unpleasant reason, but we've been friends for a long time and I felt I owed it to you to tell you in person."

Chris struggled to maintain his smile.

"As you know, I'm on the board of the Westmont Country Club. Yesterday evening, we held a special meeting. A majority of the board wanted to revoke your membership and Claire's. I was able to convince them that it would be better for everyone if we gave you the opportunity to resign."

Farrington was stunned. The Westmont was Portland's most prestigious country club. Its members were his and Claire's closest friends and his staunchest political supporters. It was a haven where he could play a round of golf in peace or have a drink without being beset by favor seekers and journalists.

"I don't understand."

Susan experienced an alien emotion, embarrassment. It took a great effort of will to look her friend in the eye.

"We've known each other for a long time, Chris. You know I've always stood by you, but this . . . this situation is too much."

"Claire hasn't been convicted of anything. This is America. She's presumed innocent."

"That rule works in a court of law but not at the Westmont. We had a special committee review the facts in her case. I don't know what's going to happen in court. Travis Holliday has a reputation for working magic with juries. But we both know that Claire is guilty of murder several times over. And your affairs, Chris. They were kids, and they're dead because of you."

"You don't think I had anything to do with the murders?!"

"I have no idea what you knew about what Claire was doing. But Pulaski was your client, Erickson was your babysitter, and Walsh worked on your campaign. If you can't see that sleeping with them was wrong I can't explain it to you. I suggest you resign from the club as soon as possible. If you resign it will leave the possibility open of rejoining in the future if your problems resolve themselves favorably."

"Thank you for helping to give me that option and thank you for having the guts to meet me face to face."

Susan reached out and touched Farrington's hand. "I wish you the best, Chris."

She stood up. "I really have to go now."

Farrington stood. "I understand."

He walked her to the door and watched the Town Car drive off. When it disappeared from sight he returned to the study. Just months ago, he'd been the most powerful person on Earth. He'd had the power to destroy the world with the push of a button. Now . . .

Farrington stared at the fire. The flames radiated heat but it could not dispel the chill in the air.

Acknowledgments

Any reader who doesn't know me personally might make the mistake of thinking that I'm a walking *Encyclopaedia Britannica* because of the technical information on medical topics, the workings of the Secret Service, dental procedures, telecommunications, etc., that you can find in *Executive Privilege*, but all of that information comes from some wonderful experts who were willing to take time out of their busy day to help me make my book more realistic. So I want to thank Dr. Karen Gunson, Dennis Balske, Dr. Daniel Moore, Ken Baumann, Al Bosco, Andrew Painter, Andy Rome, Ed Pritchard, Joe Massey, and Mark Miller. I also recommend *So You Think You Want to Be an Independent Counsel* by Donald C. Smaltz to anyone who wants to be an independent counsel or just needs to know a lot about that office.

I appreciate the time taken by Susan Svetkey, Karen Berry, Ami Margolin Rome, Jerry and Judy Margolin, Pam Webb, and Jay Margulies for reading my first draft and sharing their ideas on how I could make the book better.

A special thank-you to Marjorie Braman for her excellent work in editing *Executive Privilege*. It is a much better book because of her comments and suggestions. A special Pulitzer Prize for Titles goes to Peggy Hageman. And nothing I can say will be adequate to show my appreciation for the compassion shown to me by everyone at Harper-Collins during the worst time of my life.

Also there for me—as they always have been—were Jean Naggar, Jennifer Weltz, and everyone at the Jean Naggar Literary Agency.

No words will explain how fabulous all of my friends have been in supporting me and Daniel and Ami—my wonderful children—since Doreen passed away. Doreen was my muse and my inspiration for everything I've done in life, and she will continue to be.